'As good as Sarah Waters...
highly recommended'
HISTORICAL NOVEL SOCIETY

'Seriously impressive'
PHIL RICKMAN

'I was convinced, transfixed,
transported and I'll be keeping
these characters close to me for
a long time to come'
IMOGEN ROBERTSON

'Akin to the best of Susan
Hill, this is just the kind of tale
for the lingering cold nights'
CULTUREFLY

'With an impressive sense of
time and place at its core, this
is a spine-tingling and seductive
blend of history, mystery and
the downright macabre'
LANCASHIRE POST

'Exquisite... Clements'
characters are as vividly
evoked as the dark fate
hovering over them all'
ALISON LITTLEWOOD

'A stunning read!
I couldn't put it down'
NICOLA CORNICK

'Packed with atmosphere,
mystery, drama and
good characters'
CHOICE

'So rich in its beautifully
rendered atmosphere that
I could feel it pressing
at my chest'
JASON HEWITT

Also by Katherine Clements and available from Headline Review

The Crimson Ribbon
The Silvered Heart
The Painted Chamber (*digital short stories*)

THE
COFFIN
PATH

Katherine Clements

REVIEW

First published in Great Britain in 2018 by
HEADLINE REVIEW
An imprint of HEADLINE PUBLISHING GROUP

First published in paperback in Great Britain in 2018 by
HEADLINE PUBLISHING GROUP

3

Cataloguing in Publication Data is available from the British Library

ISBN 978 1 4722 0430 1

Typeset in Aldine 401 BT by Avon DataSet Ltd, Bidford-on-Avon, Warwickshire

Printed and bound in Great Britain by Clays Ltd, Elcograf S.p.A.

MIX
Paper from
responsible sources
FSC® C104740

Headline's policy is to use papers that are natural, renewable and recyclable products
and made from wood grown in well-managed forests and other controlled sources.
The logging and manufacturing processes are expected to conform to the
environmental regulations of the country of origin.

HEADLINE PUBLISHING GROUP
An Hachette UK Company
Carmelite House
50 Victoria Embankment
London EC4Y 0DZ

www.headline.co.uk
www.hachette.co.uk

For Paddy

1674
Spring

1674
Spring

Chapter 1

I was born with blood on my hands.

I killed my mother on the 22nd of August, in the year 1642, the day the first King Charles turned traitor and chose a battlefield over a throne. She was not murdered by musket shot or slaughtered by steel blade, as were so many during those years of war. Hers was a woman's fate. She died in blood – the blood that bore me in on its tide.

At least, that's what I was told.

I've had blood on my hands ever since. I'm elbow-deep in a thick, viscous caul of it. Though I've never sweated and screamed in my own childbed, I know life and death better than most women. And now, as ever, I'm mindful of my mother. It happens every time I birth a lamb – the weighted pause before the newborn's first breath, like a clock's final turning before the hour's strike, and I always think the same thing: how the moment of birth, of new life, so often means the death of something else.

Such maudlin thoughts are natural in the cold, lonely months when days are icicle-bright and nights are heavy with peat smoke and shadows. But the February chill has lessened lately, the sky become cloud-laden, mist-thick, and the first lamb is a sure sign that spring will soon follow. It should be a moment of celebration, of gratitude and thanks, for the closing of one season and the beginning of the next – we have survived another winter – but sight of the first suckling always reminds me of the mother I never knew, the father who was left to grieve, and the debt I owe to both. With every spring, and every lamb, I have a chance, once again, to make it right.

Up on the moor, the snow is still knee-deep and sheep huddle under peat hags. Down on the valley slopes, where this one has wandered alone, just the drifts are left. The ewe has found herself a bare hollow sheltered from the wind, against the wall of an abandoned fold, and is butting up against the stone, pawing the frozen earth.

Ignoring the familiar twist inside – my guts telling me I won't like what I find – I scramble down the steep fell towards her, scattering stones, my dog, Bracken, at my heels.

This place was someone's home once: a one-roomed cottage slowly crumbling to ruin, doors and shutters long since stolen for fuel, mist winding about the chimney in place of smoke, a dank tomb smell of lichened stone, the sheepfold now a stretch of tumbledown dry-wall. Ragged crows eye me from the naked branches of a wind-twisted willow.

Urging Bracken to keep her distance, I move slowly towards the ewe. She's unsteady, stumbling away from me, front legs buckling. I'd know her as one of my own even without the smudge of last summer's tar mark on her fleece. She's young, tupped for the first time last autumn. She should have at least two weeks until her time, but Nature has other ideas.

I call Bracken forward and she creeps into position, head low, clever, keen eyes fixed on the sheep. The ewe grumbles, panting hard as her flanks contract. She tries to move away but careers into the wall, off balance, and stands a moment, stunned, confused. I take my chance, hook her with my crook and pull her into the corner of the fold. She struggles and complains, but she's tired, lacking strength to fight.

Her hind legs are bloodied, already blackened and stiff. There's no sign of her water – it's long been broken – but her backside is red and badly swollen. One small hoof protrudes from a seeping, sore hole. The poor creature grumbles again, loins quivering as she pushes, but instead of the double legs I hope to see, the single hoof doesn't shift.

I send a curse to the clouds. I'm too far from home to go for help, and Ambrose will be indoors by now, waiting for his supper, while Dority stirs the pot and bounces the baby on her hip.

There's a sudden cacophony as the crows rise from their watch post in a flurry of jagged wings and midnight-black feathers. Bracken barks. High above, a lone merlin circles, silent, waiting. She can smell death on the wind; at this time of year, even bad meat is better than none.

The ewe rolls her amber eye to mine and makes a mournful whicker. She doesn't struggle as I hopple her front legs with a length of twine, tug her ankles and shoulder her onto one side. I run my hands over her belly. She kicks her tethered feet without conviction. The flock tends to lamb by noon, before their shadows grow short, but that hour is long gone: this lamb must be stuck, or maybe worse. I must get it out or lose them both.

Hurrying now, I strip off my heavy coat and hat, for I cannot work so encumbered. The air snatches my breath. The freezing deep of winter may be passing but it's still bitter cold. I did not wear my stays today, preferring the ease and practicality of men's clothes for my work, and the sudden chill bites beneath the rough kersey of my shirt.

I roll up my sleeves and kneel at the ewe's back end. Lifting her tail, I see it's worse than I first thought. Instead of a clean, wet opening, she's torn and bleeding. Though I see no sign, I wonder if she's birthed another before this one. Perhaps she's injured herself in the struggle to be rid of the thing inside. There's still only a single hoof in view, no sign of a second and no sign of a head.

I grip the lamb's hoof in one hand and slide the fingers of the other inside the ewe. She makes a strangled complaint. My heart tightens. 'There now, girl, let's get this out of you.'

I push my knuckles inside, then more. Hot, shuddering muscle grips my wrist as she takes me in.

I feel it at my fingertips – the hard little bud of a second hoof – and slide inward to find the joint. It slips away so I push deeper, feeling for the slime-covered fleece and bone of the lamb's leg. Then I have it in my grasp. I try to draw it gently forward but feel it pull back – a sign the lamb is alive. My hope awakens. But if it's to come, I must help it. Left alone it will die and poison the mother too.

A fierce determination surfaces in me – the same I feel whenever I'm faced with Nature's fickle ways. I know it's wrong and I should accept God's will in all things, but when it comes to my flock I'll fight like a wildcat to make sure His will marries with my own.

I push further inside, up to my elbow, encased by slick heat. It's careful work, taking all my strength and concentration as the ewe grumbles and pants. At last I have two legs within my grasp but I cannot feel the head; the lamb is lying back to front, turned away from birth rather than towards it. I have to work fast; a lamb stuck like this will suffocate before it has a chance of first breath.

I push deep and hook the second leg, trying to bring it forward to meet the first so I can start to pull. But it's too much for the ewe. She strains against me, desperate to escape the thing that pains her. With no one to hold her still and no means of gaining better purchase, my arm is squeezed out. I'm splashed and smeared with scarlet. There's something horrid about the vibrant hue – this is not the clotted, viscid stuff of birth but the fresh blood of a rupture. There's something very wrong. I'm running out of time.

I've been here before, and from the first time to this last it's always the same – the struggle only makes me stubborn. If I cannot save the ewe, I'll save her lamb; a bargain I make time and again with God.

I push my hand inside to find the hind legs once more. Flesh slides between fingers like ribbons, the sheep's channel a mess of meat. I grope blindly, no longer sure what I'm feeling. I swallow down rising panic as I feel the heartbeat pulse of blood against my hand. My arm is slick to the shoulder, shirtsleeve brightly streaked. It's not right – there is too much blood.

I find one hoof, and soon, a second. A quick check – I have the hind legs. There's no time to try to turn the lamb, so I grip both hooves and pull, gently at first and then a little harder until I feel it begin to slide.

The ewe has stopped straining and gives me no aid. She's voiceless as she fades. But I feel a faint twitch from the lamb. I hold life in my fist, so I tug harder and bring the legs out. The mother groans. I struggle to my feet, levering all my weight now, and pull as hard as I can. And the lamb is born at last, slithering forth, yellow as butter, slippery as a trout.

The animal is formed well enough, as I knew this ewe would bring, but there's no sign of breath. I have no straw or grass to rub it down, to hurry the life into its lungs, so I tear off my waistcoat and use that, ignoring the pinch of icy air. I wipe away the gore from its nose and mouth and dangle it, head down, swinging it gently back and forth, urging it to draw that first crucial breath. But the pale little body stays limp and airless.

Most often, a healthy ewe will turn about to find her young, licking it to life. Quickly, I use my knife to slice the tethers from the sheep's ankles but she just lies there, flanks heaving, exhausted and blank-eyed, nothing left to give. Bracken comes sniffing, nose to nose, but there's no response – the ewe no longer has the strength even for fear. I take the lamb to her head, hoping the scent will rouse her. Steam rises from the slick little body. The mother's nostrils quiver but her eyes are clouding: she cannot help me.

I push the lamb against her fleece and rub hard. I wrap the tiny thing in my waistcoat once again and do the same, sending both prayers and curses up to a God who likes to give with one hand and take away with the other. And at last the lamb splutters and shudders, struggles to open its eyes.

The mother lasts long enough to hear the first fragile cry of her newborn. She fixes me with those amber eyes and I see the moment that she gives up. She lays her head upon the grave-cold ground, ready to breathe her last.

There's nothing more I can do for her, out here, alone, with the dark gathering. I hate to leave her to the mercy of foxes and wild dogs. I hate to lose her, to admit defeat, but there's a chance for the lamb, if I can get it to warmth and milk soon enough. I'm less than half an hour from Scarcross Hall, where a fire burns in the kitchen and Agnes will heat the milk. I make the painful choice, as I always do.

I pull on my coat and hat, tighten my waistcoat around the small, quivering creature and cradle it against my chest, ignoring the feeble panting of the ewe. I'll send Ambrose with the cart to collect whatever is left of her in the morning. Calling Bracken to my side, I start out across the fell, making for higher ground. I hold the lamb tight for warmth, feeling it shiver, pressing its timid heartbeat against my own. I do not look back.

There's a fog gathering, sitting heavy on the hills, sinking into the valley. I know the paths across these moors like I know every stone and slate of Scarcross Hall, but when the fog comes down it's fast and unforgiving, and even us hefted ones can lose our way.

I first feel it as I crest the hill and join the old coffin path towards the crossroads. I sense it like a rabbit sensing a fox: there are eyes on me.

I'm used to all weathers and I know the tricks that Nature can play. I've scared myself at times, imagining spirits in the mist or glimpsing marsh lights dancing on the moor at midnight. But those are nothing more than half-remembered fantasies of a child with a head full of goblins and fairies, put there by a God-fearing father with a dread of the Devil's creatures. I'm not one for superstition and scaremongering and I've never before felt truly afraid.

This is different: there is a threat in it.

My hackles rise. I'm a field mouse sensing the hawk, my pursuer invisible to me but every instinct telling me to run.

Bracken slinks to my side, ears flattened, growling low.

'What is it, girl?' I ask. 'What can you see?'

She stops, glances backwards, teeth bared, then darts ahead, as if to hurry me. I quicken my pace to catch up with her, trying to shake the feeling, concentrating on the creature now in my care, telling myself I'm hurrying for him. The lamb has fallen silent, eyes closed, panting quick, shallow breaths. I pull my coat tighter and whisper to him, telling him to stay with me, that I'm taking him to a warm, safe place where I'll give him the milk he needs.

With the fog comes the quiet, the weird, echoing closeness that hushes the birds and has any sane person hurrying to their hearthside. Bracken leads me on, her small brown body disappearing and reappearing through the gloom, like a wraith. Damp air seems to press at me, walls of fog reducing the wide expanse of the fell to little more than a few strides of uneven track. I've walked the coffin path my whole life, but without landmarks it's impossible to tell exactly where I am. I feel disoriented, trapped. The muffled silence is uncanny. I fix my eyes ahead, denying my own wild thoughts. Something compels me to run, heart thumping, making a drum beat in my ears. I begin a quick, stumbling gait that has me tripping over stones I should know are underfoot. Still I feel it, like a cold hand sliding down my back: someone or something is out there. I cannot help but look behind. I see nothing save the stark black statue of a winter-stripped tree. A wild dog, perhaps, desperate and skeleton-starved? Or a beggar lost his way on the packhorse trails? I open my mouth to call out a greeting but something stops me and I'm suddenly convinced: whatever it is, I don't want to meet it.

At last the gables and chimneys of Scarcross Hall appear through the murk, the lantern burning at the casement a welcome beacon.

I hurry across the yard to the kitchen door and lift the catch.

Bracken pushes past me, skittering across stone flags towards her makeshift bed by the fire.

'Agnes!'

I hear the soft shuffle of indoor shoes in the buttery next door.

'Agnes, come quickly. I need warm milk and blankets.'

As I turn to shut the door, I see a figure standing at the gatepost. It's indistinct, a shadow-shape, swathed in a winding sheet of fog.

Silent.

Still.

Watching.

For a moment I'm transfixed. A sense of recognition, of deep and ancient dread, wells in me. Then a bank of fog moves across the yard and when it clears the figure is gone. Imagination, I tell myself, a trick of the fading light. But as I shut the door, I make sure to turn the key.

Chapter 2

Agnes is at the door to the buttery, wiping floured hands on her apron.

I open my coat and show her the lamb, pressed against my panicked heart. 'I need warm milk, quickly.'

'The mother?' she asks.

'Down by the old cottage. I couldn't save her.'

She shakes her head as she turns away. 'The good Lord may have His plan but it can be a cruel one.'

I check the key in the lock once more and take a few deep breaths, swallowing my fear and drinking in the comfort of familiarity: the glow of peat clods in the hearth, the yellow tallow casting false warmth across cold flagstones, the yeasty scent of the dough Agnes has been working for tomorrow's loaf.

I wait, impatient, while Agnes fetches milk from the churn – she moves so slowly, these days – and I long to take charge, but the lamb needs warmth before anything, so I kneel at the hearthstone, holding the small, damp body as close to the embers as I dare, trying to rub some heat into him. His fleece steams. Though I feel the rapid flutter of his tiny heart, he remains limp and shut-eyed.

I glance at the window more than once, expecting to find a stranger looking in, but there's nothing except the reflection of candle flame as the sky darkens, making a mirror of the panes.

Agnes returns with a pan of milk and sets it over the heat. Then she fetches rags to clean the lamb's fleece, still caked with his mother's poisoned blood.

Those few minutes waiting for the milk to warm seem like hours. Bracken stretches and yawns, our strange encounter seemingly forgotten.

'Did anyone come calling today?' I ask, as we wait, unable to shake the sense of disquiet.

'No.'

'No visit from Pastor Flynn?'

She frowns. 'Was he expected? No one told me.'

'No. I thought I saw someone . . . Ah, no matter.' I know how Agnes frets, and fretting makes her ill. She gives me a familiar, suspicious look. She knows I'm keeping something from her – but I decide that's exactly what I must do.

When the milk is ready, I tilt the lamb's head back and open his jaw. Agnes spoons it, little by little, into his mouth. At first it dribbles down my arms and makes creamy white rivers amid the bloody fleece, but with gentle coaxing he soon begins to swallow. After a few minutes of this I feel strength enter his limbs – a kick or two, a shiver – enough to raise a smile between Agnes and I. That's how my father finds us, knelt at the hearthstone, like two pilgrims before a shrine, praying that the good Lord might spare the life in my hands.

Sam comes clattering in first, dragging Father by the sleeve. Agnes might be slow but Father is slower and no match for this strange whirlwind boy with his head of rusty curls, piercing stare and freckles showered across pale skin.

'Now, child, I told you more than an hour past, it's time for you to run along home,' Agnes says, throwing Father a disapproving look.

He pretends to ignore her, dark eyes glowering beneath the

grey crag of his brow. He's agitated. I can tell his mind by a single glance – unlike me, he wears his moods for all to see.

'Tell them, Sam,' he says.

The boy looks up at him. 'I thought it were a secret, Master Booth.'

'There are no secrets in this house, my boy.'

Sam hesitates, a little unsure. 'We're searching for lost treasure,' he says, almost a whisper.

'That may be, but your ma will be sore worried and looking out for you,' Agnes says. 'It's twilight already.'

Father bats away her concern. 'Leave the lad be. He's safe enough with me. What have we here? Look, Sam, Mercy has a newborn . . .'

As Sam sees the lamb, he drops Father's arm and takes a few timid steps towards me. 'Will it live?'

'If we keep him warm and fed through the night, he may yet,' I tell him.

Sam frowns as he watches Agnes spoon a little more milk down the lamb's throat. The creature is responding to the feed and at last gives a hopeful bleat. Bracken raises her head at the sound, sniffs the air as she catches the scent.

'The ewe?' Father asks, placing his cane on the tabletop and leaning heavily beside it.

I shake my head.

He nods, lips pursed. I see his fists clench and unclench as he works out the frustration I know he feels. A hardy, vital man until recent years, he no longer has the strength for shepherding work and it's a grievance to him. He still blames himself for losses like this one. He stands suddenly and goes to the casement, peering out into the thickening murk as if looking for something. I watch from the corner of my eye as he rubs at his forehead and pinches the bridge of his nose, as he does when he's fighting his temper. I notice a slight tremor in his hand, a weird, distracted look in his eye. What has him so stirred up?

'Can I feed it?' Sam asks, bringing my attention back. 'I know how. I've done it before.' He leans in close, peering over my shoulder so I smell the oaty scent of his young skin.

'It's time you were away home, child,' Agnes says. 'This little one can do without you. Mercy will take care of him.'

The remnants of fear are still knotted in my stomach. I don't want anyone wandering outside the bounds of Scarcross Hall this evening. 'There's a heavy fog coming in,' I say. 'And it's near dark.'

'Let the child stay,' Father says sternly. 'The Garricks will know where he is.'

'I want to help save the lamb,' Sam says. 'Pa would want it.'

He's right. In his place Ambrose would insist upon it. Besides, I'll be up through the night and company would be welcome. The lamb is struggling to be set free, so I put him gently down on the flags where he sits for a moment before trying to stand on unsteady legs. Bracken, head resting on her paws, pretending indifference, watches, nostrils at work.

'Sam can stay in here with me,' I say. 'We'll fetch out the cot. Would you like that, Sam?'

He nods, pleased and surprised I've taken his side.

Agnes climbs slowly to her feet, rubbing the small of her back. 'Don't blame me when you have a tired, contrary child on your hands come morning.' She takes up the pan and goes to fetch more milk, muttering under her breath.

It takes several hours, some dry blankets and another good feed before I'm satisfied that the lamb is out of danger. I wait up long after Agnes and Father have gone to bed. I must be sure before I allow myself any rest and, besides, I will not sleep easily tonight. The memory of what I saw out in the fog troubles me. I tell myself I'm being foolish, creating worry out of nothing, like a girl half my age, but I cannot dispel the creeping unease, or the sense I had of being followed.

I know the perils of wandering the fells alone. These moors and valleys are a haven for those who cannot make a better life for themselves in more forgiving country. We have our share of beggars, thieves and ne'er-do-wells. But this is my land, my home, and the things that may scare others are a comfort to me. I don't see foreboding in a rain-fat storm cloud, but God's hand in helping the becks run full and free; I don't see the Devil's work in the lights that sometimes dance across the moor top or the vivid colours that sometimes fill the night sky, but proof of His majesty; I don't see a path down to Hell in the stretches of deadly peat bog, but His provision of our warmth and light. Never before have I sensed the kind of danger I did today.

I distract myself by making sure that Sam is warm, fed and night-stilled, tucked under blankets on the cot, the lamb dozing at his side. He's quiet for a long time, staring into the fire until I take a seat nearby, on the high-backed chair that Agnes favours. I kick off my boots and warm my feet, thick woollen stockings giving off a faint must. I reach my pipe and tobacco down from the mantel, pack the bowl and light it with a taper from the fire. The smoke is rich and soothing.

Sam watches me, gently stroking the lamb's ears. 'What happened to his mother?' he asks, eventually.

I take a long draw on the pipe. 'She died.'

'But why could you not save her?'

'She was already too sick when I found her. The lamb was stuck. If I'd not come along, they would both have been dead by morning.'

He nods sagely and again I see the essence of Ambrose Garrick in him. 'Will you find another to suckle him?' he asks. At seven years he already knows the shepherd's tricks. Like me, he's been tending the flock alongside his father since his first steps.

'He's the first this year and he came early, so none will take him yet.'

I can see he's fighting heavy eyelids. 'The first of the year . . . and the first is special.'

'Yes.'

'Then he'll grow into a strong tup.'

The lamb is weak, small and will make a wether at best, if he survives at all, and it does no good to keep truth from the boy, but I don't have the heart to say it.

Sam yawns and rests his head back on the folded blanket that serves as a pillow. He strokes the soft fleece at the lamb's muzzle. 'He reminds me of the first lamb I birthed,' he says. 'Do you remember?'

I expect his eyes to cloud, but they stay clear, searching and painfully innocent. 'Of course I do.'

'What do you remember?'

His lids are drooping now and I know this is my chance to be kind, to bless him with dreams of a happier time. 'I remember how brave you were, and how clever, the pride in your pa's eyes when the lamb stood so tall and strong. I remember how happy you were. I remember Will's smile . . .'

Sam's eyes are shut and his breathing deepened. I won't tell him what I remember most about that day, because we don't speak of it. That was the day before Will's accident.

My pipe is spent so I lean forward to rest it on the hearthstone, but Sam stirs, blinks, struggles to focus on the sleeping lamb.

'You should rest now,' I say. 'I'll watch over him.'

He shakes his head. 'Did Master Booth find his treasure?'

I recall Father's troubled frown, the tremble in his fingers. 'What treasure?'

When he speaks he's furtive, a little hesitant. 'Sometimes the master lets me count his coins, but today some were missing. He said three were gone – the three he found up at the White Ladies.'

I know the coins that Sam means. Three small golden discs, worn and warped, decorated with strange pagan symbols – they're not like any coin I might use to pay the traders in the village. When I was small, Father used to tell me the same story – that he'd found them up at the stone circle on the moor top, a gift of protection from the sprites. They were our secret and I swore never to speak of them, for fear it would break their spell. I liked to study them, to feel their weight, hear the tinkling chink they made if I rattled them in my cupped palms. But then I grew a little older and heard the stories, folklore and fancy, handed down to us young ones, whispered by firesides on dark winter nights. After that I sometimes wondered if, rather than protection, the coins offered an ill omen. But it's been years since I thought of them, not least because Father keeps them hidden away.

I'm surprised he's shared the secret that was once ours, though perhaps I shouldn't be – in the absence of a grandchild, he has a soft spot for the boy. And if the coins are truly missing, perhaps that's what has upset him: he's always been so possessive of them.

'Maybe the boggarts took them back,' Sam says.

'Did my father say that?' I feel a spike of irritation, a little cross with him for entertaining the boy's superstitions.

'Yes . . . he said it might be so.'

'Do you believe in boggarts, Sam?'

He presses himself up onto one elbow and looks at me. 'Don't you?'

'Sam, you shouldn't believe everything my father tells you.'

'But he said—'

'That's enough now. It's time to sleep.' I stand and go to the door that leads out into the yard, trying to ignore the swell of unease in my chest. I test the latch, as I've done three times already. It's still locked.

I return to the fireside and stoke the embers. I am being ridiculous.

'I'd like to name him,' Sam says quietly, as the lamb stirs and nuzzles against his hand.

I wrap a blanket round my shoulders and sit down. 'If you like.'

'I'll name him Will.'

'Are you sure? Will that please your pa?'

He looks away, stares into the fire, thoughtful and sad. 'It's not up to Pa. It's up to me.'

He has his father's strong opinions, and his stubbornness. 'Very well.'

Sam closes his eyes, satisfied. I watch for a few minutes until his jaw falls slack and his eyelids begin to flutter. Can there be anything more peaceful and perfect than a dreaming child? The sight calms me.

I watch the reflection of the flames in the leads and think about what might be out there in the dark upon the moor. There's nothing outside save the night, I tell myself, and the fog pressing at the panes. But I cannot sleep until I have closed the shutters.

Chapter 3

A few days later, I'm at the brook washing out my rags.

I prefer to do this work away from prying eyes – the scarlet stain of my flowers is a thing I would deny even to myself, if I could – so rather than use a tub in the yard, I choose a secluded spot near the falls, just a little way downstream. It's the place we use to wash the sheep in summer – wide enough for three or four men to stand but so an arm's reach could snare any wayward beast, deep enough to reach a man's hips, with a strong current to take the filth away. The river is watered by streams that run off the moor top. We need only dam it in years of drought, perhaps five times in my whole life; this is damp country and clouds collect in the valleys. Now, in late February, melting snow swells the streams that feed the falls, and the water is too deep and too cold for any man to bear.

To either side, the land rises steeply up the valley walls. Silvery water carves a thousand-year path between peat and rock, dropping from the fells, freezing into icicles, glazing the mosses and hazing into fine mist where it meets the valley bottom. The music of the falls is as familiar as my own breath. It's a place I've known my whole life – a playmate in childhood, a sanctuary now I'm grown, and many things between. The lofty ravine becomes my chancel, the lichened stone my altar, cascading water the whisper of prayer.

It's a place of memory, of grace, a place where Heaven and Earth seem to meet.

The fog that fell the night I birthed the lamb has stayed with us, rising and falling with the hours, turning daytime into twilight, lending a roof to Nature's chapel. I am cocooned by it.

I set to work, trying to ignore the harsh sting of icy water and lye that turns my skin sore and red. As I beat my monthly blood from the rags, I sing to myself – an old ballad that Agnes taught me as a child. The story is sentimental, and when I was young, with a head full of notions, it appealed to me. Some silly maiden falls for a rogue who treats her ill. She prays for help to catch him and keep him, claiming that, deep down, he loves her more than his life of crime and sin. She can redeem him, she says, if only God will help. But by the end of the tale, the Devil has claimed his prize, and the poor girl gives herself up to a life of sadness and solitude, forever repenting that she could not save the man she loved.

Perhaps Agnes was trying to teach me a lesson, trying to instil some caution in me, for she saw my wilfulness early on. Perhaps she was trying to save me from the lessons that life has since taught, but I didn't listen. I was made bold by the idea of so great a passion and so great a sacrifice. Of course, that was before I learned the truth about love, before I felt the torment of devotion where it is not desired, before I knew and accepted my own solitude, and before I understood that such stories are only that.

Agnes, with her crooked gait, creviced cheeks and white hair like cotton grass, needn't have relied upon tragic ballads as a warning – her very presence is proof enough of the result of a disappointed heart. I decided long ago I would not suffer the same fate.

Still, it's a pleasant tune, full of melancholy, and one I turn to often. Now, it serves to quell any foreboding I might feel, for I cannot rid myself of the memory of that day and the figure

I saw in the fog. No matter how many times I tell myself it was nothing more than imagination, that I was tired and over-wrought, I cannot cast the image from my mind's eye, or shake the creeping fear that comes with it. Deep down, I know I did not make it up.

And as I think of it, I feel it again – the slow crawl across my shoulder blades, prickling at my neck, a quickening of my heartbeat. I try to shake it off, but the sensation stays. I fall silent, stop my work and listen, resisting the urge to look around. There's no one about for miles, save Ambrose, who I know is out on the fells with his dog, Flint, checking the sheep for early lambs.

I go back to my laundry, working in the lye, rubbing at the stains. I hum the tune, quieter now, but fear is pressing in my chest and my voice comes out uneven. Bracken, who's been lazing at my feet, raises her head, one ear cocked, and makes a low growl.

I put a palm on her back, taking comfort in her solid warmth. 'You sense it too?'

Her nose twitches and she grumbles before resting her head on her paws.

I begin rinsing and wringing the sodden rags. My fingers are aching and clumsy with cold.

For a time I focus on the task, finding pleasure in monotony, pausing after each rag is wrung out to flex my fingers and bring the blood back into them. I watch the fog sink into the valley, obscuring the treetops and silencing the birds. Today I don't like the eerie stillness that descends, so I begin my song again.

And after a few minutes I'm answered by a whistle – a few distant notes echoed back to me. I strain for the sound of footfall or hoof-beat, of someone on the path that runs along the valley, but hear nothing, the fog muffling everything but the splash and burble of the falls. I'm imagining things again. It might be birdcall, or wind singing through the stones.

But when, after a few moments, I continue, it comes again, a whistle picking up alongside. This time, when I stop, it carries a few more notes before it too falls silent.

'Who's there?' I call, fear rising. I hold my breath and listen.

There's no answer.

Slowly, I put down the wet rag I'm holding and reach for my crook.

A sudden shower of pebbles scatters the hillside by the falls as if someone has disturbed the higher ground. Bracken jumps to her feet, tense and growling.

'Who's there? Ambrose, is that you?' But Ambrose is not one for tricks – it's not his nature – and Bracken knows him by sound and scent.

I feel the sensation of eyes on me, like a spider crawling up my spine, and this time I stand and spin about, trying to see through the gloom. I call Bracken to my side and try to quiet her but she begins to bark, breaks away and runs to the foot of the falls, snarling and snapping into the hazy space above.

I see what has disturbed her: a figure in the fog, a dark smudge on the crag above the falls.

For a few seconds I can do nothing. I stare at the thing, gripped by horror. The fog blurs my vision. I expect the figure to disappear as before, but it does not move. It stands and waits. Again the blood rushes in my veins and my heart is all chaos.

'Who's there?' I call again. 'Show yourself!'

The figure obeys me – moves forward to stand on a rock at the very top of the falls. Now I can make out the shape of a hat, a long coat and a staff.

Bracken is all savage eyes and sharp teeth.

Then, from above, 'Call off your dog!'

And with the order a great wave of relief courses through me, faster than the rushing water at my feet. This is no phantom.

I call to Bracken but she won't come, so I go to her, picking my way over the rocks. I catch hold of her rope collar and find my fingers are shaking.

The man does not wait for invitation. He finds a precarious path down the side of the falls, climbing from rock to rock, clinging to the heather, stones slithering away from beneath his soles. As he emerges from the veil of mist and spray, I see there's nothing ghostly about him. He's tall, made to seem more so by a long buckskin coat, sturdy leather boots and a battered brown hat. He has a pack slung about his shoulders, beneath which he's stowed the staff that I now see has the curved bow of a shepherd's crook.

He reaches the valley foot and stands a few yards from me. 'I mean you no harm,' he says. 'I heard you. I didn't expect . . .' He makes a gesture towards my clothes.

His voice has a smoky, charred tone, reminding me of the charcoal-burners who often have such a break in their voice, but now he's close, he speaks quietly.

'Who are you?' I ask. 'Why were you watching me?'

He stands and stares for a few moments. Then he takes a step forward and extends a hand. 'Ferreby. Ellis Ferreby.' I do not take it. I keep my grasp on Bracken's collar.

She's fallen quiet now but I feel her coiled energy as she watches him. I know, if I say the word, she'll snap at him, like a fox after our hens.

'I said, why were you watching me?'

'I lost the track in the fog. I heard your voice and thought to seek the owner. I didn't mean to frighten you.'

'You didn't.'

He glances at my tight grasp on the crook, the dog at my heel. 'Then I'll be on my way, if you'll put me on the right path.'

'Where are you headed?'

He shrugs. 'Anywhere there's work. Folks told me they'd be needing hands for the lambing at a place called Scarcross Hall.'

I should have guessed. The only men travelling at this time of year are those seeking a place to earn their bread and beer, those with no hearthside to wait out the winter, those wanting a place they won't be found. We don't welcome such strangers. 'Who told you so?'

He does not answer but shrugs off his pack and sets it down. 'That's a fine-looking bitch you have there.'

I feel Bracken bristle, but I won't let him see I'm so wary myself. 'I've not seen you in these parts before,' I say.

He bends suddenly, dropping to one knee, and holds out an empty palm towards Bracken. 'Come here, girl . . .'

Bracken glances up at me, questioning, just once and then to him. He says nothing more, but crouches, eyes lowered, palm still upturned in a gesture of conciliation and submission. I feel the moment the resistance goes out of her. She relaxes, noses the air for his scent, takes a tentative step towards him. I loosen my grip on her collar. And she goes to him. She goes to him and sniffs his hand.

I've seen her skip and yap around Ambrose before, I've even seen her let Sam pet her once or twice, but I've never seen her go to a stranger. Bracken is my dog and she answers to no one but me.

He pats her head, rubs her ears, then stands. She folds herself neatly at his feet. I cannot believe it.

'If you'll show me the path to Scarcross Hall, I'll be on my way,' he says.

I turn and begin to gather the rags, wringing out the last few and placing them in the waiting basket. My fingers are still trembling with slowly dissolving panic. I take my time, hoping he'll understand the message in my coldness.

He watches in silence and, though I don't look at him, I sense that he's judging me, weighing me up. There's a strange stillness about him – he makes no offer of help and is not compelled to chatter as some might, but seems content to wait for my answer.

When I've folded the last rag, I turn back and find he's donned his pack. Bracken is on her feet, looking up at him the way she looks at me when she's waiting on my word. 'Bracken, come to heel,' I say, but she doesn't move. She looks at me and wags her tail.

'Scarcross Hall?' he asks again.

I don't know why I don't send him on, why I don't tell him who I am and turn him away. The words seem to tumble out of me before I can check them. 'I'm going that way.'

He nods, taking that as some sort of permission.

At last Bracken trots to my side. I set off, following the valley bottom towards the path home. I don't look back or speak to him again but I know he follows. I can feel his eyes on my back.

Chapter 4

As we leave the valley and reach the sloped sweep of the fell we meet Ambrose Garrick and his dog, Flint. The two dogs greet each other with a volley of yaps. I'm relieved to see him. My father's head shepherd, now mine, I trust his judgement as much as my own, at least in matters of farm and flock. I'll leave the stranger's fate to him but mention nothing of the queer nature of our meeting.

We wait while the stranger climbs the last few yards towards us. I see Ambrose take the measure of him. Ambrose is a big man, red-bearded with weather-beaten skin and the curt manner of those born and bred in the hills. I know he can seem imposing, but the stranger bears his scrutiny and greets him with a solid handshake.

'Looking for work, then?' Ambrose asks.

'Yes. I was told to speak with you by John Bestwicke.'

'John's one of our best men. You know him?'

'Only in passing. Said he was headed up here himself in a few days. Told me to try my luck.'

'What's your name?'

'Ellis Ferreby.'

'You're not from these parts. I'd know you if you were.'

'I worked these last years on the moors above York and as far as the Cumbrian fells. I know hill country.'

Ambrose shoots me a questioning look, raises an eyebrow, but I just shrug, passing the decision back. I'm not shy of my responsibility, quite the contrary, but I prefer to leave these matters to him. I've learned the hard way that shepherding men prefer to strike an accord with their own kind.

'We've no quarters, but you can sleep in the hayloft till the hay is in,' Ambrose says. 'Your bread and beer, and twopence a day.'

The stranger nods.

'Well, then, Master Ferreby, follow me and I'll see you housed and fed. You can start with me in the morning. One week to begin and we'll see how you work.' Ambrose assumes agreement – no man desperate enough to wander the fells in the fog would turn down the offer – and starts along the path to Scarcross Hall.

I stride ahead, the basket of rags heavy in the crook of my arm, eager to leave them behind. Though I trust Ambrose's instinct, I'm not sure it matches my own this time. We've employed many men like Ellis Ferreby over the years and I know the type. The hills are full of them: men without history, without a home, who keep their counsel when questioned about their past. Often they're good workers, grateful enough for the chance we give, but some bring their troubles with them. I'm always glad when the harvest is done, the sheep are put out for winter and we are left alone once more.

Reaching Scarcross Hall, I hear raised voices and recognise the sound of Father in a rage. I find him in the kitchen, puffed up with fury, gesticulating wildly – an echo of the formidable man he used to be. His temper has not abated with age: rather, it's grown worse. At times, it gets the better of him. The smallest incident can ignite explosions of irrational anger. Agnes knows to tread carefully but has grown peevish and impatient after so many years. The fights they have can be fearsome.

'You are lying, woman!' Father yells, as I enter. 'By Christ,

I swear I shall turn you out into the night if you don't tell me the truth.' He's been threatening this for years. We all know it will never happen.

'I told you, I know nothing of it,' Agnes says.

'You've taken it, haven't you? Taken it to sell to the tinkers. This is what I get for keeping you all these years, for not insisting that you know your place – nothing but lying and thievery!'

Agnes rolls her eyes and turns away, exasperated.

Bracken, usually keen to curl up by the fire whenever I allow it, slinks away and sits by the door. I'm unwilling to put myself at the centre of one of their squabbles but curiosity gets the better of me. 'What's happened?'

'The Applegarth woman' – as Father calls Agnes when he's angry with her – 'the Applegarth woman has stolen my inkwell and won't admit it.'

She turns to me. 'He's worked himself up over a piece of brass.'

'That inkwell belonged to Merion Booth, the man who raised this family up from nothing, who made our fortune, whose riches paid for the very flags upon which you stand and the slates over your head.' As he speaks, he jabs Agnes with the end of his cane. 'So don't you dare say it's just a piece of brass.'

'Raise a hand to me again, Bartram Booth, and I'll bring curses down upon you.'

I know she'd never do this. Agnes would never wish harm on anyone, but this is the game they play – petty bullying and empty threats.

'Was it you took my coins too? Will you use them against me in your spell casting? Do you think I'll allow such witchery in my house? Do you think I'm so old and forgetful that I would not see what you're about? I've said nothing about your heathen ways before but I'll keep silent no longer.'

'I haven't touched your precious coins neither.'

'I don't believe you,' he says, leaning over her, eyes dark with threat. 'You have no idea what you are toying with.'

I put my basket on the table. I'll have to deal with this before I address the wet rags. 'Calm yourself, Father. Where did you last see the coins?'

'In a safe place, away from prying eyes and thieving fingers,' he says, stepping away from Agnes with a sour look.

'And the inkwell?'

'It was on my desk, of course.'

I cross the room and put a soothing hand on his forearm. 'Are you sure you didn't move it yourself, to fill it perhaps, or to make space on your table?'

Father glowers. 'Do you think I'm a fool?'

'Then, come, we'll find them together.'

I lead him across the hall towards his study, Agnes trailing after us. The cold pinches as we leave the warmth of the kitchen. It's always chill in the hall, even in summer. The room should be the heart of the house, with a ceiling stretching to the rafters, a large, open hearth and a big window that reflects spirals of sunlight on rare days of sunshine. At one time, with beeswax candles burning in the sconces, rich tapestries stopping the draughts, minstrels in the gallery and a fine feast spread on the heavy oak table, it might have been splendid. But now the table is pushed up against the panelling and any useful furniture has been moved to smaller rooms that are easier to heat. There are no candles, and no tapestries or rush mats to soften the stone-flagged floor. We never set a blaze because the chimney is fallen in and the wind whistles through the cracked panes in the window, straight off the moor. I've often wondered what kind of people might have had need of such a space, for we certainly have no use for it.

My father's study is at the back of the house with windows that look out over the old walled garden. Since his health failed, and his sight began to fade, it's become his sanctuary and the room in which he spends most of his days. There's bare light through the panes and no candles burning, the only brightness cast by a few flames from a timid fire.

I take a taper, light it and touch the candles in the stick on the desk. Though Ambrose and I manage the flock, Father is still head of the household. He likes to oversee the account books and keep up correspondence with the cloth merchants in Halifax and Leeds. The desk is strewn with ledgers and bills of sale. His reading glass teeters precariously close to the edge. I find at least three quills with snapped nibs, all dripping ink onto the wood. But Father is right: there is no sign of the inkwell.

He is triumphant. 'Who else could have taken it? No one else comes in here, save Ambrose and yourself. She must have it.'

Agnes shoots him a dark look but keeps her silence.

We search on bookshelves, under rugs and in boxes filled with old bones and rocks – Father likes to collect these things – but we cannot find the inkwell, nor any sign of the missing coins.

He stands by, drumming his fingers on the desk. I don't understand why the loss of these things has vexed him so when he has not mentioned them for so long. I've not seen the coins since I was a child, and Agnes is right about the inkwell: I doubt it has little value beyond that endowed by Father's sentiment.

Still, I'm frustrated by the mystery. These things cannot have disappeared. I think of Sam and his questions about the missing coins just a few nights before. The boy is always in and out of Father's study – the only one allowed such licence – and he's been in the house these last few days, tending the lamb. Could he be playing some sort of misguided game?

'Where's Sam?' I ask.

'He was in the kitchen earlier,' Agnes says, 'mewling on about that milk-stinking creature and getting under my feet.'

'Well, then, let's ask him.'

Back in the kitchen, we find the lamb curled up in a crate by the fire, but no sign of Sam. I hear movement upstairs – the creak of boards and a low, regular *thunk*, as if someone is tossing a ball onto the floor of the room above.

I go to the foot of the kitchen stairs and call Sam's name into the dim-lit space above. There's no answer, but the thudding continues, interspersed with a low scraping sound of something heavy being dragged across the boards.

I climb a few steps, peering into the gloom, and call again. He cannot hear me. I mount the stairs, irritated now by everything that has come to pass today. There is still so much to be done before the light fades and I have no time to play nursemaid to my father or his charge. He does wrong to indulge the child – it encourages disobedience. I've indulged Sam too, letting him cosset the lamb in the way that Father cossets the boy. I should have sent him home days ago and seen to the creature myself.

I reach the upper floor and realise the sound is not coming from the room above the kitchen as I thought. The room where Agnes has her bed is empty. Instead it's coming from the chamber opposite.

This chamber was once a fine bedroom with a grand old tester bed and a large window with far-reaching views. We never use it now – we never have visitors in need of it – and in these last years it has become a storeroom of sorts, gradually filling with disused farm equipment and forgotten odds and ends. Last year we used it to store fleeces when the barn was too damp, and the room still holds the dense, greasy smell of sheep.

The sound is louder now, a rhythmic *thunk*, a pause, a heavy, grating *ssshrrrrrsssst*, as if Sam is tossing a ball or hoop and dragging it back across the boards before repeating.

I lift the latch and open the door. 'Sam?'

The noise stops.

The shutters are closed and there's scant light through the cracks. I doubt they've been opened in months.

'What are you doing in here? Come downstairs. My father has something to ask you.'

There's no answer.

I step inside.

The curtains are drawn around the tester bed, the ancient embroidered vines and flowers now ragged, decayed by moths and mould. A stack of crates in the corner is draped in cobwebs and wisps of fleece. At the hearthstone, a pile of soot and muck has spilled from the disused chimney, but there is a distinct, acrid smell of burning – wood smoke tinged with animal tallow. There's a thick carpet of undisturbed winter dust on the floorboards. Somehow it feels wrong to stir the silence.

Though I can see he's not in the room, I speak Sam's name.

Of course, there's no response. I leave and shut the door. As I begin to make my way back down the staircase, the noise starts again.

Thunk . . . ssshrrrrrsssssst . . .

Angered now, I storm back up the stairs. 'Enough, Sam. This is no time for games.'

Silence.

I swallow the unease that threatens and stride into the room, tug back the drapes on the bed and am lost in a flurry of dust that chokes my throat. Sam is not there.

I go to the window, squeezing behind an old chest and dislodging a moth-eaten Turkey rug that releases a storm of sooty smuts. I prise open the rusted hinge on the shutter. The murky daylight is not much help but is enough for me to see that no one is in the room.

With a weird tightness in my throat, I close the shutter and listen. Nothing. The room is strangely still. Even the ever-present breath of the wind is absent. But it's cold – the kind of snow-bound chill that creeps into the bones – and the charred stench in the air stings my nostrils. My skin shivers into goose bumps.

Perhaps the noise is just rats in the walls, now quieted by my entrance. I picture them, jet eyes glittering, noses quivering with my scent, waiting until I leave.

'Down here, Mercy,' comes Agnes's call from below, and I'm glad to answer, fastening the door and hurrying down the steps, ignoring the hard pulsing of my heart.

In the kitchen Sam is kneeling next to the lamb's box, stroking the creature's small white head.

'He says he knows nothing about it,' Father says, still scowling at Agnes.

'Where have you been, Sam?' I ask, crouching, one hand on his shoulder, welcoming the human warmth of him.

'Out in the privy.'

'You weren't upstairs?'

'No.' He doesn't look at me but goes on petting the lamb. I sit cross-legged next to him.

'And you didn't move the inkwell?'

He's silent for a few moments.

'Or the coins. Are you sure you didn't take the coins?'

No answer.

'You won't be in trouble if you tell the truth.'

He cannot hold my gaze. '*I did not take them.*'

I'm tired of this. I run my hand over the lamb, its dense fleece warm beneath my palm. It gives a bleat. 'You've done well with this little one, but I can manage now. He's out of danger. You can go home with your pa tonight.'

Sam's eyes are a conflict of childish indignation and pleading. 'I didn't take them. Please don't send me away.'

'See what you've done? You've upset the boy,' Father says to Agnes, but she doesn't retaliate – she's closed in on herself, as she does when she knows she won't win a fight and there's nothing to gain in trying.

'I'm not sending you away, Sam. You can come back and check

on the lamb in the morning. But you must be missing your ma. And what about your little sister? They need you too.'

He gives me an accusatory look: *You have failed me. You don't understand.*

As if summoned, the outside door opens and Ambrose enters, stamping his feet, the stranger, Ellis Ferreby, in his wake.

Sam runs to his father and flings his arms around his hips. Ambrose ruffles his red curls, so like his own, though these days Ambrose keeps his own scalp as close-shorn as a summer sheep.

Ambrose nods to Father, who has softened a little at the sight of Sam's dismay, then asks, 'Agnes, can you spare some bread and cheese for our new man?'

But Agnes is leaning heavily against the table. She's turned the colour of three-day-old milk. She stumbles a few steps towards the buttery, where she stops, steadying herself against the wall.

I'm up and by her side in a moment.

'Just one of my turns . . .' she whispers, under her breath. I hold her hand and feel her heart racing. 'Leave me be.' She gives me an imploring look.

I glare at Father as I send Sam to fetch bread and a hunk of cheese. His anger has brought on Agnes's troubles – these attacks have happened before, often after a quarrel. I blame him for it.

'Ambrose, help Agnes to her bed.' Ambrose comes forward and puts an arm around Agnes's shoulders, gently guiding her towards the stairs. As they leave, she glances back at Ellis Ferreby and I read her shame and horror at her frailty exposed before a stranger. But all the time Ellis Ferreby is silent. He makes no offer of help and shows no concern. Save a grudging nod towards Father, he says nothing at all, but hovers at the side of the room, like a shadow, watching and waiting until he's watered and fed, as if it is his due.

Chapter 5

'What do you make of him, the new man?'

Dority pushes a lock of hair behind her ear, leaving a dusting of flour across her cheek. 'He's all Ambrose has talked about these last two nights. I think he's taken a liking.' We both know that Ambrose never admits to friendship with any of the men we employ; he considers complaining about their failings his duty and his right. 'So . . . what's he like?'

'I've barely seen him,' I say, though this isn't true.

I had come across them that morning, Ambrose and Ellis, building byres behind the barn. It will be Ellis's job to tend any orphan lambs and recuperating mothers by night and he wants them close, so the dogs will help keep foxes away.

Bracken ran ahead to greet them, greedily licking the fingers that Ellis offered. It had taken me several minutes to bring her to heel. I cannot understand her fancy for the man. I felt his eyes follow me. He stares at me whenever our paths cross. There's no lechery in it, but no respect either. I'm a curiosity, to be peered at and made sense of. If I were a more timid sort of woman, it might unnerve me, but it's not the first time I've been looked at this way.

I think back to our first meeting at the falls and wonder why I did not send him on. Even now, when I could settle his wages and tell him to go, I choose not to. It seems to me there are secrets in his silence, and purpose in his stare. But he's proved a good worker and, though he's not said so, Ambrose is pleased. I was bred to be wary of strangers and ever since the day I saw the figure in the fog, I'm more watchful and less certain of my own judgement. My nerves have begun to play tricks on me. I find myself starting at Bracken's barks and shying at shadows like a spring-green stripling. I'd laugh at myself if the memory did not conjure such a sense of misgiving.

'Where did you find him?' Dority asks.

'He found me.'

She puzzles. 'What do you mean?'

But I need not answer. We're interrupted by Sam racketing through the door with a pail of peat clods.

'Where have you been?' Dority puts aside the dough she's been working, wiping her hands on her apron. 'Mercy's come to see you.'

Sam puts the bucket down by the hearth and sidles over to his mother. She puts a protective hand on his shoulder.

'Why have you not come to see us, Sam?' I ask. 'We've missed you at the Hall these last few days.'

He stubs the toe of his boot into the earth between the flagstones.

'Do you not wish to care for your lamb?'

At this he looks at me. 'I do.'

'Then why not come?'

Dority strokes his hair. 'Have you something to say to Mercy?'

He shakes his head.

'Sam, we agreed . . .' There's a tightening in her voice.

'No, we didn't.'

'Sam . . .'

He pulls away from Dority growing red-cheeked. 'Why won't you believe me?'

'Sam, you must do as your father said.'

'No! Why won't anyone listen to me?' Sam glares at us both. I'm shocked by the frustration and hurt in his eyes. He turns and runs outside.

Dority sighs. She crosses the room and checks on the sleeping child in the cradle – the baby, Grace, born just half a year since – then picks up a small object from the mantel above the hearth and places it on the floured tabletop. It's a gold disc, blinking jewel-bright amid the barley dust. I recognise it immediately: one of Father's missing coins.

'I found it under his pillow, but he swears he didn't take it. I'm sorry, Mercy. I don't know what to say.'

I pick it up. The metal is frostbite-cold.

'It belongs to your father, doesn't it?'

'Yes.' I stare at the coin in my palm. It makes my heart heavy to think that Sam would lie to me. 'Is this the only one you found?'

'Yes. Are there more?'

'Three are missing.'

I see a flicker of dismay as she takes this in. 'I can't understand why he would do such a thing,' she says, barely able to meet my eye. 'I've tried to persuade him to take it back, to confess and apologise. I even threatened to take him to Pastor Flynn for penance, but he refuses. He swears he doesn't know how it came to be there. I can't understand it at all.'

'Perhaps he's scared. Father has been in a temper of late. You know how he can be.'

'Sam's become so secretive. He never tells me anything.'

'What does Ambrose say?'

She shakes her head. 'Oh, he's no help at all. Says the boy is just growing up. Says I worry too much. But of course I worry, especially since Will . . .' She stops herself. Ambrose forbade us to speak of what happened, as if to do so would tempt the Devil a second time, and Dority is loyal to a fault. 'Is worry not a mother's job?'

Ambrose may be right. I've noticed creases appearing on Dority's brow, the hollows at her collarbones, the greying beneath her eyes, and put it down to winter's hardship and the trials of nursing a babe.

'To think he's stolen from your father,' she goes on, 'who's only ever been good to us . . .'

'There may be more to it. I'll take this back to Father and see what he says. Don't punish Sam until we have the truth.'

'But if he's taken anything from Scarcross Hall—'

'Father will forgive him. Father would forgive him anything.'

She sighs again, thinking. 'He said he doesn't want to be blamed for things he hasn't done. What does he mean?'

I tell her about the disappearance of the coins and the missing inkwell, and Father's fiery outburst over the whole affair. She listens, twisting her fingers in her apron. When I'm done she goes to the door and stands at the threshold, looking out. After a time, she turns back, fear in her eyes, and wipes a tear from her cheek.

'Well, one thing is certain,' she says, forcing a smile. 'Someone is not telling the truth.'

Though she will not say it, I know what she's thinking.

There's an old rhyme, well known in these parts, that the weavers teach their children. On dark nights, you can still hear it sung from rush-lit cottages, chanted in time to the *click-clack* of the loom. When we were young its macabre message delighted us and we would dare each other to sing it aloud, dancing about the White Ladies like heathens, the wind tugging at the heather wound into our hair:

> *One coin marks the first to go*
> *A second bodes the fall*
> *The third will seal a sinner's fate*
> *The Devil take them all*

Chapter 6

Ellis Ferreby is used to the rain. He knows that up on the moors it can be deceptive. A light mist can drench the thickest cloth, leaving it heavy and sodden; a spring shower can creep beneath collars and under cuffs, find cracks in the sturdiest boots. A day begun in sunshine can end in a soaking. He has seen men beaten by it – softer men, southern men – men whose fingers chap until they bleed and whose feet rot and stink until they lose toes. To spend a lifetime up here, you have to be born to it.

The two newcomers, John Bestwicke and Henry Ravens, are born to it.

They had arrived yesterday, at dusk, taking up their berths in the hayloft alongside his own. Bestwicke, the man he'd met in the tavern in the village, seemed pleased to find him there and keen to share the paltry portion of pie he'd brought. The hills are full of hardy men like Bestwicke, a widower, with decades of shepherding behind him, and Ellis feels comfortable in his company. He's small and wiry, dressed in patched, mended breeches and worn boots. His smile is all black gaps and brown teeth, but it's honest, and there's something youthful about his sharp blue eyes.

The other, Ravens, is younger, shovel-fisted and loud-mouthed, with a lean, handsome face. He's only silenced this morning by the sore head he must be suffering from the drink he'd put away. After half a bottle of spirits, Ravens had chattered and boasted, liquor-laced breath steaming in the cold night air every time he laughed at his own joke. He talked of himself, and of other local men that Ellis doesn't know, as if making a point: *I am known here. This is my territory*. Ellis will have to tolerate such displays, if he is to stay.

Today they will bring the flock down from the winter pasture to the in-bye land nearest the house, ready for lambing. The fog has lifted but the sky is heavy with fat grey-bellied clouds. In the copse by the house, wet-feathered birds hunch on bare branches. Up on the fell, where the sheep are wintered, the ground is marshy with melting snow, strewn with hoof-churned hay. But, here and there, unlikely green shoots reach through the soil, and this morning, when he pissed outside the barn, he had watered a patch of winter wolfsbane, the scent of spring sharp in his nostrils.

Once out on the land, Bestwicke and Ravens prove themselves fit and sure-footed. He follows their lead. They know this country. They know where to find the flock, the best routes to drive the sheep down, the unmarked boundaries between the Booth land and the common grazing on the moor, the smits that mark Booth's animals from the hundreds of others that share the space. More importantly, they know the traps: the bog that can swallow a man whole, the hidden becks, hags and hollows that might cause a fall, a broken bone, or worse. He trusts them because he trusts the unspoken bond between shepherding men. He puts his faith in them because he has no choice.

She is here too, of course, with Garrick, and the two dogs, Bracken and Flint. She was waiting for them beneath the sparse shelter of the copse. When she saw them coming she set off up the hillside so Garrick had to stride ahead to catch her.

Thick as thieves, Bestwicke had said, of the lead shepherd and the mistress. Ellis watches them, the way their bodies move in tandem, barely speaking, communicating by gestures and nods, in the language of sheep and fell and dogs. He notices the way she turns her face into the wind and shuts her eyes, breathes deep, the way another woman might breathe in the scent of a flower garden.

He's heard things, collected rumour and gossip in alehouses up and down the valley. *A rare one*, they said, with nudges and laden smiles, *not many like her*. He knows better than to believe everything he hears over a pint pot but she's not what he expected.

She is taller. Broader. Her gait has something manly about it. Plain-featured, drab-haired, with colouring that matches the winter-leached heather – it's only in the slim jaw and in her voice that he detects anything womanly. He noticed her voice on their first meeting – low and rich, with a hint of gentility.

He watches her backside as she climbs the hill ahead of him. The clothes – breeches and boots – almost hide her shape but there's a telltale tapering at the waist, a widening at the hips. Good teeth – he noticed that too – straight and white. He judges her as he would judge a breeding ewe.

He had not meant to frighten her that first day. He had crossed the moor slantwise, losing a drovers' track some miles back and finding himself without sure footing as the fog came down. The murk had made him blind. The mud sucked at his heels. He turned an ankle and wondered if he would last another night warmed by nothing but the few sips of liquor in his spent flask. But he has a keen sense of direction, and even without a horizon to fix upon, or sun and shadows by which to right himself, he had found his way to her.

Her manner with him is still curt, her suspicion marked. That is to be expected – only a fool would welcome a stranger without question and he sees she's not easily taken in. But he saw the change in her when the dog came to him so easily and he knew that something so simple to him was extraordinary to her. He's always had a way with animals. Betsy used to joke that it was a quality he never mastered when it came to people. But he saw the alteration in her and understood that the dog is a weakness, a way in.

* * *

Even with the dogs, it takes most of the day to find, sort and check the flock, bring them safely down and drive them into the lower grazing. Ellis finds his place in the group easily enough under Garrick's direction, working alongside Bestwicke and Ravens to collect strays and runners, while the dogs do the brute work of gathering.

Coursing the edge of the moor top, where the rough grassy hillocks of the fell give way to stunted heather and rain-drenched peat, he catches the true scent of the land for the first time. Every place and every season has its own smell, he's found. Pay attention and he'll come to know it, just as he'll learn the way the sun fades to shadow at a certain time of day on a certain hillside, the texture of the grasses on this fell and the next, the particular course of the breeze as it travels down the valley. Now, in this moment, the wind brings it to him: the rich savour of damp peat, must and decay, the metallic, coppery scent of snow and ancient, rain-washed stone, a hint of salt and sea storms. He recognises it, he thinks, though that is impossible. He knows it by some deeper sense, then: in his bones, in his blood.

He pauses, looking back down the fell towards the chimneys of Scarcross Hall.

You can't mistake the place, he'd been told by the tavern keeper. *Find the church and follow the old coffin path that runs up towards the moor top. You'll not miss it.*

The man had been right: the house commands attention. It's grander than he'd supposed, with the high chimneys and crenellated gables of an older age, mullioned windows and two jutting wings on either side of a central hall, clearly designed with more than practicality in mind – a statement of wealth and power, one man's attempt to make his mark in this wild landscape. If it were another house he might despise it. He might feel contempt for the arrogance of the wealthy, with their propensity to tame things that cannot be tamed. But on first sight, his feeling had been of surprise and something like awe.

Then, as he had followed Garrick past the decrepit half-timbered barn and drew closer, he saw that any days of grandeur were long faded. There are slates missing from the roof, cracked panes in the leads and a crumbling central chimney. A high wall lends poor protection, pocked and lichen-stained, ravaged by years of storm and gale. It has the air of a shipwreck, abandoned and disintegrating amid the great wild ocean of the moor. Even now, the dark windows seem to stare back at him, soulless, like the eyes of a destitute. Despite all his resolution, he shivers.

Mercy Booth keeps her distance. Aware that both she and Garrick are making silent judgement upon him, he keeps his mouth shut, his eyes and ears keen. Doing so seems to win Garrick's approval, for once the day's work is done, the pregnant ewes counted into the field, the man comes up to him and slaps a hand on his shoulder – a gesture in place of words he does not need to hear.

She comes to stand beside them, leaning both elbows on the willow gate. Her cheeks are wind-whipped. Strands of damp mousy hair straggle across her neck. He watches from the corner of his eye – watches her watching the sheep – and knows she's calculating which will lamb first, which might need separating from the rest, looking for signs of foot rot and milk fever. He knows because he cannot help doing the same.

When Garrick leaves, she turns to Ellis and takes a breath as though she's about to speak, but says nothing. He's suddenly aware of her arm, so close to his on the gatepost, and moves away.

The boy he's seen around the place, Garrick's son, rounds the corner of the barn with a bundle in his arms – a lamb wrapped in a blanket – the same coddled specimen that he saw before the kitchen hearth on the night he arrived.

The boy is rushing, breathless, mumbling when he speaks. 'I've brought him to see if any of the ewes will take him.'

Mercy's expression softens in the boy's presence, a hand to his copper curls. 'It's too late for that, Sam. We missed our chance.'

The boy frowns. 'Then what'll become of him?'

'You'll have to feed him until he's ready to go to grass, then we'll put him in with the others.'

'So you'll keep him for a tup?'

'He's small and not strong. He didn't have the best start.'

The boy is disappointed and she sees it. 'Well, let's see how he stands,' she says. 'Show Master Ferreby what a fine shepherd you've become.'

It's the first time she's acknowledged him all day and the first she has used his name – a sign he's done well. It sends a small, pleasurable ripple through him.

The boy unwraps the lamb tenderly and places it on the ground. It bleats and looks around, confused to find itself on cold, damp earth. A few of the ewes raise their heads at the sound.

The boy is looking at him, expectant and hopeful.

'How old is he?' Ellis asks.

'Nine days.'

'Mistress Booth is right. He's pretty but he's small. Best make him a wether.'

'What did I do wrong?' the boy asks, looking from one to the other.

'Nothing,' she says. 'It's God's way, that's all.' She crouches next to the creature and runs her hands over its back and belly, down its legs. 'We should see to the gelding. There's some salve in the barn.'

'I'll do it,' Ellis says.

They both look at him, questioning.

He draws a knife from his belt. 'I always have a keen blade about me.'

She nods. 'There now, Sam. You help Master Ferreby.'

She signals their intention to Garrick and the three of them walk to the barn, where she ferrets in a stack of chests and trestle tables, then brings out an earthenware pot of sheep salve.

Ellis pulls one of the chests towards the door, into the last of the daylight, sits and takes the lamb into his arms. It bleats and struggles but he can tell he's right – this animal is not strong enough, not well formed enough to make a good tup, might not even grow big enough to make a decent fleece, but it's worth saving, if only for the boy's sake.

With his blade between his teeth he flips the lamb, gripping the hind legs between his knees. He has Sam hold the lamb by the forelegs, and draws out the cods. The creature wriggles and kicks.

'Hold him still, lad.' Quickly he makes two small slashes, one in each pouch. He bends and pulls out the stones one at a time with his teeth, slicing away the sinewy strings that bind them. He tastes blood, spits onto the floor, then dips his fingers into the salve pot, feels the rich, waxy fat under his nails, and smears it on the wounds. The thing is done.

He sets the creature upright, checks it over, releases it. It staggers sideways, bleating, and collapses to its knees, where it sits, panting hard.

Mercy is watching him intently. 'Say thank you, Sam, for a job speedily done.'

Ellis picks up the stones and holds them out to the boy. 'They're small but it'll bring you luck to have the first of the season. Get your ma to fry them with a little fat and parsley.'

The boy takes them shyly, examines the pale, veined globes in his palm. Ellis feels the need to reassure him. 'And I have something else for you.' He reaches into his pocket and brings out a coin. 'I've rarely seen such a steady hand, even on a grown man, and you should be paid for your work.'

The small gold disc glints in his palm. He means it as a token, an offering of friendship, but the boy recoils.

'Where did you get that?'

Her tone leaves no room for doubt: he has made a mistake.

'I found it. Up there, in the hayloft.' He points upwards to his berth.

Confusion shivers across her face. 'When? When did you find it?'

'The night I arrived. I thought someone must have lost it long since.'

She snatches the coin from his hand. 'It belongs to my father.' She's angry, her usual cold composure shattered.

The boy begins to cry.

'I didn't take it, if that's what you think,' Ellis says.

'Sam, did you—'

But the boy turns away, gathers the lamb into his arms and bundles it back into the blanket.

'Keep a keen eye on the wound, Sam,' Ellis says. 'Tell someone if you see aught amiss or if he does not rally.' But the boy is not listening. He's already halfway out of the door and making for the house.

She stays, staring at the coin in her hand. 'Show me where you found it,' she says.

He points upwards again. 'Just beneath my bed, there.'

He watches her climb the ladder and hears her move overhead, shifting his things about. He waits until she comes down.

'You should have given it back when you found it,' she says, as she leaves, tossing him a blameful look.

He doesn't respond. Perhaps he should have returned the thing but he had thought it worthless, fool's gold, a trinket. He cannot fathom the strength of her reaction, her anger. He understands her sheep better than he understands her, he thinks, as he cleans the fresh blood from his blade.

Chapter 7

He does not like Henry Ravens. Too full of bragging and lies. John Bestwicke, though, he has time for. The old shepherd has proved himself the equal of the younger men today, matching them in strength, outranking them in experience. And he knows when to shut up.

All day Ravens has been baiting Ellis, getting in his way and taunting him with knowledge of the flock, as if they must work in competition. They are similar in height and girth, and would probably make a fair match in a fistfight. Ellis thinks about this, about how much he would like an excuse to land a well-aimed swing at Ravens's good-looking jaw. But he dare not risk his place here, and Garrick is not a man to take kindly to bickering among the workers.

He just wants Ravens to be quiet, so he can ask the important questions. But Ravens has been swigging from a bottle of sour-scented liquor – unshared, he notes – and is interrupting Bestwicke's train of thought.

They've passed the time since nightfall gathered around the brazier, talking mostly of sheep, of the Booth flock, of Garrick's qualities as lead shepherd and of the work that is to come. Both Ravens and Bestwicke are local men and work for Garrick every summer, coming up to the fells in spring, staying for washing, clipping and the hay harvest, and returning to their homes when the work runs dry, or when Garrick tells them to go. There's no work through the winter, Bestwicke says, and it's best not to stop up on the moor past harvest time – the hardship and loneliness can drive a man mad.

They are interested in him, in where he's from and where he's worked, but he keeps his answers short and vague until the questions stop. He learned long ago that if you keep quiet, people soon lose interest; most only want a reason to talk about themselves. Bestwicke is one of them and that's exactly what Ellis wants.

'Old Sutcliffe was head man before Garrick,' Bestwicke tells him. 'Must be ten years since he passed, maybe more. Garrick was young when Booth gave him the job and some from the village refused to work under him. But I've always got on with him. He's one of us. He's been working this flock twenty years, just as long as me.'

'He must have been a boy when he began.'

'Aye, and the mistress just a girl. I remember her, running about, skirts muddied to her knees, but she had the way of the flock even then. Born to it, I'd say.'

'She's always been the filthy sort,' Ravens says, and is ignored.

'Was she born here?' Ellis asks.

Bestwicke shakes his head, the brazier casting shadows across his face, adding crags upon crags. 'You'd think so, but Bartram Booth came out from Lancashire some time during the wars. Brought the girl with him.'

'Just him and the girl? No mother?'

'Just the Applegarth woman – she's been here as long as I remember.'

'What brought them here?'

'Now, lad, that's a question with a hundred different answers. Some folks said Booth was running from the law, others that his business had gone bad because of the fighting. Lord knows, we were all running from something in those days. There was even a story that he'd been cast out from some godly sect, and came hoping to set himself up in a New Jerusalem, but none of that came to pass. Must be thirty years ago. It's all forgotten now.'

'Which do you think true?'

Bestwicke shrugs. 'So long as I get what I'm owed it's not my business, and he's always been a fair master. But, for what it's worth, I think Booth bought up the Hall and the land because no one else wanted it. He saw a good chance and took it. He's a canny sort.' He takes a swig of ale. 'It'd been empty a good while before that. Stories, you know . . .'

'Ah, here we go!' Ravens laughs. 'He loves a tall tale, don't you, John?' He gives Bestwicke a slap on the shoulder and stands. 'I've heard this a dozen times . . . and I need a piss.'

Ravens walks unsteadily to the far side of the door, unties his breeches and pisses into the night. Ellis can see the arc of it glittering in the firelight. It makes his fists twitch.

But he doesn't want Bestwicke to lose his thread. 'What stories?'

'People talk – you know how it is. Rumours get passed down over the years. Some of the lads still won't stop up here at night – prefer to find shelter in the valley or go all the way back to the village rather than pass by the crossroads after dark.' He takes another drink and smacks his lips. 'There's been tales told about this place for longer than anyone can remember. My own pa was one of them wouldn't pass by without saying a prayer – swore the land was cursed.'

'Cursed?'

Bestwicke lowers his voice. 'There are stories go back long before our time, but the one I was raised on, the one you'll hear in the taverns, is of the man who built the Hall – a rich merchant from Halifax, with his wife and child. Must be a hundred years ago or more. There's been a farmhouse up here for much longer – but that old place had its own share of troubles and was long abandoned, so he tore it down, built the grand house you see now. He was set on making a fresh start. Wouldn't listen to the warnings.'

Ellis thinks of the house, alone and incongruous on the edge of the moor, the folly of it.

'But the first winter after the family moved up here was a rough one. The master sent all but the wife and child to take shelter in the village, but he wouldn't leave, no matter how they begged. The storms were so savage and the snow so deep that no one could get in or out for months. When the melt came, they found all three of 'em dead. Dead for weeks, they said, though the cold had kept 'em from rotting where they fell.'

'What had happened?'

Bestwicke shakes his head and sniffs. 'Ah . . . you'll find as many versions of that tale as you will folk willing to tell it. Some say they starved to death, some that a fever took 'em. Others say the man was driven mad and murdered his own kin. Strangest thing was, each had a gold coin in their mouth, as if someone had come along and put 'em there. Those that found 'em swore to it.'

Ellis recalls the cold glint of gold in his palm, the conflict of anger and fear in Mercy's eye. He feels suddenly, inexplicably, troubled.

'Poor souls didn't know what they were in for,' Bestwicke goes on. 'They brung the bodies down by the coffin path. Buried 'em at St Luke's and tossed the coins into the grave – you can still see the stone, just there, on the north side of the church.' He flaps a hand in the direction of the valley. 'People have come and gone since then, but Bartram Booth is the only one that's stuck. They say there's something up here, something evil, older than the Hall itself, or even the farm before that. They say the house should never have been built, that the land has some ancient curse upon it. But I've been coming up here these fifty years and I've seen nowt more than boggarts.' He pauses, leans forward, serious. 'I remember the Hall before Booth came. Abandoned, falling to ruins. A lonely spot, sure enough. Us local lads would drink a pot or two and dare each other to set foot inside, and I did so, often enough. The place had a queer feel to it, but I never saw aught to scare me. If Old Nick was ever at work on these moors then Bartram must've scared him off. Made it clear from the start: he'd have no such nonsense in his household or among his workers – banned us all from speaking of it, especially when the young mistress was about. You wouldn't think it now, but he was quite a fearsome man back then, with a black scowl that scared the ladies.'

'So there's no truth in all this?'

'I didn't say that, lad.'

Ellis waits, wanting more.

The older man stares into the dwindling flames, lips pursed, contemplative. Then, 'Booth's right. Best not to speak of it.'

'Why would the land be cursed?'

But Bestwicke won't be drawn. 'That's enough, lad. It's time I turned in.'

Ellis realises that Ravens has not come back. He gestures to the door. 'Where's he gone?'

'Best not to ask,' Bestwicke says, raising a brow. 'Best not to know.'

Ellis stands anyway, stretching his legs, and wanders to the doorway.

'Come back inside, lad. Leave 'em to it.'

He hears something above the crackle of flame and the buffet of wind – a scuffling, voices.

He follows his instinct, taking a few steps away from the fire, eyes adjusting to the dark. He's certain now: he can hear a voice, a female voice. He knows it's her.

'I said no, Henry. Not now. That's not why I came.'

He rounds the corner of the barn and sees them – two figures pressed up against the wall.

'You're drunk,' she says.

'That's never stopped you before.' Ravens holds her by the waist and pushes against her, trying for her mouth with his.

She struggles. 'Leave me be . . .'

'What's the matter? I thought you'd be pleased to see me again.'

'Just . . . not tonight.'

'Come take a drink, then. That'll warm you up.'

'I told you, I'm not here for that.'

She pushes at his chest and Ravens sways, takes a step backwards. Ellis sees that the man's breeches are unlaced and pulled open – that he's ready for her.

'What's the matter with you, woman?' Ravens moves closer again, hands on either side of her, so she cannot escape.

Ellis steps forward, making a crunch in the dirt, and the pair of them snap their heads in his direction.

'Christ, man, get away!'

Ellis says nothing, just stands and stares.

Then she ducks beneath Ravens's arm, out from under his grip and slips away. Ravens curses but makes no attempt to stop her.

As she comes past him, refusing to meet his eye, she gathers the flaps of her coat about her, but not before he glimpses the white fabric of an unlaced nightgown and a sliver of silvery skin.

Chapter 8

The lambs come thick and fast. For the next few weeks Ellis goes to bed late and wakes early. Life shrinks to nothing but the touch of slick new bodies, the stench of blood and sheep shit, days measured in the rapid pulsing of tiny heartbeats.

Some time towards the end of March, the murk lifts to reveal a pale blue, cloud-streaked sky. He's woken by the chatter of starlings in the beams of the hayloft and is out with the dawn. The air is sharp and bright, smelling of damp earth and dew-soaked grass. Green weeds nose their way through the soil. Crows squabble in the copse. Hens scratch and chuckle, skittering from beneath his feet as he makes his way to the byre. He has come to treasure the brief snatches of time when he's alone: early mornings and wakeful nights.

He leans on the willow gate, watching the new mothers feed their young. Two newborns that must have come in the night, still bloodstained and unsteady on brand-new legs, try to suckle, tails wagging. He notices one ewe, standing alone in the corner, pawing the ground – it's her turn this morning. He counts them. Pauses. Counts again.

He walks the length of the fence, checking for gaps.

She and Garrick come out of the house and make their way towards him.

Garrick greets him with a nod.

There is no point in hiding it. 'There's two missing, a ewe and her lamb,' he tells them.

He waits while Garrick takes this in and runs his eye over the sheep in the byre. Mercy stares at him, suspicious. No doubt she'll find a way to blame him for this.

'Have you checked the fences?' Garrick asks.

'No breaches. The gate was tied fast.'

'Did you keep a watch in the night?'

'Of course.'

They are silent awhile. He knows what they are both thinking: thieves. But no sheep thief worth his salt would be satisfied with one old ewe and her newborn – more likely passing vagrants, desperate for meat.

'I'll check on the fell, in case they got out somehow,' she says to Garrick, nodding towards the paining ewe. 'You look to things here. I'll take Bracken.'

'Take Ferreby too,' Garrick says. 'Cover the ground faster with two.'

She does not reply. She glances dismissively in his direction, then stalks off to fetch the dog.

'Go with her,' Garrick says quietly. 'Do as she asks and she'll warm to you in time.'

They spend a couple of hours searching the land above the Hall. No conversation passes between them. For the most part, she is too far distant to speak, so he watches carefully and takes his cues from her.

Long morning shadows begin to shrink. They check every ditch and beck that criss-crosses the fell side, flowing down to meet the stream in the valley bottom. In one lea he finds the skeleton of a hare, bones stripped and curd-white, and a scattering of feathers where a fox has taken a bird. But there's no sign of the ewe or her lamb.

She leads him up onto the moor top. The ground is hard going here, sodden with the last of the melting snow, the sleeping heather rising in thawing clumps to turn and snap ankles. On the crest of the hill the ancient circle of pale, weathered stone stands sentinel over the moor.

Mercy is ahead of him. He sees her start at a sudden flurry of wings: a curlew rising from the undergrowth, its call unearthly. The dog runs after it, snapping at the air, a streak of tan fur. When the creature reaches the stone circle it stops, sniffs at something on the ground, then yelps, bounds away and back again.

Mercy beckons. He picks up his pace.

The dog has found the lamb. Its small body is torn almost in two, oily guts oozing, though the flesh of its shoulders and hindquarters seem untouched. Its eyes are closed, tongue lolling in a twisted smile. It might be comic if it weren't so grotesque.

But one lamb looks much like another. 'Are you sure it's yours?' he asks.

She nods. 'Bracken knows the scent.'

He looks about, taking in the wide sweep of hillside and valley, the waste of moorland, and beyond that, on all sides, miles and miles of fell and dale. Below, the Booth land falls away, stretching back down to the fields, dotted now with tiny white specks of fleece. Lazy peat smoke rises from the chimneys of Scarcross Hall. There is no sign of the mother. He's found the remains of plenty of lambs before, mostly just a few bones to tell their fate.

'If a fox took it, why bring it up here?' he says. 'I've never seen a lamb taken like this and not a good part of it eaten.'

'Maybe something disturbed it.'

'Don't seem right to me.' He wanders away, searching for the mother. A lone fox could not take a full-grown ewe.

She crouches by the body, studying it, the colour drained from her cheeks. The dog is close by, eyes fixed on the lamb, ears flattened.

'No sign of her,' he says, shielding his eyes as the sun emerges from behind a cloud. 'What is this place?'

'We call it the White Ladies.'

Slowly, he paces the circle, touching each stone as he goes, running his fingers over the lichened surfaces. He has seen it before, of course, but never this close or in brightness and understands now why it is so named. Thin spring sunlight catches tiny white flecks in the gritstone, making a pale gemlike glisten. He leans against the tallest, pushes it to test its purchase. One of the slabs has toppled and lies flat. He goes there and climbs on top of it to get a better view. Up here, the wind is constant.

'Do the sheep graze here?'

'Yes. It's common land.'

He turns slowly, making a full rotation.

From here he can see down the scar of the coffin path, past the crossroads to the dark snake of track that leads to the village and after that, far beyond sight, to the soot and clamour of Halifax and Leeds. He notes the smoke from Garrick's chimney, snug against the fell-side, and the budding green sea of new leaves on the trees in the valley. In the distance, hills fade to purple and blue, disguising the point where land and sky meet. Here and there, he makes out dwellings: small farms, cottages, weaving huts, other folds with new lambs. The world, shrouded in winter by fog, cloud and rain, is revealed, but from up here it feels distant and apart. There is a silence despite the wind, a stillness that is uncanny. He realises: there is no birdsong.

He sits, leans back on his hands and watches her. She stands, still staring at the lamb. It's a common sight – they will always lose newborns to foxes – but she is clearly unnerved.

She walks over to him. 'My father used to tell me that the circle was built by sprites – for who else could have magicked these great stones up here?'

He nods slowly, waiting for her to go on.

'Through his stories he tried to make it safe for me, but this place has a bad reputation. Most folk won't come up past the turbary fields.' She looks at him as if challenging him to ask questions. 'This stone . . .' She reaches out and flattens a palm next to his leg. 'We call it the Slaying Stone. They say the pagans used to make sacrifices here and the spirits of those poor dead folk still haunt this place. They say the terrible things they did then opened a path for the dead.' She pauses. He senses sadness in her reflection. 'Bad things have happened here. And people have seen strange things by night. Lights, and suchlike.'

'Have you ever seen such a thing?'

'Once or twice.' She hesitates, studying him from the corner of her eye, considering whether to go on. Then, 'I've seen lanterns burning up here at midnight.'

'Just lads up to no good, surely.'

'No. They move too quickly, too fast for it to be done by one of us. And they're a strange colour – bright white, almost blue, like the sparks from a smith's hammer.'

She stands awhile, watching as the dog sniffs tentatively at the mauled body of the lamb, then creeps away with its tail between its legs.

'That coin – the one you found in the barn. My father found it up here. He found three of them, in fact.'

He recalls Bestwicke's tale: three frozen dead, three golden coins. He says nothing.

'I must know if you told me the truth that day. Did you truly find that coin in the barn?'

He stares into the sky. 'What reason would I have to lie?'

She frowns, then climbs up onto the stone and sits next to him. He can hear the rhythm of her breath above the whispering wind. He watches clouds whip across the sky and pockets of sunlight spiral across the distant hills, lighting them many shades of ochre, tan and deep peaty brown. The dog is sitting some yards from the carcass, eyes fixed upon it, as if it cannot be trusted to stay put.

To the east, far off by the crossroads, he sees a procession of men, women and children begin to make their way up the coffin path.

'What are they about?'

She follows his gaze and her composure falters: confusion, then a curse. 'It's Cross Day. I've been so busy with the lambing, I forgot that Easter comes early this year.'

'What do they want with us?'

'They're beating the bounds of the parish. They'll take the coffin path past Scarcross Hall, as they do every year. Do they not do the same where you're from?'

He considers. 'Perhaps. Why do they call it the coffin path?'

'It's the path they use to bring down the coffins from the dwellings on the moor. It leads to the church in the valley. You would know that if you went on Sundays.'

He doesn't miss the scornful look she throws him.

'And it's the path they used to bring the coffins down from Scarcross Hall. You've heard the stories, I suppose . . .'

'Some.'

'And what do you make of them?'

'You're better placed than I to know the truth of them.'

'A careful answer, Master Ferreby.'

He waits, enjoying the sound of his name on her tongue. Then, 'If we're to work together all summer, I'd have you call me Ellis.'

She glances at him in surprise. Perhaps he has stepped too far. But then she inclines her head – a small gesture of assent – before turning away.

They watch as the little band takes the path from the crossroads and begins to wind up the hillside towards the Hall. Ellis spies the pastor from the village at the head of the procession, black-clad and sombre, carrying a wooden crucifix. Behind him, the men of the parish, dressed in their Sunday coats, snowy collars and tall hats. Their wives follow, in dusty skirts and lime-white caps. A gaggle of children run and dance to the clamour of tambourines.

Mercy squints, frowning against the sun. He sees the moment that her eyes cloud and her frown returns. 'I must go back,' she says urgently.

She climbs down from the stone and calls the dog to heel. The creature, still staring at the body of the lamb, whines.

'Why hurry?' he asks.

'I can't see Father. He should be with Pastor Flynn. Every year they pass by to give a blessing at the Hall and he likes to lay on bread and ale outside the gate, but he's not given instruction this year. It's important to him . . .'

She whistles to the dog and it slinks slowly towards her.

'You'll stay here and bury that . . . thing.' She waves a hand in the direction of the body.

'Why not leave it for the foxes – let them finish what they began?'

'No. It must be buried.'

'I've no spade.'

'Then find a way,' she snaps, her usual terseness returned. She begins to walk away but then stops, turns back. 'And you'll not mention this to anyone. Not even Ambrose. We found nothing. Is that clear?'

He does not understand why something so commonplace should be hidden – he knows the dangerous power of secrets – but this is a chance to prove the value of his word. He nods. 'And the ewe?'

'Keep looking. No doubt you'll find her.'

But she knows as well as he they'll not see that animal again.

Chapter 9

When she comes to him and asks him to take the letter to the pastor, he considers it a promising sign. Perhaps she's beginning to trust him. Though he knows he has little choice – he cannot refuse an order from the mistress – he's pleased to accept the errand, for it will give him some time away from Bestwicke and Ravens. Time to think.

She tells him he'll likely find the pastor in his cottage at the edge of the village. He understands from Bestwicke that Pastor Flynn adds to his meagre living by tutoring and has a passion for the education of the rougher sort. In the free school along the valley – endowed by godly merchants in Halifax who rely on the local weavers for cloth – he strives to teach the children their numbers and letters. They're lucky to get them at all, most of the cottagers preferring their offspring to farm crops or work looms from an early age. Ellis imagines the battles that Flynn must fight on his ill-fated crusade. Though he usually has little time for men of the cloth, he's disposed to suspend judgement for this one. As a man who understands the value of letters he knows life could have gone so differently had one kindly soul not done the same for him.

The coffin path takes him from Scarcross Hall to the crossroads, where he pauses. A tall boundary stone marks the place, slanted, like a drunkard leaning outside an alehouse. On its eastern face he traces the indentations that show the direction of the village and, opposite, the tilted *S H* that points back the way he's come. To the south a little-worn path drops 'sharply into the valley, its destination hidden by trees. Worn letters are carved into the stone, though they are so weathered it's hard to make them out: perhaps a *D*, perhaps an *H*. He does not know what this could signify – another hall, another village, or some other place long abandoned and forgotten. The fells are scattered with decaying remains of the past.

The north face of the stone is blank. He runs his fingertips over it to find any trace of lettering that has been worn away by a hundred years of storm and gale. Nothing. There is nothing to the north except the wild sweep of moorland, all mud browns, mossy greens and black peat, and the rise of the hill to the moor top where, on the horizon, he can make out the stark uprights of the standing stones. The path that way is narrow and overgrown, barely wide enough for a packhorse to pass, winding away for a short distance to be lost between rising clumps of heather.

Over the stones the sky is overcast, low clouds moving in. He thinks of the dead lamb and of stories he has heard about the place and shivers at a breath of cold, rain-damp air. He feels suddenly that he should not linger there.

When Ellis reaches the falls, he stops. Nature is kinder in the valley and spring has come sooner. The rocks are bright with patches of primrose yellow and sea-green moss. Beneath the trees the ground is scattered with crocuses, bright amid last year's rotted leaves. The sweet echo of a cuckoo resounds – the first he's heard this year. Ordinarily, these things would calm him, but nothing will quiet his mind.

He sits awhile on a boulder by the bank of the stream where he first saw her, listening to the burble of water. Barely a month has passed since that day. He marvels at how so brief a time, so quickly flown, can also seem so long. He almost cannot remember a time before he knew her, has forgotten what it was like not always to have the image of her in his mind.

When he's in her presence, he can think of little else. It is not some fleshly attraction, as he has felt for other girls – God help him, it cannot be that. She is not pretty or womanly. Her face is plain, her manner cold. She seems to think herself apart, better than him, and though the world might see it so, he does not. In fact, he recognises her aloofness for what it is: a mask. What is it, then, that has consumed him, so he finds himself studying her, painfully aware of her proximity, or lack of it, and, despite his better self, craving some sign from her?

Perhaps it is simply that he's never known another like her. He thinks of Gretchen, as he always does; he cannot help but compare every woman to her. He remembers the dimpled plumpness of her backside, thighs parted, the tang of her on his tongue, recalls her complicated expression when they parted, and feels the usual stirring of desire and guilt: still potent, even now.

But with Mercy it is different. It is nothing so base as that. As the days slip by, he becomes more convinced that the affinity he senses is God-given proof: in her he has found what he has been seeking. There is a strange stretching and bending of time that occurs with such meetings. There is a before – as he shifts his stiffening cock, he is only too aware of that – but it seems remote and indistinct in the after.

He takes the letter from his pocket, runs his fingers along its folds and studies the seal: an interlocked double *B* with a curled tail, impressed into the scarlet wax. He had noticed the signet the moment she gave the letter into his hands. Now, he stares at the arched backbones and fat round bellies of the letters, a weird churning in his chest: he knows this mark. He recognises it.

He breaks the seal and reads:

Dear Sir,

I beg you to accept my sincere apologies for my absence at yesterday's proceedings. I must urgently enquire whether you were so good as to bestow the usual prayers and blessings upon my house and lands, for I cannot find out the truth of it among my people. You will understand how essential it is to the safety and prosperity of all within my care and I trust that I will hear upon your reply that our Blessed Lord protects us all for another year. If not then I must have you here again to perform that rite upon your earliest convenience.

With humble respect,
Bartram Booth

Ellis stands and holds the letter over the fast-flowing water, the curled script of Booth's signature like a taunt. He makes a fist, crumpling the paper, feeling the wax seal crack to fragments in his palm. For so long those intertwined letters had meant something else. He feels the blackness of the past begin to rise: anger, dark and consuming. He cannot afford to let it overtake him now. It is too soon to take that risk.

If he fails to deliver the letter there will be questions. He steadies himself, mind alive with his own: *Does this confirm his suspicions? Is Booth the one to blame?* And why is the old man so concerned with spiritual protection? What does he fear will happen if he does not receive it?

He takes a deep breath, looks about him to check he is still alone, then flattens the paper, folds it, and sets off towards the village.

Later, he drinks. The liquor is sharp, abrasive and stinks like the cattle trough it was probably made in. It burns Ellis's throat, heating him in a way that the smouldering peat in the brazier cannot. Booth provides them with small ale but he's grateful for his first taste of spirits in weeks. He craves the comfort of it, longs for the liquidity of limbs, the gradual sink into silent contemplation, though there is not much hope of that now: drink makes Bestwicke and Ravens more talkative than usual.

While Ravens becomes lewd and boastful, it takes John Bestwicke a different way. For half an hour he's been recalling his youth, eyes gleaming with sentiment, but he's moved on now to his years as a soldier and the rosy sheen has gone, replaced by something baleful and unsettling.

'You young 'uns don't understand what it was like to fight for something you believed in,' he says, shaking his head. 'It was everything to us – life or death. It gave a man a higher purpose, to be fighting for God and country. We prayed before every battle. It didn't matter how much drinking and whoring went on between times – and the Lord knows most of us had to be drunk to fight – we always prayed before we took to the field. Lord, how we prayed!' He raises his cup to the sky, toasting the heavens. 'It's not the same, these days. So long as you've a warm bed, a hot dinner, and enough pay to get drunk once in a while, you're happy. Selfish and lazy, that's what we've become, God help us, just like our king.'

Ravens is eager, bottle swinging from his fist, knuckles gripped white. 'Did you ever kill a man?'

Bestwicke shrugs. 'Hard not to when you're on the field and they're all trying to kill you. I was in Fairfax's Foot. I'd no musket to hide behind and no horse to raise me from the fray. It was pikes and swords and whatever we could lay our hands on in those early days. By Christ, for a time, when I first joined up, I had to make do with a club and a butcher's knife.'

'What does it feel like? To kill a man?'

Bestwicke takes a long draw on his pipe.

Ellis watches a coil of smoke drift upwards, mingling with the grey smog in the rafters, and waits for Bestwicke's answer.

'At the time, it felt like nothing, lad.'

'But to put a blade in a man . . . to know you've ended him. That must be something,' Ravens says.

'Sounds like you've a fancy for it.'

'You must've felt . . . powerful.'

'Tell me, how many times have you killed a sheep, a rabbit or a chicken?'

'Plenty. Or oftentimes my brood would not eat.'

This is the first mention of any offspring and Ellis is surprised: so the man is married, an adulterer as well as a drunkard. Does she know?

'And it's no more than that at the time,' Bestwicke explains. 'You can't think on them as men. We're feeble beings, as easily ended as a new lamb, and it's not difficult to kill a thing that's trying to kill you. But afterwards . . . it's different afterwards . . .'

Ellis is interested now. He leans forward, beckoning for the bottle from Ravens. 'How so?'

Bestwicke considers. 'Some men are born soldiers. They kill and never think on it at all. Some glory in it. But others do not. Others kill because they've no choice and *they* carry it with them – the memory – the knowledge of the lives they ended.' By the regret in Bestwicke's eyes, it's clear he's one of them. 'You find yourself thinking on their sweethearts and their mothers, pondering on their little 'uns. You find out it's not the same as slaughtering a hog for the spit or twisting the neck of a chicken. But you only find out when it's too late.'

'Even when what you've done is right?' Ellis asks. 'Even when it's God's work?'

Bestwicke sighs. 'God's work? Aye, we thought as much. Our killing was done in the name of justice, freedom and the Lord. There were many would've made themselves a Joshua or a David, but you suffer for it in the end.' He looks thoughtful, staring up into the night sky. '"Whoso sheddeth man's blood, by man shall his blood be shed."'

Ravens takes back the bottle, drinks and grins, greedy for more. He does not seem to notice the older man's melancholy. 'You must've killed a few to get through unhurt.'

'Not unhurt. Marston Field was my last fight. I was injured there and after that was too sick to fight again. In truth, I didn't want to go back. I was glad to leave the bloodshed to others.' He puts a hand on his thigh and rubs the muscle there – an action of unconscious habit.

Ravens is impressed. 'Ah, what it must have been to be part of that great victory, to have routed the Royalists from Yorkshire. I must shake your hand, John.' He leans over and does so. 'I had an uncle under Cromwell, killed at Dunbar.'

'We all lost someone in those years.'

'It was before I was whelped but my mother talked about him till the day she died. He was a hero to her.'

Bestwicke gives Ravens a sudden kick to the ankle.

'What?'

He nods to the doorway, where Bartram Booth leans up against the big oak doorpost, watching and listening.

It's the first time Ellis has seen the master up close. He's spoken of as a formidable man, so he's surprised to see how old he looks, how stooped and grey-haired, how ashen-faced and rheumy-eyed. The three men fall silent as Booth comes forward.

'Of what are we talking, gentlemen?'

Bestwicke stands. 'We were talking of the old war, Master. Will you join us by the fire?' He clears a space on a sack of grain but Booth does not sit. He hovers next to the brazier.

'A sad topic indeed, and not one I have occasion to talk of often.'

'Do you remember it well? With respect, sir, my guess is that you were of an age to fight.'

'I was . . . I was . . . but I did not fight. I was too much engaged with business at that time. Too much engaged . . . But you are a veteran, I think, John?'

'Yes, sir.'

'It's good to have fighting men about you in times like these.'

'Been a long time since I was a fighting man, Master. I've contented myself with the farming life for many years. I was just telling these two young 'uns, seems nothing much to fight for, these days.'

Booth frowns. 'On the contrary, John. There's always something to fight for. I'll concede we live a quiet kind of life here and have not much to do with matters of King and Parliament. The fight that concerns me is the battle for our eternal souls. You'll understand, John, that men of our years must be prepared. Satan's army is the one we must concern ourselves with now.'

The men are silent. Ellis studies Booth as he stares into the fire. Perhaps there is something of the man he imagined after all, in the jut of his brow, the loose-fitting coat, as if it had been made for a bigger, prouder man, a fierceness about his stare. He thinks of the letter he slipped beneath the door of the pastor's cottage, and Booth's desperate plea. What is it that the old man fears so much? He recalls the waxy seal beneath his fingers, the intertwined double *B*, the choking recognition creeping over him.

Booth shakes himself from his reverie. 'It was all such a long time ago. This quiet life suits me better. I never was one for warmaking, John, though I do remember how it was. These young ones will not understand your stories. They don't remember how it was back then. They will not recall the fire that consumed us all.'

But Booth is wrong. Ellis does remember.

He remembers cobbles beneath his feet running red with blood. He remembers an upturned barrel of offal, spilling across the street from the shambles and not being sure if the guts were those of beasts or men. He remembers the thunder of cannon fire and chunks of stone falling, splintering like earthenware pots. He remembers horses that seemed huge, snorting and sweating, as though they would breathe flames. He remembers the men on their backs with blank, iron faces. He remembers people running, shouting, screaming, and the warm wet piss seeping down his leg.

He remembers arms lifting him and someone – a woman – saying, 'Don't cry . . . don't cry,' and not being sure if she was talking to him because he had not known he was crying. He remembers how tightly she held him and the chafe of a bone in her stays that had broken free of its seam and stuck into his leg as she ran.

Yes, he remembers exactly how it was.

Chapter 10

Weeks run by.

Ellis stands high on the fell and looks out over the chimneys of Scarcross Hall, down the mud-black snake of the coffin path to the crossroads, the crooked boundary stone beckoning like a finger, and across the valley to the distant hills beyond. Already he's beginning to feel a bond with this landscape. White, pillow-plump clouds chase across an expanse of blue, grey-edged and rain-tainted, as if stained by coal smoke from the towns to the east. Every so often the sun breaks through. Up here the wind has a bite, redolent of winter and far-off storms. It pinches and raises the skin, then the sun soothes it. He takes off his hat and lets the breeze shift his hair, feels it drag at his beard, whisper against his eyelashes. The warmth ripples over him, bathing him from head to toe.

He's reminded of the sea – he saw it once. He stood on a beach, in the surf up to his hips, felt the push-pull of the waves and the tight salt-sting in his eyes. He had pissed where he stood and enjoyed the momentary heat as it curled around his legs, before the current eventually snatched it away. Today's sunlight has that same caressing quality. He enjoys the promise these early bright days bring, with lambing behind them and the knowledge that summer is almost here.

A bark from the dog draws him back.

Mercy suggested that he take the creature, which surprised him. She's possessive of the dog and proud of its loyalty. But it makes sense to have a helpmate out on the fell, and Garrick has the other dog, Flint, with him. Garrick and Ravens have taken two dozen shearlings to sell at the May Day fair in Halifax and will be gone at least three days. Bestwicke, mending walls on the northern slopes, has no need of company.

He likes this time of year, when the lambs are gone to grass, starting to get fat and strong, and there's nothing much to do except watch and think. His practised eye can spot signs of trouble – an ailing wether or a grass-poisoned lamb – from a hundred paces, but a dog is always useful for snaring strays and can get into nooks and burrows that a man cannot. Besides, the animal seems to like him, responding well to his whistles and calls. They work together in a way that is unusual without years of training and trust. He feels proud of this and childishly triumphant that the dog will go to him when it will not go to Ravens.

Not a week since, Ravens had tried. He'd asked her if he could take the dog out with him. Ellis saw her hesitancy and the way she wouldn't meet Ravens's eye. But Ravens pleaded – he sneers to remember it – went up to her, lifted his fingers to stroke her cheek, grazing her breast, before she batted him away. She had glanced at Ellis, to see if he'd noticed the intimacy, and said: *Oh, very well. Take her.*

But the dog would not go to him. Bracken sat by the barn, tail sweeping the dirt, ignoring Ravens's attempts to seduce, then trotted to Mercy in flat refusal. But she comes to Ellis with no question.

He does not understand the hold that Ravens seems to have over their mistress. There must be some reason she would let a man like that use her in such a way. He knows how it is between them, no matter how she tries to hide it. He knows where Ravens goes when he leaves the barn in the pitch black of night. He reads it in Bestwicke's silence and in the way Ravens returns, shifting himself about inside his breeches. He's heard them, once or twice, on his own night-time wanderings, the slow circuit of the Hall he makes when he cannot sleep. Or, at least, he's heard him – there is never any sound from her.

If she were a different sort of woman he might feel sorry for her – he understands the things some women must do to survive – but he cannot find that sympathy in himself. In every other respect she seems strong, self-sufficient, so why this weakness? The thought of them together repulses him. He's known many men like Ravens – men who are too shallow and too weak to rise above the urge to rut anything, any time they can. They are so many, those men who seek it out, who will lie and joke and brag about it, who see their conquests as proof of their manhood, their strength, when in fact it's quite the opposite. There are the self-righteous ones – the ones who swear chastity, pretend they are better than that, only to find themselves fallen back in some filthy stew, begging for it, paying for it, or just taking it, with fists and threats, because they cannot help themselves. He considers these men pitiful animals with no self-control, no better than rutting hogs. Then there are those who come with some romantic notion, some pretence of love, who wheedle and worship before their chosen female idol, but when it comes to it only want the same thing – to stick their swollen cocks into a slippery hole, all thoughts of higher sentiment, honour and consequence cast aside for a fleeting moment of escape from the hate they feel for themselves.

He has seen them all, knows them for what they are and despises them.

He feels anger rise in him now as he thinks of her with a man like that. Perhaps she's no better than the rest of her sex for allowing it, even welcoming it, when she has no need. Why does she give away what others would sell? But she is a woman so she is weak, more susceptible to the Devil's temptations than he. What had he expected? Something more. He had hoped for someone better than the rest of the squalling, fornicating masses. Someone more like him. He is angry with her too.

The dog barks again and he turns to follow the sound. Bracken is up on higher ground near the White Ladies, a small brown streak amid the wavering sea of cotton grass, growling and snapping at something he cannot see. He puts his hat back on and makes his way towards her through the peat hags.

The sun hides behind clouds. A curlew starts up from the heather in a burst of squawks and feathers. There is a nest cradled at his feet, three small speckled eggs nestled there, like the crowns of three tiny skulls. He has almost trodden on it.

He sees what has disturbed the dog from several paces: a dead lamb.

Its body has been torn at the belly, a great chunk of guts missing, as if something has taken a bite out of it. Its legs and head are untouched, eyes open and glassy, jaw hanging. Most likely it did not die immediately but lingered, suffering, while life leaked from its innards. He stares at it, unease shifting in his belly.

Bracken is off, heading towards the stones, and he sees, perhaps twenty feet away, another still white fleece.

The second lamb has injuries to its hindquarters, bloodied and mauled, a hunk of flesh savagely ripped. It lies in a wine-red pool. This one would certainly have bled to death, if the shock did not end it.

He looks around. Usually, when a lamb dies, the mother will stay with the body. He's seen pitiful displays from ewes refusing to accept they cannot resurrect their young with a nudge of the head or the kick of a hoof. He once found one standing guard over a half-eaten, rotting carcass that must have been dead five days. But there's no sign of any mother here.

He sees the third corpse before Bracken reaches it, puts her head back and howls, as if she knows and feels the tragedy and the strangeness that is starting to creep beneath his composure and worry at the threads of his understanding.

This one has no head. The front of the body is gone, leaving a three-legged mess of muscle and bone that is somehow obscene. He's not squeamish and has seen his share of death but something about this makes his skin crawl.

Bracken sniffs the lamb and whines. Her hackles are up. She backs away from the carcass, snarling, ears flattened. He looks about him, expecting to find something that will make all this fall into place. He feels a sudden unnerving sense that he is not alone and listens hard, scanning the ground for tracks or signs. But there is nothing, save the still, silent figures of the White Ladies, the breath of wind through the heather: the constant song of the moor.

He lifts the small body, shoulders it, and makes his way back to do the same with the others. He keeps one eye on the stones, suspecting now that whatever creature did this is still here, hidden, watching him. He has no weapon to protect himself, save the small blade at his belt: he should leave. Now.

The lambs have been dead long enough to stiffen and for the wounds to congeal, but as he collects the carcasses, he feels the leak of blood down his back, sees spots of it arc across his chest. Bracken falls in at his ankles, keeping close, cowed and silent.

He sees Mercy at the window of her chamber as he nears the Hall, a lone, pale figure, indistinct behind the panes. She's in her night-gown, hair loose, looking out towards the moor as if she's been waiting for him. He wonders briefly if she's ill – it's unlike her to be in her chamber at this hour – but then she moves away and the glass is nothing but reflected sky, darkness within. She must have seen him coming.

Sure enough, by the time he's decided to dump the bodies behind the barn, away from the byre where a couple of ailing lambs are separated from the flock, and has settled Bracken to guard them, he finds her in the kitchen, already fully dressed in uncustomary skirts, and attending to the day's indoor work. It's the first time he's seen her in women's garb, apart from when she goes to church on Sundays, and he's momentarily struck by how different she looks at close quarters, how unlike herself. The old woman and the child are there too, and he's suddenly aware of the gore-splattered state of his shirt. He should have washed and changed.

'Oh! Lord above!' Agnes cries, as he enters. The three of them stare at him. The boy, helping at the table, gawps, flour-dusted fingers creeping out to find Agnes's.

Ellis touches his hat, averts his eyes. 'I've something to show you.'

Mercy steps forward. 'What is it? What's happened?'

'Better come with me.'

She wipes her hands on her apron and pushes a loose strand of hair behind her ear, face grim.

The two of them stand behind the barn, looking at the pile of pathetic, torn bodies.

'Where?'

He'll spare her the details. 'At the White Ladies.'

'All three?'

He nods.

Her colour drains. 'If you're lying to me . . .' She gives him a hard stare, challenging him to look away, but he holds steady. He is not lying about this.

'It makes no sense at all,' she says. 'And you say there was no sign of any mother?'

'No ewes within two hundred yards or more.'

She touches her hand to her forehead and he notices that her fingers are trembling. 'I've never seen anything like this, except that one time, but never before that, and now three in one night. Who . . . What would do this?'

He shakes his head. 'It can't be foxes. Dogs, perhaps. A large one could do it.'

'A wild dog would kill for food, surely, and whatever did this was not hungry.'

'I knew a pack of them once, big enough to take lambs, shearlings even, but they would always eat them, tear them apart, fight over the meat. We'd find bones scattered. This is not the same.'

'Do you think . . . a human hand? Thieves?'

'For what purpose? What would be the gain?'

She sighs heavily and turns away, thinking. 'We must tell Ambrose this time. Hide them in the stables. Keep them away from the horses. Find a sack to cover them. And don't tell anyone else. Not John or Henry.' She fixes him with an uncompromising stare. 'It's important. Do you hear me?'

'Yes.' She should know his word can be trusted – he's not mentioned their previous find to anyone.

She takes a few paces away from him, comes back. 'We'll have to start a night watch. Ambrose gave you a pistol.'

'Yes.'

'And you know how to use it?'

'Yes.'

'Then you'll take first watch tonight. Ambrose will be back the day after tomorrow. Say nothing till then. And change your shirt. You do have a clean one?'

He nods.

She starts to walk away, shoulders bunched. He watches her go, noticing the curve of her waist pinched by stays, the sway of her skirts. As she reaches the corner of the barn she stops, turns back.

'What do you truly think?' she asks. He sees urgency in her

eyes, the seeking for answers that will not come – he recognises it. 'What could have done this?'

'I don't know,' he replies, and shrugs, because he cannot bring himself to tell her the whole truth. What good would it do?

As he'd collected the small mauled bodies he'd tried to ignore the creeping sense of dread he'd felt, the growing conviction that he was not alone on the moor. The dog had kept silent, slinking close to his heels, tail between hind legs. He told himself he'd done this a hundred times before. But he knew he'd never seen anything quite like it, and as he'd walked down the fell he did not dare look back, for fear of what he might see. Bestwicke's words had stalked him: *They say there's something up here, something evil . . .*

Chapter 11

I cannot sleep. I lie in bed and study the coins.

Each is small, about the size of a buttercup head, decorated with strange patterns and the crude impression of a horned beast – perhaps a stag, or something more sinister. In the honeyed glow from the tallow candle they have a rich golden sheen. Though I cup them in my palm, they remain icy cold.

I'm sure they are two of the three lost coins but cannot bring myself to return them to Father. I want to keep them with me a little longer, as if by touching them, brooding over them, I'll be able to fathom how this came about. I feel the need to keep them close. Lately, Father's temper is frayed and I do not want to give any cause for worry or reason for it to flare. I've noticed how he frets, how he's nervous and unsettled. Perhaps their return would calm him, but I doubt it. The mystery will surely plague him as much as it plagues me. And if he gives any heed to the old stories, it will only make things worse. In his current mood, I think it best to wait. When I have answers, I'll give them back.

One coin marks the first to go . . .

The first, found beneath Sam's pillow. It would have been easy for the child to take the coins but I cannot understand his reason or why he would lie once his wrongdoing was discovered. There was something in the vehemence of his denial that makes me think he was telling the truth. He's been at the Hall since, the lamb following him around like a pet, but has not mentioned the coin again, and I dare not bring it up.

A second bodes the fall . . .

If Ellis Ferreby is to be believed, the second was found beneath his bedroll. If Sam took the coins, why would he hide one in the hayloft? The coins went missing on the day I birthed the season's first lamb, before Ellis ever came here, so it cannot be anything to do with him. I think again of that day and the wraithlike figure I saw in the fog. Was it a thief? A footpad? Someone who found his way into Scarcross Hall unseen? But, if so, why take only these tokens, and how so, when they were well hidden? And that does not explain how they have found their way back to me.

Above all, there is one constant nagging question: where is the third coin?

The third will seal a sinner's fate . . .

The image of Ellis Ferreby in his blood-streaked shirt comes to the fore. I did not say the things I wanted to this afternoon when I had the chance. I'm prevented from speaking my mind because he refuses to speak his. I want to know every detail of what he found, exactly what he saw. He must have some opinion on who or what could have killed those lambs with such unaccountable violence. I think he was not honest with me. But he's not from these parts and won't know the ill omen of his find.

The Devil take them all . . .

Ellis Ferreby will not know why such a thing must be kept quiet. How can I trust him when he hides his mind from me? I see no reason why he should lie, but in his silence I sense the space for secrets.

I slip from beneath the coverlet and tiptoe across the room. In the corner there is a small hole in one of the floorboards. I slide a finger inside and prise up the board. Beneath is a small, dusty nook – a secret hiding place I discovered as a girl. Here I keep the two objects I treasure most: a red velvet pouch, now worn and threadbare, holding the wedding band that belonged to my mother, and a pretty ebony box, decorated with bone-white vines, flowers and a fancy golden lock plate.

Father gave me this box on my tenth birthday. It was a wedding gift to my mother, made to remind her of the day she became his. On the lid, inlaid in ivory, is the double intertwined *B* of his signet. The key was lost long ago and the box has never been opened in my memory. When I was younger, the contents were a source of great frustration to me. I would shake it, feeling the shift of something inside, and hold it to my ear as if expecting it to whisper its secrets, but I was forbidden to force the lock. Father said that would sully my mother's memory and so be the worst sort of betrayal to him. In this, he would not bend. So, though I came close a few times in my childish tempers, I never dared. And as I grew older, the mystery of it faded. Years go by when I don't think of it at all. But these things are still special to me, the only keepsakes I have of the woman who gave her life for mine.

Now, I lift the velvet pouch, untie the drawstring and take out the ring. It is a simple gold band that barely fits on my finger. I put it to my lips – a habit since childhood – and murmur a prayer, then slip it back into the pouch along with the two coins. They will be safe here, until I decide what to do with them. I place the pouch back beneath the boards, metal chinking against metal, and replace the slat.

As I sit, thinking, a sound comes to me, quiet at first, pushing its way to consciousness:

A dull *thunk* . . . a pause . . . a long, dragging *ssshrrrrrrsssssst* . . .

Suddenly alert, I listen hard. Night sounds become all too loud: creaking timbers, the wind sighing through missing slates, something scurrying in the chimney.

Thunk . . . *ssshrrrrrrsssssst* . . .

It cannot be Sam this time. Sam is at home, safe in his bed, with Dority and Ambrose.

Without pause, I take up my candle and pad out onto the gallery.

As before, the noise is coming from the old bedchamber.

The hairs prickle on my arms, a chill dances down my spine. I wait a few moments, expecting Agnes or Father to emerge, sleepy-eyed and disturbed too, but there's no sign from either room.

I make my way along the gallery, the candle spinning shadows ahead of me. Thin blue moonlight filters in through winter's dirt on the big leaded windows in the hall, spilling puddles on the grey flags below. Fearful compulsion drives me on.

I pause outside the door to the chamber. The noise seems quieter now. How can it have reached me when it has not disturbed Agnes, who sleeps just across the stairwell?

I put my hand on the door and the noise stops. I hold my breath. I have an inkling that whoever or whatever is inside the room can hear me, is listening to me, just on the other side of the door.

I lift my hand away. A few moments' silence and the noise starts again.

This time I don't wait. I lift the catch and push the door. Through the crack the room exhales a sigh of damp air but it resists me, as if something is braced against the other side. Perhaps boxes have fallen against it.

Again, the noise has stopped.

With my heart in my mouth I put my shoulder to the door, meaning to heave whatever is behind it out of the way, but this time there's no resistance and the door swings open on its hinges.

Candlelight spills across the floor, joining the milky patches of moonlight. The bed hangings have been tied back – Agnes must have done that – but otherwise the room seems unchanged. There's nothing at all behind the door.

I force myself to go inside. The air is musty and chill, with the faint traces of sheep grease and dung. But, just as before, there's another smell, charred and acrid, like smoke from a bone fire, and a heaviness, such as hangs in the valley just before a storm.

Shaking off my foreboding, I make my way around the room, turning over empty crates, peering into corners. I find nothing – no rats' nest or trapped bird. But then, when I turn back towards the bed, my eye falls upon the figure of a child.

It is standing by the bed, next to the wall, silent and utterly still. The blood turns in my veins.

For a few seconds, terror has me mute and frozen.

Then I lift my candle and the indistinct form takes shape. This is no human child – it's a wooden carving – a fire screen, fashioned and painted to look like a small boy.

I remember it, next to the hearth in the parlour when I was young. Father used to tell me that it was another child, a brother to me, who misbehaved so badly that the fairies trapped him inside the wood. I would chatter to this ill-fated sibling sometimes, running my fingers over the strange, old-style clothes he wore and, once or twice, stuck needles into his flat, rosy cheeks to see if he would cry. I've not seen it for years and thought it long gone. Agnes must have found it and set it out, not wanting it to rot and decay with everything else.

The memory of Father's joke brings me back to myself – how he must have laughed at me. What a fool I've been, conjuring spirits in the night.

I go to the open shutter, put my candle down upon the sill and look out into the night, my mind alive with questions.

A movement by the gatepost catches my eye. My heart tilts, leaps into my throat to choke me again. There, obscured by darkness and moon shadow, is a figure. I strain to see past the reflection of the candle flame in the glass. My God – I swear this time I'm not imagining it. I can make out a pale shape, face tilted upwards to meet my gaze. And I'm suddenly sure it's looking for *me*, waiting for *me*.

I do not stop to think. I snatch the candle, run from the room and fly down the staircase, flame snuffed in my haste. I tug back the bolts on the heavy front door and run barefoot out into the night.

No one is there.

I go to the gatepost, straining to see into the blackness along the coffin path.

Nothing.

I spin back, heart racing, searching the windows of the house for the telltale glow of moving candle flame – Father wakeful and wandering, or Agnes in her nightgown, fetching a sleeping remedy from the herb patch – but there is nothing: no shade at the gatepost, no face at the window, no lights, just a lone owl, swooping silently from the barn, body silhouetted against the moon-spun underbelly of the clouds.

Chapter 12

The rest of the night remains sleepless.

Every time I close my eyes I see that pale impression in the dark. My ears strain for sounds from the old bedchamber. There is nothing but the screams of a vixen, somewhere far off, and the rush of wind through the willows in the copse. I rise before dawn and am warming the porridge pot over the kitchen fire by the time Agnes enters. She looks surprised to see me but asks no questions and I give no explanation.

I try to distract myself. I take Bracken out onto the fell to watch the flock and walk the gullies to check for lambs in trouble. But it does not work. In the morning calls of moor birds I hear the moan and chatter of spirits. In the yelp of a dog, echoing from the valley, I hear the howl of demons. And I see small, mauled bodies in patches of white cotton grass.

I know the stories. Though Father forbade talk of it, children will always disobey their elders. In the woods and the graveyard at the church, up on the moor at the White Ladies, we scared ourselves silly with tales of ancient curses, of wandering spirits and gruesome slayings, of the ancient dead rising from the bog. We dared each other to scream and sing and taunt the Devil with our dancing.

The three coins. The slaughtered lambs. The figure in the fog.

These things are familiar to me, the stuff of whispers in the schoolroom and tormented childhood nightmares. But as I grew older I put my trust in God and never really believed that the stories might hold truth.

I decide it's time to speak to Father.

Back at the Hall I find Agnes in the kitchen mixing batter for the oatcakes. 'Where's Father?'

She shrugs. She has that look on her that says she neither knows nor cares. They've probably quarrelled.

I hear the creak of floorboards overhead and the uneven rhythm of Father's footsteps.

'Now, what's he doing up there?' she says. 'I found him in the buttery yesterday, licking curds from his fingers. He's no better than a child at times.'

I follow the sound as Father paces back and forth across the room above, where Agnes sleeps. She tuts and huffs to herself. I haven't the patience for Agnes's moods today so I leave her and go up by the kitchen stairs. When I reach the room I find it empty. Back out on the gallery I hesitate by the door to the old bedchamber, reluctant to enter. I press my ear to the wood for a moment, the memory of last night causing cold fingers to brush my neck, my heart to beat faster. Then, telling myself I'm being foolish, I go inside.

That room is empty too. The air is thick and mote-heavy. There are pathways in the dust where I shifted boxes. I go to the window and look out: nothing. When I turn back my eye falls upon the fire screen. The boy's gaze is blank and staring, seeming to follow me. I turn the thing towards the wall and leave.

I search the rest of the upper floor. Father is not in his bedchamber, but finally I see him from the window of my own. He's standing amid the kitchen beds in the walled garden behind the house, staring at something on the ground. How he can have got there without passing me is a mystery I'll have to puzzle out later.

By the time I reach him, he's kneeling in the dirt, beside a row of onions. Their green shoots are just starting to sprout. He grips one thin leaf between finger and thumb, leans forward until his nose almost touches it, sniffs long and hard, then sighs and sits back on his heels.

'Father?'

He's startled by my sudden interruption, turning to me with a wistful, faraway gaze. 'Do you remember the gardens at Wickford?' he says. 'They had the most exquisite roses. I've never found a scent to match it.'

Wickford was my grandfather's house – my mother's father, whom I never met and who is long dead, his estate entailed away to a distant relative. Father rarely speaks of it, but when he does, he might be speaking of a fantasy – a mythical place of beauty and ease. I've never been there.

'Do you remember how we would walk there?' he goes on. 'And we would stop and smell the scents. I would grow roses just as fine for you if I could, my dear, but the soil here is not right for roses. See how they falter . . .'

'I've never been to Wickford, Father. You know that.'

He hesitates, eyes clouding, daydream dissolving. 'Forgive me, child. For a moment I was lost in memory. You remind me so much of your mother at times. We used to walk in the gardens at Wickford in our courting days. Her father grew the most wonderful roses. I'll never be able to match them here, no matter how I try. The soil is not right.'

'We've never grown roses here.'

'Have we not?' He climbs slowly to his feet and looks about him, taking in the freshly weeded soil where we've planted beans, carrots and turnips, the bed of herbs that Agnes tends, the little patch of primroses. 'No, of course not. The soil is not right at all . . .' He prods the earth with his cane, distracted, lost in thought.

'Are you unwell, Father?'

'I've never been heartier.' This is clearly untrue but there's no sense in challenging him: he will deny his failing health till he takes the coffin path.

'Then I must speak with you.' I indicate a low stone bench against the wall of the garden. 'Will you sit with me?'

He does so, following me to the seat. I notice how he looks about, frowning, confused, as if surprised to find himself outside.

I'm not sure how to begin, so I wait awhile, gathering courage.

'Have we received a reply from Pastor Flynn?' he asks, sitting, leaning his cane against the bench. 'It's been . . . how many weeks now?'

'He spoke to us at church.'

'We must have that blessing.'

'But he assured us it had taken place. Don't you remember?'

He frowns again. 'I must see the thing done with my own eyes.'

A flicker of concern rises in me. 'Why?'

'I've been remiss in my duties of late. How can I have forgotten about Cross Day? What will the good Lord think if the first man of the parish cannot show his face on such an occasion?' Then, agitated, 'Yes, I must be sure we have that blessing.'

'Pastor Flynn is a man of his word. He wouldn't lie to us.'

'Even so, it would put my mind at rest to have a man of the cloth to pray with us.'

His eyes wander across the face of the house, searching for something. Then he turns to me. 'My dear, I'm glad to have this moment alone with you. There's something I've been wanting to ask.'

My stomach clenches. Does he know I've been keeping the coins from him?

'Have you ever thought to live a different kind of life?'

I hesitate, surprised. 'What do you mean?'

'We live a mean existence here. Sometimes . . . sometimes I wonder if I've done right by you. We never have much in the way of company.'

'I've no need for company. I have you and Agnes.'

There is regret in his eyes. 'I always did what I thought best for you, but perhaps I've not done as I should. Do you never wish to live among others? Do you never wish for friends? Perhaps a husband?'

He's never asked me this before. The question is like a pinprick in my heart. But the feeling is fleeting and quickly stilled – it's been many years since I allowed myself to think that such a thing might be possible, or desirable.

'I have all I need,' I say, and I mean it.

'This place . . .' he says, looking again towards the house. 'Have you never wished to leave?'

'How can you ask it? You know Scarcross Hall is everything to me.'

'Have you never wished to see more of the world?'

'My world is here. I want no other.'

He takes my hand and grips it tightly. 'I've done my best to protect you but I think, perhaps, I've failed.'

'What do you mean? Why are you talking like this?'

'There are things you don't understand, my dear . . .' He tails off and stares into the distance. 'Yes, it's imperative we have that blessing at once. We have need of God's good grace, now more than ever.' There is a quaver in his voice. Could it be fear?

I think of the coins, the missing inkwell, the dead lambs. I've an instinct he knows more than he's willing to say. Why else this sudden idea? The prospect of leaving Scarcross Hall fills me with horror, more real and more urgent than any night-time terror I may have conjured. 'Father, why do you need to protect me? What could harm me here?'

At the question his face crumples, as if he might cry. This is unlike my father, who is usually so sure of everything. I've never seen a tear from him in all my years. Even in temper he's always been as solid and steadfast as the scar above the vale and I don't recognise the weak, melancholy man before me. It shocks me to the core. I don't know how to comfort him.

Whatever reason he has for saying these things, I must not give him further cause for concern. I must give him no reason to doubt our place here. Everything I know, everything I love, is in these walls, these fells, this wild, open sky. The thought of leaving makes a hollow ache in my innards that no prayer could fill. In that moment I decide I'll not share my fears with him. I'll not encourage such thinking. I must stay silent.

Father gathers himself, drops my hand. 'I want only what's best for you. What's best for us all.'

'I know that, Father.'

'I'll speak to Pastor Flynn on Sunday. I'll ask him to pray with us. What do you say?'

'Whatever you think best.'

He seems satisfied with that. He sits, seeming absent. He's forgotten I wished to speak with him and that suits me now.

The breeze is getting up, sending chill fingers beneath my neckerchief. I shiver, and not just from the cold. I stand and hold out my hand. 'Come, let's go inside.'

'Is the fire set in the study?' he asks. 'Tell Agnes to bring me some broth, will you?'

'Of course.'

We walk slowly across the garden. Though our arms are linked it seems to me there is a new distance between us.

As we go towards the door I catch a glimpse of something

gleaming at the casement of my chamber: a pale figure that quickly moves away. The hairs at the nape of my neck bristle. I pause a moment and wait for it to reappear, straining to see into the dark interior, until Father asks, 'What is it, my dear?'

'Nothing,' I tell him. 'Nothing at all,'

I tell myself the same: it was just the reflection of the clouds, racing across the broad springtime sky.

Chapter 13

That night, I sit with the coverlet bunched up to my neck, until the candle burns low and splutters in a pool of thick yellow tallow, the stink of mutton fat in my nostrils. I cannot settle to my Bible or to darning my holed stockings or any other useful thing because my mind is too restless.

I'm concerned about the rain that has fallen every night and most days in May. The ground is too wet and marshy for our oats and barley to prosper. The fell seems a mess of mud and new-sprung brooks. And Agnes complains that a plague of slugs has destroyed most of her summer crop. In a few weeks we need to wash the sheep, ready for clipping, and we need fine weather for that.

But these worries are the usual ones, of farm and flock and family. There is another reason I cannot sleep: I am listening.

I hear the night sounds of wind in the gables, the dash of rain against the casement, rats beneath the floorboards and the creak of old timbers in the walls. I'm listening for all the sounds I'm used to and for those I'm not. My senses seem heightened so that the smallest noise I might otherwise disregard takes on an unexplained and sinister meaning. The tap of a branch against a window becomes a ghostly hand rapping upon the pane; the whine of wind in the chimney becomes a ghoulish moan; the drip of rain from the eaves becomes the steady tread of unfamiliar footsteps. And all the time I'm straining to hear it, expecting to hear it, dreading to hear it – that sound, the memory of which sends freezing fingers playing up and down my spine: *thunk . . . ssshrrrrrrsssssst . . .*

Most of all, I'm fretting about Father, who spent the rest of the day locked away in his study, poring over old documents. I'm sure now that he's keeping something from me. I've never seen him so distracted and unsure. What is it he fears? Like me, he's not one to give credence to the old stories, but it's clear to me that something has shaken him in a way I've never witnessed before.

I cannot blame him for hiding his fears: I've not spoken to anyone about my own. To do so would make them real and I cannot countenance that. So I spend the darkest hours listing the recent unsettling events and trying to explain them away. Of the missing coins – two now returned and in the pouch beneath my floorboards: this must be Sam playing tricks. Father's inkwell, still not found, I put down to his recent absent-mindedness. The dead lambs must be the work of wild dogs; it's just that we have not seen or heard them yet. The noises in the empty bedchamber can be nothing worse than rats. The figure I've glimpsed is mere imagination, my own fear taking shape in the moorland mist. And the unnerving sensation that I'm being watched can be accounted for when I think of Ellis Ferreby and his strange, unsettling stare.

Even so, there is a new and rare unease in me, a haunting instinct that tells me to pay these things heed. In the end I can bear my unceasing questions no longer. I rise, throw my thick coat over my nightgown and pull on stockings and boots.

Out by the byre the air prickles with storm threat. It is not yet midnight. The clouds hide stars and race across a high, hazy moon. I need the light of my lantern.

I climb over the gate and make my way to the corner where we've folded several ailing lambs. There is shelter here, a low stone wall and the straggling boughs of the willow copse. I slip and slide in hoof-churned mud, cursing myself for not dressing properly.

As I near the sheep, I become aware of that same creeping sensation: the feeling of eyes on my back. I've been thinking on strange things too much and have brought my fear outside with me. I stop and search the darkness. The lantern cast makes me blind outside its beam. The dim, cloud-covered moon does not give enough light to see by. Behind me, the sheep begin to stir and bleat. Something disturbs them.

My heart begins to climb into my throat.

I open my mouth to speak but hold back at the sound of someone moving towards me. I have an urge to run, to snuff my lantern and hide, but find I cannot move. My body thrills with fear. I'm alone, with no weapon, facing danger in the darkness. Someone is out here. Someone is watching me.

'Who goes there?' The voice is deep, male and threatening, but I know it at once: Henry Ravens. A flood of relief unlocks me. How foolish I'm being.

'I said, who goes there?'

'Henry, it's me.'

I hear the creak of the gate, the soft squelch of footsteps. 'Mercy? What are you doing?'

I'm almost trembling, but I must not let him see. 'Checking the sheep.'

'At this hour?'

'I couldn't sleep. I thought to look them over.'

He enters the circle of lamplight and comes to stand by me, a little too close. 'I see,' he says, a slow smile showing wolfish white teeth. 'Is that not my job? Don't you trust me?'

'Of course I do. I couldn't sleep . . . that's all.'

'I thought you were a thief. You should be careful – I could have shot at you. Garrick has given us a pistol, you know, to use against thieves, and we carry it loaded.'

'I ordered it.'

I realise how absurd I've been, to be driven from my bed by thoughts of spirits and spectres, seeking comfort in something real and commonplace.

I've always found solace in the flock. I like to do the same work year in, year out, and know that those who've gone before me did the same. Even with the trials that Nature sends, I find a perverse consolation in knowing that, no matter how hard I try, we are at God's mercy. When my hands are wrist-deep in fresh-clipped fleece, or slicked with the birth-slime of a trembling newborn, or I stand at the crest of the moor and look out over my land, I know I'm in my right place. This life is all I've ever wanted and all I shall ever need. The conversation with Father has disturbed me deeply and I'm seeking that same reassurance now. But what do I think I will find on a hillside at midnight?

The rain starts to come down. The candle hisses.

'I know why you're really here,' Henry says, as if he can read my mind. 'I know what you really want.'

He takes the lantern, fingers heavy over mine, then grasps my free hand. 'You're shivering. Come, leave the sheep till morning.'

Now he's close I can smell the drink on him, pipe smoke, warm hay, and the strong musk of a working man. As we walk back across the field, my hand in his, I'm drawn towards that scent, and I know he's right. I desperately want to forget myself.

'You've not come to see me these last few weeks,' he says, reaching the gate. 'Am I to know why?'

I have no answer for him.

'You know I can't come to the house. There are plenty of other girls I could have for sport if I wished it. I needn't wait on you. So what's changed?'

The glow of the lantern softens the hard lines of his face. He's a good-looking man with a straight jaw, a head heavy with brown curls, and sky-blue eyes that glitter when he laughs. He has a strong, well-shaped body too. I think of that now.

Since the first time, some five or six years back, I've told myself I should not go to him. He's not a good man. He's an adulterer and a drinker. But he's a keen shepherd and he knows sheep. He knows women too – or, at least, he knows me. It has been a simple exchange, each of us taking something from the other, and it has suited me.

There is never any lovemaking or flattery with him. He never kisses me. He is quick and hard. When I'm with him I become nothing but flesh and bone and sensation. I abandon the self that wakes each dawn to work and live by God's strictures and, just for that brief time, I am wild and I am free.

It's true I've avoided him in these last few weeks and I cannot say why. It seems to me that every year he grows rougher. At times, I catch bitterness in his expression and a hungry look in his eye. This year, one of his teeth is missing, his smile not so perfect.

I cannot pretend that I hold back out of finer sentiments. I'm not concerned about the scandal should my behaviour become known. After all, why should a spinster like myself care about the gossip and scorn that can harm a younger girl, when shame and judgement are already forced upon me? It's not even for the sake of my soul that I hesitate. The one thing that might give me pause is Father, for I know the heartbreak and disappointment he would feel if he were to know how short I've fallen of his own moral standard.

But none of these things has stopped me before and I don't think they will stop me now.

'Is it Ferreby?' Henry asks. 'Do you grow tired of your old friend? Do you mean to have a new one instead? You might find that harder than you think. What makes you think he'll want you? You're not so young any more and you've never been pretty.'

'No . . .'

'And I'll not step aside as easily as all that.'

'It's not him.'

'Some other easy mark, then?'

'No, Henry, there's no one else.'

'I won't share you.'

'Even though I must share you?'

'That's different.'

'Is it?'

'I don't like being ignored.'

I will not indulge his petulance. I put my hand on his chest, feel the firm curve of muscle beneath his shirt and the beat of his heart beneath that. Something stirs in me – desire, a sudden need, respite from the fears, real and imagined, that keep me sleepless.

He looks at me and puts his hand on top of mine. 'Well, I'll forgive you, if you'll come with me now . . .'

I nod. That is all it takes.

Chapter 14

That Sunday, after the sermon, I wait outside the church door, hoping to speak with Pastor Flynn. Father is making himself ill with fretting, insisting that we have Flynn to pray with us as soon as possible. When I ask him why it's so important, he calls me a heathen and shuts himself in his study.

The church in the valley is a mean, tumbledown place – a single room with cracked, mildewed walls, stone-hard benches and small high windows letting in thin grey light. The altar is an old trestle covered with tattered grey cloth. Pastor Flynn is a true Puritan, eschewing any kind of adornment or ritual in his church. His sermons are all scripture and forceful warnings about the dangers of ill-living. He's a sinewy man in middle age with enough vigour still to stir himself into a frenzy every Sunday and bring at least part of his congregation with him.

Father likes his hellfire preaching, but I think he prefers the man who sometimes leaves off his parish duties to sit in the study at Scarcross Hall in a haze of pipe smoke, debating passages of scripture and bemoaning the state of morals in his flock.

Today, during his preaching, he fixes his fiery gaze on me until I have to look away. Sometimes I feel the man knows my sins. I still do not feel the guilt I ought but it does make a queer sensation build inside me. I will myself to defy his judgement – he cannot possibly read my secret thoughts or know of my transgressions – but, inevitably, I always yield.

As I wait, I watch Henry's wife, Annie, gossiping with some of the women from the village. She's a thin, stringy bint, with sly eyes and a beaten-down look – old before her time. It's no mystery that Henry strays. I see her attention wander to her two boys, now throwing stones at a bedraggled roost of crows in the horse-chestnuts, and then to me. There is venom in her stare. This is no surprise: she's suspicious of every unwed woman this side of Halifax. Still, the sight of her always makes me uneasy. She says something to her friends and they all throw scornful looks my way. I pay them no heed. I'm used to it.

Dority comes up to me, baby Grace swaddled and slung across her chest, dragging Sam by the hand. He is surly and red-eyed. As she releases him he runs off to join Henry's lads.

'I swear I'm at my wit's end with him,' Dority says, watching him pick up a large pebble and fling it into the branches. It crashes to the ground in a shower of twigs and leaves, narrowly missing one of the other boys. 'He spent the whole sermon whispering to himself and cried like a babe when I took him outside and spanked his legs.'

At the front of the church, lost in my own reverie of guilt and sin, I'd not noticed this little drama play out. I watch Sam shouting and whooping as a big black bird rises from its nest, his upset forgotten.

'Ever since that business with the coin he's been difficult. What did Master Booth say about that?'

I've still not returned the coins to my father. I cannot give them back without some explanation; I dare not provoke his precarious temper. I'll not be the cause of more talk about leaving Scarcross Hall.

'Oh, it's all forgotten,' I lie. 'Sam should come up to the Hall and see for himself.'

'I don't know what troubles him. I can't make any sense of it. He still swears he knows nothing of how the thing came to be in his bed. But how can that be true? He's lying to me and I don't know why.'

The baby starts to whimper and Dority coos and jigs. She looks exhausted, frayed at the edges.

'Perhaps he's afraid,' I say. 'Father has a temper and Sam has seen it at work. He's seen how he can be with Agnes and how he shouts at me.'

'It's as Pastor Flynn says. If he's truthful and sorry he'll be forgiven. Anyway, your father dotes on him, you know that.'

'That's true.'

'I can't help but feel there's something more, something he's not telling me. He was always such a happy, honest boy before . . .'

I put a hand on Dority's shoulder. The gesture makes her eyes shine wet.

'I try my best but it feels like I'm losing him and it's my fault.' She bites her lip and looks down at the grizzling child in her arms. 'The baby doesn't sleep well. Ambrose is out at all hours, sometimes all night with the flock, and there's so much to be done in the house, with the animals and the crops. Sam's been avoiding his work, running off without a word and staying away all day. I don't even know where he goes. I don't know what I'm doing wrong.'

'It's not your fault.'

'I'm just . . . very tired.' It's true – her once-smooth cheeks have lost their rosy plumpness and there are parchment-thin lines feathered around her eyes. 'I can't bear to feel I'm losing him. Not after . . .' She stops, unable to go on.

'I'll take Sam home with me today. Agnes will look to him and he can help with the flock. He can stay awhile. It might do him some good. What do you say?'

'I don't mean to pass my burdens on to you.'

I hush her. 'I'll hear no more. I like to have him around the place.'

Just then Father and Pastor Flynn come out of the church, already deep in debate.

Jasper Flynn looks me up and down, taking in my old worsted skirts, my patched bodice, my darned shawl. Though I must wear these things for Father's sake, I know my attire is not truly fitting for the mistress of Scarcross Hall. I care nothing for this, but others do, and I feel Flynn's scrutiny upon me.

'I trust you're well, Mistress Booth?' he says.

'Yes, thank you.'

'Will you come, Flynn?' Father says, worrying at his neckerchief. 'I'll rest better if I see the thing done with my own eyes.'

The man is still staring at me. 'I'm sure Pastor Flynn has more important concerns,' I say.

'Bestowing God's protection upon the deserving is a pleasure,' Flynn says. 'I'll be happy to hold a special prayer meeting. We can never be too mindful of the Devil's ways, especially in these troubled times.'

What does he mean? For a moment, suspicions crowd in. Does he know something? What has Father told him?

'Yes, do come soon, Flynn—'

We're interrupted by a woman from the village, determined to have the pastor's attention. As he talks to her he gives little glances my way until I have to turn from his small ferrety eyes, wondering what he has heard that makes him look at me in that way.

I'm up at the White Ladies. It's midnight. A chalk-white moon sits high in the sky, silvering the clouds. I lie on my back on the Slaying Stone, feeling its rough surface and hard edges through my nightgown. The wind sings through the heather. All is peace and calm.

I sense that someone is here. Someone is watching me. I raise my head. The stones glow a weird furnace-blue, sending moon shadows out across the moor, but I see no one in their cast. I lie back. Now I can hear someone – the crunch of footsteps across frosted ground. I dare not look. I close my eyes and the footsteps come closer. A single hand grips my naked ankle. A chill crackles through me like lightning. I look up into the fierce dark eyes of Ellis Ferreby.

I wake with a start. I've thrown off the coverlet, and am shivering with cold. The sheet is wound about my leg. I kick it free, pull the bedding up to my chin and rest back on my bolster. But I cannot dispel the dream so easily. I did not close the shutters and moonlight spills across the floor.

Then I hear a footstep on the boards.

My heart spikes. It comes again – one step, then another, at the foot of my bed.

I stare, motionless, into the darkness, but see nothing. Am I still dreaming?

Then a run of steps, away towards the casement, quick and light; the footfall of a child. I cannot separate my waking senses from my dream world. Fear stifles my breath. Pressure builds in my lungs as they crave air. My body prickles all over and yet I dare not move.

Again – a flurry of steps from the casement back towards the bed. I squeeze my eyes tight shut, expecting to feel the touch of that cold hand once more, but whatever it is suddenly swerves away towards the door. The latch clicks and there's a low creak as the door swings open, no wider than a hand's breadth.

I force myself to speak. 'Sam?' It comes out whispered, ragged, my tongue turned dry. I'm met with silence. 'Sam, is that you?'

I lie still a few moments, straining for any sound, but all I can hear is the rushing of my own blood. I force myself from the threads of nightmare as the world begins to right itself. I find my tinderbox and, with clumsy fingers, strike at the steel until the charcloth ignites. I light a candle and straight away the warm glow chases away the demons. My door is open, no more than an inch. Perhaps I did not secure it. Perhaps the draught has caught it.

I pad across the room, bare toes on cold boards, catching a slight whiff of something burning. I open the door. There is a small chamber next to my own, just big enough for a pallet bed and washstand, meant for a maid. The door to this room stands open. I lift my candle and peer into the shadowy corners, but there seems nothing out of the ordinary so I continue to the gallery.

I see faint light at the door of the old bedchamber. Foreboding rises again, and for a moment I consider turning away, locking my door and retreating to my bed, but this time I've enough waking sense to challenge the feeling. Besides, I'll never sleep now. So I tiptoe along the gallery, my candle sending long shadows ahead, my reflection bounced back at me a hundred times in the mullioned glass of the big window.

As I reach the door, my heart rises and falls with raw panic. But I will not be beaten.

I put my eye to the crack, seeing nothing save the glow and waver of candle flame. But I can hear something: a whisper, a voice. I cannot make it out. Very gently, I push the door.

Sam is there. He sits on the floor at the foot of the old tester bed with his back to me. There is a candlestick on one side of him, flame stretched high in the chill, and on the other, the old fire screen – the child-shaped fiction that was my father's warning. Sam is muttering to himself. I cannot tell what he's saying but he does not seem to hear me.

'Sam . . .'

He starts and turns, eyes wide with shock and fear.

'What are you doing?'

He stares at me as if he does not know me.

I step into the room. 'What are you doing in here, Sam?'

His expression is a stew of fear and flight. Furtive, desperate, he glances around the room, searching for something: an excuse? A way out?

'What is it? What's the matter?'

He shakes his head. He does not want to tell me.

'There's no need to be afraid. I'm not angry.'

Then, 'Don't tell Pa.'

'I won't. I promise.' I wait, hoping this offering will encourage some confidence, but he stays silent. On the floor he's placed two piles of pebbles, one before himself and the other near the fire screen. Some sort of game?

'What are you doing?'

Again, mute silence.

'Come, you should be in bed.'

Reluctantly, he climbs to his feet, eyes still darting about the room. I follow his gaze but there is nothing to see.

'Put out the candle,' I tell him, but he just stands there so I do it myself. I take his hand and lead him away, closing the door firmly behind us.

Back in my room I secure the shutters and leave a candle to burn on the chest. Somehow I cannot stand to be plunged back into darkness. I tuck Sam beneath the coverlet and climb in beside him. His copper-curled head rests on the bolster, hazel-green eyes watery and scared.

'You know you're safe here, Sam. You know that, don't you?' My own doubt makes the words sound like a lie.

Nothing.

'Is there something you're afraid of? Something that's making you unhappy?'

He shakes his head.

'Will you tell me what you were doing in that room?'

His lips tighten.

'Please, Sam.'

'Please don't tell anyone,' he says, eyes welling once more. Why is he so afraid?

'Did you come into my room tonight?'

'No.'

'You must tell me if you did. I won't be cross.'

'No.'

'Are you sure? You must tell me the truth now. You mustn't lie to me.'

'I was never in here before. I'm not lying. Why doesn't anyone believe me?'

I look at him. There is nothing deceitful or cunning about him. He's just a boy with a troubled past and fear in his eyes. A sad, lonely child. My heart swells with pity and affection. 'Very well. I believe you. You can sleep now. You're safe here. No one is angry.'

He blinks a couple of times, then allows his weariness to take over. Of course he's lonely. He has lost his only playmate. I can understand that. My own childhood friends were few: the shepherds who tolerated a precocious tomboy, Agnes and my farmyard pets. I cradle him against my shoulder and stroke his hair, thinking of the coin found beneath his pillow, praying it does not foretell his fate. After a while his breath deepens and he sleeps.

I know that I will not.

Chapter 15

As the sun sinks, Father calls Agnes, Sam and me into his study to pray with Pastor Flynn. He is insistent, ignoring my pleas to be excused, so we kneel on the worn rush mats, the hard-flagged floor bruising our bones, eyes closed, hands steepled, the very picture of Puritan penitence, while Flynn speaks of sin, humility and the Lord's protection. Father is placated by Flynn's presence, so we follow him from room to room, bowing our heads while he prays for us, until we end in the hall, on our knees once more, before the draughty fireplace.

The sun is beginning to set and, beyond the window, the sky is stained scarlet. Shafts of reddish light make the dust motes glow and wash the walls with shifting cloud shadows.

Flynn's voice fills the space. I kneel, joints aching, annoyed that I've wasted the last light of the day. God does not speak to me through prayer learned by rote, or by self-denial and fasting. I'm with Him when I'm out on the moor, when I see His hand at work in life, death and the turning of the world. I have a miserable feeling that, this year, we need more than Flynn's passionate invocations.

Through half-closed lids, I watch Flynn, arms raised to the heavens, eyes screwed shut, expression somewhere between ecstasy and anguish. '"Whoso dwelleth under the defence of the most High shall abide under the shadow of the Almighty. I will say unto the Lord, Thou art my hope, and my strong hold, my God, in him will I trust . . .'"

A chilly gust climbs in through the broken panes and weaves its way around my neck, bringing with it the scent of burning, charred wood and peat smoke. I glance at Agnes but her eyes are closed too, lips moving in a silent echo of Flynn's.

"'For he shall deliver thee from the snare of the hunter and from the noisome pestilence. He shall defend thee under his wings, and thou shalt be safe under his feathers . . .'"

It's quiet at first, a rasping scrape beneath the deep timbre of Flynn's voice; the sound of something dropped and dragged across upstairs boards.

No one moves. Flynn does not falter. A sense of dread flutters in my chest.

It comes again, louder now: that dull *thunk* . . . a pause . . . the long, dragging scrape.

Flynn raises his voice.

"'Thou shalt not be afraid for any terror by night nor for the arrow that flieth by day; nor for the pestilence that walketh in darkness nor for the sickness that destroyeth in the noon-day . . .'"

Flynn's familiar recital takes on new, forbidding meaning. I open my eyes and look at Father. He's rocking gently to and fro, beads of sweat rising on his forehead. Can he hear it too?

Louder still.

Thunk . . . ssshrrrrrssssst . . .

Thunk . . . ssshrrrrrssssst . . .

Surely they must hear it. Only Sam has his eyes open, staring into the far corner, smiling to himself as he watches cloud patterns dance across the plaster. Something in his expression is unnerving – knowing, almost triumphant. Is he laughing at us? I open my mouth to speak but a sudden thought stops me: perhaps no one else can hear it. Am I imagining it? I think of the figure in the fog and the sensation that I'm the one being watched, as if the threat is meant for me alone. For the first time, I doubt my own mind. Queasy dismay roils in my belly.

Thunk . . . . ssshrrrrrsssssst . . .

Thunk . . . . ssshrrrrrrsssssst . . .

I close my eyes and echo Flynn's words. For once, I'm in earnest.

'"There shall no evil happen unto thee, neither shall any plague come nigh thy dwelling. For he shall give his angels charge over thee to keep thee in all thy ways . . ."'

Thunk . . . ssshrrrrrrsssssst . . .

Thunk . . . ssshrrrrrrsssssst . . .

Flynn, completing the psalm, falls silent.

We remain on our knees and I know beyond doubt that we are all listening, waiting, but nobody says a word. The noise has stopped. There is only the wind in the empty chimney, the faint crackle of the kitchen fire and the galloping pulse of my quickened heartbeat. The last light of the sun fades and we are dipped into twilight.

Slowly, quietly, we stand and go on as if nothing has happened.

Later, instead of leaving Sam to Agnes's care, I tuck him beneath the covers of my own bed. When I bend to blow out the candle he clings to my hand and looks at me with frightened eyes. He's said nothing of Pastor Flynn's visit but, of course, it must have upset him. I cannot get the image of his peculiar expression out of my mind.

'What is it, Sam? Is something wrong?'

He shakes his head. 'Will you leave the light to burn?'

I nod, bending to kiss his cheek. 'Don't worry. I won't be far away.'

I sit awhile, till he starts to doze, then go down to the kitchen, seeking something to still my nerves.

Agnes has the same idea. I find her settled in her chair before the hearth, intent on cutting short lengths of twine, a pot of caudle warming over the embers.

I go to the casement and look out. The horizon is streaked with claret wine and violet, the glimmer of early stars. Somewhere out there Ellis Ferreby keeps watch.

Is he scared up on the moor alone? He's used to solitude and lonely nights on the fells – it is a shepherd's life – but I'm glad of my warm hearth and bolted doors this evening. As far as I can tell, he's told no one of the slaughtered lambs, or the coin he found beneath his bedroll.

Though he's kept his word, I still cannot find it in myself to trust him. He keeps himself so closed. I pray he does not know the power of our shared secrets because he could use them against me, if he so wished. I curse myself for allowing that to happen.

When I told Ambrose about the lambs I saw fear shadow his face, like a kite swooping across the sun. He said nothing. To speak it would only make it real. But I sense a new wariness in him and two days ago I came across him at the White Ladies, when I thought he was safe at home with Dority. He was on his knees at the Slaying Stone, praying fervently. I turned away before he saw me and left him alone with God, swallowing the old regrets that threatened to overcome me.

I pull up a stool. Agnes ladles a portion of caudle into a cup and hands it to me, then resumes her work. I drink it, relishing the comforting sweet savour of sack, honey and cloves, and pour more, desperate for something to stem the tide of my thoughts.

Agnes watches me sideways, taking three twigs from a basket at her side. She snaps them into equal lengths and ties them together with the twine to make a small six-pointed star, like a tiny version of the cages we make to train the vegetables.

'What are you doing?'

'Nothing more than any Christian soul would do.' She sets

another little construction down and fetches up another three twigs. 'I'll wind them with herbs . . . for protection.'

I put my cup down, my throat suddenly squeezed. What does she know? 'Why would we need such a thing?'

She does not falter. 'You may think so, but I'm no fool. I've still sight enough to see. That man, coming in here, covered with blood, looking like he'd done the slaughtering himself.'

So, she's guessed about the lambs.

'How did you know?'

She gives me a withering look.

'You don't think Ellis is to blame?'

'I couldn't say.' Thirty years of isolation have made her mistrustful of strangers.

'You don't like him, do you?'

She does not raise her eyes. 'Let me tell you something, Mercy. There are more wicked things on these hills than even Pastor Flynn would have us believe.'

In the past I would have dismissed such a comment. When I was young, I delighted in her tales, intrigued by the old ways she spoke of, the charms and amulets she would scatter about the boundaries of the house to keep out sprites and fairies. Like any child, I trembled beneath my coverlet to think of witches, demons and the Devil's familiars – Father instilled in me a natural fear of such things. Once I discovered a pair of battered child's shoes in a tangle of brambles and Agnes sealed them beneath a block in the hearth so that witches could not come down the chimney. I've not thought of them for years. As I've grown older and become taken up with the everyday concerns of flock and farm, I've seen the real horrors of life and thought her stories the fabrications of a lonely old woman. Now her words take on new meaning.

'What do you mean by wicked things?'

She puts her work aside and squints into the fading firelight. 'You've always been the same,' she says. 'Concerned only with the sheep and the crops and the weather, thinking only of the next season, the price of fleece, the day's tasks. And it serves us well – I see that. But it makes you blind. Sometimes you refuse to see what's right under your nose.'

'That's not true.'

'If it were not so, you wouldn't need to ask such a question. You would know.'

I'm struck by the sudden and pressing need to unburden myself. I'd thought that in keeping my counsel I was protecting Agnes, sparing her, but now I see my error. If anyone knows the truth in the tales, it is she. I should have come to her when this began.

But then I don't know how to start. I don't know how to confess the things I've heard and seen. I want to tell of the feeling that plagues me, of eyes watching, of someone there, just out of sight. I want to speak of the noise I've heard from the bedchamber, that dreadful, dull *thunk* that plays out in my dreams, like my own heartbeat. And the footsteps that sound like Sam, the child who has begun to inspire such conflict of maternal protection and peculiar wariness. But how can I say these things? How can I express them when I cannot explain them to myself?

Agnes sits back, fixing me with her wise grey eyes. 'The other day I went to take your father his dinner. Lord knows, he'll not come into the kitchen for it, these days, and if I didn't take it to him he'd let himself starve. But he wasn't in his study. I could hear you walking about in your chamber above. And I could hear Sam, running to and fro. So, I went upstairs to find you both. Well, there was no one there. You were out with the flock, your father was in the garden and Sam was with him. When I went out to fetch them he said he'd been there all morning, smelling the roses, of all things.'

I'm not as surprised as I should be. 'Who do you think it was that you heard?' I'm a child again, pulling at her skirts, asking why the rain falls from the sky. There is a tight feeling in my chest, a sensation that I'm on the cusp of something bad. I'm dizzy, as though I'm high on the precipice at the crags, looking down the steep sweep of the vale. I want answers, yet I fear them.

She sighs, takes a draw on her cup. 'I've never said aught to you, but when we first came here – you're too young to remember – I didn't like the place. It seemed to me that we weren't wanted. It was always cold, even in summer, and folk stayed away. We saw no one from one month to the next. Even so, I always felt there was someone else here, someone watching. I'd turn a corner and catch a glimpse from the corner of my eye. I'd hear strange footsteps when there was no one about. And, once or twice, my things went missing only to turn up in places I'd not put them. I accused Bartram of playing tricks but, no, he was not one for jokes in those days.'

Despite all her stories, she's never mentioned this before. The echo of my own experience causes strings of dread to tug at my heart.

'I heard things I didn't much care for – at market, at church. People will talk.'

'What things?'

'Tales of those who lived here before us.'

'The family that died?'

'Not just those poor souls, but folk that came before them too. Tales about this house, and the White Ladies, and the ill fate of any poor body who tries to make a life here. I was sure the stories must be made up just to scare children home to their beds by nightfall. Even so, something in them had me fearful. Those first few winters were bleak. I don't mind saying, I almost left, but you were still in your cradle. I couldn't leave you alone, and Bartram wouldn't hear of it. Then, as the years went by, he roused himself, employed Sutcliffe to manage the farm and began to grow the flock. The war ended, the men came back to farm the land and make families again, and I told myself it was just stories. I'd heard too many silly tales about this place, and allowed myself to believe them. I told myself that for a long time, and I've had peace enough. There's been nothing to change my mind, till now.'

'So, what has happened?'

She looks at me with her shrewd gaze. She has more to tell.

'Please, Agnes.'

Without a word she reaches into the pocket tied at her waist. She brings out a coin.

I know before I see the glint of gold, the strange markings.

The third will seal a sinner's fate . . .

My stomach tilts and knots. I flush cold. 'Where?'

'Beneath my pillow,' she says.

I sit for a moment, then get up and pace the kitchen. I go to the window, trying to ignore the scouring sickness in my gut. The sky has darkened and I see nothing in the panes but my own reflection. I have a strong urge to close the shutters, to bar the night.

'Dority told me of the coin she found in Sam's bed,' Agnes says. 'And another, offered to Sam by the new man.'

I'd thought I was keeping the secret so well. 'Who else knows?' I ask.

She shrugs. 'Dority is loyal to this family. She wouldn't say a word to anyone. She only spoke to me because she thought I already knew. You have the other two, haven't you?'

Of course – I'd told Dority that I'd spoken to Father and returned the coin she gave me. She would have assumed that Agnes knew. I've been caught out.

I nod. 'I suppose you think I should return them to Father.'

Agnes considers, then shakes her head. 'When we first came here, I told him this house had its secrets. I warned him. And he flew into one of his rages and forbade me ever to speak of such things again. Promised to cast me out if I did. Seems no sense in changing that now.'

'But what if he's seen things, or knows things? He's been so strange of late. Is that why he was so keen for Pastor Flynn to visit?'

She lowers her eyes. 'To my mind, a life of prayers and fasting never did anyone any good. He's so changed in this last year. His mind is all adrift. I'll not speak of it to him. I'll not make him unhappy. But you must do as you see fit.'

'No, you're right. We mustn't worry him. We'll keep this between us.'

She holds out the coin and I know she's asking me to keep it safe. I take it. It's as cold as hoarfrost. There's one thing I cannot fathom. 'Why have you never told me this before? Why have you kept quiet for so long?'

'Like I said, your father forbade it. Besides, the Devil feeds on fear – what sense is there in inviting him to sup?'

'The Devil? What business would the Devil have with us? We are godly people.'

She raises an eyebrow. Though she never speaks of it, I know she questions my conscience.

'There are many kinds of devil, Mercy. There are those that dwell inside, poisoning a body from the core. We can try to cast them out with prayer and fasting and good deeds, but some are too strong. They might lie quiet, sleeping, waiting for their chance, but we cannot escape them. They will always be part of us. Well, this house is the same. I knew it then and I know so now. There is some kind of devilment here.' She pauses, looks at the golden coin in my palm. 'I always knew, deep down, it would come for us in the end.'

Summer

Chapter 16

Ellis takes the coffin path to the crossroads and, from there, follows the track that leads down into the valley. Garrick's cottage is set snug against the hillside, sheltered from the worst of the weather and far enough from the path to avoid notice by the beggars and vagrants that sometimes come to Scarcross Hall, seeking charity. He has seen it from a distance, its grey slate tiles and chimney coil of peat smoke visible from the moor top, but has never visited.

He was surprised when Garrick suggested it: *supper. Dority has killed a chicken.*

A welcome change, then, from the bread, cheese and broth that is staple at Scarcross Hall. He wonders why he has been singled out. Garrick does not seem the type to be familiar with the workers, not garrulous, like Bestwicke, or boastful, like Ravens, and in no need of their approval because he already has Mercy's good opinion.

Ellis's natural instinct is to keep his own company and folk usually understand this: if you make no friends there is nothing to tie you to a place, no regret when the time comes to move on. He has lived most of his life in this way, refusing the invitations of farmers' wives, rejecting the hand that has sometimes been extended. But he is curious and, he reasons, what is the harm this time?

It is a pleasant summer's evening. For three weeks Nature has treated them well, bestowing the sunshine needed for the grass and grain to ripen and the lambs to flourish. Now, the sun is gilded, sinking slowly to the west, and the air is still warm. Cuckoo-spit clouds glow rose-petal pink. Rooks muster in the treetops, their squabbles echoing in the valley. Above him, swifts wheel and peep, plying their deadly trade with the insects. The ground has dried at last, the endless marsh and spring-silvered mud of winter firmed beneath his feet. The heather is budding and the willows shiver with new leaves.

As always, his eye is drawn to the flock scattered over the hillside. The lambs are fattening, fleeces growing to curl. They have lost a few to grass sickness, and one drowned in a beck, but there has been no repeat of the carnage he found at the White Ladies. No more limp, mauled bodies spilling blood.

She has not mentioned it again, the killings or the coin, though the men are instructed to carry the pistol with them on their nightly vigil. He dislikes the gun and, when it is his turn, has begun hiding it beneath his bedroll. He does not think that the rusted old flintlock will protect him against anything he might encounter on the moor.

He noticed Bestwicke's reaction when the gun was first given into his hands – *Never thought I'd have cause again* – and supposes that the man knows all too well how such instruments hold a certain power, a power that can drive a man to recklessness and catastrophe. He assumes that Bestwicke must have been witness to such things in the wars, though he does not ask with which end of the barrel the old soldier is more familiar.

Garrick's cottage is like so many others on the lip of the moor: a laithe house with two rooms below, two above and a small barn attached at one end to shelter whatever livestock might be afforded. There is a single, mournful goat tied to a stake. A clutch of scruffy chickens scratch and argue. Flint is tethered on a long rope and starts to bark as Ellis approaches, bringing Garrick outside. Sam is sitting on the wall, kicking his heels. He jumps down and runs off into the trees without a word.

Garrick, though, greets him like a friend.

The wife is small and slight with the narrow shoulders and hips of a girl. She has neat, delicate features and, creeping from beneath her cap, hints of abundant, tawny hair. She lacks colour, he notices, and grey shadows cup her feline eyes. She blushes when he takes her hand, which makes her prettier. He thinks of a kitten, something sweet and harmless, to be petted and coddled. But as the evening progresses he feels her watching him, appraising him, and realises there is more to her than that. She, like her son, regards him warily, with judgement. Of course, Garrick would not choose a stupid woman, though a biddable one, perhaps. He wonders what it would take to make her flex her claws. He must be sure to remain guarded.

The chicken is eaten and good ale has been supped. Matters of farm and flock have been discussed. Sam is lured indoors by hunger and the smell of roasted meat, but he wolfs his food in silence, then creeps upstairs to bed. Ellis should leave, but is surprised to find he does not want to. He has never really known the simple pleasures of hearth and home and is fascinated by the way husband and wife are together, following each other's thoughts, anticipating each other's actions in a kind of synchronicity: Dority will fill Ambrose's cup just as he finds it empty; Ambrose moves aside to let her tend the fire. The little exchanged glances loaded with unspoken meaning.

'Where are you from, Ellis?' Dority leans forward, elbows on the tabletop, eyes keen.

'No place in particular,' he replies. 'I've travelled a lot.'

'But where were you born? Where are your family?'

'I've none to speak of.'

'Your parents?'

'Dead.'

'Oh . . . I see.'

'Not many who choose a shepherd's life have steady work to keep them settled, like your husband.'

'That's true. Master Booth has been good to us. Mercy too. We owe them so much.'

'The mistress is a friend to you?'

'Ambrose has known her a long time, since childhood. They grew up together.'

'I've worked for Bartram Booth since I was ten years old,' Garrick says, 'and I've never known a fairer man.'

'I've heard he was different back then. People were scared of him.'

Garrick considers. 'It's true he's got a fearsome temper on him, but he's mellowed with the years. He used to be out with us most days, but it's been a long while since. These days, he likes to keep himself warm indoors and leave the mistress to run the place.'

'She seems to like it that way.'

'Scarcross Hall is her home,' Dority says, 'and her whole life. She would make any sacrifice to keep the farm profitable.'

'But she has no man to help her.'

'She has Ambrose.'

'I mean, she never married.' He voices it as a statement but she takes it as a question.

'No. She's chosen not to.' She shoots a glance at Garrick, who avoids her eye, reaches for the jug and begins to fill their cups. It is fleeting but he catches some meaning in her tone. He allows an uncomfortable pause, hoping she will fill it with explanation, but she does not.

'A man might think there would be suitors enough for the heiress of Scarcross Hall,' he says, thinking of Ravens. He wonders for the first time how many like him have come before and feels a flicker of jealous disgust at the thought.

'Once perhaps . . .' Dority is studying the cup in her hands, refusing to look at him. She must know about Ravens, he thinks, if she is as good a friend as she claims to be. 'But Mercy is a singular sort. She knows that to marry would change her standing. As it is, she is Bartram Booth's only child, so she will inherit, but if she were to marry, her husband would own Scarcross Hall.' She stands and begins to gather the plates.

'Such is the way of the world,' Garrick says.

'So, she's his only heir?' Ellis asks.

Garrick shrugs. 'We've never known of other family. Booth is a private man. Keeps such cards close to his chest—'

'Of course Mercy will inherit,' Dority interrupts. 'Scarcross is everything to her and the master knows it. He wouldn't give it away to a stranger.'

'It's not always so simple,' Garrick says. 'If the law favours a male line, it might be entailed—'

'There is no male line.' She sits down again, clearly agitated.

Garrick reaches out and pats her hand – the kitten again. 'My wife is protective of her friend, as you can see.'

Dority pulls her hand out from under his. 'I just believe in what's right. I know Mercy expects that Scarcross Hall will be hers some day and it'd be wrong to take it away from her, no matter what the law says. It'd break her heart.'

'I fear the law has little sympathy for heartbreak,' Garrick says.

Dority glares at him, then turns her attention to Ellis. 'But what about you, Master Ferreby? Has there never been a wife waiting for you?'

He feels the usual flare of guilt. 'I find this life is not favourable to keeping one.'

'Many of the men manage it. John Bestwicke was married,

though he's a widower now, and Henry Ravens has a wife and two boys in the village.'

Perhaps she does not know about Ravens, after all. 'That may be, but I've not been so fortunate.'

She smiles at him. 'If you were to settle here, I'm sure Ambrose would see to it that you had regular work.'

'It's not the life for me.'

'Well,' she says, fixing him with those wily eyes, 'that's a sore shame.'

'I'm sorry about my wife. She falls prey to gossip – the curse of all women.'

With Dority gone to bed, Ellis has accepted Garrick's offer of more ale to see him home. 'We don't get many strangers, and certainly not unwed ones, so you're a fascination among the womenfolk. She's been vexing me for weeks. I'd no rest till you'd agreed to come.'

So, it was not Garrick's idea, after all.

'Women are so curious about the detail of things.' Garrick continues. 'She must seek out the why of everything. I've no patience for it. There are only a few questions that fill my mind: when will there be rain? How much can we pay the clippers this year? Should we wash early while this good weather holds?'

Ellis smiles. 'As it should be, then.'

Garrick laughs, pauses, growing thoughtful. He takes a mouthful of ale and swirls it from cheek to cheek before swallowing. 'There's one question I would have answered. What was it killed those lambs you found?'

There has been no discussion among the men, despite the presence of the pistol; as promised, Ellis has not mentioned the dead lambs to Bestwicke and he would not give Ravens the satisfaction of his confidence. He knows that Mercy told Garrick, showed him the bodies in the bloodstained sack, but this is the first that Garrick has acknowledged it to him. Darkness shadows the head shepherd's brow.

'Could it have been dogs?' Garrick asks. 'You found the carcasses. You must have some thoughts.'

Ellis feels the weight of expectation, but he has no answers. 'If there was a pack loose around here, we'd know about it.'

Garrick rubs at his forehead as if it pains him. 'There's something I've not told anyone. Not even my wife. You don't strike me as the superstitious sort, and I'd never have considered myself as such, but . . .'

Ellis feels a swell of foreboding. Instinct tells him he doesn't want to hear what Garrick is about to say.

Garrick thinks for a while, fingers twisting his beard. 'I've lived and worked this land my whole life. I've gone to church and said my prayers and never doubted my faith. I know there are stories about the moor, and about Scarcross Hall, but I never saw or heard anything amiss. At least, nothing that could not be explained. Then, a few months back – it must've been January, yes, a few weeks before you came – I was up at the White Ladies, looking for sheep caught in drifts, when something strange happened.' He pauses, swallows. Ellis watches the constriction of his Adam's apple. 'I was sure someone was there – someone who wished me harm. I felt a sense of dread like I'd never felt before, in all my years, and I couldn't shake it. It was a presence, a threat, like no earthly thing I've ever known. It didn't leave me till I walked away and was safe inside this house.' He leans back. 'It plagued me for a time but I put it down to illness of mind – the winter can do that to a man, you know. And I almost forgot about it, till you found those lambs.' Garrick refills both cups. 'No doubt you've heard the story of the slayings by now.'

'The family that died at Scarcross Hall?'

'Before that. Before the Hall was built.'

Ellis shakes his head.

'Then you'll wonder why the mistress is so insistent we keep this thing quiet. It's said such killings are a sign that the Devil is walking the moor once again.'

Ellis ignores the prickle that runs up his spine. 'Once again?'

Garrick's smile does not reach his eyes. 'I've not paid it much heed since I was a pup, but some of the old folk around here talk of a curse – a curse that goes back a long way.' He gulps his ale. 'There's no one old enough to know the truth of it now, but these stories are told to us in our cribs. Some still won't take the coffin path or go up to the Ladies for fear the place is tainted.

'It's said that some terrible wrong was done here, against the heathens that lived in these parts and practised their sorcery at the Ladies. Strangers came, tried to claim the land with violence and slaughter. In revenge, those that were left summoned up spirits of the dead and put a curse upon the land so that no man could ever tame it. They made sacrifices of their animals and placed the bodies about the moor as a warning.'

Ellis thinks of the golden coin, its strange markings, with the look of something ancient and pagan, the unusual, deliberate injuries that killed the lambs.

'It's said that when sheep are found slain like that, and with no good reason, it's a sure sign of their witchery at work again, a sign that the path down to Hell has been opened, that the dead will come back to claim any poor soul who dares try to tame the land here.'

There is a distant, sad look in Garrick's eyes. Ellis stays quiet, allows the ale to loosen Garrick's tongue.

'They say sheep were found slaughtered before that terrible winter when that poor family died at Scarcross Hall, and that wasn't the first time neither. The man who built the Hall did so hoping to banish the past, because that spot has an ugly history.'

Bestwicke had referred to such before he'd refused to go on.

Ellis feels an uncomfortable mix of excitement and fear, but stays silent, willing Garrick to continue.

'Before the Hall, there was an old farmhouse. One year, the family who dwelled there had lost near half their flock that way by autumn. Then, one night when the snows came, they were murdered in their beds, torn to pieces in the most gruesome way, as if all Hell's demons had run amok. Those who found them said they had to walk over floors frozen with blood. Lord knows how much is truth, but when it happened again . . .'

Garrick leans back, cradling his cup. 'They're just old stories, but you see why folk in these parts are easily afeared. You see why it's best to keep word of these killings between ourselves.'

'Do you believe these tales?' Ellis asks.

Garrick ponders. 'That's not the point. Many do. But I've known bad things happen at the White Ladies. Things that make a man ask questions of God. And now, since you found those lambs, I think perhaps I didn't imagine it that day. Perhaps I did sense something, some kind of evil. I pray I did not.'

Ellis thinks back to the day he found the small, mangled bodies. He had sensed it too, had walked steadily down the fell with the conviction that someone was watching him go. He had not looked back. He had not mentioned it to Mercy, and had certainly not spoken of it to the other men. They would have laughed at him, and rightly so. He had convinced himself that such fancy was weakness, brought on by the shock of his find and Bestwicke's yarns.

Garrick is watching him closely. 'You've felt it too, haven't you?'

With the warm ale in his belly, he's tempted to confess, but what would be the use? He's witnessed it before – the hysteria that can spread like flames through a summer hayrick. Once, he wintered in a small village near the old north wall, where confinement and poverty bred resentments and bad blood. It had taken only a spark – one cry of witchcraft – to send the whole place into a frenzy of lies and retribution. He had left before the roads cleared, risking his life in the snowdrifts rather than be consumed by fear and fury. He will not be the one to encourage that kind of thinking here.

'I've never felt aught amiss,' he says.

Garrick nods slowly. Ellis knows he doesn't believe him.

He senses it as soon as he leaves the warmth and smoke of the cottage: the weather is about to turn. The stars are cloud-covered. He can smell rain in the air.

He feels the first drops as he reaches the crossroads and pauses by the signpost, compelled to turn towards the White Ladies, though the pale stones are shrouded in darkness.

He thinks of Garrick's admission. He had pressed for more. What bad things had Garrick witnessed? But at that Garrick had closed like a casket, and it became clear, soon after, that it was time for him to leave.

He stands, feeling the rain on his cheeks, the earthy scent of the peat bog strong in his nostrils. He feels the presence of the stones, but will not countenance the fear that crawls upon his skin, like lice. He forces himself to walk the coffin path steadily. He will not hurry.

By the time he peels off his breeches and climbs into his bedroll in the hayloft, he is soaked to the skin. He lies, staring up into the blackness of the eaves, listening to Henry Ravens's snores, the lament of owls, and the sluice of water over the tiles.

Chapter 17

Despite the warm midsummer air, the brook, fed by a hundred tiny springs that rise on the moor top, is icicle-cold. The rain that has fallen for a week has finally ceased, but the deluge leaves the streams brimming with a current that both helps and hinders the task: the fast-running water carries away the filth but it's harder to find sure footing, harder to stay upright with a thrashing, panicking sheep on your hands. He has already fallen more than once.

Garrick came to the barn late last night to tell the men they would begin the washing today. Ellis was out with first light, ready to bring the flock from the fields, where they have been folded, down to the valley and into the large willow byres that have been built to hold them. It had taken hours but now the byres are crowded with jostling animals, all stinking of peat, excrement and fear, all unwilling to take their turn in the brisk, chilly flow. Ellis feels some sympathy for them.

He collects another animal from Ravens, who has the task of checking each one – teeth, feet and fleece – before feeding them, one by one, into the brook.

This one is strong, a big wether with a patchy, peat-stained fleece, and Ravens smiles as Ellis struggles to control it. He tugs its horns, keeping its head above water as it fights, sending spray across his face. Sam, waiting on the bank to collect any loose fleece, laughs as Ellis curses. The boy has been bursting with self-importance all day, glorying over the new lads who are older than him but given lesser tasks.

They have two new boys, one working alongside Ravens and the other tending the washed sheep in the fold on the far bank. They remind Ellis of himself when he first worked the hills, reeking of poverty and a troubled, violent past. Brothers, come to find labouring wages, they have the tawny hair and blue eyes that betray their Irish blood. The eldest, Tom, carries the awkwardness that comes with the verge of manhood, and a marked protective instinct for his brother, Nat, but both are keen for the work, and for the coin. He envies their wiry bodies that do not seem to tire. His own is aching, legs numb from the cold water, back and shoulders nagging, fingers puckered and rubbed sore.

Ellis manoeuvres the sheep to a shallow spot, where it can find a footing. It settles, allows him to tug away dags, burrs and dried grasses, and separate tangled loose strands of fleece that will find their way into Sam's basket, and eventually to the looms of the poorest weavers, who come begging for scraps.

As he works, he watches Mercy from the corner of his eye. How different this place seems now, a few months on, from the eerie, desolate spot where they first met. Today it's full of noise and chatter: the banter of men, the din of complaining sheep, women come to keep company, their children to watch. The trees are heavy with greenery, foxgloves swaying on the slopes, rocks shining yellow with new moss, a carpet of tiny star-shaped flowers blooming in the hollows. The air is rich with sunshine and birdsong. Somewhere, far off, a woodpecker is at work.

Lost in the hum of activity, he could almost forget the haunting sense of foreboding that has dogged him since he found the slaughtered lambs – increased since his conversation with Garrick – and the questions that keep him awake at night. True to his word, he's not mentioned any of it again, but feels perversely glad of the shared secret, bound to Garrick, and to her, in unspoken collusion. The threat hanging over them draws her closer.

When he's sure the fleece is clean, he drags the sheep over to the far bank where Mercy waits.

'Contrary creature, this one,' he says, catching her eye. 'It'll bolt given a chance.' He sees her surprise – they've exchanged no words all day.

She nods and calls Bracken to her side, then takes hold of the sheep's horns and hauls it clear of the water. The animal, glad to be on firm ground, calms at her touch. Mercy stands astride, gripping its head between her legs, fingers deftly plucking away the dirt that has been missed: the cleaner the fleece, the better the price.

Earlier, he had watched her laugh with Dority, who came with Agnes to bring food for the workers and has stayed to keep an eye on Sam. The women had sat apart from the men while they ate, gossiping and laughing in the conspiratorial way that makes a man feel judged. Ravens had played up to it, had stripped off his shirt, swaggered and preened for them, slugging a pot of ale and competing with the boys, who turned cartwheels and threw themselves about like tumblers. Ellis noticed the way her eyes followed Ravens, but she did not smile at his show.

Ellis prefers to watch her work. He admires her strength, which could match that of most men, and the way she handles each animal with firmness but care – her fastidious concentration returning several creatures to the brook for a second wash. She is unselfconscious, caring for nothing but the task. He has never known a woman work so like a man while seeming to have no need of one. He does not see the fickleness he's witnessed in other women but, then, life has given him little comparison.

* * *

Sapling, the whores had called him, *green wood*. Wherever they went he was petted and teased, persuaded to play his part in their bawdy tricks by a pretty smile, the cushion of a moon-white breast, a devious tear. He was pet of them all, and Betsy didn't mind. She took pride in her boy. Then he grew tall and strong with a few straggling hairs upon his chest and chin.

One of them – Gretchen – took him into her chamber and sat him down upon a straw mattress strewn with filthy blankets. She had hair the colour of honey and the skin of her large breasts was freckled, like eggshells. Pink nipples peeped above her low-cut stays. She stared hard at him while she undressed. He hadn't known what was happening until it had happened. And afterwards she said: *We drew straws*.

He was fourteen years old. At least, that was what he was told.

A sudden shout from Ravens draws his attention. Tom, whose task is to keep each sheep inside the narrow run until Ravens is ready, has let one slip through the gate. He makes a lunge for it, but too late. It cannons into the backside of the wether that Ravens is checking, sending it headlong into the barrier on the far side of the pen. Ravens struggles to stop both animals charging blindly into the water, while Tom looks on, panicked and helpless.

Once the sheep are under control, Ravens is fuming. 'Christ alive! If you can't do your job, stay out of my way!' He clips the boy's head. Tom, caught off balance, stumbles backwards and falls, his head meeting a jutting rock.

There is a moment when his face crumples, lip quivering, and Ellis sees the child that he still is – the mewling infant that resides beneath the bravado of youth.

Then the boy gathers himself and sits, scowling at Ravens, one hand pressed to his skull. Dority rushes to him. 'Are you hurt, Tom?' She offers a hand, but the boy ignores her. He's staring at his fingers, now slicked with scarlet.

'Let me see,' Dority says, trying to assess the wound.

'No.' He bats her away, climbing to his feet.

'Tom, please . . . you're hurt.'

But he will not show distress in front of Ravens. He slopes off along the run towards Bestwicke.

Dority watches him go, hands on hips. 'That was cruel, Henry.'

'Then he shouldn't get in my way,' Ravens says. 'Besides, it might knock some sense into him. I don't know why we're giving work to their sort when there are boys in the village would welcome the wage. We don't need them.'

Garrick looks up from the sheep he is washing. 'Hold your tongue, Henry, if you cannot hold your ale.'

Mercy pretends to ignore them but Ellis knows she's listening.

'Tell me, then,' Ravens goes on, 'why you're squandering good coin on this papist scum when there are local boys going hungry?'

'We always use travelling labour for the hay harvest, you know that.'

Ravens snorts. 'Aye, for hay cutting, but not shepherding. Keep them in the fields or, better still, turn them out, send them on their way. There's little enough work as it is. Why should we go hungry to feed them?'

'We cannot bring the grass in yet – it's too wet. Am I to pay them to sit and do nothing?'

'As far as I can see, that's all they're good for. My boys would do twice the work with half their years. Their sort don't belong here. Why give them reason to stay?'

Bestwicke makes a grumble of agreement. Tom is sending daggered looks towards Ravens.

'Where I find workers is not your business,' Garrick says.

But Ravens is only encouraged. 'There's a papist plague on this country, I tell you. Folk thought there was an end to it when

Cromwell had his way over there, but seems to me there's more and more of them each year. What right have they to take our work? This is our land and they're not welcome here.'

'Calm yourself. I need your mind on the work,' Garrick says, handing the sheep he's washed to Mercy.

'It's not just the Irish,' Bestwicke says. 'I've heard there are vagrants in the old cottage now. They'll be up here begging for charity before the week's out.'

'And no doubt the master will spare what he can, as would any good Christian,' Garrick says.

'But why should he?' Ravens counters. 'Why should we give away what we've worked for when these people have not the sense and pride to do the same? They travel the roads, settling on our land, taking our work. We don't need strangers round here.'

Ellis feels the slice of Ravens's words and knows that some part is meant for him. Anger begins to flex a fist in his belly.

'A little kindness cannot be a bad thing,' Dority says. 'And Master Booth has a kind soul.'

'More fool him,' Ravens replies. 'See how he likes it when his land is swarming with papists. Let's see how his pastor preaches hellfire then.'

Ellis glances at Mercy. She is feigning concentration on the sheep in her hands but her lips are pressed together in a tight line. Why does she stay so silent? A single word from her would end this and return everyone's attention to the work. Does she refuse to play the mistress out of some twisted loyalty to Ravens?

He wades to where Ravens has the next sheep ready for him. It's a ewe this time, a bedraggled shearling with an untidy fleece. He takes it by the horns and pulls it towards the water. It makes a half-hearted attempt to resist, bleating, hooves sliding on the wet bank, but then staggers into the brook and begins to kick and swim.

Ravens is ranting now: 'Why don't we find some Spaniards for harvest? Or ask the gypsies to clip the sheep?'

Ellis turns his mind to the work, leaving Bestwicke and Ravens to debate the worst kind of worker – the Irish or the gypsies. He feels the sharp edges of a storm cloud gathering and shuts his ears. He cannot afford to lose his temper.

The sheep is weak, struggling to keep its head above water and he has to hold it up by its horns as he begins to work the dirt free from its fleece. It rolls its eyes and bleats piteously. Instinct tells him something is wrong. He runs his hands over its flanks. Towards the rear, he can feel the flesh is uneven and soft; the creature makes a low grumble as he presses there. Its fleece is matted. The stink of rot rises.

'Hold!' he calls. Garrick, just about to collect another animal from Ravens, signals a halt.

Ellis drags the creature to the far bank where Mercy meets him, and hauls both himself and the sheep out of the water. He knows he's right before he sees it – the sheep is fly-struck.

There is a patch of filth-stained fleece on its hindquarters and as he parts it, a great ooze of maggots spills from a festering wound. It's worse around its backside, the skin there already putrid and stinking of rotting meat. No matter how many times he's seen it – and there have been plenty – the sight of a maggot-infested sheep still makes his stomach turn.

'Oh, Lord . . .' Mercy whispers, under her breath.

The sheep is frightened and confused, straining to bite at the wound it cannot see.

'Hold her,' he says to Mercy, and she takes the ewe between her legs, calls Bracken to her side in case she loses her grip. He goes to his waistcoat, fetches his knife and is back in seconds. Before Garrick reaches them and before she knows what he intends, he lifts the ewe's jaw and draws the knife deep across the veins in its throat.

He feels the sinews split. An arc of violent crimson catches the sunlight. Drops of it patter his face. He tastes it on his lips.

The sheep slumps to the ground, twitches and quivers, burbling its last breath.

Mercy is speechless, staring at him in undisguised shock. There are spots of bright scarlet on her cheek.

The women are all gawping, the children fallen silent. Ravens snorts, makes a weird, twisted smile.

Garrick reaches them, dripping wet and fuming. 'By Christ, what are you thinking? You've no right to destroy another man's property. I should dismiss you for this.'

'I only did what must be done.'

'You've no right.'

'It was as good as dead.'

'No one makes that decision but me.'

'It was fly-struck. It should never have been in the brook. It might have poisoned the water.'

All eyes fall to the stream as if expecting a plague of flies to rise from it, but of course there is nothing.

'The wound was too far gone. We could not have saved it.' He appeals to Mercy. 'Tell him.'

But she is still looking at him with disgust. He feels fury rising. It has been a long time since he felt the strength of it. She saw the wound. Why will she not speak up for him? She knows Ravens has failed in his duty, knows the man is a drunkard, an incompetent, but would she punish him in Ravens's place? Would she stand by and say nothing while he is cast out?

There is a buzzing in Ellis's ears, a dark pressure simmering in his chest. Ravens is leaning against the byre, enjoying the scene. Ellis goes towards him, knife still gripped. Ravens squares up.

Ellis shoves him, leaving a bloody handprint on one shoulder. 'This is your fault. That sheep should never have been in the water.'

Ravens holds up his palms. 'Don't blame me if you've a taste for blood.'

'You're drunk. Drunk and useless.' Ellis pushes him again, harder this time, and sees the response in Ravens's eyes. He wills him to throw a punch, to be the first. 'What are you afraid of?' he says, under his breath.

Ravens is mocking. 'You think I'm afraid of you?'

Ellis pushes him once more. He sees the clench of Ravens's jaw, the slight flare of nostrils.

'Don't do that again.'

He does it again.

'Stop this!' Garrick shouts. 'I'll not have fighting among my men. Stop now or I'll turn you both out.' But neither is listening.

Ellis is deafened by the rush in his ears. He longs to feel the crunch of bone, the give of flesh, the warm wet slick of blood on his knuckles. Before he knows it, the knife is at Ravens's throat.

Then Mercy is between them, pushing them apart, one hand on his chest. He feels her touch like a punch.

She throws him a pleading look, then drops her hand and takes hold of Ravens's forearms. 'Please, Henry, stop this. Ellis is right. That sheep was done for. I would've done the same.'

'You take his side over mine?' He pulls away from her.

'It should not have been in the brook. You should've stopped it.'

Ravens's mouth twists into an ugly grin. He looks from her to Ellis and back again. 'I see how it is. You're just like the rest of them. Whore.'

The word alters her face, like a slap. She draws herself up, almost as tall as him. 'You will not talk to me like that.'

'That's enough,' Garrick interrupts. 'How dare you speak so, Henry? Take it back.'

But Ravens is staring at Ellis, eyes fiery with hatred.

'Apologise,' Garrick insists. 'We've work to do.'

'Well, then, let's see how you do it without me.'

Ravens spits at Ellis's feet, then turns and gathers his things, slings his shirt over one shoulder and stalks away down the path towards the village.

'The alehouse has a keen customer there,' Bestwicke mutters.

Ellis, fists twitching, muscles coiled and shaking, watches him go.

Chapter 18

Agnes is a creature of habit. I used to think, when I was very young, that if she did not wake to kindle the fires, the day would not begin. If she did not fetch the water in before nightfall, the moon would not rise. If she did not dig the kitchen beds soon after Candlemas, the first lambs would not come and spring would stay sleeping beneath the snow. I believed that she commanded the rising and setting of the sun, the whole order of my world dictated by the many small tasks that filled her days, weeks and years.

Even when Pastor Flynn taught us about God's will and I began to understand just how much the turning of the seasons and our survival through each one is a matter of His mercy, I still took comfort in the familiarity and ritual of Agnes's routine. I still do. So, when I return with the men to Scarcross Hall for our midday meal and she's not waiting in the kitchen to greet us, I know something is amiss. Though we have not spoken of it again, she has not been the same since the night we confessed our fears to one another.

We have had a long morning herding the flock into the lower pasture in preparation for clipping, and the men are hungry. There is no warm loaf on the table, no slab of cheese or pots of beer. A steaming cauldron of pottage bubbles over the fire, hissing and spitting into the flames.

The men are tired and grumbling. The rain has been pouring all morning, and if it does not stop, we shall have a hard time with the shearing. The clippers will be here within the week, skilled men who are in demand and will not sit idle waiting for the clouds to clear. It's the same every year. Ambrose and I spend a lot of time watching the sky.

Ever since the argument between Henry and Ellis, there's a new tension in the air. Henry returned, as I knew he would, chastened and contrite, full of promises I suspect he'll not keep. The two men keep their distance, circling each other, like bristling dogs.

'Why did you take his side?' Ambrose asked, later, when we were alone.

I told him the truth: 'Because Ellis was right.'

In a way, I was glad to witness the flash of anger in Ellis – first proof of something real and human, after so many weeks of dour silence. But the cold-hearted calm with which he dispatched the animal was unnerving. I still cannot make sense of him.

I take charge, telling the men to sit while I rescue the pot from its stand, fetch bowls and spoons and find the bread, still warm beneath its linen wrappings in the pantry. I leave them jostling for a serving and go upstairs.

Agnes is not in her room. I find a heel of pie and a slab of white, crumbling cheese forgotten on her bed. I collect both and make to return to the kitchen, but when I reach the top of the staircase I notice that the door to the old bedchamber is ajar.

I pause a moment, listening, straining to hear above the rumble of men's voices from below.

'Agnes?'

No answer.

I leave the food on the top step, creep to the door and peer through the gap.

She's there, sitting in the gloom on the far side of the bed, her back to the door, motionless and silent.

I watch for a few seconds. There's something peculiar about her stillness, as if she's deep in daydream. Agnes never rests in daylight hours.

The board creaks beneath my foot and breaks the spell. Entering, I find the room in chaos. Boxes and crates have been shifted about. A large chest has been dragged into the centre of the room and thrown open, mildewed fabric spilling like entrails. The fire screen is pushed up against the wall, the boy's dead eyes hidden. The air is choked with dust and there is a sharp scent of charred wood. Despite the milder weather, it's chill.

Agnes turns slowly. 'Mercy . . .' she says, voice thick with emotion. I see now, her eyes are red. Her apron and cap are streaked with soot and dirt. There is a small wooden box opened on her lap.

'What's the matter? What are you doing in here?'

'I . . . I was looking for something.'

I indicate the upturned crates, the stack of split pails that have tumbled across the floor. 'I can see that.'

I walk over to the bed and she quickly shuts the box and stands, but not before I catch a glimpse of something inside. 'What have you there?'

She looks to the casement where, through one opened shutter, the dull light of a rain-washed sky filters through streaked panes. Then, 'Oh! The pottage!'

She skirts the bed, trying to secrete the box beneath her shawl.

I bar her way. 'I've seen to it.'

'I must go down. The men will be waiting on their dinner.'

'I said, I've seen to it. Agnes, tell me what's the matter. What have you there?'

'I was looking for something, that's all. I forgot the time.'

'Can I see?' I stretch my hand towards the box but she holds it out of reach.

She hesitates, defiance in the set of her mouth. But her eyes tell a different story. I can see her thinking, trying desperately to concoct an explanation.

'We agreed – no more secrets,' I say.

'You'll think me an old fool. It's just some shoes that belonged to you when you were a babe. I kept them . . .'

She opens the box, revealing a pair of child's slippers, made of the finest leather, stitched with gold thread, nestled on a scrap of red brocade. They are no bigger than my palm, barely worn.

'I don't remember them,' I say. 'Why have I never seen them before?' I go to touch but she moves away and shuts the box.

'You were too young,' she says. 'I'd forgotten about them. Then I couldn't find them. I thought they might be in here.' Following her gaze I see that she's placed a talisman in the grate, amid the waste of soot smuts and the tiny white bones of a dead bird that must have tumbled down the chimney. She has begun to push a large chest across the fireplace to block it. 'Then I thought perhaps they might be beneath the bed and, sure enough, that was where I found them.' She looks with distaste at the old oak bedstead, its rotting drapes and worn bolster. 'I've never liked that great thing. If it were up to me, I'd burn it. We never use it now, not since—'

'But it's not up to you, is it?' The sound of Father's voice makes us both start. He's standing by the open door, leaning heavily on his cane. 'That bed is as much a part of this house as the stones in the walls.'

He takes a few steps into the room, sniffing the musty, charred air. 'What has happened here? Why is this room in such a sorry state?'

Agnes is staring at the floor. I'll have to answer or Father will blame her and they'll fight.

'We shut up this room some time ago, upon your word. Don't you remember?'

'I think I would recall that. It's a fine chamber, with fine views. Why would I have allowed such a thing?'

'We used it to store the fleeces last year when the barn was damp. You suggested it yourself.'

He goes to the casement, almost tripping on a pile of old linens, and tugs at a rusted shutter. It refuses to open.

'Mercy, take this.' He thrusts his cane in my direction and pulls on the catch with both hands. It gives, showering him with dust and cobwebs. He seems not to notice. Outside, the sky is heavy. Rain patters against the thick leads and low cloud obscures the valley.

'There . . .' he says. 'I always did say this was the finest view from the house.'

Agnes and I exchange glances. He turns back to the room, surveys the jumble of battered old chests, pallets covered with teasels of greasy fleece, the scatter of grime at the hearth, the rusted blades of three old scythes that have somehow made their way here. In the dim light his face is lined and haggard. I'm taken aback by the desolation in his eyes.

'How did it come to this?' he says. 'We must do something about it. Where will we put our guests?'

'Father, we never have guests.'

'What are you talking about? I've a great many friends. Your mother and I . . .' His hand lifts, flutters slightly, drops to his side. He's staring at the box in Agnes's hands. I can see his confusion, then the moment his eyes spark and temper takes him. He glares at her with venom. She cowers behind me.

'No one will remove the bed, do you hear me?' he says, stifling anger.

'Yes, Father, but—'

'This room will be cleaned and put to rights. The Applegarth woman will do it.'

'Father—'

'That's my final word. I'm still master here, Mercy, no matter what you think. I'll not speak of it again.'

I know there's no point in arguing with him. I watch, wordless, as he stalks across the room and snatches the box from Agnes's hands, then turns and walks the length of the gallery to his own chamber. He slams the door, the noise echoing in the empty hall below.

Agnes, wiping away a tear of frustration, is resolute. 'I won't do it.'

'He'll have forgotten about it by morning.'

'Perhaps you should tell him.'

'Tell him what? That we're afraid of rats in the walls?'

'About the coins and the dead lambs. You heard what he said. If he will be master of this house still, he should act like the master. It's time. I'll not suffer in silence. That man knows more than he lets on. You must speak with him. He'll not hear it from me.' Agnes is herself again. As she reaches the door she looks back at me over her shoulder. 'I don't care what he says. This room should be locked up for good, and if you'll not see to it, then I shall.'

She goes into her room and changes her apron. I wait until she gathers the food I left on the steps and descends. I hear the sounds of welcome and Henry's laughter below. Then I shut the door to the chamber, promising myself I'll find the key. Agnes is right. It's time to confront Father.

I know what I must do. I go to my bedchamber and, checking that no one follows, prise up the loose floorboard. I'll take the coins and return them, along with the mystery of where each one was found. Though I've spent sleepless nights searching for an explanation, I've found none. I'd thought that in keeping them from him I was sparing him the same worries, but perhaps I was wrong. He knows the old rhyme as well as anyone. And when he hears of the dead lambs and the nature of their killings, he will have to listen. Perhaps he will have answers. I'm sure he's keeping something from me. What did Agnes mean when she said he knows more than he says?

The red velvet pouch is where I left it, next to the ebony box. As soon as I lift it I know by the absence of weight that something is missing. There's no chink of metal on metal. I untie the drawstring and tip the bag upside down, hoping beyond sense that I'm wrong. My mother's ring falls into my palm, but the coins are gone.

Chapter 19

I do not tell Father about the coins. Instead I seek out the key to the old bedchamber, turn the lock, thread the key through a length of twine and knot it around my neck. I put the red velvet pouch back under the floorboards, next to the ebony box, swallow my horror, and say nothing at all.

No one knows of my secret hiding place, not even Agnes, and I can find no reasonable explanation this time. It cannot be rats in the chimney, a gust of wind or a stray branch tapping at the windowpane. I tell no one. I go to bed each night expecting to be woken by fleet footsteps, or strange sounds coming from the old bedchamber. I sleep badly, if at all.

These thoughts plague my mind as I walk the fell-side, looking out over my land. It's dusk, a midsummer sky of apricot and swallows, peat smoke and the trill of stonechats. The breeze carries the rich charred scent of the tar pot from the field behind the barn where we've been clipping the flock for the last three days. Thin rain threatens to soak the fleeces, so we clear a place at the back of the barn, beneath the hayloft, to lay them out. My hands are red and raw from picking them over, folding and rolling them into a stack where the floor is dry. I do not want to store them in the house this year, so the barn slowly fills with the sweet, oatmeal smell of wool.

We have two clippers, men we know and trust, and they work fast. We are all up at first light, the days passing in a blur of glittering shears and the clamour of the waiting flock. The air is thick with the smell of tar and the stench of scorched fleece as we mark each newly shorn sheep with the Scarcross smit.

These few days will determine the year ahead as the quality of the fleece and the price it will bring come clear. A good year will mean a profitable portion from the worsted weavers and coin enough to see us fed through the winter, perhaps a little more to put by. A bad year will mean a lean season, and little bargaining power for years to come. I've known farms suffer sorely from rot and fly-strike, the poor fleeces that result and bad word of mouth. A good reputation takes years to build and can be lost in a single summer. But the signs are good: the men are making progress and tonight Ambrose has let them finish before dusk. It's midsummer's eve and they must have their time to drink.

I do not join them. Instead I walk the fell. I want to be alone with my flock, my thoughts and the moor. As I stop and look over the chimneys of Scarcross Hall, dark fingers pointing skywards against a horizon of brilliant orange, and the fell, dotted with pale bodies – the brand-new fleece of the shorn sheep – I cannot feel the joy of it. My burdens press too heavy.

It's not just the mystery of the coins, or the unexplained noise in the old bedchamber, or the slaughtered lambs, or even the uncanny sensation I've had of being watched – it's what Agnes said about the Devil that stalks my thoughts tonight.

I am a sinner. This is true. I've sinned in thought and deed, with Henry Ravens and others before him. And, though I put my soul in peril, I'm not as sorry as I should be. I've questioned the Bible's teachings and discarded my father's piety in favour of a different kind of worship. I've made an idol of the land, my passions, my own selfish desires. Could it be that this devilment in me is the reason for these strange events?

Satan is known for his trickery. He takes on other forms and sends his demons to do his work. He's drawn to those with moral weakness because they are easier to corrupt. Pastor Flynn preaches of the dangers of temptation, of the trials we must undergo on the path to salvation. Am I the one being tested? Am I being punished for my sinful past?

Some way to the east I see a figure silhouetted on the skyline, making slow progress towards the White Ladies. Ellis Ferreby has volunteered for the night watch. It seems he has no thirst tonight either. For a brief moment I'm tempted to go to him, to tell him the full scope of my worries. I long to confide in someone and he's so closed and silent I'm sure he would not repeat my secrets. But, no. I must shoulder this alone.

By the time I return to Scarcross Hall the twilight is fading. I walk towards the gate in the wall nearest the kitchen and watch the hens roosting in the old coop by the outhouse. From here I can see the glow of a fire in the brazier outside the barn, hear the merry hum and chatter of the men. I pause a moment and watch, hidden in shadow where they cannot see me. They're seated on upturned troughs and pails, faces lit by flame. There's a peal of laughter and one man – one of the clippers – stands and begins an unsteady jig while the others mock him. Even if I wanted to join them, I cannot, forever divided by who and what I am.

'I knew you'd come.'

Henry is drunk, slurring, but he's managed to creep to my side without my knowing. He thrusts a half-drained bottle towards me. 'Don't look at me like that, Mercy. Have a drink with me.'

The desire to lose myself is strong. I take the bottle. The liquor is rough and stings my throat, but it feels good.

'I haven't seen you for weeks,' Henry says.

'You see me every day.' I take a good mouthful.

He comes closer. 'Don't be coy, Mercy.'

'I've been busy.'

He smiles, takes the bottle and drinks. 'Hard work usually gives you an appetite. Come on, it's midsummer's eve . . .' He sways a few steps closer and puts a hand on my waist, drawing me towards him so I catch the potent scent of his sweat and the tobacco on his breath. 'I knew you'd come back to me. You always do. You can't help yourself.'

'You're drunk.'

'Come.' He puts the bottle by his feet and places both hands on me, runs one down to grope my buttock. He glances back over his shoulder towards the men outside the barn, then noses my neck. 'Let me have you here – they can't see us.'

Suddenly it seems to me that I'm in the arms of a stranger. I've always known that Henry Ravens is not a good man. I've no romantic notions about him and tell myself no lies, but now I see something I've not seen before – something sordid beneath the well-made cheek, the cajoling eyes, the greedy smile. He's a handsome man with an ugly heart. I knew this deep down, but it has never mattered to me before.

'No. I don't want that.' I push him away but he holds on tight.

'Let's not play this game. Let's go to the stables.' He gives me that smile, but instead of melting me, it hardens me. I know suddenly that I no longer want him and it is over between us.

'Henry, this has to stop.'

'You always say that, and you never mean it.' He raises a hand to my breast and squeezes.

It has no effect. I push myself away. 'I mean it this time.'

He must see I'm in earnest because he stops his pawing. 'Why are you angry? How can you be pettish on a night like this?'

'I'm not angry.'

'Then what's wrong?'

I barely understand this sudden change myself but I know I owe him no explanation. 'Nothing's wrong.'

'Mercy . . .' He reaches for me once more but I sidestep out of reach.

'I won't come to you again, and you must not seek me out. Do you understand?'

'What's the matter? Has Jasper Flynn scared you with his sermons? Are you frightened for your soul?' He laughs, a horrid, grating sound that contains no humour. 'It's far too late for a whore like you.'

'I mean it. We must stop. And you won't talk to me like that. Do you understand?'

His laughter dies and instead a hard glint comes into his eye. 'I see. So, you mean to have him, then? Or have you had him already? I expect so.'

I don't need to ask who he means. 'You misunderstand me.'

'I think not. I see how he stares at you.'

'You're imagining things. I'll hear no more of this. You'll not come to me again. From now on you'll leave me be.'

'You can't tell me what to do. And you can't expect me to stand by and watch some other man take my place.'

'You'll watch your tongue, if you want to keep your wage.'

'You think threats will buy my silence?'

'I won't bargain with you. It's over between us, that's all.'

'It's not over till I say so. What would your father think, if he knew? And Garrick? And your godly pastor? There are names for women like you. Women are hanged for less.'

'What are you saying?'

'That you should think well before you threaten me. I'm not done with you, Mercy Booth, and if you think Ellis Ferreby a better man than me, think again.'

'You cannot force me. I'll turn you out.'

He laughs again and in that moment I despise him.

'You won't do that. You've too much at stake.'

Though I've every right to banish him from my land, I know

one word from him could bring the fury of the world down upon my head: adulteress. The law has little pity for unwed women, especially those like me. And I would be powerless to stop the terrible consequences, because his accusations would be true.

I have done this to myself. I've not been careful, or prudent. I've taken my selfish pleasures with no thought for others, no mind for justice. I might say I'll take my punishment gladly, but that would be a lie too. I've no wish to end my days at the end of the hangman's rope. And I cannot do it to Father. The disgrace would destroy him. If he knew what I truly am, it would break his heart. And what would become of the farm, with no one to take my place? I realise, with horror, that Henry Ravens has the power to destroy everything I've built here. How did I ever allow it? How could I have been so blind?

'All lovers quarrel,' Henry says. 'It increases the heat between them. Can you not feel it?'

He comes closer again and grips both my arms, fingers digging in so hard the flesh will bruise. 'Come to the stables with me now . . .'

I am trapped. Though the thought repels me, I will have to do as he says.

Just then, I hear the kitchen door open and Agnes, panicked: 'Mercy, is that you?'

'Yes, I'm here.'

'Thank the Lord. Come quickly.'

I look Henry in the eye, bolder now. 'Leave me be. Don't come to me again.' Then I pull myself from his grip and slip quickly through the gate.

Agnes stands on the threshold, lantern aloft, squinting into the darkness. 'Have you seen your father?'

'No.'

'Where have you been?'

'Walking the fell.'

She frowns. 'And you've not seen him, in the barn or the stables?'

'Agnes, what's wrong?'

I follow her inside where she sets the lantern down on the table, returns to the door and locks it. She looks distressed, eyes darting into the shadowed corners of the room. 'I can't find him.'

'Is he not in his chamber? There's a light at his window.'

'You don't understand. He's gone. I don't know what to do.'

I recognise the look in her eye – the same I saw the night she told me about the coin beneath her pillow. She's afraid – afraid deep in her bones. The hairs at the nape of my neck prickle. 'Agnes, what's happened?'

She snatches up the lantern and leads me out into the hall. The candle casts long shadows, the flame mirrored in the windowpanes. As I pass the empty fireplace I catch the scent of ash and charred wood.

Agnes takes the back stairs up to the gallery, avoiding the steps that lead past the old bedchamber. Instead she makes her way to Father's room.

The door is ajar, a stub of candle burns on the sill. The bedclothes are in disarray and the chest beneath the window has been thrown open. The contents – old clothes and boots – are strewn about the room, as if he's been frantically searching for something. I notice the wooden box that Agnes found in the old bedchamber lies open on the bed, empty, the small leather shoes gone. The air is chill – at midsummer we need no fires – but again there's an acrid, burning smell beneath the greasy scent of tallow.

'I found it like this,' Agnes says. 'And look . . .'

She goes over to the window and bends, holding the lantern up to the panelling. This was a fine room once, but the paint is flaking off the oak and damp is creeping down the wall from the casement. Near the floor, rising in an arc, is a set of sooty marks, each one the shape of a hand. They run from the floor, like birds rising to flight, up to the side of the chest where a single print rests.

Thin fingers of dismay tighten around my throat so it feels suddenly hard to breathe.

I reach out but Agnes slaps my hand away. She's trembling. 'No! Don't touch it.'

I hover my palm. The hand is much smaller than mine – the size of a child's.

'I found him weeping,' Agnes says. 'Here, on the floor, weeping as if his heart were broken. I've not seen him cry like that. Not since your mother . . .'

The thick, charred scent reminds me of the tar pots. There are children about the farm, Sam and a couple of others come to watch the clippers at work. Perhaps one of them did this. Tentatively I extend a single finger and touch one of the marks while Agnes cowers. My fingertip comes back dry, not sticky and black as I expect.

'When I asked him what was wrong, he flew into a rage,' Agnes says. 'He pushed me out of the door and I fell.' She rubs at her knee as if to prove the hurt. 'So I left him.'

I run my finger over the other prints. There is no tarry residue, nothing at all to the touch, except a strange emanation, a peculiar sensation that reminds me of the sickroom, an atmosphere of rot and decay. A terrible thought rises – a memory of the deathbed.

'I was angry,' Agnes goes on. 'But after a time I felt sorry and brought some caudle up to comfort him.' She indicates a cup at the bedside, long since turned cold and congealed. 'But he was gone and the room as you see it. Then I saw this.' She clutches at my sleeve with desperate eyes. 'What does it mean?'

I have no answer for her.

Chapter 20

He hears her before he sees her, the sound of someone moving through the heather jolting him from his reverie. His senses are attuned to the night sounds of the moor – the whisper of the wind, the *pit-pit* of the peewits, the eerie *churr* of the nightjar, the crunch and tear of foraging sheep – and the sound of something other calls to him.

He sees the candle lantern she carries and knows instinctively that it's her by the flare in his chest. He feels relief at the presence of something human. Even cocooned by the mild midsummer air and lit by a bright moon, the White Ladies make him uneasy. He has taken to avoiding the place but something drew him here, on this night when the year hinges. As he approached he had ignored his quickening heartbeat and the sense of disquiet, hoping to find answers, and had been almost disappointed to find the stones silent and deserted. There is no forbidding presence, no mutilated lambs, just the moor and moon shadows. Lulled by the heady night scents of damp peat and solstice bonfires, he had rested against the Slaying Stone and sunk into half-dream – a respite from the pressing thoughts that fill his head.

He straightens as she approaches. She's wearing the look she has when something is wrong and she's trying to conceal it.

'Ellis, have you seen anyone up here tonight?'

'No, Mistress.'

She holds the lantern high and peers into the darkness beyond its cast. 'I was sure . . .' She places the lamp on the Slaying Stone, then strides to one of the uprights and circles it, peering out across the wide stretch of moor.

He watches for a while. 'There's no one here but me.'

She does not reply, but moves around the circle, then returns to his side. Within the glow of lamplight he feels held, protected, but it's harder to see beyond its beam. Suddenly, where the moon had given light enough, all is shadow and pitch.

Her face is cross-hatched with worry lines. 'My father is gone from Scarcross Hall,' she says. 'I don't know where he is.'

'Master Booth knows this land better than anyone,' he offers. 'If he's taken a night-time stroll, he'll find his way back.'

'He never goes out after dusk.'

'Perhaps he went to the village. The tavern will be merry tonight. Is his horse gone from the stables?'

'My father does not like to drink, these days, or to ride. He hasn't taken Sailor out in a year or more.'

'To visit the pastor, then. I hear they're friendly.'

'You don't understand.' She puts both hands to her temples, paces back and forth. He watches in silence while, some distance away, a curlew makes its lonely cry.

Then she comes closer, the lantern casting crags across her face. She looks exhausted. 'Something happened. I think it upset him.'

She bites her lip. For the briefest second he thinks her eyes grow wet, but perhaps he imagines it, perhaps it's just the moon's shine, because she shakes her head and is stern again.

He waits for her to occupy the space he creates. Restraint can be more effective than questions: people cannot bear a silence and will tell you their secrets to fill it.

'You've sensed it, haven't you?' she says eventually, searching his face. 'I think you have.'

A hundred thoughts spark in his mind. What does she mean? How much does she know?

'They say there's something up here, on the moor,' she says. 'Something ancient. Something evil. I never believed it. I never saw anything to make me believe it. But now . . .'

'The lambs,' he says.

'Not just that. If only it were just that. There's more you do not know.'

Again, he waits. Even in the dim light, he can see real fear in her eyes. 'I think my father is afraid. Something is plaguing his mind.'

He likes to think of himself as a man of reason, not given to the superstition that breeds among the hill people: it belongs to an older time, a time before the wars changed everything, but he has no doubt that she is in earnest, and she is not a woman given to delusion. He remembers Garrick's confession. He remembers the bloody bodies of the lambs. He recalls the sensation of eyes on his back and feels daggered claws sink into his innards as his own fear begins to mirror hers. He struggles to push it down.

'What can be done to find Master Booth?' he asks, keen for some distraction.

She looks about, as if expecting all the demons in Hell to rise up from the peat bog. 'I must search for him.'

'Without a horse he'll not have gone far.'

'I suppose.'

'I'll help you.'

'What about the flock?'

'They'll do well enough for one night.'

'Do you have the pistol?'

He shakes his head. He had left it hidden in the hayloft. 'Where might he have gone?' he asks.

'As you say, he may have sought refuge with Pastor Flynn. Will you go? Across the moor will be quicker than the coffin path. Do you know the house?'

'Yes.' He gathers his hat and crook. 'And you?'

'To Ambrose. My father has a fondness for Sam – perhaps he went to the cottage. If not, I'll circle back to the Hall. I must be there if he returns.'

'If I find him, I'll bring him home or, if he cannot travel, I'll send word.' He nods a farewell, turns and begins to walk away, but a question stops him. 'Why did you come here first?'

'I don't know. But I was sure he would be here.'

He knows why. If evil is at work upon the moor, then this is the place to find it.

He watches the lantern bob and sway as she makes her way back down the fell towards Garrick's cottage – a small dot of lambent gold in a landscape washed lunar blue. He can see well enough by the moon as he picks his way across the moor top. He follows an old drovers' track for a while and knows by the stars that he's headed east, and will drop down the fell-side into the valley before he reaches the church. As he crests the summit of the moor, he loses sight of her lantern. The heather is alive with the scurry of small, nameless creatures. The moor smells different by night – damp peat and ancient wood, iron, blood and bone. Everything is washed pure. He feels, for a moment, not on top of the world but beneath it – a strange night-time otherworld of darkness and starlight and the fine line between life and death.

She used the word 'father'. It is a word he dislikes, a word that conjures confusion in him, a feeling he dulls with drink and denial. Any other course is weakness. A man should be strong and hard, without sympathy or remorse. He was taught this by the man who raised him, lessons delivered by fist and blade. As a boy, he swallowed them whole, though at times they made him sick to the stomach, made his body bruise, his flesh split, his heart bleed and then, finally, become a cold, dead thing.

Betsy had suffered with him and, somehow, that had made it all right. She did not have the strength to fight back. By the end, it had all been sucked out of her, drained dry, like a bottle of sack.

He remembers the last time he saw her. He remembers the pistol. He can see the powder keg and the pouch of bullets on the tabletop. His father had been cleaning it, had loaded it, ready to fire.

He remembers Betsy afterwards, shaken and spat out, slumped in the corner, like a hare mauled by a hound. Gretchen too, bruises stippling her throat, eyes brimming with horror. But most of all he remembers the words.

If he ever doubted that words have the power to cut, to slice and maim, he does not now. He carries those words like a wound that will not heal: *You are nobody's son. You are nothing.*

He remembers the heft of the gun in his hand.

The first time is the worst.

As he begins to follow the track down the fell-side, he's surprised to see the faint glow of firelight away to his right. He stops, checks his bearings. It must be coming from the old ruined cottage. *Vagrants*, Bestwicke had said.

He leaves the path and cuts down the slope, heels sliding as he meets the dew-drenched grass of the lower fell. An owl swoops, snowy underbelly a sudden shock of white feathers.

The light is coming from the ruin. He can see the flickering of a fire through unshuttered windows. Smoke is escaping through holes in the roof. He can hear the low tones of a male voice.

There is no gate or door to rap upon so he creeps to the entrance and peers in, not keen to disturb the kind of men likely to find shelter here.

Bartram Booth is seated on the earthen floor, his back to the door. He's talking, animated and gesticulating. Around the fire are several figures – not the brigands and thieves that Ellis expects but a family: a man, a woman and four children – the youngest a babe, asleep in its mother's arms, no older than a year.

They are dressed in rags and have the shrunken, desiccated look of poverty. One of the children, a girl, is poking at the embers with a stick.

'But you must not do business with the wool badgers in these parts,' Booth says loudly. 'If there was ever a bunch of untrustworthy scoundrels, I tell you it's them. I would not part with my fleeces even if they offered me the best price. No, deal straight with the weavers. Leave out all that bartering and nonsense. Fix a price and stick to it, that's my advice to you.'

The man is staring, uncomprehending, nodding along.

Ellis steps into the room, into a yeasty stench of old hay and dung. Gaunt, hollow-eyed faces turn to stare at him, but Booth does not notice.

'A badger might promise you a higher price,' Booth goes on. 'But who's to say you'll ever see the coin? I don't mind telling you, I've been cheated before.'

Ellis touches him gently on the shoulder. 'Master Booth.'

'Well! Good day to you, sir,' Booth says, as if greeting a friend over a flagon.

'Your daughter is waiting upon you. I'm come to fetch you.'

'Have a seat, sir. You look like a shepherding man. Have a drink with us.' Booth raises a battered wooden cup, slopping thin liquid.

Ellis sees a pan of something by the fire that smells of wild garlic and nettles. 'We've no time for that, sir,' he says carefully.

'Don't worry, there's plenty to go around. Come. Sit. Mistress Goffe, spare a drink for our new friend.'

The woman leans forward to ladle broth into her own cup. She has a pinched, skull-like face, which tells of hardship and hunger, and cold, accusing eyes. She stares at Ellis with distrust. He holds out a hand to refuse.

'This is Silas Goffe,' Booth says, flapping fingers in the direction of the man.

The man nods at Ellis, eyes vacant, beaten by ill fortune.

'And this is his good lady, Mistress Joan, and all his brood, see? And who are you, sir? You are not familiar to me.'

'I'm Ellis Ferreby, Master Booth. I work for you at Scarcross Hall.'

Booth frowns, bewildered. 'Ah, yes, Scarcross Hall. Of course . . .'

'I'm sent by your daughter. I'm come to fetch you home.'

'My daughter?'

'Yes, sir. Your daughter, Mercy.'

'Mercy . . .' Booth looks at the cup in his hand, then in surprise at the faces around the fire. He laughs, forced and uncertain. 'Yes, of course.' He puts the cup down. Ellis notices his fingers are shaking. 'I've trespassed upon your hospitality for too long. Forgive me, Mistress Goffe. I must be on my way.'

Ellis helps him to his feet. Booth, unsteady, leans heavily against him. Silas Goffe stands, wipes a hand on his filthy breeches and offers it to Booth. 'God bless you for your kindness, sir.'

Booth declines it, but nods. 'Yes, yes, I shan't forget. I shall see to it. You and your family shall have work.'

Silas Goffe sinks in an obsequious bow and Ellis hears, distinctly, the woman make a splutter of disdain.

They leave the wretched family huddled by the fire. As they walk away Ellis turns back, just once, and sees the woman at the doorway, watching them go.

Down in the valley they follow the stream to the falls and from there along the coffin path, the way he had first come to Scarcross Hall. Booth moves slowly and offers no conversation. He mutters to himself, seeming lost in thought. When they reach the cross-roads, he wants to take the packhorse trail to the White Ladies and it takes Ellis some time to persuade him to wait until morning. He has no desire to revisit the stones tonight. When he asks why it is so important, Booth falls silent and will say no more. But as they go, he talks to himself, and draws a small leather shoe from his pocket, cradling it as if it were made of gold. Ellis catches the names of strangers and the words, repeated over and over: *I must find them. I must go to them.* The man is surely not in his right mind.

By the time Ellis sees the outline of Scarcross Hall, the sky is brightening to the east and early-morning dew glistens on the fell-side. How differently this night could have ended, he reflects. One wrong step can put a man in the peat bog, leave him sinking and drowning in thick black mire. One slip could send him tumbling into the brook: a broken bone, a stray rock, a body dragged down to the bridge in the village. Such things can end a man. Especially a man like Bartram Booth. The moors are not kindly. They tempt tragedy.

Mercy comes running from the house, eyes fearful and ringed with shadow, telling of a night spent waiting and fretting. Once they are inside and Booth is safe before the kitchen hearth, blanketed, hot caudle pressed into his hands, Agnes fussing, she comes to where Ellis is lingering by the door.

'Later, you shall tell me all.' She puts out a hand and rests her fingers lightly on his forearm. Her eyes meet his and she smiles. 'Thank you.'

And, in spite of himself, he is glad.

Chapter 21

His back aches. His shoulders smart. He pauses, straightens, upturns the scythe and rests the blade at his feet, the sharpened edge, a gleaming iron smile. Sweat trickles and pools in the curve of his back, his rough kersey shirt damp and clinging. 'Rest awhile,' he tells the girl.

She looks at him with round, vacant eyes.

'Fetch me a drink,' he says, holding out his flask.

She cocks her head, unsure, as if she does not quite understand him. He wonders if she is simple.

'You see that woman?' He points to the corner of the field, where Agnes doles out small beer from an earthenware jug. 'She'll give you drink. Bring some back for me.'

The girl takes the flask and scurries off, stoatlike, through the tall grass. He's forgotten her name and she has not spoken all day, but that suits him. So long as she rakes the cut hay evenly, so long as she picks out the ragwort, ryegrass and hemlock that would poison the sheep, he is satisfied. The work is hard but he enjoys the pattern of it, the rhythm of breath, muscle and blade that is almost musical. Without interruption, he has peace and time to think.

He was not surprised when he recognised Silas Goffe and his ragged family among the handful of workers Garrick has employed to help with the hay cutting. He remembers Booth's promise that night in the ruined cottage and supposes that he likes to be seen as a man of his word, a man of Christian charity. Garrick has put the older girl and the mother to spreading and picking over the grass in other fields while the man and his young lad are given a scythe and put to work nearby. They are a listless, beggarly bunch with little strength. He saw how hungrily the girl tore at the loaf Agnes gave them at midday and felt a pulling in his chest that might have been pity, or at least recognition.

Still, he is making good progress, almost half his section now laid flat, the long grasses fanned behind him in the sunshine, freckled with the rainbow bloom of wildflowers. The girl is making a fair job of it. He shields his eyes from the glare and scans the fields that stretch up the valley side to the lower fell. Above them, on the slopes and crags, the sheep are scattered wide, left to fend for themselves on the higher ground until autumn. He feels bound to these pale, skinny creatures in their new-clipped coats in a way he has not known before, as if his own well-being is now tied to theirs. He is beginning to see how it might be to stay still for a while, to throw in his lot, and is surprised that he feels none of the usual desire to unhitch the shackles and move on.

Garrick has waited almost two weeks for sunshine, but he could not delay any longer. Last night, after one bright day and a fiery sunset, he sent word: they would begin. His instinct was right – it's the first real summer heat in weeks, and though heavy-bellied clouds threaten to the west, they stay away from the hills. But the earth is damp. The grass still holds rain and will not dry easily. They need a good clear week or two, maybe more, before it can be gathered and moved inside the barn where it will fill the hayloft.

He, Bestwicke and Ravens have already moved their bedrolls, making camp on the dirt floor that feels bone-achingly cold after the comfort of the loft. Ravens has already picked out two small fleeces to fashion a mattress, but the fleeces will be gone soon too, sold at the big summer fair in Halifax.

Other workers are gathered from the village – women and youngsters who leave off their looms and their livestock to bring in a few extra pennies – or from among the travelling labourers who seek work in the wild, desolate corners where farmers are more likely to turn a blind eye.

He notices the two Irish lads, Tom and Nat, have returned and are set to work with Ravens. Garrick's unspoken punishment amuses him. He's sure, now, that Garrick does not like Henry Ravens, and cannot understand why the man is still in his employ, unless this is not Garrick's choice. Mercy Booth is mistress after all.

She is here too, of course, working in a nearby field. He watches her as he rests, noticing the low, clean sweep of her scythe, her steady rhythm, and the strength in her swing. If it were not for her narrow waist and the curve about her hips and buttocks, you would mistake her for a man. He catches glimpses of Sam's ruddy curls, bobbing behind her as he spreads the hay.

The girl comes back across the field carrying the leather flask. The beer is watery and tastes a little sour, but he relishes it. 'Here.'

The girl eyes the flask warily, pushing dirty blonde hair away from her face.

'Drink – you need it.'

Her big eyes sidle from his to the neck of the flask. She sniffs it.

'What? Do you think I'll poison you?'

She shakes her head.

'Then drink.'

She takes the flask and does so, never taking her eyes from his. Strange little thing, he thinks. She can be no more than eight years old but has none of the natural levity of childhood; her grave, suspicious manner seems well beyond her years. He feels a twinge of kinship.

He hefts the scythe, ready to begin again, when there is a sudden shout and a child's scream close by. It's the vagrant boy – the younger brother of the girl, with the same muted blond hair and scrawny frame. Ellis watches the shrieking child run towards his father, who drops his scythe and gathers him in his arms.

Ellis turns to the girl. 'Stay here.' He hands her his own scythe and hurries towards them. *Please, God, don't let him be badly cut.* He once saw a dog swiped in half and has witnessed enough bloodied calves and lost fingers to know the dangers of this work, but not everyone is so experienced, or so careful.

The boy is screaming, battling against Silas Goffe's grip. Others stop work, stand and shade their eyes, peering towards the commotion.

Joan Goffe is running too, stumbling in bunched skirts, but Ellis reaches Silas first. 'Is he hurt?'

The child is still wailing and twisting about.

'No. I don't think so.'

'Then what's wrong?'

Silas points to the ground a few feet away.

Almost hidden by the long grass is the body of a lamb – small, with the unshorn fleece of this spring's newborns. It is lying belly down, legs awkwardly splayed, atop a pile of its own guts. Its head has been removed and placed a few inches away, turned back to face the body, glassy black eyes unmoved by the sight of its own remains. Around the carcass, where the grass has been flattened in a circle, there are several pale objects – the flesh-stripped skulls of other animals.

Despite the sticky heat and his thumping heart, Ellis feels his blood run chill: he recognises the lamb.

Joan Goffe reaches them, sees the mess of bloodied fleece. 'What evil is this?' she says, eyes brimming with horror.

A small crowd gathers, each person gasping and exclaiming, repulsed by what they find. Children push between legs to see. A village lad reaches out to pick up one of the tiny skulls, his hand slapped away by an adult.

Joan, taut with anger, turns to her husband. 'I told you – I told you we should never have come here. Didn't I say this place is cursed?'

'Keep the children away,' Ellis says, attempting to take charge, but no one is listening. He looks about for someone with more authority. Where is Garrick? Where is Mercy? And then he remembers Sam.

He sees Mercy climbing over the low wall of the field, Sam running ahead, and goes forward to meet them.

'What's happened? Is someone hurt?' Mercy says, clearly panicked, as she nears him.

'No one is hurt. It's a lamb,' he says, but he does not know what to say next, does not know how to explain what he's seen.

He catches hold of Sam's arm. 'Don't look, Sam.'

The boy searches Ellis's face for some understanding. Ellis sees the moment he knows. Sam struggles, tugs his arm free and sprints to the gathering circle. When he reaches it, he does not scream or cry out like the other children. He does nothing, just stands and stares, the muscles at his temple twitching.

Mercy raises a questioning eyebrow. 'Is it . . .?'

'See for yourself.'

When they reach the body she tries to hide the blow but he sees it. He sees the colour drain from her cheeks and the way she clenches her fists so no one will notice her trembling hands. She kneels down next to Sam and puts an arm around him.

'Don't be afraid, Sam,' she says, but the quaver in her voice betrays her.

Sam remains transfixed.

Joan Goffe is ranting to anyone who will listen. 'There's evil at work here. I've a sense for these things and I knew it at once. I told my husband. "This place is tainted," I said. And here's the proof.' She points at the dead lamb. 'He told me to keep my silence, for the master promised us work, but I won't keep my silence now and I won't keep my children in such danger.' She looks about her at the shocked, fearful faces. 'We're leaving, and if you've a care for your lives, you'll do the same.'

Garrick reaches them, quickly takes in the carcass on the ground, the aghast, unnerved expressions of the workers. 'Wait. Don't be hasty,' he says. 'We don't know what's happened here.'

'I know well enough,' Joan says. 'There's devilment upon this land. This is witches' work.'

There is muttering among the onlookers. One of the children starts to wail.

Mercy stands, a hand resting protectively on Sam's shoulder. 'I'd thank you not to say such things when we do not know the truth.'

'The truth?' Joan says, rounding on her. 'The truth is plain to see, and I'm not afraid to speak it, not even to the likes of you.'

Ellis watches Silas Goffe, now carrying the sniffling boy in his arms, turn away with resignation, but his wife is not done.

'I've seen it before,' she says. 'There's something ungodly at work here. I'll not wait around for the Devil to come calling.'

'If you leave, who else will give you work?' Garrick says.

'Work or no work, I'll not stay here to be witched.'

'Would you rather go hungry? Think of your children.'

'I'll look to my bairns and you look to yours.'

She nods towards Sam, eyes alight with fury. They settle on Ellis – he feels her glare as a pinprick behind his eyes – then move on to Mercy.

Joan appeals to the crowd. 'I say this as a warning. If you're God-fearing people you'll leave this place. This is sure sign of a witch at work.'

Mercy steps forward. 'Don't listen to her. She's a stranger. What does she know of us?'

'I heard this is not the first such slaying to be found,' says one of the local men.

'You've given your men a pistol. Is that not true?' asks another.

'I heard the same,' adds yet another. 'And you have them keeping watch by night. Why would that be?'

How do they know? The drink-loosened mouth of Henry Ravens has been at work again, no doubt. Ellis wonders, momentarily, if Mercy has shared their secret with him, and feels a pulse of jealousy at the thought.

'There's no reason to be afraid,' Mercy says.

'Then why the gun? What are you hiding?'

'Tell us the truth!'

Already some of the women are gathering their children about them. One – a woman Ellis recognises from the village – speaks up: 'She's lying. We know the stories well enough. We know the signs.'

There is a murmur of agreement.

'Tell us,' the woman says, voice wavering in dread of the answer. 'Is the Devil risen once more?'

A ripple of horror at the fear made real.

'They are just stories,' Mercy says.

Ellis wants to speak, to stop the spreading accusatory looks, but they're right: she is not telling the truth, not even half of it.

Instead, it's Garrick who steps forward. 'Enough of this,' he says. 'Any man, woman or child who wants their pay will stop their mouths and get back to work. There'll be no more talk of witches or the Devil.'

The threat quiets them a little. But not Joan Goffe. 'Ask yourselves, whose land is this?' she says. 'Who stands to gain from your labours? Who will profit from your silence?'

'I said, enough,' Garrick says.

But she won't be silenced. She points at Mercy. 'It's her. She's the one. She did this.'

There is a hush as Mercy steps up. 'How dare you? You know nothing of me.'

'I know what I see. I knew it the first time I set eyes on you. You have the stink of Satan about you.'

Mercy's voice is as hard and brittle as ice. 'You will leave my land and never return. And if you say one more word against me, I shall have you cast out from this parish. Your children will starve. You'll find no work, no shelter and no help from a single soul.'

Joan glares at her, all hatred and spite, the sinews in her neck straining as she swallows whichever curses threaten to fly. 'I would not stay in this godforsaken place if you begged me.'

'Do not test me. I've the power to do it.'

Silas steps to his wife's side, the whimpering child still in his arms. 'Come, Joan,' he says. 'We must move on.'

There is a moment when Joan falters, trembling with anger, but then Silas puts a hand on her shoulder. 'There are other places,' he says quietly. 'Safer places.'

Mercy turns away and crouches to comfort Sam. As the little crowd begins to disperse, muttering and casting fearful backwards glances, she catches Ellis's eye and he knows what she's asking of him. He will take the body of the lamb and he will burn it, just as he did the others.

Joan turns back to her husband. 'Get the pay we're owed,' she says sharply. 'And where is Anna?'

Anna. That is her name – the silent girl who has followed him like a shadow all day. He looks for her. She has done exactly as he asked. She has not moved from the far side of the field, where she has picked up the scythe, as if impatient for him to resume work. She stands, watching them all, a tiny tatterdemalion, dwarfed by the half-moon of the blade.

Chapter 22

'It is a matter of sin.' Jasper Flynn takes a large pinch of tobacco, fingers it into the bowl of his pipe and brushes away the stray strands that fall to his lap. 'And a matter of justice. The souls of the departed do not wander this realm unless God desires it.'

Father, seated close to the flames with a blanket over his knees, leans back. 'But what do the Scriptures say? And what do you, as a man of God, make of what I've told you?'

'Ah, the Scriptures . . .'

'What of Samuel? Did his spirit not appear to Saul?'

'Beware, Master Booth. Remember that the spirit of Samuel was summoned by a witch. Likely it was not the soul of Samuel at all, but one of Satan's creatures in disguise.'

'Yes, yes, I see.' Father frowns, deep in thought.

Flynn puts a taper to his pipe and draws deeply, the tobacco flaring. 'Ah, here is Mistress Applegarth.'

Agnes greets him, then doles out cups of steaming broth. She offers one to me but it's too stifling in the room to drink. Father is still recovering from the chill he caught the night he spent on the fell and must have a fire, despite the summer heat. The stench of burning peat mingles with the tobacco fug, making the air dense and oppressive. I long to be out on the hills but Flynn insists he speak with us all.

'What do you make of it, Agnes?' Flynn asks, as she lowers herself awkwardly onto a stool by Father's chair. 'What do you have to say about these unsettling events?'

Agnes shoots a look of surprise at me and then to Sam, who sits in the corner of the study playing with a box of animal bones. He's ignoring us, engrossed in his game, trying to fit several of the bones together to form some semblance of a living creature; a macabre puzzle. He's barely spoken since the discovery of the lamb.

'I'm not sure what events you mean, Pastor,' Agnes says carefully.

'I speak of the lamb that was found in the hayfield. People in the village have come to me. There's talk of witchcraft, devilry and heathen curses among my congregation. And now Master Booth tells me that he's heard unexplained noises about the house and strange marks have appeared on the walls. Have you experienced these disturbances too?'

Agnes hesitates, looking to me. I see she is as shocked as I that Father has admitted these things to Flynn. I wish he'd told me of his intention to do so because I would have persuaded him otherwise; I know Agnes believes, as I do, that we must keep what has happened between us. The more people who know, the more danger there is of real damage to our chances of a good year at market. Still, it's done now, and perhaps Flynn can help: he will not want these rumours to spread any more than we do. I nod, giving Agnes my permission to share what she must.

'Yes, it's just as you say, Pastor. Though the master taking ill is the worst fright of all.'

Flynn looks troubled. 'And what do you suggest is the cause of these things?'

'I couldn't say. But I don't think it should be discussed in front of the boy.'

'Nonsense,' Father says. 'He's old enough to learn the ways of the world, are you not, Sam?'

Sam looks up.

'Come here by me, child.'

Sam stands and crosses the room warily.

'He's a good boy,' Father says. 'Knows the ways of the flock, just like his father. What have you there, Sam?'

Sam splays his palm to reveal the small, brittle skull of a newborn lamb.

'He's fascinated by the workings of the world. A student of nature, are you not, Sam?'

Sam says nothing but stares at the skull. I notice a film of sweat spring on his upper lip.

'He'll make his father proud.'

'Stop mithering the boy,' Agnes says. 'Sam, come into the kitchen.'

'Please stay awhile, Agnes,' Flynn says. 'I want you all to hear what I have to say.'

'Sam, come and sit by me,' I say.

He comes gratefully, still cradling the skull, and folds himself on the floor by my feet, leaning against my knee. At the touch of his warm, soft curls I feel a swell of motherly tenderness. I would protect him from this, if I could, but Father is right: he's old enough to learn the threat of the Devil.

'Teachings tell us that the souls of the dead cannot return,' Flynn says, taking a slow, solemn draw on his pipe. 'We die and are received into Heaven – if we repent of our sins and God grants us mercy – or, if we do not, we are damned to an eternity in Hell. Scripture tells us that there is no middle ground, no place for wandering souls, as the papists would have us believe. There is no mention of Purgatory in the Bible.' He pauses, sucking at the last of the tobacco, then rests the pipe in a dish beside him. 'But I cannot deny that I've heard of such cases before, where some wrong has been perpetrated on earth and the departed cannot rest, cannot make their way to the Lord's mercy until justice has been

served. Could it be that, in such cases, the Lord allows these souls
to return? Is it His way of helping us to see justice done? The
things you've told me today – the strange noises, handprints – do
they not suggest a human presence? Perhaps someone who has
come to right such a wrong?'

I understand him but this does not tally with the malevolent
presence I've felt, the sense of ill will.

'I must ask you all to look to your consciences. Is there some
wrongdoing, some sin for which you have not atoned? Secrets
work like poison within the soul. But, remember, there are no
secrets from God. He already knows all. He knows your sins. I
would urge you to confess them and repent.'

Henry Ravens springs to mind. Since my altercation with him
he's done as I asked and stayed away, but that does not change the
sin, or the threat he has hung about my neck. I think of all those
nights I wanted him. All these years I've not felt as guilty as I
should. Then I think of the time, two summers since, when I did
not bleed for almost four months. My breasts ached and my
stomach churned at the smell of roasting meat. But I'd begun
bleeding again and the thing that came out of me was left to rot in
the pit beneath the privy.

Father's eyes are stormy. 'You think I've brought this on
myself? I've done all I can to protect this house and those in it.
You know that, Flynn. All these years, I've kept us safe.'

I think of how Father has fretted over the lost coins and
the missing inkwell, how, ever since they first disappeared, his
mind has seemed distracted, unanchored. I've not mentioned
the coins to him, or to anyone, since I discovered them gone
from beneath the boards in my chamber – that is my own secret
and I see no sense in making things worse by sharing it. I'll not
be the one to cause more worry. I do not even want to admit it
to myself.

'I'm not suggesting you are at fault,' Flynn says, 'merely saying that the truth will out, in this life or the next, and if there is some wrongdoing, God will have His justice in the end.'

'You're frightening the child,' Agnes says.

Lost in my own reverie, I'd not noticed that Sam has turned white as the bone in his hand.

Father ignores her. 'You know the stories, Flynn, about this place. You know what they say about the White Ladies. They say that sorcerers used to gather there – witches of the worst sort.'

'And they are the Devil's creatures indeed, Master Booth.'

'Could they have returned? Who else would slaughter that lamb in such a deliberate way?'

'Such questions are being asked, but be cautious before you take that line of thinking. I'd not encourage it. Do you have any reason to suspect a witch at work? Is there someone who would wish harm upon you or your family?'

'You think there was purpose in this?'

'It's not for me to say, but surely all possibilities must be considered.'

Father says nothing.

'My father is not a man to make enemies,' I say. 'And I see no reason why anyone would wish him ill.'

Flynn turns his penetrating gaze upon me. 'Can you all say the same?'

I think of Henry's wife and try to hold Flynn's eye. 'I know of no one who would do this.'

Strained silence. I hear Sam breathing unevenly.

Flynn hangs his head, thinking. It seems to me he's holding something back. Then, 'My concern now is with the peace and well-being of my congregation. I'll do all I can for you, but, if you're convinced the threat is not an earthly one, your best protection is your faith.'

Father is insistent. 'But how do we proceed? How do we protect ourselves?'

'Look to your consciences. Many a learned man would say that any apparition is the work of Satan – his creatures, manifested in the image of those we have lost, or the things we desire most, sent to taunt us, sent to tempt us to sin.'

I think of the presence I've felt, the glimpses of a pale figure from the corner of my eye. I shiver, sensing a cold breath upon my neck, despite the heat.

Father is leaning forward now, one hand pressed to his temple, hiding his face.

'Enough of this,' Agnes says gently, putting a hand on his arm. 'You haven't the strength.'

He bats her away and looks at Flynn. 'What must we do?' he says. 'What must we do to be rid of this?'

'If Satan is at work here, your best protection is prayer, Master Booth, prayer and penitence. I recommend a fast.'

'And if there is witchcraft at work?'

'Then my advice would be the same.'

'Is there nothing you can do to cleanse the house? Have you not the means to drive out any evil that lingers here?'

Flynn looks offended. 'I do not perform the Catholic rite of exorcism. You should know that, Master Booth. Prayer and penitence is my advice. God is your best protection now.'

Before he leaves, Flynn asks to see the handprints. Father has refused to return to his bedchamber since Ellis Ferreby brought him home, so we have set up a truckle bed in the front parlour and he sleeps there.

Agnes has cleared away the mess and made the bed. I show Flynn the marks upon the wainscot. By daylight they do not hold the terror they did by night. They now have little more density than a shadow. The clarity of the marks is gone too, the outline of palm and fingers no longer so evident.

Flynn crouches and examines them. 'Your father seems convinced they are the handprints of a child.'

'Yes. It seemed so at the time, but they've faded.'

'Is there any reason he would claim this? Anything to cause him such distress? Anything in your family's history that might explain it?'

'You mean . . . a child?'

He nods. 'A child that passed on.'

'No. I was my mother's first and she died when I was born. Of course, there was Will . . .'

'Yes. A sad business.' He stands and stares out of the window, pensive. I'm uncomfortable. I don't want him here, prying and meddling, no matter how well meant his intention. He turns to me suddenly. 'I'm glad to have this moment alone with you, Mercy. There's something I must say to you.' He fixes me with his forthright stare, the way he does in church – the way that makes me feel he can read my thoughts. 'I'm concerned about your father,' he says. 'He does not seem quite himself.'

'He's been ill. The sickroom does not agree with him.'

'It's more than that. I understand that he's had a shock, but I've been noting a decline in him for quite some time. Tell me, Mercy, are the things he says really the truth of it? I'm no physician but I see his strength failing, and perhaps his mind too. I would not blame you or Mistress Applegarth for humouring an old man in his dotage, for easing his path, however misguided.'

'I don't know exactly what my father has seen or heard but I can tell you that it's not wholly imagination. Many people saw that lamb.'

'But have you seen or heard things within this house?'

Part of me wants to unburden myself, to tell him everything – the unexplained noises, the footsteps, the dead lambs, the missing coins, the figure in the fog – but I fear what will happen if I do. He'll think me mad, or worse. I say nothing.

'God's world is full of mysteries,' he says. 'Did you heed me, Mercy, when I spoke of sin, just now?'

I suddenly feel as if I'm six years old, caught stealing sweetmeats from the pantry. I force myself to meet his eye. 'Of course. Though I don't believe that any of us is carrying such a burden.'

He takes a deep breath and releases it slowly, noisily. 'My advice to you is to marry.'

I'm taken aback. 'Why so?'

'These problems aside, your father is unwell and a woman cannot manage this place alone. A husband would offer you . . .' He searches for a word. '. . . protection. You need a man beside you . . . and a child, if Scarcross Hall is to be yours when the time comes. You understand that the heir must be male.'

'Father has promised me many times that all will come to me.'

'Your father tolerates your freedom because it has suited him but do not think that he will stray from the accepted path for you.'

'I've Ambrose Garrick to help me. Nothing need change.'

'Ambrose Garrick is not the man. You will need another. Another who is free to make you his wife.' He puts a hand on my shoulder. 'I only say this because I care for you. You must prepare yourself. I've seen such cases before. It will get worse before the end. I do not wish to see you turned out of your home. A marriage would smooth your path. You are an unusual woman, Mercy, but even you cannot fight the natural order of things.'

I show him to the door and watch as he mounts his little hill cob and sets off towards the crossroads. The clouds are low. The air is thick and crackles with the threat of a storm. I wonder what he has heard about me to make him say such things. Has Henry Ravens been boasting in the tavern? And what has Father told him? Why should Flynn be concerned with my future? My future is certain, and always has been.

When I was young, I would walk in my sleep. I would rise from my bed and wander the corridors in my nightgown. To my mind, it was always winter and snow made the moonlight bright and blue. I would walk from room to room in the silent, empty house, making dust tracks with my fingertips on the furniture, feeling the floorboards shift beneath my feet, my breath misting in the chill night air. I was completely alone. Everything was peaceful and still. I would go to the old bedchamber, which in those days was still kept clean and comfortable, and lie upon the mattress. My head would sink into the pillows and I would drift there, secure and content, knowing that Scarcross Hall was for ever mine, and that no one could take it away.

Agnes would find me there in the morning, stiff and aching with cold, but the feeling would stay with me, and I know in my heart that day will come.

Chapter 23

Just as I feared, gossip and rumour run wild in the village. Joan Goffe has moved on, but not before she spread the fear of the Devil. That sly cat has cost us dear. We have to cajole our workers to stay and finish the hay harvest with promises of higher wages we can ill afford. They do stay, but only out of want, not loyalty.

I see how they look at me now, avoiding my eye, fearful I'll wish curses upon them. I'll need them to return to bring in the barley but instead I spend the money on extra wages now, praying we'll get a good price for the fleeces this year. I hope that time will see the whole thing forgotten, but now, when I go to church on Sundays, people whisper and turn away from me.

Father decides to fast. I argue with him – he needs to build his strength – but he's determined. Once he sets his mind to something, there can be no dissuading him, and he is more contrary than ever. For a fortnight he exists on nothing more than thin gruel and prayer.

His fervour seems to rub off on Agnes. I find her on her knees when she should be churning butter or salting what little meat we can afford. We do not speak of the things that have come to pass, as if to do so would encourage their return. But the weeks pass, the hay is in and, for a time, I'm not plagued by footsteps or strange noises in the night. I keep the door to the old bedchamber firmly locked. There are no more dead lambs. I begin to hope that Father is right and that God is protecting us.

I'm at the fold behind the barn with Ellis. He's brought three sheep down from the summer grazing near the White Ladies, all afflicted with fly-strike. We work together, carefully cleaning the wounds, none of which is deep, and burning the maggots. We will keep the sheep away from the rest of the flock, tend them daily, and hope that there are no more eggs burrowed in places we cannot find.

The flies are usually at their worst in the late-summer heat, when the sun is fierce, but the damp this year seems to have brought them early, and the worse for it. Summer storms make the air dense and prickling, and then there are days of flat grey skies when it feels that the seasons are turning, though it is not yet August.

I never asked Ellis what he did with the body of the slaughtered lamb. I watched him gather the parts, the guts slippery and crawling with flies, and put them in a sack. People stared as he walked away towards Scarcross Hall, but once Ambrose had forced them back to work, no one seemed to notice his figure in the distance, climbing the drovers' track towards the White Ladies.

I watch him now, carefully digging maggots from a fleshy wound in a ewe's backside with his blade, a firm hand and quiet words keeping her calm.

'Did you burn it?' I ask.

He looks up. He knows what I mean. 'Yes.'

'And the bones?'

'Buried.'

'At the stones?'

'Yes.'

'That was not the work of a wild dog.'

He finishes cleaning the wound and inspects the sheep's fleece. 'No.'

'When you burned it, did you see anything?'

He picks a maggot from the sheep and drops it into the brazier. 'No.'

'Nothing at all?'

He stands, lets the sheep go. She careers away from him into the willow fence of the byre. I can see his mind working. 'I've not seen the boy here of late. Is he well?'

'Sam?'

'Aye. Garrick's boy.'

'He's stopped coming. He has no reason now.'

Ellis nods slowly.

'Dority says he spends most of his time alone, out on the moor.'

'He's just a lad. The moor is in his blood.'

'As it is in mine,' I say. 'And yours too, I think.'

He frowns, turns away. Have I said something wrong?

'I'll fetch the salve,' he says.

'No, I'll go.'

I jump the gate of the fold and make my way towards the barn, wrapping my leather waistcoat tight around me to keep off the thin drizzle that has begun to fall. It's true – there is something about Ellis Ferreby that is familiar. I see in him a bond with this life that is a mirror of my own. I know so little about him but that does not matter: there is an affinity that comes with shared understanding. I've never felt it with Henry, or any of the other men who have come before. It has crept up on me over these last weeks, while Ellis has done as I asked without question and kept his silence. Perhaps his quietness is just reticence. Perhaps, like me, he does not show his true self easily. Perhaps I've been too hasty to judge.

The barn reeks with the fetid smell of damp hay. I'm afraid that our scant harvest will rot and the flock will have to survive on thistles and heather when the snows come. The fleeces are piled beneath the hayloft. If this rain keeps up we shall have to move them inside the house, but I do not want to put them in the old bedchamber this year. Perhaps we could pile them in the hall and light the big fire to keep them dry. Father likes to keep the hall clear, tidy and ready to receive visitors, but what is the point when no one comes?

I go to the chest where I keep the salve, open it and take out a pot. The scent of the liniment is soothing: honey, tansy and beeswax.

There is movement in the hayloft above. I'm nervous, these days: any strange noise makes my heart leap.

'Who's there?'

It comes again – rustling, scraping – something too large to be a rat.

'Who's there?'

I take a few steps back and peer upwards, afraid of what I might see. The face of Henry Ravens appears above the lintel.

'Mercy.' He makes a lazy smile. 'So, you're come looking for me after all.'

'What are you doing here? You should be out on the fell.'

'Ah! John will look after the sheep. He doesn't need me.' He stands and swaggers to the ladder. 'Why don't you join me? A little tumble in the hay . . .'

'You're drunk.'

He laughs, shows me the bottle in his hand. 'As a lord.'

Anger flares. 'You cannot behave like this, Henry. I won't pay you to spend your days in drink.'

He wobbles and I think for a moment he might topple, but he manages to grasp the rail and begins to climb down, feet groping blindly for each rung. 'It's time you and I had some sport. You remember what good times we used to have before he came, don't you?' He grapples with the last few rungs. 'I know you miss me.'

I glance over my shoulder towards the door of the barn, making sure we are not overheard. 'I told you, that's over, and I'd thank you not to speak of it.'

'And I told you, I think not. Come, have a drink with me.' He offers the bottle.

I should cast him out for this, but his past threats prevent me. There is too much at stake. 'Henry, you must stop this or I'll have no choice but to tell you to leave. If Ambrose knew—'

'Oh, I need not worry about Garrick. He's your little pet. He'll do whatever you say. And you don't want me to go.'

'I cannot pay a worker who does not work.'

'Is that all I am to you now?' He touches a twist of hair that has fallen loose from my hat.

'Don't touch me,' I say, pushing his hand away. 'You are not to touch me again.'

'Saving yourself for him, are you?' He fixes me with a drink-blurred smile. 'I told you, I won't share.' He runs his fingers down the front of my waistcoat, tries to slip a hand inside to circle my waist.

'You're not listening. Sleep it off, but this is your last chance.'

His smile dissolves and is replaced by something darker – a look I've seen before: anger mixed with lust. 'You can't threaten me.'

'I'm mistress here, Henry. And you must do as I say.'

'They're already calling you witch down in the village. Did you know that? Should I add whore to their insults? Slattern? Adulteress? What will they make of you then?'

He grabs my arm, hard this time, so I cannot shake him off. 'Let me go.'

'Refuse me and I'll do it, I swear. I'll tell the world what you are. I'll tell them how you witched me.'

'I said, let me go.'

He tosses the bottle aside, sending a shower of spirits over the fleeces behind us, then lunges for me, one arm about my waist and the other pressed tight to the back of my neck. He forces his mouth to mine.

He's never kissed me before and I'm stunned for a moment while he knocks my hat to the ground and his tongue fills my mouth. He has a sickly, unclean taste of yesterday's liquor.

I try to push him away but his grip is tight, fingers digging into my neck. He pushes me backwards, his feet tangling with mine. We fall onto the fleeces.

'Henry, stop!'

He breathes heavily against my neck – a rasping, panting sound like an animal – then sinks his teeth into the flesh above my collarbone.

I cry out, curse, and try to push him away but his weight and sudden strength are too much.

'I know it's me you want,' he says. 'It's me you want, not him. Say it. Say it's me.'

He climbs on top of me, pinning both arms to the ground, knees digging into my thighs, grinding bone against bone.

'You're hurting me.'

He leans forward so his face is next to mine, the scratch of stubble against my cheek. 'You can't send me away. You can't do that. I'll tell them what you really are, whore.'

He grips my jaw and looks me in the eye. There's a desperate fury in him that frightens me. 'Say it. Say you're a whore. Say you want me.'

I struggle to raise a knee, a foot, anything, but I cannot move. I say nothing and it angers him more. His hair falls forward into his face, spittle drooling from the corner of his mouth. 'Say it – or you'll pay.'

Instead, I spit into his face.

He makes a wild roar and begins to tear at my clothes.

'No! Stop!' I shout, but he's too lost in rage to heed me. His hands are at my belt. I pummel his shoulders but he takes the blows, spitting out curses. He tears at my breeches so they come loose. He moves to pull them down, begins to fumble with his own. As he releases my arms I raise a knee and kick out, landing a blow to his chest. He reels backwards, loses his balance a moment and that is all it takes. I lash out again and the heel of my boot connects with his cods. He yelps and doubles forward on top of me. I struggle and manage to wriggle out from beneath him but he grabs my ankle and pulls me back so my cheek scrapes across the floor.

Rage wells in me, fuelled by his threats, his poison, and the disgust I feel at myself. I twist and kick his hands away, climb to my knees. The first punch is true, my fist landing on his jaw so hard that my knuckles crunch. He reels, but then smiles, a horrid mirthless grin, as blood trickles from his split lip. I don't even see him draw his own fist back but the blow makes bright light flare behind my eyes. For a few seconds I'm stunned. He takes his chance, flinging himself on top of me so I'm belly down, face pushed into the dirt. He tugs at my breeches and, with the tear of stitching, pulls them down. But I'm not beaten yet. His head is at my shoulder and I reach behind, fingertips finding flesh. I feel the firm wet give of an eyeball. He cries out, clutching his face and I take the chance to heave him off me. Disoriented by drink, he slumps to one side. I get to my knees and stay there, catching my breath as I see a figure appear at the door.

Ellis is across the floor before I can warn him off. He grabs Henry's shirt, pulls him to his feet and drags him into the centre of the barn. He does not wait for explanations or excuses, but throws a powerful punch that catches Henry in the gut.

Henry takes the hit, a mean, unrepentant grin spreading across his face. He throws himself, full body, at Ellis and they tumble to the floor, rolling, sprawling in a tangle of flying fists.

I'm on my feet, stumbling forward, but I don't know how to stop this. The two of them are well matched, and even though Henry is disadvantaged by drink, they push and punch with bloodied knuckles, grasping at hair and limbs, landing blows. Both become panting, desperate things. I've seen Henry lose his temper many times but he's never tried to hurt me, or force me before. Still, the sweating, grunting brute I see now does not surprise me. But I never imagined that such violence would lurk inside Ellis. He is a thing possessed, wild and savage – I think he means to kill Henry.

He soon has the better of him, sits astride his chest, hands at Henry's throat.

Henry splutters, face turning red, eyes beginning to bulge.

'Stop!' I shout, but Ellis is deaf to me. His face is contorted in hatred and rage. I've never seen him so before. How can this murderous, feral creature be the same man I spoke to just minutes before?

Henry is choking, tongue lolling. He rolls his eyes to mine and I can see he's terrified.

'Stop it! You'll kill him!'

I grab Ellis's shoulders and try to pull him away. For a moment he resists, but then releases Henry with a frustrated cry, climbs to his feet and staggers a few paces. Henry rolls onto his side, coughing up blood. Ellis goes back to him and pulls him to his knees. He drags him by the hair to the door of the barn and shoves him roughly onto the ground outside.

'You touch her again, you'll not live,' he says, towering over him, a boot on his chest to keep him down. 'Do you understand me?'

Henry gives up and curls into a ball, moaning, vomiting bile and blood.

'You nearly killed him,' I say.

Ellis's eyes flash with dark fire. 'What would you have me do with him?'

With horror I realise he is asking for my permission. What would he do? How far would he go? Would he burn him and bury him beneath the White Ladies, alongside the slaughtered lambs? Would he do that for me?

My racing heart stops my words.

Ambrose comes running, face flushed. He pushes Ellis away from Henry and stands between the two of them. 'Both of you, get your things and be gone from here.'

Ellis wipes the blood that drools from his chin. He catches my eye but I look away.

Henry makes a sound that might be protest.

'I'll hear no excuses,' Ambrose says. 'I'll employ no man who acts the savage. Both of you, be gone by nightfall. I care not what becomes of you.' It's rare that Ambrose is moved to such outrage, but neither is he a man for idle threats.

Henry groans, tries to pull himself up to sitting, but he cannot. I do not care. All I know is I want him gone. Any sympathy I might have felt, any shred of compassion I might once have persuaded myself was real, is dead. Let him spread his lies and be damned – I cannot stand to have him near me.

I step forward and see Ambrose catch his breath as he takes in my torn shirt and breeches, the bruise I can feel swelling across my cheek. 'No,' I say. 'Henry must go, but Ellis stays.'

'You cannot condone this,' Ambrose says, but I see he understands something of what has taken place.

'Henry goes. Ellis stays,' I repeat.

'But, Mercy—'

'I will not argue with you. Do as I say.'

I turn and walk towards Scarcross Hall.

I hear Henry appealing to me but I no longer have any pity for him and will not allow myself to be cowed by the shadow of his threats. Ambrose calls me back, begs me to reconsider, but I've made my choice. I am mistress here and Ambrose will do as I wish. Only Ellis is silent, but I know he watches me as I go. I can feel his eyes on my back.

Chapter 24

The first thing he notices upon waking is the smell: charred, acrid, pungent.

Next is the light. It should be devil-dark in the barn but there is light – not the cold blue flood of the moon but hazy, golden, and flickering, like candles through mist.

A weight presses on his chest.

Is he dreaming?

He props himself up on his elbow, blinking, confused.

Then he tastes it: smoke.

He's on his feet in seconds and is lost in thick smog that suffocates him and stings his eyes. Flames crackle and leap at the far end of the barn. The fleeces are ablaze.

His first thought: save them.

He grabs his blanket and tries to beat the flames but the blaze is already too strong. The heat scorches his face and hands. The blanket begins to smoke, fire catching a corner, racing up the seams. He surrenders it to the flames, drops to the floor, coughing and hawking.

'John!' He crawls over to the bedroll where Bestwicke sleeps. 'John! Wake up!'

There is no response. He shakes the man, tugging him onto his back but he does not stir.

There is a loud creak as the flames lick the underside of the hayloft, the wooden platform beginning to bend and blacken in response to the heat.

He shakes Bestwicke hard. 'John, wake up!'.

Still nothing. Is he alive? He cannot tell. He drags Bestwicke from his bed. The man is shrunken and wiry with age, but he's a dead weight. He hooks an elbow under each armpit and drags him towards the door.

The smoke is thickening, filling his chest and stifling his thundering heart. Charred wood mingles with the stench from the wool as the hayloft catches fire. Above, the hay is beginning to smoulder, releasing the familiar scent of hayricks and bonfires.

He reaches the door. It is kept closed by night to protect the valuable fleeces from thieves and stop wild animals seeking shelter. He dumps Bestwicke on the floor and pulls back the big wooden bar that keeps it secure. He pushes against it. It will not move. He tries again, uncomprehending. It cannot be barred from the outside. He remembers shutting the door himself – the last thing he did before lying down and snuffing the lantern. He pushes again, puts his shoulder against it, panic rising. He begins to kick at it, shoves it with all his weight, but it's stuck fast.

There is another door at the rear of the barn, close to where the fleeces are stored, but he cannot see it through the smoke. Flames are licking upwards, drawn by the holes in the roof, the hayloft now consumed. That way out is lost to them.

He begins to kick and hammer at the door, yelling for help. Surely the sound of the fire will rouse someone. Mercy. He knows she does not sleep well. He sees a light at her window more often than not, when he cannot sleep himself. Garrick keeps watch on the fell tonight, but even if he sees the flames, he's too far away to help.

He never thought he was afraid to die but he is afraid of the fire, afraid of the pain. He saw a soldier burned alive once, set alight by a misfiring musket. The man had run through the camp, heading for the river, but the flames were too fast. He had fallen not ten feet from Betsy's tent and lain there, screaming and gurgling, as the flesh melted from his bones. He has never forgotten the sound of that suffering. The stink of roasting meat had hung over the camp and made Ellis's belly rumble for days.

He runs over to a pile of tools in the corner of the barn and fetches an axe. Each breath makes his throat sting and his eyes stream. He can barely see, bright points of light fizzing at the edges of his vision, his head spinning.

He strikes the lower panels of the door. The barn is old, the wood made almost as solid as stone by years of weathering. The planks splinter and crack but he cannot get through.

He keeps going, not daring to look behind. He can feel the heat on his back, hears the crack and groan of the old wood as the beams in the roof feel the lick and kiss of flames. If the roof falls, they will both die.

Frantic now, he hacks at the door and at last it fractures. He kicks at the wood, smashing away two planks, then three, at the bottom. He crouches, squeezes through, ignoring the splinters scraping his shoulders, and falls, sprawling, coughing, into the night air. Quickly he's on his feet again. He was right – the door has been secured from the outside, the wooden bar fixed in its holding. He tugs it back and pulls the door open. A great belch of smoke rushes forth, covering his face with smuts that blind him. The blaze flares bright, the far end of the barn now lost in flame.

Half blind, he stumbles to where Bestwicke lies and drags him out of the barn by the ankles. He pulls him clear and stands, doubled over, retching, choking, panting hard.

Then he remembers.

There is no hesitation. The flames are taking the roof and he has only seconds. He takes a gulp of clean air and goes back inside. He fights, sightless, through the smoke, keeping low, the barn creaking and hissing around him. The heat sears like a furnace. He trips over a bedroll and casts about until he finds his pack and his crook. He snatches both and runs, lungs screaming, to the door.

He hears her calling his name as he stumbles out.

She is standing next to Bestwicke, a solitary bucket from the well slopping water at her feet.

She sees him and runs forward. He thinks she will run into the barn, she will try to save that which cannot be saved, and as she reaches him he catches hold of her.

'Let me go!' she yells.

'It's too late.'

She twists against his grip but he holds her tight.

'Let me go!' She kicks his shin, her face utter anguish.

There is a great roar and a crash as the roof at the end of the barn collapses. They are showered in hot red sparks. He pulls her away, back to where Bestwicke lies.

He puts his head to the man's chest. There is a quiet, slow beating.

'He's alive,' he says, 'He needs help.' But she isn't listening. She's standing, watching in silent horror as the flames curl up through the gaping roof.

Booth comes hobbling, dressed in his nightshirt, Agnes behind him, like a shadow. He can hear Bracken, barking wildly, shut in the stables, and the horses kicking at their stalls. They can sense the danger.

'Quickly!' Booth shouts. 'Something must be done!'

But there is nothing to be done.

Next to him, Mercy drops to her knees. She does not scream or weep. She does not pray or call out to God. He sees in her eyes not disbelief, but pure, fathomless despair, as the future is reduced to ashes.

Chapter 25

'We go on as before. What choice have we?'

There is a pause. All three men look at me, and in each one I read the questions I'm asking myself.

'Without the income from the fleeces, there'll not be enough to pay the workers,' Ambrose says. 'Harvest is almost upon us and it won't be long before we need more help with the flock. Without John . . .'

'We've had lean years before and have weathered them, have we not, Father?'

Father is gripping the table edge, fixed on the misshapen lump of metal around which we sit like points of a compass.

'Father?'

He looks up and stares hard at Ellis. 'The Booths have been through worse than this and survived.'

'Then how will you pay wages?' Ambrose says. Dority will urge him to stay loyal to Scarcross Hall, but he must feed his family and he cannot do so without coin.

I have already decided what must be done. 'We'll have to sell the best of the lambs at the All Hallows fair. That will raise enough to keep us fed, if we are frugal, and perhaps leave a little for labour. I'll do the rest of the work myself.'

Ambrose snorts. 'You can't bring in the barley alone. Even you can't do the work of ten men.'

'Then I'll do as much as I can.'

'I'll stay,' Ellis says. He still has not washed, having kept vigil at Bestwicke's bedside through the day, and his eyes are strangely white against cheeks still blackened by ashes and fire.

'I can't pay you what we promised,' I say.

'I'll work for bed and board.'

'Why would you do that?' Father asks. 'Is this the voice of your conscience? Seems to me only a guilty man would feel the need to make such an offer.'

'Father . . .' I put a hand on top of his to silence him but he ignores me, sitting forward and fixing Ellis with a condemning glare.

'You say you were the one to bar the door from the inside. You say you snuffed the only candle, but how do we know that's the truth?'

Ellis leans back in his chair, expression grim.

'Father, John Bestwicke would be dead if it were not for Ellis. We should be thanking him, not accusing him.'

'We have only his word. Had you been drinking, Master Ferreby? Pastor Flynn tells me there is much drunkenness among the workers of this parish – indeed, among my own men. He tells me they're to be found in the taverns, wasting their wages on liquor and wenches. Are you one of them?'

'Ellis does not visit the tavern, Father.'

'We shall see what John Bestwicke has to say when he wakes. Now, there is a good man. An old soldier like him knows the meaning of loyalty. He'll tell the truth.'

'I doubt even John will be able to answer this riddle,' Ambrose says. 'Mercy, did you see the door barred on the outside? I did not.'

'No,' I admit. 'But I've no reason to doubt Ellis's word. And I don't wish to speak of it again. We cannot change what's happened. We're here to decide what's best for all of us now.'

'Then it'll stay a mystery,' Ambrose says, giving me a scathing look.

Ellis is avoiding my gaze, but he must be thinking the same as Ambrose and I: there is only one man who has reason to seek such revenge. I cannot say his name aloud, not while Father is here, for he does not know the reason Henry Ravens left us. Does Ellis stay silent to save my shame?

I know Henry Ravens to be a selfish, violent man but I never saw a killer in him. Despite the quarrels of recent weeks, I cannot believe he'd wish such harm upon us all. To set a blaze, to bar the door, knowing the catastrophe that would befall – that takes a cold, heartless calculation of which I'd never have thought him capable. I wonder if I've been mistaken all these years, blinded by lust and sin. I thought myself cannier than that, immune to such things. Surely I would see the signs of the Devil in a person.

A picture comes to mind of Ellis, standing over Henry's sprawled body, brimstone burning in his eyes, but I force it away and bury it beneath the weight of more pressing worries.

It was the noise that woke me. I sleep lightly, these days, disturbed by the slightest sound. I ran out onto the gallery, where, through the big windows in the hall, I saw the orange glow of flame lighting the night sky. I know the signs. I'm bred to watch for them, to fear them. Fire can mean disaster – the end of everything.

By the time I found Bestwicke, slumped and insensible on the grass, I knew it was too late to save the barn. When I saw Ellis emerging from the flames, like a demon from the depths of Hell, the useless pail of water I carried slipped from my hands.

Afterwards, I realised he must have dragged John outside and gone back in. At the time I assumed he was trying to stop the spread of the flames, giving up only at the final moment, but now I'm not so sure. His pack and crook sit in the corner of the kitchen, the only things untouched by the fire. Why would he risk his life for these few belongings? And why is he so silent now? Why does he not defend himself?

'I told you it was stolen,' Father says, nodding towards the twisted lump of soot-stained metal in the centre of the table.

'If it were stolen, why would the thief hide it among the fleeces?' I say. 'They would have sold it long since.' But he has no answer. His brow is black and craggy as rain-slicked rocks on the moor top.

It had been found by one of the men from the village – one of the meddlers and gossipmongers who've been trekking up the coffin path all day. The first arrived before dawn, from farmsteads and cottages, drawn by the horror of flames in the darkness, the rest, since then, lured by curiosity, the column of thick grey smoke rising from the embers, and the stench of burned fleece. They come to ogle our misfortune, pretending sympathy, but, I notice, once they see there are no goods to scavenge, no remains to be picked over, no bodies to mourn, they leave, sighing and shaking their heads, secretly glad it did not happen to them.

But that one man, poking around the charred skeleton of the barn, found the molten metal in a pile of ashes that had once been our year's yield of fleece. Seeing no value in it, he gave it to Ambrose. Its four legs are bent and crooked, the body of the thing smutted and dirty, the engraving run to nothing in the furnace of flames. The glass inkpot is gone, shattered in the heat, and the hinged cap is now welded into place, but it is unmistakably my father's missing inkwell.

Now, when he looks at me, his eyes are wet. 'It's all my fault,' he says.

There is a long silence. For one horrid moment I think he's about to confess.

'Why would you say that? It's not your fault. How could it be?'

His eyes are desperate, appealing to me, but I've no idea what he wants me to say.

'It's all my fault. All of it . . .' He buries his head in his hands and suppresses a sob as tears drip from between his fingers to make dark spots on his breeches.

I'm shocked. Where is the strong-willed, determined man I know my father to be – the man who would never show weakness or defeat in front of others?

Ambrose and Ellis are staring, embarrassed, at the inkwell.

'I'm so sorry, my child,' he says, muffled through wet fingers. 'I've brought this upon us all.'

Tentatively I reach out a comforting hand to his shoulder but he shrugs me off. 'It's not your fault,' I say. 'Perhaps it was nobody's fault. Perhaps it was an accident.'

Ambrose huffs and rolls his eyes. I don't blame him. I do not believe it myself.

Father shakes his head. 'I have prayed and I have fasted, just like Pastor Flynn said, and still I cannot find peace. What must I do, Mercy? What must I do?'

'You must calm yourself, Father. Despair will not help us.'

A shudder moves through him. He takes a deep breath and sighs it out slowly, recovering himself. 'Yes, you're right, of course. I must have courage. I must be patient. This is a test of faith. Forgive me. Forgive my moment of doubt.'

I squeeze his hand and this time he does not pull away. He sits awhile, thinking, Ambrose and Ellis both silent and awkward in the face of his frailty.

'Mercy is right. We will go on as before,' he says eventually. 'We will do the best we can and have faith that our Lord will provide.' He turns to Ellis. 'Master Ferreby, your offer of service is appreciated. If you wish to stay, then we will keep you. Mercy will see to it that you have berth in this house.' And, to me, 'The small room next to your own is not used. That would be suitable.'

He pushes himself up to standing. I notice how it pains him. 'You'll forgive me but I must retire to pray.' He splays his fingers atop the inkwell, lifts it, and leaves, taking the warped, ugly thing with him.

Two weeks later, John Bestwicke leaves us. The smoke has poisoned his lungs. His breath is laboured and he coughs up thick, malodorous spew whenever he tries to speak.

One of his sons comes with a cart to take him away. He's said little about the night of the fire, speaking only to corroborate Ellis's story and whisper his prayers, but once he's seated in the cart, he takes hold of my hand. His fingers feel papery and withered, like autumn leaves. 'Be ever wary of the Devil's tricks,' he says, eyes turned dull and watery with illness. 'Don't be alone, Mistress, remember. Don't be alone or he'll find you when you least expect it.' Perhaps his malady has turned his mind as well as his body, but his words chill me. I wonder if he felt it too: that ill-omened presence, watching us as the fleeces burned. He lifts my hand to his lips and kisses it. 'God be with you, Mistress. God be with you.'

I stand by the gatepost, watching the cart trundle down the coffin path, past the black bones of the barn, cold and damp now in the rain, roof beams pointing skywards, like a fallen crucifix. Beyond that, up on the fell, lost in cloud, the flock is waiting for me.

Ellis, watching him go too, raises a hand in solemn salute. There is an ache in my chest. We both know we will not see John Bestwicke again. He looks at me and, for the briefest moment, I see real sadness in his eyes. Then he rests his hand gently upon my shoulder.

I am not alone, I think. I am not alone, because Ellis Ferreby is by my side.

Autumn

Chapter 26

Scarcross Hall is quiet.

Ellis checks the bolts on the front door and rattles the shutters at the kitchen window to make sure they are secured. Each night, when the rest of the household has retired, he paces the corridors, checking the catches and poking at embers, unable to rest until he is sure there is no danger. Only then can he creep silently to the small chamber next to hers and fold himself into the truckle bed to drift in half-sleep, wakeful and stirring through the small hours, knowing she is doing the same.

But tonight, as he crosses the hall and opens the dog gate to take the stairs, he notices a dim glow from beneath the door of Booth's study. He expects to find an unsnuffed candle – the man has a habit of leaving them to burn – but the door opens and he finds himself face to face with Booth himself.

'Ah, it's you,' the old man says, relieved.

Ellis waits, unsure how to respond.

'Do you like brandy, Master Ferreby?'

'Yes, sir.'

Booth steps back, beckons him. 'Come. But keep your voice down. We must be careful not to wake the ladies.'

Inside, a lone high-backed chair, with elaborate carved armrests, is set before a dying peat fire. A single candle burns on the mantel.

Though Ellis has included this room on his nightly rounds, he has done so quickly, furtively, and in darkness, with a sense of trespassing. Now, invited for the first time, he has leisure to take it in.

The flagstones are strewn with worn rush mats, crowded with boxes, chests and mismatched furniture. He notices several small piles of rocks on the floor: grey moorland gritstone, flints and stream-smoothed pebbles of the sort the boy, Sam, likes to collect. The walls are panelled, once brightly painted, now drab and smoke-stained. The rich tang of peat smoke cannot hide a denser, mildewed scent: he recognises the pervading reek of the house, dank and decaying, as if the damp of the moor has crept into the stones.

Booth drags another chair, similarly decorated but older still, the wood darkened and cracked with age, from behind his desk and places it next to his own. He indicates that Ellis should sit. Then he goes to a low chest and fetches a stoppered brown bottle. He picks up two pewter cups from a small cupboard in the wainscot and returns to the fireside.

'*Aqua vitae*,' he says, placing the bottle and cups on a low table between them. 'Will you take some?'

'Mistress Booth told me you don't approve of drink.'

'I don't approve of drunkenness. That is not the same thing.' Booth smiles conspiratorially and Ellis is compelled. The old man is clear-eyed tonight, the addled, absent look seemingly gone. He sees a flash of Booth as a younger man and wants to stare, wishing he could watch him unobserved.

Ellis takes a cup and drinks, enjoying the rare burn of the liquor as it heats his blood.

'I'm glad to have this chance to speak with you,' Booth says, sitting. 'Something has been preying on my conscience.' He takes a sip and leans back, holding Ellis in his gaze. 'I should not have blamed you for the fire that night. And I've not thanked you for what you did for John Bestwicke.'

'I did what any man would.'

Booth shakes his head. 'You risked your life for another. Not every man would do the same. Many would fail such a test.' He contemplates his cup for a few seconds, then drains it. 'I'll admit I know nothing of you, Master Ferreby, and for many years I've not had much to do with strangers. So much time alone makes a man suspicious. But your actions speak well of you. And Mercy tells me you're a good man to have about the place. Now, I don't know about that, but I trust my daughter and I'm grateful that you've chosen to stay when you needn't. Others would have sought better wages elsewhere. It shows loyalty. It shows determination. But it occurs to me that perhaps you have some other motive for staying.' Booth eyes him, then picks up the bottle and refills both cups.

Is this Booth's attempt to take the measure of him, now he's part of the household? So be it. Ellis leaves the silence to be filled by the hiss and grunt of the fire, the gust of wind in the chimney. He has no need to defend himself.

'Will you take a pipe?' Booth asks.

'Gladly.'

Booth stands, groaning as he straightens, then hobbles over to his desk. As usual it is covered with papers, wooden boxes, several quills and a stained inkpot. He takes up one of the larger boxes and returns, laying it open on the table. Four unused clay pipes nestle bowl to bowl, their clean white stems reminding Ellis of flesh-stripped ribs. He thinks of the small scorched bones of the lamb, burned and buried up at the White Ladies. Booth takes out a smaller box, opens it, and Ellis catches the strong, earthy scent of tobacco.

Booth fidgets, searching the floor near his chair, kicking and upturning a pewter tankard. A puddle of liquid soaks the matting, the smell of piss rising, but Booth ignores it. He goes to the desk and begins to shuffle through papers, muttering to himself. 'Bring the candle, will you? I cannot find the tapers.'

Ellis stands, takes the candle from the mantel and joins him. Amid the jumble of news books, pamphlets and scrawled ledgers, he notices a number of maps, crudely drawn and sparse in detail.

Booth is distracted, turned away to search for the tapers on a sideboard, and Ellis has a few moments to study the largest map. Across the top of the paper is the inscription *Scarcross Hall*, but he would know that anyway: here is a building with a central hall, a squat wing at either end, and here another, smaller, rectangular, where the barn once stood, and several more nearby – the stables and outbuildings. A faint line winds away from the house – the coffin path. He runs his finger along it until it meets with another to form a cross. Beyond that, a stretch of white space and a little dotted circle: the White Ladies.

'You're interested in my maps, I see,' Booth says, at his shoulder. 'This is Scarcross Hall, as the birds must see it.'

'It's strange, is it not, to see our little world so reduced, all God's creation represented by a few lines on a piece of parchment?' Booth points to the collection of buildings. 'Here, the very walls in which we stand, this room no bigger than my thumb. And here,' he traces the line of the coffin path to the crossroads, 'our link to the wider world. To think that all our friends, all good news and bad, comes to us and leaves us by this faded trail. How insubstantial it seems.'

Ellis runs a fingertip along a broken line that encircles the land and buildings, runs down into the valley and up the fell-side, almost to the circle of stones.

'Ah, now! *That* marks the boundary of my land.' Booth spreads the paper and lifts the candle so that light falls across the page. 'It's too dark for me, but you have younger eyes. This shows everything I own, everything I've worked for. It contains everything most dear to me. How strange to think so.'

Ellis finds himself entranced. Out on the fell, it's impossible to tell where the Booth land begins and ends. The common grazing on the moor top, the boundaries with other farms, are not marked out by walls, byres or brooks: they are kept by promises and ancient knowledge that passes from father to son and cannot be written down. This is the land that bred her, the land she loves and fears in equal parts, and it cannot have edges because, out there on the moor, it seems boundless and untameable.

He has a sudden urge to snatch up the paper and toss it onto the fire, and another, competing, to steal the thing away, to hold the knowledge close, to translate it to heath and beck and crag. 'The Scarcross land stretches further than I thought,' he says, feeling a flush of heat rise to his cheeks. 'And yet it does not seem big enough.'

Booth looks at him, surprised. 'You have it exactly. Ah! Here they are.' He brandishes several thin rush lights. 'Come, take a pipe.'

Booth says nothing more until he is seated with a smoking pipe in hand. Ellis watches as little curls of tobacco flare and float upwards, dying as quickly as they are lit. 'How many acres is the farm?' he asks, when his own pipe is burning, the charred, woody smoke curling in his nostrils, the taste bitter on his tongue.

Booth seems not to hear. 'Can you keep your silence, Master Ferreby? I think you can. You do not seem the chattering sort to me.'

'You're not the first to say so.'

'Then I'll tell you of the plan I have for Scarcross Hall. Mercy will fight against it, of course, but it will be better for her in the end.' Booth squints at him through red-rimmed eyes. 'Can I trust you?'

Ellis recognises the signs of a man not used to drink. 'Why would I spill the secrets of the man who keeps me in brandy and tobacco?'

Booth laughs. 'Indeed. Here, have some more.' He takes up the bottle, leans forward and pours clumsily.

Ellis holds his eye for a second, feeling a flutter of portent.

'There are men – rich men – looking to buy land,' Booth says. 'These men are sending agents about the country, looking for places where they might acquire it. Now, this is harsh land, as you know, and it's not an easy living, but it's still worth something, and with the house it would bring a tidy sum. My daughter would have enough to settle elsewhere – to try a different sort of life. She's not too old to do that, is she? She's not too old to start again?'

Ellis shakes his head. Why is Booth telling him this?

Booth goes on: 'I must prepare for the day I leave this life – no, do not protest, Master Ferreby. I'm an old man and my health is not what it was, there's no sense in denying it. That day will come soon enough. But when it does, God forgive me, Mercy will discover I've not been entirely truthful with her. I've let her believe that all in my possession, everything on that map there,' he flaps a hand towards the desk, 'will come to her. But, my dilemma is, I must leave Scarcross Hall to a male heir. And I do not have one. So, what am I to do?'

Ellis's heart is thumping. Booth looks at him, bleary-eyed now, as the brandy takes hold. He seems suddenly older, worn down.

'I always thought she would take a husband, you see. Then, in time, a child would come. A boy. But she has always refused. And now the hand of time is upon us. She's no longer so young.'

'Does she not know this?' Ellis asks, recalling his conversation with the Garricks some months ago and Dority's fierce insistence that Booth would do right by his daughter.

'I never thought there was need. I never doubted that there would be a grandchild to take my place. And now I find I do not have the heart to tell her.'

Ellis knows why. It would break hers.

'She will fight against my decision, but I can see no better path. Besides, I think it best to give her a new start. That was my hope when I first came here. I wanted to be somewhere I was not known. And it worked, for a while. I made a good life for us here. But now . . . things have changed.'

'How so?' Ellis asks carefully.

Booth draws on his pipe, frowns. 'I was a much younger man then. I thought I could keep the past at bay. I believed that, with God's blessing, it was possible here. I find I no longer have the same convictions.'

There is a pause and Ellis waits in silence, hoping for more, but it does not come. He may not have such a chance again to ask the questions that run through his mind, but he must be cautious. 'Why the need for such a place?'

Booth sighs. 'I sought peace. The first time I came here I felt the presence of God. Somehow, the divide between the corporeal and the spiritual seemed more fragile here. I thought there was nothing between a man and his Saviour on these moors. It was during the wars and that kind of peace was hard to find back then. I could not stand the idea of another town – all those people bickering and blaming – and I could not bear to stay where I was.' He stops suddenly, takes a deep draw on his cup. 'Tell me, were you ever a fighting man, Master Ferreby?'

'Never.'

'I thought not. You've the look of a shepherd, not a soldier. Let me tell you this: war turns a body into someone he is not. I came away to forget that time and to make a new man of myself. A quiet life . . . a godly life – that's all I wished for, for myself and my child.'

'I thought you did not fight in the wars.'

'Not by choice. I did not seek it out. I did not offer myself up for King or Parliament, as others did. But then the war came to me.'

He sucks at his pipe again but it is spent. He lays it aside and swills the brandy. 'I'll never forget that day. Nor will any who were witness. They rode through the streets, cutting down anyone in their path. Punishment for defying the King, they said, for defying God. They slaughtered any townsman who dared raise a sword. They killed women and children in the marketplace. I saw a man with a child's head on a pike. I ask you, what kind of man does that? And what kind of devil allows it? I'm not squeamish, Master Ferreby, but the things I saw that day still haunt me. And afterwards it was never the same – it never could be the same.'

Ellis swallows hard. 'Did you lose people?'

'Yes.'

'Your wife?'

Booth's eyes dart to his, face made younger by the vigour of anger. Then he looks away. 'My wife had already left us, God rest her soul.'

A sudden flurry of wind sends a belch of smoke down the chimney and into the room. The house creaks, timbers groan. Booth turns his face towards the ceiling and Ellis becomes aware of a low, rhythmic tapping from above. He's not sure whether it has been there all along. He's still unused to the myriad noises of the sleeping house. He shivers, pushing away unbidden suspicions.

'Tell me, Master Ferreby, do you think the dead can return?'

'Perhaps.'

'Pastor Flynn tells me they can do so, if God wishes it. He also tells me the Devil sends demons to mimic the dead, to play tricks upon the living, to taunt and tempt us. "So," I asked him, "how do we know the difference? Which manifestation should we heed and which cast out?"' Booth drains his cup and reaches for the bottle again. 'Do you want to know his answer?'

Ellis nods.

'He did not know.' Booth leans back in his chair, resting the bottle in the crook of his arm. 'For once, I outwitted him – he did not know at all!' Booth laughs, chuckling at first, then louder, until his eyes water and he sounds crazed, unhinged. There is no mirth in it.

Ellis has never heard him laugh before – he realises he has not heard anyone laugh like that since Henry Ravens left – and it stirs something in him, pulls at threads of memory buried so deep he did not know they were there.

Booth gathers himself, wipes his eyes, solemnity returning. He splashes brandy into his cup and offers more to Ellis. 'You know the stories about this place, I suppose.'

'I've heard tales.'

'Folk hereabouts like to dwell on such things. Lord knows I've tried to quell the talk over the years. I've tried my best to protect my family. But now, what hope have I? With the things that have happened of late . . .'

There is defeat in his tone, that of a man beaten by his burdens. But Ellis feels no sympathy. He feels the stirring of old emotion, the shift of something dark, deep inside.

'It was one hundred years ago this very winter when that poor family died here,' Booth goes on. 'You can see the headstone in the graveyard if you so wish, and the year is there, writ plain as day: 1575. That's when they were buried, of course, in the spring. I choose not to draw attention to it. And you'll say nothing of it – not to Mercy nor to Agnes. We cannot have the womenfolk any more riled up than they already are.'

Ellis nods assent.

'Flynn knows, of course, and I asked him – is that why? Is that why they've come back? He had no answer for me. He thinks I'm losing my mind.'

'Who has come back?'

'Do you think I'm losing my mind, Master Ferreby?'

'Do you speak of the family who died here? Do you believe their spirits have returned?'

'I said, do you think I am mad?'

'That's not for me to say, sir.'

'They can take me. They can carry me down the coffin path, but they'll not have my daughter.' Booth's eyes are as black as the shadows. 'I'll sell. Then she'll be forced to leave. She'll hate me for it, but it's the only way to keep her safe.'

As he watches Booth stare into the fire, the melancholy of drink upon him, Ellis is struck dumb by his own conflict, by the questions burning like the peat in the hearth. He does not trust himself to speak. Is it a coincidence that Booth has chosen him to be the keeper of this secret? Is it the brandy talking, or is it his way of saying the things he cannot say, of acknowledging the past?

When Ellis leaves, he takes the stairs and stands for a moment outside Mercy's chamber. There is no chink of light beneath the door, no sound from within. He wonders if the door is locked and waits, hesitating, willing her to wake. Then he turns away, and goes into the small, windowless room next to hers, where he lies on the bed and waits for dawn.

Chapter 27

These days, sleep takes me like death. I'm exhausted from working in the fields with Ambrose and Ellis as we try to bring in our small barley crop. My limbs are heavy and complaining, hands blistered and raw, and my head pounds so I cannot follow my thoughts. Each night I fall into darkness, only to wake, time and again, thinking I've heard a shout, someone crying out in fear, or the crackle and pop of burning wood.

Even though I know the dangers, sometimes I fall asleep before snuffing the candle and when I wake I cannot distinguish shadows cast by the dancing flame from spirit form. I'm taunted by my imagination.

Tonight I'm woken by a whisper. I swear someone has spoken my name.

I lie still, listening, struggling to clear the fog of dreams. Did I conjure the sound in sleep?

Then I hear a step upon the floorboards.

I strain to make out the hush of soft-soled shoes above night sounds, the breath of wind rising on the moor, the stir and rustle of turning leaves. It comes again – one step, then two, then a flurry, the trip of a child moving from the casement to the foot of the bed.

I hold my breath, close my eyes and shrink beneath the coverlet as my blood runs chill. My skin shivers as if doused in icy water. I want to draw my knees up, away from the foot of the bed, curl into a ball and hide my face, but I dare not move. It cannot be Sam this time.

Once more, quick – up and down, up and down – at the foot of the bed.

My lungs begin to ache and a breath shudders out of me. There's a sudden bluster at the window as the wind drives rain against the panes. In my fear, it seems again that someone whispers my name.

The footsteps move closer, along the side of the bed, so that the thing, whatever spirit this is, comes level with my face. It stops. I squeeze my eyes tight shut. I hear the rasp of ragged breath – perhaps my own, I cannot tell.

I pray, simple words, in earnest: *Please, God, save me. Forgive me. Have mercy.*

I feel sure that the thing is reaching out towards me – I sense a hand hovering, about to pull the coverlet from my face. A sudden, profound sadness swells in my chest, threatens to overwhelm me. Fear recedes as sorrow matches it. My heart aches.

Gathering all my courage, I draw the coverlet down. I see nothing, blinded by darkness.

Then the footsteps patter away towards the door and are gone.

I lie still for a few minutes, listening to the rain, waiting for my breath to slow and my heart to cease racing. I hear the branches of a tree scratch against a downstairs window, the gurgle as water runs from the eaves to pool in the yard, the creak of timbers as wind buffets the house. A tear leaks from the corner of my eye, trickles past my ear to my neck. I know I did not imagine it this time. I cannot deny it: something is haunting this house. Haunting me.

Eventually I pull the coverlet down. The room is still and dark, shadows pitched in corners. Trembling, I force myself to sit and strike the tinderbox to light the candle at my bedside. But as the light floods the room, I see – there, at the foot of my bed – the old fire screen.

I stare at the hideous thing in disbelief, flooded with fear. All my reason tells me this cannot be – I must be dreaming. But it's as real as the key to the old bedchamber that still hangs about my neck.

With my heartbeat deafening, I get out of bed and force myself towards it. The painted boy's eyes seem fixed upon me; his empty stare, his mirthless smile. I shove the thing with my foot, almost expecting to feel the soft, warm give of human flesh. But it's solid and cold. Desperately, I try to find an explanation. Could Agnes have brought it into my room? Does she have another key to the bedchamber? Or perhaps Sam. I've found him playing make-believe with the thing before. Is it possible I was so exhausted that I did not notice it when I retired?

I know, deep inside, that these are vain attempts at comfort. It cannot be a coincidence – the footsteps, now this.

I sink to my knees, staring at the boy's face. I see the needle pricks in his cheeks that I made myself, the paint cracked and falling away at his temple, the lifeless eyes that seem to stare back. For a brief second I'm convinced there is animation in them: a look of knowing accusation and blame.

I take hold of the screen, my fingers curling around the boy's shoulders. It is madness but I feel as if he might hold the answers I so crave.

'What do you want? What do you want from me?'

There's no reply save the wind, wailing from the moor top.

A sudden noise below makes me start, heart faltering. But this noise is familiar – the sound of Father moving about in his study. All of a sudden I feel like the young girl I once was, the carefree child running wild on the fells, whose tears were all for a scraped knee or a stillborn lamb. I've a violent need for the company and reassurance of someone who can make everything good again. I want to be with my father.

I grab the candle, hesitating only a moment, afraid to open the door for fear of what I might find. I force myself onward, hurry past the door to the small room where Ellis sleeps and run down the staircase that leads to the hall. Just as I turn the stairs I catch a glimpse of something outside – a pale figure looking in through the window, moving swiftly out of sight. Fear spikes, sending my heart into frenzy, but there's nothing to see, save the night pressing at the panes and my own reflection, the white smudge of my nightgown in the halo of candle flame.

As I thought, there's a light in Father's study, and I rush towards it, bursting into the room without warning. But it's not Father I find there, it's Ellis Ferreby.

He's bending at Father's desk, rummaging among the papers, and starts up, shocked and guilty.

My surprise casts other thoughts aside. 'What are you doing? Where's my father?'

He says nothing, composing himself, face regaining its customary blankness.

My heart is still pattering hard. I close the door behind me and lean against it, partly so he cannot get out and partly so nothing else can get in. 'Answer me.'

He turns and tries to slip something into his pocket unseen.

'What have you there? What have you taken?'

'Nothing.'

We stare at each other, defiant, unsure who will make the first move. I'm torn, part of me horrified by his trespass, the other frightened and yearning for human company. I want the childish comfort of arms about me and it matters little whose. But I cannot indulge the thought. I'm suddenly aware of my old nightgown, my hair loose about my shoulders, my bare feet and ankles.

'Explain yourself.'

'I was looking for something.'

'If you're looking for money, there's none to find.'

'It's not what you think.'

'I saw you put something in your pocket.'

'I'm not a thief.'

'Then turn them out.'

He does nothing. He glowers at me as if I'm the one in the wrong, then comes from behind the desk and walks towards me. For a moment I expect him to strike me or take hold of me, and as he comes close I brace myself, but he does not touch me. He reaches past me, turns the key and takes it from the lock. As he does so I catch the scent of tobacco, brandy and sweat. It's something real, human, and I cling to it.

'Sit,' he says, indicating the chair by the hearth.

Breath catches in my throat. 'What are you doing? Unlock the door at once.'

'Mercy, please, sit.'

His use of my given name pierces my insides. 'I could turn you out for this.'

'I know.'

Though I should not, I cross the room and perch on the edge of the chair, put my candle on the table beside me. I would rather submit than go back to my chamber alone. The room is cold, the fire dead, and I shiver, searching the shadows for I know not what. I'm still trembling like a maid. I take the blanket that's folded over the chair back and wrap it around my shoulders to cover myself, the worsted cloth rough against my neck.

Ellis stands next to the hearth, face shrouded in shadow. He studies me, frowning. 'You seem troubled.'

I do not answer. I do not know how to respond.

He sighs. 'I'll tell you what I was looking for, but in doing so I must break a promise to your father. Would you have me do that?'

'My father?' Why on God's earth would my father entrust Ellis Ferreby with anything?

'Would you have me do that?' he repeats.

I nod.

'I was looking for land deeds.'

'What? Why?'

'Because your father intends to sell Scarcross Hall.'

I think at first I've misheard. The idea is absurd. The night's events have addled my mind. 'What are you talking about?'

'He told me so himself, not two nights since.'

'I don't believe you.'

'He told me in confidence. I gave my word I wouldn't tell you.'

'This is nonsense. I won't listen to lies. I must fetch him. Unlock the door.' I gather the blanket around me, rise and take up my candle, but he comes forward and puts a hand on my shoulder to stop me.

'Please, listen. I came here looking for the land deeds, thinking to hide them till I decided how best to go on. He can't sell the land if he can't prove he owns it. It was a poor attempt to buy time.'

He seems in earnest.

I hesitate. 'My father would never sell Scarcross Hall. It's everything to him, as it is to me.'

'You may ask him yourself. He'll know I've broken his confidence, but that's in your hands now.'

Ellis holds my eye. There's none of the slippery avoidance I've witnessed before.

'But what reason could he have?'

'He's afraid of something . . . afraid that he cannot protect you from it.'

That I can believe. The thrill of fear twines up my spine and makes the hairs on my neck prickle. I recall the strange conversation I had with Father some months ago, how he'd asked if I ever dreamed of a different life, somewhere far from Scarcross Hall.

Has he been planning this? Could he have been trying to warn me? But still . . . 'No. He'd never do that without telling me.'

'He wants to save you the heartache he knows it will cause, till the deal is done and cannot be undone. I think his mind is . . .' He searches for the word. '. . . I believe he may not be thinking clearly. He spoke of the things that have happened of late. He didn't say so but it was clear to me that he believes the threat is very real.'

There is a hollow ache in my chest. The fear that followed me from my chamber is joined by another, more earthly and even more daunting. I think of the faraway look in Father's eyes that I've noticed more and more recently, the way he seems lost in memories, the way he talks to me of a past in which I have no part, when he struggles to remember the simple thread of each day. I think of his precarious tempers and the obsessive rumination over the missing coins and the old inkwell, of how he went missing, wandering the fell distracted, the night he found the handprints on his bedchamber wall – the chamber he still refuses to enter. 'He's just tired,' I try to reason. 'And since the loss of the fleeces, things have been so hard . . .'

'Why would I lie?' Ellis says quietly, no hint of deception about him.

How can I trust him? I cannot even trust myself, these days. I barely know what's real and what's imagined. And if I could so misjudge someone close to me like Henry Ravens, how can I trust this stranger? But Ellis Ferreby does not seem a stranger to me. I find it hard, now, to remember a time before he came. I've a powerful instinct he's telling the truth.

He crosses the room and picks up several papers from the desk. 'I can't find the deeds, but I found these.'

I spread the letters in my lap. The first is from a man I know to be a lawyer, with whom Father deals from time to time. It's clearly a reply to a request, offering apologies and regrets that he's unable to visit Scarcross Hall in the coming months. But there's nothing to suggest a sale. Still, what would Father want with a lawyer?

The second is a set of scribbled notes in Father's unsteady hand:

> *Three hay fields*
> *Two of barley*
> *Grazing acres?*
> *Ask Garrick how many lambs this year.*

But this proves nothing.

Ellis hands me one final document: a letter from a man I do not know, who signs himself as land agent to Master Pollock, requesting an inventory of Scarcross Hall and all surrounding land. He states that a price for the whole will be negotiated upon receipt. As I read this, I begin to feel sick. I read it over again, holding it up to the light as if the words will change on the page.

'Your father is afraid of something,' Ellis says again. 'Something here, at the Hall. He wants to protect you. He knows no other way.'

I sit, staring at the paper in my hand, unable to take it in. 'But why would he tell you this?'

Ellis shrugs. 'I don't know. He was a little worse for liquor.'

'My father doesn't drink spirits.'

Ellis goes to a chest behind Father's desk. I watch, wordless, as he opens it and draws out a bottle, finds two cups, pours a measure into each and hands one to me. Even before I put it to my lips I smell the sharp scent of brandy. I wonder: what else does Ellis Ferreby know about my own father that I do not?

I drink deeply, my hand shaking. If Father has witnessed the same things as me, I can hardly blame him for trying to protect us. There's a part of me that understands his reasoning. But I will never agree to this scheme, or sanction his secrecy. 'He cannot do this. I won't allow it.'

'He knows you'll fight him.'

Suddenly I'm angry. 'All my life he's told me that Scarcross Hall is to be mine. It's mine by right. It's not his to sell.'

Ellis, perched on the edge of Father's desk, gazes at the floor. I wonder why he should care so much.

'You said you were looking for land deeds,' I say. 'Why? What is it to you if he sells?'

He takes a drink, stares into the corner of the room, refusing to meet my eye. 'If the land is sold, and the flock with it, then I'll have to leave. I find I do not want that.'

'Why not?'

He refills his cup, then mine, and comes to stand by the hearth once more, staring into the grate as if contemplating invisible flames. 'When I was a lad, I never lived in one place for long. We moved around, following the camp.'

'The camp?'

'The King's army. I've lived my whole life like that, moving from one place to another. I fell into shepherding work as a young man, and as I watched the flocks in my care, I saw how the sheep are hefted to the land, knowing the place they belong, finding their way to that particular fell, that particular grazing, year after year. It's an ancient knowledge they have without thinking. It's in their bones. They know the place they belong and are glad to return to it. I never thought to find that. Till I came here.'

His voice has dropped almost to a whisper. I've never heard him speak so many words together.

'That's the reason I'll never leave,' I say. 'This land, this house, the moor – it's where I belong. I'll never leave it.'

He holds my gaze for a moment and for the first time I see the stir of emotion beneath that stony exterior. 'Even if your father is right?'

I swallow hard, the memory of the evening's horrors causing my heart to thrill. 'Even then.'

'So you must talk to him,' he says. 'Persuade him that you'll do whatever it takes to stay.'

Silence as I consider. I need to think this through carefully. I need time alone. 'Do you promise you'll not say a word of this to anyone?' I ask.

He makes a wry smile. 'What's my promise worth when you see it's so easily broken?'

'All the same, I would have it.'

He nods. 'You have it.'

And I know that he means it.

The next morning, as soon as Agnes wakes, I ask her if she moved the fire screen to my chamber. She looks at me as if I've lost my mind. 'Why would I do that?'

I don't want to tell her about the events of the night. I'm not ready to speak of the reason for my fright, or my conversation with Ellis, until I'm sure of the truth.

'Get rid of it,' I tell her.

She gives me a look that says she knows I'm concealing something, but she doesn't ask for an explanation. She knows I'll not speak until I'm ready. 'What am I to do with it?'

'I don't care. Just be rid of the thing.'

And when I return to my room later that day the fire screen is gone.

Chapter 28

He finds the grave in a neglected corner of the churchyard. Brambles have taken root, fed by the richer soil, straggling across lichen-stained gritstone, almost obscuring the inscription. It is in the place where no one goes, on the north side of the church – the Devil's side – tangled in bracken and thorns beneath the shadowy boughs of a spreading horse-chestnut. The space is set aside for burials that leave a question in the church ledger, the deceased respectable enough to warrant sanctified ground – no criminals, suicides or unbaptised here – but interred by night, with no ceremony. Still, all those years ago, someone had paid for a stone to mark the spot.

Here lieth the body of Thos Falconer
of Scarcross Hall
and
Jane his wife
and
Thos their son
who departed this life
1575

He has wanted to come here ever since Booth told him –

wanted to see for himself – but this is the first chance he's had. The farm and the flock keep him busy from first light till well past moonrise, she and Garrick working each day until they are fit to drop. Between the three of them, with a little help from the boy and the old woman, they have cut and sheafed the barley. The crop is sparse, at least half of it rotting in the field because of the damp summer. They have reaped what they can from the kitchen garden and sown onions and collards and black cabbage. She works alongside the old woman into the night, boiling and preserving whatever can be kept. He spent a whole morning picking apples from the three stunted trees in the walled garden, plucking maggots out of windfalls. The trees do not thrive in this soil, even in the shelter of the garden, and offer up small, bitter fruit.

It will be time, soon, to bring the flock down from the moor top, to grease the lambs they are keeping and choose which will go to market. There have been no more dead sheep, save the two they have butchered and salted. She had asked him to do the killing and watched, hawkish, as he slit throats, quickly, efficiently, and collected the red fluid in pails, to be saved for blood sausage. At least there will be a supply of salt mutton, winter hares and moorland birds when all else runs dry.

They had not heard the news until after the funeral, so no one from Scarcross Hall had been present as John Bestwicke was put into the ground. The miserable wooden cross that marks the fresh grave is on the opposite side of the churchyard, waiting for the headstone that Booth has promised. As Ellis lingered beside it, the familiar angry flame igniting in his belly, all he could think of was the fire that killed the man, how close he had come to the same fate, and Henry Ravens's sneering smile.

Now he kneels, the damp soaking through his breeches, and tugs brambles away from the Falconer stone, pushing aside a pile of fiery yellow leaves that have gathered at its base.

Was it the weather that beat them? he wonders. Was it the

winter? Did they suffer and starve, trapped by drifts of blinding bright snow, suffocating inside Scarcross Hall? Or was it something else? Something more sinister?

They've come back, Booth had said. Is it possible that the things that have happened – the dead lambs, the ancient coins, the fire in the barn, the strange rhythmic sounds he sometimes hears at night from behind the locked door of an empty chamber – could have been caused by something as insubstantial as spirit? They have the taint of forewarning, of ill will, of witchery – the reek of the Devil.

She's afraid. She fights hard not to show it, and others would not see it, but she cannot conceal it from him.

He thinks of the promise he made. Perhaps he should not have done so. He does not believe in promises: he has known too many broken and the word has lost all meaning. But, in that moment, he had meant it.

She stirs a strange conflict of feeling in him, of which he has never known the like. He feels an urge to protect her, to offer himself into her service, like a knight in the stories of chivalry that Betsy used to tell him, but in doing so, he betrays himself. Sitting there, her large bare feet turning deathly white with cold, he was aware of her nakedness beneath her gown; the broad sweep of her shoulders, the hard, lean muscles of her thighs. He could smell her: brine and spice, a faint yeasty tang of fermenting grain and sheep grease. He felt a twitch between his legs and had to turn away.

It has been a long time since he knew a woman, but he despises himself for this sign of weakness. He must not let himself think in this way, not even for a moment. And yet the thoughts come. He cannot prevent them.

Instead, he looks again at the headstone and pictures the three dead bodies, with the three golden coins in their mouths.

Garrick had spoken of others: another tragedy, an earlier horror.

Are those poor souls here too? Behind the grave, in the tangle of thorns and nettles, there is no sign of another stone. The Falconer inscription proves relatives and riches; he doubts those that came before – simple farming folk, as Garrick told it – had either. He stands and pushes his way to the centre of the patch, feeling the soft moss beneath his boots, the telltale give in the ground. He squats, pushing weeds aside, ignoring the nettles stinging his hands, and exposes a small tumbled cairn of riverbed pebbles: a grave marker for those who could not afford one.

He feels the low pull of guilt: he had not been able to give Betsy even that.

Pushing further through the thorns, he finds more collections of stones – smaller, half buried and moss-covered, easily mistaken. But he knows this is the place. He senses the same at the White Ladies: the corruption of unnatural, brutal death.

A presence. Someone is watching him.

The first drops of rain patter in the canopy. He knew it would rain again today, could smell it. There is a dull thud as a spiked green seedpod lands next to him and splits open to reveal the gleaming russet nut within. As another lands, this time to his left, he hears the crack of twigs snapping underfoot.

He freezes, listening hard. Silence. His hand creeps automatically to the hilt of the knife tucked beneath the ties of his breeches.

The crunch of dried leaves. Slowly he stands, still facing the graves, senses alert, quivering. A cold breath on his neck. There is someone behind him. He can feel it.

When he turns he does so suddenly, spinning about, blade drawn and ready.

The boy yelps, tosses another horse-chestnut. This time it hits Ellis in the chest.

'Sam,' he says, feeling the tension leave him, almost laughing in relief.

The boy is glaring, face curd-white and angry. Then he turns and darts off between the headstones, a rabbit chased down by hounds.

'Wait!'

But Sam disappears into the trees on the far side of the coffin path. Ellis can hear him crashing through the bracken.

He goes to where the boy was standing. Next to him is a small headstone. A little pile of objects has been arranged upon it: three tiger-striped feathers, one pure white, trapped beneath a fist-sized lump of rock. On top of that is a small bird's skull with a coal-black beak – a magpie.

He picks up the skull and the rock, turning them in his hands. The underside of the rock glints copper, almost the same colour as the boy's hair.

Then he looks at the gravestone.

William Garrick
Buried 1672
Aged 5 yrs

A brother? A twin?

A breath of wind ruffles the feathers and lifts the downy white one into the air. Ellis watches it ride the breeze for a moment, then catches it and puts it back with the others, arranging the strange offering exactly as Sam had left it.

Chapter 29

I find Father in the walled garden, standing between two rows of ragged cabbages, prodding at their small green heads with his cane.

It's one of those rare bright mornings when the mists disperse to reveal swift strings of white cloud at the horizon. The trees are turning flame orange, ochre and yellow, shaking off leaves that collect in the crannies. Autumn ivy streaks like wildfire across the face of Scarcross Hall. New holly berries shine like glass raindrops. The crisp air is scented with wood smoke from the charcoal fires in the valley. Usually, I would relish a morning like this, delight in the turning of the season, but knowing it could be the last time serves to increase the sickness in my gut.

Bracken is lively, desperate to get out on the fell. She bounds down the path to meet Father, who greets her with surprise. 'Well, who do we have here?' He bends to rub between her ears as if she's a lapdog. She bounces away and back again, takes a nip at his cane. 'Where have you come from?' he says. 'And what brings you to my garden?'

'You know Bracken, Father,' I say. He looks up and I see he has the faraway expression of which I've become so wary, when he seems to gaze right through me, as if I'm flimsy as a spider's web. He looks back at the dog: she has the cane between her jaws, tugging at it, backside wriggling.

'Bracken,' he says, no hint of recognition.

'Yes – my working dog.'

He's suddenly irritated, flapping a hand at me and wrenching the cane from Bracken's jaws. 'I know that.'

I call her and she comes to heel, waits until I give the signal, trots away to worry a pair of roosting pigeons.

'What are you doing out here in the cold?'

He looks about, distracted. I notice there's a darker patch on his breeches, spreading from his groin and down one thigh.

'Are you unwell?'

A flare of temper. 'Of course not, child. Why should I be unwell? When have you ever known me to fall ill?' He's already forgotten the chills and agues that have plagued him lately, the periods of fasting that have left him weak. He turns and prods at the head of a nearby cabbage. 'Look here. Slugs. We must tell the gardener to be more vigilant.'

'We don't have a gardener, Father. We have only Agnes, and Dority comes to help when she can. You know this.'

He mumbles something to himself, walks away and sits on a low stone bench at the far side of the plot, resting his cane across his knees. It's made from his old shepherd's crook. Ambrose shortened it for him when it became clear he'd no longer need it to work the flock. He likes to run his hand over the smooth, worn bow, an unconscious habit, and does so now, lost in thought.

I sit next to him and for a few minutes we stay silent, watching Bracken follow the scent of some small creature, quarrying in the dirt. I can smell the acrid tang of urine rising from his clothes. A surge of concern and tenderness swells in me but I must ask the questions that have been burning since my conversation with Ellis. I've been waiting for the right time, but ever since, Father has been either absent-minded, angry or both. I realise there will never be a right time, and I cannot wait any longer.

'Father, who is Master Pollock?'

He ignores me, smiling as Bracken finds a stick to chew.

'Can you hear me, Father? I said, "Who is Master Pollock?"'

'Of course I can hear you, child. I'm not deaf yet. Pollock . . . I don't know any Pollock.'

'You've been writing to him.'

'I think not.'

'I've seen the letters.'

'Is he a merchant? One of the cloth men from Halifax?'

'Don't lie to me.' Impatient, I struggle to keep my voice level. 'He's the man who wants to buy Scarcross Hall.'

He looks to the sky and sniffs the air. 'When is it St Luke's Day? It cannot be long before we must put the ewes to tup.'

I cannot believe he would continue this pretence. I fail to keep the anger from my tone. 'I know, Father. I know what you're planning. How could you even think of it?'

He turns to me at last. 'Why would you say such a thing?'

'I know you're lying. I've seen the letters.'

'What letters?'

'From Master Pollock's land agent. I found them on your desk.'

Now it's his turn to be angry. 'What were you doing in my study? My correspondence is private.'

'Why are you lying to me?'

'You dare call me a liar?'

'You always promised that Scarcross would be mine one day.'

He turns away, hiding his face. He cannot deny it.

'Scarcross Hall is my home,' I go on, frustration fuelling my fire. 'I've never known any other. I'll not leave it. You promised me. Ever since I was a girl, you promised it would be mine. I've spent my whole life believing it. Believing *you*.'

He's silent awhile, his face in conflict. Then he stands and paces. I can see he's battling with something.

'Please, Father. Please tell me the truth.'

Eventually he returns to my side. His expression seems clearer, as if my upset has fetched him back to his right mind.

'My dear, it will be better for you in the end.'

'So you admit it?'

'I admit I have considered it.'

'Then why conceal it from me?'

'I must think of your future. When I go to meet God, what will become of you?'

'I will go on as before. Just like we always have.'

He shakes his head. 'That will not be possible.'

'But that's what the Booths do. You said so yourself—'

'I know what I said. Did that man tell you this?'

'What man?'

'The dark one . . . Ferreby. I knew I should not have trusted him. I see the way he looks at you . . .'

There's no sense in dragging Ellis into the argument. He only broke his word to help me. I must protect him. 'No. I told you – I found letters.'

'Hmm.' He takes a deep breath and sighs, weary, defeated. 'Well, perhaps it's time you knew the truth. Mercy, I cannot leave Scarcross Hall to you, and nor would I if I could. It's not safe here any more. You know this by now.'

My first impulse is to argue but he holds up a hand to silence me. 'I've thought for some time that my best course of action is to sell and leave you with a sum of money to begin again elsewhere. But I know how you love your old home . . .' He reaches out as if to stroke my cheek in a rare display of affection, then drops it back to the bow of his crook. 'I do not do it to hurt you, child, but to protect you. Something evil is at work here. For a long time I thought I could keep it at bay . . .'

I see he is truthful, and deep in my heart I know he is right. He's sad and scared. I know I should not be angry when he's trying to be a good father to me, however misguided his thinking, but the thought of leaving all that matters to me brings a hollow ache to my chest, more real and urgent than the fear I feel, and his duplicity makes me furious.

'Of course I heard the stories when I first came here, but I dismissed them. I believed that God would protect us. I thought *I* could protect us. And while I live, I may yet, but when I'm gone . . .'

'What do you fear will happen?'

He says nothing, just shakes his head. He is so sorrowful, so resigned, he can barely keep tears from his eyes. I cannot stand to see him like that – where is the strong, wilful man I have depended on for so long?

'Please, Father. I could not bear to leave. Scarcross Hall is everything to me.'

He studies me sadly.

I swallow my anger and take both his hands in mine. This is my chance to persuade him. 'I promise, Father, that if Scarcross Hall is to become mine, I shall protect it as you have done. I shall bring the pastor here every week. I shall pray. I shall fast. I shall live as you wish, and God will keep me safe.'

He sighs and hangs his head. 'I believe you would try, but it's not as simple as you would have it.'

'Why not?'

'Even if I could reconcile myself to the thought of your staying, my hands are bound by law. I must leave all my property to a male heir.'

My heart seems to rise into my throat, then plummet, to thump erratically against my ribs. 'But I am your only heir.'

He's silent for a few moments. Then, 'I've no choice, Mercy. Merion Booth, your great-grandfather, insisted that any fortune be entailed to the male line. I made that promise to my own father.'

'But there is no male line.'

'The lawyers have a way of finding one. I had a cousin once. I know not what became of him but I believe he had sons. Besides, even if a male heir could be found, I think it best to cut the ties completely.'

I don't know what to say. The thought of Scarcross Hall in the hands of some stranger who has no care for the place, who has never even set eyes upon it, makes my blood boil. And not just that: I'm shocked at the calm, matter-of-fact way in which he speaks, as if he has not just admitted to a lifelong deception.

I cannot control my feelings any longer. I stand and face him. 'How can you speak so? Do you not understand that you have betrayed me?'

'Mercy—'

'All my life I've put you above any other. I've done as you asked. I've trusted you. To find out you've lied to me all this time . . .' I have to pause for breath as the true scale of his falsehood hits me. My trust in him, my reliance upon him, shatters about my feet. He has been the lodestar around which I have centred my life. I feel unsteady, as if my whole world is shifting. 'I know there's something amiss here. I feel it too. But how can we protect ourselves if you keep the truth from me?' I turn away from him, more determined than ever. 'I won't leave. I can't. This place is my life.'

He looks shocked. 'Then it has worked its wicked magic on you too.'

'I want nothing else. This is all I know and all I need.'

'You need only your faith . . .'

'It's God's will that I remain here. I know it.'

'Oh, my child, how can you be so sure? How can you know it's not the Devil that draws you?'

I've asked myself the same question, but what does it matter if I lie to him, as he has lied to me? 'Father, I'm in no danger. You must believe me.'

He sighs deeply, and leans forward, head in hands, guilt at his lies written in the cleft of his brow. 'Oh, Lord, what should I do?'

'There must be a way,' I say. 'And we will find it together, if you forget this plan. Please, Father, let me stay.'

He sits for a time, lips moving in silent prayer. Then, 'There is a way. If you were to marry . . . a child . . .'

In truth, I'm not surprised, but my heart sinks. When I was younger he often urged me to seek a husband but, witnessing my broken hope, and the death of it in the years since, he gave up, as I did. I thought he understood. 'You've said yourself, I'm not the sort of woman men take as a wife.'

'In the past perhaps I have said that, but you're still of childbearing age – it's not too late. And, until your son comes of age, you could manage affairs on his behalf. It could be arranged. A match could be made.'

'I don't need a husband. I need Scarcross Hall to be mine, as you promised.'

'If we pick the right man, little need change.'

'Everything would change. Scarcross Hall would not belong to me.'

'Mercy, I cannot change the law. I do not have that power.'

Pastor Flynn's warning comes back to me. I'd not heeded him at the time, but he was right: Father will not break his covenant, even for me.

And as if Father can read my thoughts he says, 'What of Jasper Flynn? Now there's a godly man who knows your disposition, and who has been a good friend to our family. To have a man of God in the house, surely that would bring great peace of mind.'

I think of Jasper Flynn with his thinning whiskers and weasel's face. The thought of his skeleton fingers upon me makes me shudder. 'Father, I do not want to marry Pastor Flynn.'

But there is a new light in his eye. 'Yes, a man of God. What better protection could there be?'

'Father, listen to me. I'll not marry Jasper Flynn. I don't wish to marry at all.'

'I'll speak with him. I'll write at once and ask him to come. Will you send Ferreby with a letter?'

'For God's sake, listen to me. I don't want to marry Jasper Flynn – I want Scarcross Hall to come to me. I want to take your place as master here, as you promised.'

He shakes his head and fixes me with a determined stare. In it, I see traces of the forceful man I recognise, the father I once obeyed without question. 'That dream is one you must give up. This has come as a shock to you and I'm sorry for it, but you must see I'm driven by my duty to protect you. It's my one remaining wish to see you secured before I go. If you are so determined to stay at Scarcross Hall, I will do everything in my power to make sure you are safe. A suitable marriage would be the best way. The only way.'

'You speak as if there is urgency.'

He lowers his voice. 'You know as well as I, all is not well here. I'll not speak of it now, I'll not invite it, but you're right. I fear my time here is coming to an end.'

'Why would you think so?'

He straightens and takes a deep breath, then searches the face of the house, eyes lingering at the casement of the old bedchamber. 'Will you grant an old man his final wish and do as I say, so that I might go to my grave with some hope of peace?'

Yet another dismal thought presses in. 'Is there more? Something you're keeping from me? Are you unwell?'

'Will you promise me?'

'Father?'

'Answer me, Mercy.'

I see he will not be pressed. 'If I were to agree to consider it, would you forget the plan to sell?'

'I will pray on it, child. I will pray on it.'

There is a small, young part of me that yearns to obey him, but

I've not been that child for a long time and the keen blade of betrayal still cuts. 'I cannot make any promise . . .'

'Very well. I shall give you some time to consider. I will pray on it, Mercy, and you must too.'

And with that, it is clear the conversation is over.

By the time I reach the kitchen I'm fuming. I find Agnes and Sam bringing in a fresh pail of milk. Bracken skitters across the flags to her spot before the fire and settles there. Agnes reads the fury on my face.

'Set it down in the buttery, Sam,' she says, raising an eyebrow at me. 'Which one is it?'

'What?'

'Only a man could cause that black scowl, so which one is it?'

I sit down heavily in Agnes's chair. 'Father. He's lied to me, betrayed me.'

Her eyes roll skyward. 'Those are strong words, Mercy. That man may be troublesome but he cares for you. He cares for us all.' She wipes her hands and follows Sam into the buttery. I listen as she shows him how to scoop the curds from the old milk into the muslin, ready for pressing, my thoughts racing.

I dare not tell her all I know, about the letters and Master Pollock, because she will worry herself to sickness. So I stoke the fire angrily, a cauldron of water hung above beginning to steam. Bracken watches me.

Agnes comes back, goes to the table and begins to slice onions and carrots, putting them into a bowl beside her, ready for the pot. 'Don't fret,' she says. 'Whatever he's done, it'll be forgotten by morning. He cannot hold on to a thought for long.'

'This is different,' I say. 'He wishes me to marry. He tells me that Scarcross Hall must pass to a male heir, so I must provide one.'

I expect shock but Agnes just nods slowly.

'You knew?'

'It was about time he told you.'

Agnes too? Am I the last to know? 'My God, why did you never tell me?'

'It was not my place, Mercy. Not my secret to tell.'

'My whole life, you've both lied to me. He promised me I would inherit. Why did you let me go on believing it?'

She says nothing.

'So, if I'm to have any hope of keeping what should be mine, I must find a man to marry. What choice have I? You have trapped me.'

Agnes darts a look at the door to the buttery. 'Would it be so bad to have a new master about the place?'

'There should be no master but me.'

'You would still be mistress. That need not change, if you pick the right man.'

'That's what Father said. He doesn't understand.'

'Then at least in that we agree.' She eyes me sideways as she chops the vegetables. 'Did he have someone in mind?'

I take a deep breath, trying to calm myself. 'Jasper Flynn.'

At this she snorts. 'Oh, that man knows little of women. And you? Do you have anyone in mind?'

'No.'

She waits awhile, studying me, then stops and puts the knife down, suddenly serious. She glances again towards the door of the buttery where I can hear Sam at work, muttering to himself.

'Mind you pick carefully. Choose a local man, someone born and bred here. Do not even think of a stranger. Hearts are broken that way.'

'Why do you say so?'

'I know who it is you think on. Not him, Mercy.'

Her forcefulness surprises me but I don't need to ask of whom she speaks. 'He's a good man.'

'You know nothing of him.'

'I know more than you.'

Her nostrils flare. 'He's not the man for you.'

I think of the promise Ellis made me, the feeling revealed in his eyes. I will not be swayed from what I know to be true. 'Why do you dislike him so? Ever since he came here you've taken against him.'

She turns back to the vegetables, her mouth tucked in a thin line, and begins to hack at them viciously. 'Your father may not know women, but you know even less of men.'

'And you do, I suppose? A barren old spinster who has devoted her whole life to a man who does not love her back.'

She looks as if I've slapped her.

My venom is interrupted by an almighty crash from the buttery. Sam cries out. I leap from my chair and cross the room, Agnes at my heels.

A second crash – the sound of pottery shattering on flagstones.

The buttery is a mess, swimming with spilled milk, the churn overturned, the curd pot splintered across the stones. A jug lies in pieces, belly rocking back and forth, small beer foaming amid the blue-white flood.

Sam is crouched against the wall, hugging his knees, face as pale as the milk. 'I did not touch it,' he whispers. 'I did not touch it.'

As I stand there, aghast, taking in the waste, my quarrel with Agnes forgotten, there's a strange scraping sound behind me. I turn back just in time to see the bowl of cut vegetables slide across the tabletop, as if pushed by an unseen hand, tip and smash upon the floor.

Bracken is on her feet, hackles up, teeth bared.

Agnes grips my arm, eyes fearful. 'See?' she says. 'The Devil thrives on discord.' She drops to her knees, skirts soaking up the pooled milk, and begins to pray.

Chapter 30

The bench is as cold as stone. The chill creeps through his breeches to numb his bones.

The church is cool at midsummer, set on the north side of the valley, under shadow of fell and scar, but now, with dark patches of damp seeping across the limed walls, and wind moaning through missing slates, it is as cold as an ice cellar. He cannot imagine how it will be, come deep winter. Surely the congregation will perch on hoarfrost and kneel in snowdrifts.

He has never been one to attend church often, finding his own place of prayer on the slopes and summits of northern hills, but now he is part of the household, Booth insists upon it: *I will not have a heathen under my roof.*

So he takes up a place on the pew next to Mercy and shivers with the rest of them through Pastor Flynn's hellfire sermons.

He sneaks a look at Booth now, seated between Mercy and the old woman. His eyes are closed, lips moving in fervent prayer. Agnes is staring at Flynn, hands clasped in her lap, the wattle beneath her chin wobbling as if she is chewing cud. She never speaks to Ellis if she can help it, but he does not care. He is not concerned with her. Her place in the Booth household may exceed his, but he's becoming certain this will change in time.

Next to him, Mercy shifts in her seat. He feels the brush of her thick worsted skirts against his thigh. He cannot get used to the sight of her in women's clothes, white cap covering her hair, her shape enveloped by a thick woollen cloak. She looks like every goodwife in the place, demure, plain and ordinary. He hates it almost as much as she does. She is not like the rest. She is better than them.

She looks sideways at him, catches his eye, the corner of her mouth curling. Her eyes flit to Flynn, then back, rolling in mockery. He smiles too, wanting to reach out and take her hand in his.

These moments of shared understanding are becoming frequent: a look, a smile, a single word. They are sinking into an ease that he has never known with any woman, not Betsy and not Gretchen. At times, he catches himself thinking of how things might be between them, if circumstances were different. That confusion rises in him now and he squashes it down. Not here. Not now. Not with that man watching.

Flynn eyes him with disdain and mistrust, as if he has found a rat nesting in his mattress. He knows that look – the look that men give each other when they first meet, sizing each other up like dogs – and has already cast his own judgement: men who claim to be so godly usually have something to hide.

He notices how others look at him too – the exchanged glances and comments behind hands. He knows what they are saying. Who is the usurper who dares sit in the front pew with Bartram Booth of Scarcross Hall? Where has he come from, this nobody, with neither family nor wealth? What claim has he on Mercy Booth? The thought is darkly amusing.

Today, though, he feels their interest keenly: it has a different timbre to it. As the Booth party had entered the churchyard, a thin woman had thrown them a scowl and herded her children out of their path. Henry Ravens's scrawny wife had turned her back as Mercy passed. The family who most often sit behind them chose an empty pew – one of many, he notes – at the back of the church, leaving only space across which whispers rustle like the crisping leaves on the birches.

After the sermon the congregation lingers in the churchyard as usual. The only chance that many have to meet with their neighbours, it is usually a wasps' nest of rumour and gossip, but today there is a hush, as if they are waiting for something. Ellis stands near the door, watching as Mercy greets Garrick's wife and takes her bundled baby into her arms. He idles over and is met by the first warm smile of the day.

He likes Dority Garrick, just as he likes Ambrose – in spite of himself.

'Master Ferreby,' she says, beaming at him. 'Ambrose tells me you're to see out the winter with us. How glad I am to hear it.'

He raises a finger to his hat, nods acknowledgement.

'Well, you must come and break bread with us once more, if Mercy can spare you. Or perhaps you could come together, if Master Booth could manage alone . . .' She trails off as Mercy gives her a hard stare.

'We were talking of Sam,' Mercy says, 'and finding some real work for him on the farm. I say we could use him. What do you think?'

Before he has the chance to answer, Jasper Flynn interrupts. He tips his hat to the women, ignoring Ellis. 'Mistress Booth, may I speak with you?'

Mercy hesitates, smile dissolving. Ellis sees something – apprehension – pass behind her eyes. 'Of course.'

She hands the baby back to Dority, the small pink thing squirming inside its wrappings, and is led away, towards the old graves. Ellis watches all eyes follow, the crowd of villagers, Henry Ravens and his wife among them, and, standing apart from the rest, Bestwicke's son, hat in hand over his father's grave.

'So, what do you think, Master Ferreby?' Dority asks. 'Might there be some use for Sam up at the Hall? I know how hard you're all working. I barely see my Ambrose these days.'

'Surely that's for your husband to decide.'

'He's not a large boy for his age but he's plenty of spirit. Too much, perhaps . . .'

She looks over to where her son is standing, alone, scuffing his feet in a pile of leaves.

'We'll be bringing the flock down from the moor this week. There'll be plenty of work to stem his boredom.'

'You've hit upon it.' She jiggles the baby, who has started to whine. 'He needs direction. Guidance. Someone to take him under his wing.'

'He has his father. There's no better man.'

She smiles, and he's struck again by how pretty she is, how small and girlish in comparison to Mercy. 'He doesn't listen to his father. You know how boys can be. Ambrose was the same when he was young.'

Ellis looks over at Mercy. She and Flynn are turned away. He sees the man reach out and touch her shoulder but she shrugs him off and moves apart. He can see only her profile yet he can read the anger in her stance – feels a stab of it as if it's his own. He can sense vitriol building among the villagers. He picks out Ravens among them, sees him speak to those nearby, though he cannot catch the words. Annie Ravens's expression is brooding, black as coal smoke.

'The truth is, Master Ferreby,' Dority goes on, seemingly oblivious, 'Sam has turned a little wild of late, and ever since that poor lamb of his was found, he's been impossible. He ignores all his tasks about the house, disappears for hours on end and won't tell me where he goes. Nothing I say makes any difference. Indeed, I'm at my wit's end.' She looks to the grizzling child in her arms. 'And I'm afraid for him, spending hours out there, all alone, after everything that's happened . . . Some time at Scarcross Hall and a guiding hand from someone other than his father might be what he needs.'

She looks up at him, hopeful, and Ellis nods, but he is not listening. He's watching: watching the rest of the congregation watch the conversation between Mercy and Flynn. Small huddled groups turn their backs as Agnes and Garrick guide Booth towards the cart, and help him up onto the seat. It's clear that Booth's strength is failing but no one comes forward to assist as he struggles. Instead, daggered looks are sent their way.

At last, Mercy and Flynn shake hands and she starts back towards them, grim-faced. As she passes, Annie Ravens rushes forward.

'You're found out, witch!' She raises a hand to strike a blow, but Ravens catches her, pulls her back.

'Not now, Annie. Not here.'

Mercy is stunned into silence as Annie begins a weird animal shrieking. 'I know what you are! I know what you did!' She fights against her husband, clawing as if she would scratch out Mercy's eyes.

Ellis leaves Dority open-mouthed and strides to Mercy's side. He tries to stand between her and Annie, but Mercy, gathering herself, shoves him roughly aside. 'Whatever you have to say to me, I'll hear it.'

'Witch! Whore! I know what you are! I know what you've done! Henry told me everything!'

He sees a flicker of shock in Mercy's eyes.

'The pastor told me what you've been saying,' she says, raising her voice to be heard above Annie's rage. 'And it's lies. I did not kill my own sheep or burn down my own barn. I'm not the one who killed John Bestwicke. Ask your own husband who should pay the price for that!'

It's the first time she's expressed Ellis's own suspicions, but everyone knows what she means. There is a ripple of shocked muttering. It rushes back to him: the dreadful heat of the flames, the choking smoke, the stark, urgent fear of that night. He feels the tinder of anger, sees it mirrored in Ravens himself.

'You've no proof,' Ravens says. 'And I'm not the one accused.'

'We all know it's you! It's your fault!' Annie cries. 'We all know what you are! We don't want you here.'

Ellis's fists curl. One hand moves to the hilt of his knife. He could do it now. He could finish what Ravens started that day in the barn. He knows it would not serve him, but the urge is powerful and seductive.

Jasper Flynn steps forward, pulpit voice raised above the throng. 'I'll have no violence at my church!' A restraining hand outstretched towards Annie. 'I've done as you asked. Now go home, all of you. I'll hear no more of this.'

Annie spits and growls like a dog, tethered by the pastor's wrath.

'I said, go home!'

Ravens whispers something in his wife's ear and, reluctantly, she sinks back against him, allows him to drag her away. The man must know that he cannot afford more questions to be raised.

Mercy turns and walks quickly away, eyes stormy, sending a quick glance in Ellis's direction – a call to heel. He stands for a moment, sure to catch Ravens's eye, then follows.

'We must leave, now,' Mercy says, reaching Dority, who stands, shocked and horrified. 'Tell Ambrose to bring Sam up to the Hall tomorrow, if he'll come.'

'What's happened?' Dority asks. 'What does Annie mean?'

But Mercy does not reply.

She says no more until they are away from the church, following the coffin path out of the valley. It had taken some time to reassure Booth, who had seen the whole altercation from his perch in the cart, but is now settled, grumbling quietly to Agnes.

Mercy walks beside Ellis. The road is wet, turned to mud in places – slow going for the old carthorse – but at last they pass the crossroads and gain the higher ground.

He waits while she broods. He does not expect thanks for his poor attempt to protect her and knows better than to press for confidences but eventually she turns to him.

'No doubt you're wondering what the pastor wanted with me.' She glances ahead to make sure her father cannot hear. 'You've probably guessed – we're no longer welcome at church.' He can hear the suppressed rage in her tone, notes the clenched muscles in her jaw. 'The villagers are demanding that Flynn banish us.'

'For what reason?' Though he does not really need to ask.

She snorts. 'I've known these people all my life. We've given them work and charity, and now they abandon us. Now, when we need them most. There's nothing godly about that.' She is silent awhile. Her cheeks are flushed but he cannot tell if emotion or exertion is the cause, or just the whip of the chill October wind.

'Flynn says there's been trouble brewing ever since summer, and worse still since the fire. They say there's a witch at work at the Hall. They say that the old curse is rising again and we're to blame, that we've summoned it. Some of the wives came to him, demanding that he bring in the law. They think it's one of us. They think it's me.' She looks at him. 'Tell me, why would I murder my own lambs? Why would I burn down my own barn? Why would I destroy my own livelihood? Dear God, how am I going to calm Father now?'

He is not surprised to hear it. He has been waiting for something like this ever since the day Sam's lamb was found dismembered in the hay field. He recalls the woman, Joan Goffe, and her spiteful accusations – her fear spreading to others, quicker than mice fleeing a blazing hayrick. In her absence, Annie Ravens has done a fine job of fanning the flames.

'What does Flynn say about it?' he asks.

'I've never much liked that man but he's been a friend to my father all these years and it seems he's a friend still. He's quieted them for now. He refused to bring in the law without proof and, of course, they can prove nothing. But they agreed to let the matter drop only on the condition that no one from Scarcross Hall attends church. So, we are to be cast out, made guilty, sentenced without trial.' She pauses a moment, allowing the cart to go on ahead. 'He knows it's all lies. He knows we need God's grace now more than ever. As our pastor, he should speak up for us, but he's weak. I never knew it before. He's a cowardly man. To save his own position he's chosen compromise over justice and truth.'

'But you shook hands with him.'

'Yes.' She sighs. 'For Father's sake, he's agreed to hold a private prayer meeting once a week at the Hall. We'll tell Father that it's for the good of his health. It'll not be long before we cannot bring him in the cart – the path will be too bad – and he can no longer manage the walk. I'll not tell him the real reason.'

Ellis knows why. She will not give Bartram Booth any more reason to sell.

'I've attended that church every week for my whole life. I've known these people since I was a child. Does that mean nothing?'

'They're afraid. Folk will always look for someone to blame.'

'They're wrong about us, but they're right to be afraid,' she says, looking ahead to where Booth sits in the cart. Ellis wants to console her but he does not know how. He feels guilty, knowing he can never give the answers she craves.

For a time she walks with her head down, dragging the hem of her skirts in puddles, the damp creeping almost to her knees. Then she looks up to the crest of the moor where the White Ladies are just coming into view, the rugged stones pale on the skyline, heights pointing to Heaven, roots buried Devil knows how deep.

Chapter 31

The smell of sheep grease is a comfort, something real and constant. The wiry texture of lambs' fleece, grown thick and coiled tight, underbellies peat-stained russet brown after a summer on the moor, as familiar as the fell itself.

As always, I find escape in my work, savouring the strain of muscles as I struggle to keep a beast still enough to apply the grease, the aching back, the chapped fingers, the mix of sweat and steaming breath in the cold autumn air. I welcome the golden leaves on the willows, the October scents of rot and peat smoke. I try to put aside the creeping fear that plagues each sleepless night, the ominous sense of dread when morning comes, and lose myself in the work.

We brought the sheep down from the high moor two days ago. They knew it was time. We found them huddled under peat hags against the driving rain, grey and ragged among the last of the purple heather. Now they are scattered over the low fields.

Ambrose and Sam have the task of gathering and sorting the sheep: this year's new lambs that need greasing, the shearlings, the older ewes that will go to tup, the wethers that need to be checked over before they can be turned out for the winter and the ones we are forced to sell.

Ambrose and I pick out the best, the ones with the fullest coats, good teeth and a strong, square stance, hoping for the highest price. It might seem senseless to sell our best new lambs – the future of the flock – but we have no choice. Without this year's fleeces, we need the coin the best animals will bring. It's the only way we'll last the winter.

Sam is given the task of bringing the lambs into the small pen we use for greasing. He's been taught how to check them carefully for signs of foot rot and fly-strike, separating any that might be ailing. He works quietly, sulking and dejected.

For the last week he's slept in my bed. I want him close. Last night, when I climbed beneath the coverlet, he was so still and silent I thought him sleeping, but he was watching me with big, tear-filled eyes.

'What's the matter?' I asked, as he turned away and curled into a tight little ball. As I stroked his hair he flinched. 'There's no need to be afraid. Nothing can hurt you here. I'll make sure of it.' The lie choked me.

Each night I've lain awake, waiting and listening for that light step upon the boards, praying that whatever spirit visited me does not do so again. I've a sense that while Sam sleeps in my bed it will stay away, and I'm become superstitious – selfishly so – in keeping him by my side.

Eventually he turned back and let me cradle him in the nook of my arm. In the morning there was a patch on my nightgown where his tears had dampened the linen. He has shadows beneath his eyes, as if he too has barely slept.

Ellis works with me and we take it in turns to hold and grease the lambs.

'Sam, send in the next.'

Sam is idling by the gate, staring into the distance. He turns slowly and shoots a petulant look towards Ellis. Then he opens the gate and wrestles another sheep into the run.

'Have you checked this one?' Ellis says, but Sam does not seem to hear. He's staring up the fell-side towards the moor top.

Ellis shakes his head and begins picking leaves and clods from the lamb's fleece. 'If the boy hasn't the wits for the work, is it wise to keep him here?'

'He can do the work,' I say, taking the sheep's head between my knees to hold it still. 'He just finds it hard to trust strangers, and you're still a stranger to him. He'll come round in the end.'

Ellis is silent awhile. When he's satisfied the sheep is ready he dips his fingers into the grease pot, scooping a fistful. 'Who is William Garrick?' he asks.

I glance back over my shoulder at Sam and lower my voice. 'Where did you hear that name?'

'There's a grave in the churchyard.'

'Then you know that William Garrick is dead.'

Ellis bends to the work. I can tell he wants to know more. I've not spoken of it for so long, even with Dority, but I think Ellis should know, now he's one of us.

'He was Sam's twin brother.'

Ellis doesn't seem surprised; he must have guessed as much. 'How did he die?'

'An accident. Ambrose doesn't like anyone to speak of it.' Again I glance at Sam to make sure he cannot hear, but he's working now, checking over the next lamb. 'No one knows what really happened.'

'Was the lad alone?'

'No. The twins went out on the moor one afternoon and didn't come home. Dority thought they'd stayed at the Hall, as they often did, so they weren't missed until the next day. We sent out men to search and they were found up at the White Ladies. Will had fallen and broken his back. He died three days later.'

Ellis nods towards Sam who is now dragging another reluctant sheep into the run. 'What does he say about it?'

'He's never spoken of it. Not once. He didn't say one word for a full month after Will died.' I don't like to think of that time. Before the accident, the twins were inseparable. Dority called them her red devils, for the tomcat-orange hair that was so like their pa's, but she stopped afterwards, in case it tempted Fate. Sam was like a ghost, silent and watchful, a shadow of himself, haunting us while his father tried to work away his grief and guilt. Ambrose barely slept that season and was present for almost every lamb as if by birthing so much life into the world he could stave off his own loss. Instead, it salted the wound.

Ellis is silent for a time, seemingly focused on his task, but I know he's adding poor Will's fate to the list of bad things that have happened at the White Ladies. I watch his hands – strong hands, working hands – tending the sheep with gentleness and patience. Unbidden, an image comes to mind of those hands on my body.

Then, quietly, he says, 'The guilt of such a thing is a heavy burden for a young boy to carry.'

'Yes. We all feel the burden of it.'

'Why should you? The child was not yours.'

'He died at Scarcross Hall. We did all we could for him but . . .'

Ellis straightens, finished with the lamb, and gives me a forthright stare. 'The bedchamber that's kept locked. He died in there, didn't he?'

Of course he would guess. I've heard him, wandering the corridors by night, as sleepless as me.

'You've heard it, then? The noise?'

He nods but says nothing. I know what he's thinking, because the same thought plagues me, though I dare not put it into words: *Is the spirit of William Garrick returned?*

I think such things in the dead of night, as I wait and listen. I've an urge, now, to tell him everything, to confess my fears. They say a burden shared is a burden halved. But it seems to me the more I give credence to this thing, the worse it gets, as if by speaking of it, acknowledging it, I give it power. So I say nothing more, and Ellis does not press me. I fold and pack the longing away, along with all my other unspoken desires.

That night, the noise begins again.

Sam is asleep beside me, chest rising and falling, one foot twitching. I pull the coverlet up over his ears, hoping he will not wake.

I lie still and listen to the lament of the wind as it finds its way through cracked panes, beneath doors and down chimneys, and the Hall's answering creaks and groans. And there, alongside the familiar night sounds, the rhythm I've come to dread: the dull *thunk*, the dragging scrape.

I hear the click of a latch and a rasp as a door opens nearby. The glow of candle flame lights the inch beneath my chamber door. I watch the shadows as Ellis steps out of his room and pauses, a single floorboard creaking as it bears his weight.

Does he know I'm awake? I feel sure, somehow, that he's waiting for me and the feeling causes a blizzard in my chest.

So as not to disturb Sam, I slip silently from the bed, pad across night-chilled boards and open the door.

He's dressed hurriedly, in breeches and undershirt, and holds a candle lantern. He says nothing.

I step out of the room, closing the door behind me, and for a moment we stand, looking at each other, listening to the rise and fall in the dark.

Thunk . . . ssshrrrrrrssssst . . .

Thunk . . . ssshrrrrrrssssst . . .

I take the key to the bedchamber from around my neck and hand it to him. His fingers curl around skin-warmed iron and he gives a determined nod.

I'm already shivering as we skirt the gallery, but I do not know if the cause is cold or fear. I cannot bring myself to look out into the black night so keep my eyes fixed upon Ellis's back, as if his company alone will ward off any danger. I am braver with him than alone.

As we reach the chamber, the sound ceases. The silence seems heavy, the sudden absence unnatural.

Ellis presses an ear to the door. I do the same, so we are face to face and I feel his breath on my cheek. The blood beats in my ears, wave upon wave, but I hear no more.

He moves away first, then puts the key in the lock.

The mechanism is stiff, scratching and clunking as it turns. It seems loud and I cringe but there is silence from within.

I hold my breath as Ellis lifts the catch and opens the door.

He steps inside, holding the lantern high.

The room is exactly as I left it. Dust has settled in the spaces where Agnes pushed boxes towards the chimneybreast, and part of one of the wooden shutters has rotted and fallen away. It smells of must and mould, the faint density of sheep grease and an acrid, familiar scent of burning.

The bed is empty, drapes pulled back, coverlet scattered with wisps of fleece and curls of flaked paint from the bedstead. One of the bolsters is split, feathers spewing.

'Is this where the boy died?' Ellis says, indicating the bed.

I nod. He holds the lantern up over the coverlet, inspecting it. He sniffs the air. Then he makes a slow circuit of the room, peering behind boxes and tilting the lamp into dark corners, just as I have done so many times before. At the chimney, he squats and retrieves the talisman that Agnes put there. He stares at it for a moment, then crushes it in his palm, dry twigs snapping.

'Fear breeds fear,' he says, coming to stand by me. 'Such trinkets belong in the fire.'

'Agnes does what she can to protect us.'

'Sticks and twine will not help.'

'Pastor Flynn says that the spirits of the dead can return only if God allows it. Those not sent by God are tricks of the Devil.'

He looks around the room. 'And you think this is such a trick?'

'I don't know. But . . . Annie Ravens is right. That woman, Joan Goffe, she saw it too. Everything that's happened these last months has the taint of evil about it. There's something here. Something that wants us gone. I feel it. You feel it.'

He does not respond.

'Agnes thinks we should find a popish priest to cleanse the house. She says they have a particular gift.'

'What would your father think of that?'

'He'd never allow it.'

'Agnes is afraid.' He unfurls his palm and shows the crushed talisman, drops the twigs to the floor and kicks them beneath the bed with his bare foot. 'Fear will not help.'

'Then what should I do?'

He looks at me with surprise. 'You ask my advice?'

'Yes.'

'Whatever visits here, whatever its intent, you cannot keep it at bay with a locked door. You must not give in to fear. You must confront it.' He holds up the lantern so its light is cast across his face. 'At times, it pays to hold a candle to the Devil.'

And for a moment, fuelled by the intensity of his gaze, I am strengthened. I am bold.

He reaches out towards me, as if to touch my shoulder. His hand grazes the linen of my nightgown then drops back to his side but I feel the sensation as if he has brushed my naked skin. I see something pass behind his eyes: a yearning that reflects my own.

It is all the sign I need.

I take the lantern from between his fingers and place it on the floor. I turn back to face him and put my hands flat against his chest.

He looks down at my fingers as if surprised to find them there and for a few seconds we are fixed like that. Then, his hands come up to cover mine, pressing them close until I feel the cadence of his heart beneath warm, firm flesh. My own is soaring like a skylark's song.

He closes his eyes but does not move. He does not wrap his arms around me or bring his lips to mine. He does not reach for my body, as Henry Ravens would have done.

His stillness causes my courage to falter and, as it begins to slide away, I catch at the tail of it, slipping a hand from beneath his and placing it gently against his cheek. I cradle his face, his beard soft as fleece in my palm. I run a finger along the flesh of his earlobe. His lips part and I touch my thumb to his mouth, feel the damp heat of his breath.

I slide my fingertip down to the small thumb-sized hollow at the throat that cradles the pulse of lifeblood. I notice a cord about his neck, a thin twine of old leather, much like the one upon which I carry the key to the chamber. Curious, I begin to draw it from beneath his undershirt and catch a glimpse of fine golden metalwork before his eyes snap open and his hand clasps mine, preventing me from lifting it further.

He stares into my eyes – his are all confusion – and I think he will lower his mouth to mine but then the familiar shadow descends and he becomes taut and brooding once more, cold as first frost.

He pushes me away roughly, as if I'm suddenly abhorrent to him, turns and goes towards the door. There he pauses, twisting back, though he does not look at me.

'I cannot,' he says, throwing the words over his shoulder as if they are nothing.

And then he is gone.

Chapter 32

Ellis kicks off his damp, heavy boots and leans back in the chair, the heat of the kitchen fire easing his aching limbs. Steam rises from the boots, the leather so cracked and sodden that when he pulls them on each morning his legs are leaden, and each night he is aware of the itch and stink rising from between his toes.

'You must be tired.' Dority Garrick stands at the kitchen table, laying out trenchers and bread. He cannot get used to her presence in the old woman's place. At least Agnes does not bother him with chatter.

'I'll hang your things to dry,' she says. 'I can't let you catch a chill when we're all depending on you. Have you clean clothes?'

'Later,' he says, resting his head on the chair-back and closing his eyes.

While Mercy, Garrick and Agnes are gone to Halifax, to sell lambs at the last fair of the year and bring back supplies for the winter, the care of the flock falls to him. He has spent a rain-lashed day out on the fell. She has been gone only three days yet he feels her absence as a nagging ache in his centre, a space where she should be. He curses himself for such a failing but, at the same time, finds himself encouraging it, allowing the sensation to grow and fester in his chest, like a canker, because it is the only thing he has of her that belongs to him.

Sometimes he longs for the days before he knew her. He remembers it as a time of solitude and peace before this serpent began to twist within, this double blade that sharpens with each day, though he knows that is not a true memory because he has never known serenity, not the sort that godly men speak of, only the false impression of it found at the bottom of a bottle.

'You must be hungry for some supper,' Dority says, carving hunks from a dark, dry loaf. 'I expected you back at midday.' Her tone is unmistakable: she is annoyed with him.

He rubs his eyes and props himself up, watching as she prepares three trenchers of bread and cheese, then goes to the door and calls Sam's name into the hall beyond.

There is no answer, other than the chaos of rainfall and the wind whistling down the hall's dead chimney.

After a few minutes she gives up and returns, collects two of the trenchers and brings them to the hearth where she places one in his hands. She drags a stool across the flags and sits, wrapping a shawl around her shoulders. 'He'll come when he's hungry,' she says.

They eat in silence, accompanied by the sound of rain driving against the panes, as it has done for a week or more. Every so often a drop splashes down the chimney, making the fire hiss and spit. The bread is heavy, made with bitter rye, crumbling between his fingers, but it is better than nothing.

When he is sated he sets aside the trencher and leans back once more, listening to the crackle of flame, the gentle rustle of Dority's skirts as she moves, the creak and groan of the house. He picks out the regular beat of footsteps from above. He glances at Dority and sees she is listening, head cocked, eyes following the sound to and fro.

'How is my boy doing?' she asks, when the footsteps stop.

He shrugs, takes a swig of ale. She thinks it is Sam she hears, but he doubts that.

'I'd hoped he might be happier here,' she says. 'I'd hoped you might be a friend to him, but he seems as sad and lonely as ever.'

'He does not much like me,' he says.

'Why would you think that?'

'It's the truth.'

'The truth is more complicated.' She puts down her trencher, her supper barely eaten, and dusts the crumbs from her lap. 'He finds it hard to trust people. Lord knows, that poor boy has had his share of troubles.'

His irritation rises. 'I know something of his losses, Mistress Garrick, as I know something of yours, but I don't see how I can heal them. As his mother, surely you should be the one to do that.'

She stares at the floor, face pinched. 'I've tried – of course I have – but I'm not able.'

'I cannot be a father to him. He has a father already.'

She folds her hands in her lap. 'Mercy cares for Sam a great deal. I thought that might mean something to you.'

'Why should it?'

She stares at him for a few moments, as if trying to read something in his features, then stands, collects the trenchers and returns to the table. 'Why are you still here at Scarcross Hall, Master Ferreby?'

He says nothing.

'It can't be for the coin, because I know too well there is none. It can't be for the love of the work because it is gruelling and tiresome. I can't believe that you've nowhere else to go, because a man like you will always find a bed somewhere. So, why do you stay?'

He shrugs, wishing she would leave him be.

She sighs, exasperated. 'You might fool the rest of them, pretending you care for nothing and no one, you might even fool her, but you don't fool me.'

He's surprised by her temper and finds his own rising to meet it. 'My choices are no business of yours.'

'Perhaps not, but the welfare of this family is. I've lived too long beside them to keep silent.' She turns to him. 'Let me tell you one thing. Mercy Booth may pretend she cares for nothing but her flock, but she's as much a liar as you. If the two of you can't see the truth in each other then you must be blind. But I don't think you *are* blind, Master Ferreby, any more than she is.' She comes towards him and jabs a finger at his chest, feline eyes sparking. 'I know there's a heart beating in there and I see for whom it beats. It takes a brave man to own his heart. But I think perhaps you're a coward. Are you a coward?'

He stands, towering over her, tumult roiling in his chest. His fists clench. He could strike her now – it would be just punishment for speaking so plainly, for touching so raw a truth – but some small part of him wants to fall at her feet and confess all.

Alarmed, she steps backwards and reaches out a hand to steady herself on the tabletop.

'You think you know me,' he says, failing to keep the jagged rage from his voice. 'You think you see the truth. But you know nothing of me. You know nothing of the truth.'

Before she can respond a great howl echoes through the hall.

'Sam,' she says, faltering, turning to the door. But the howl has become a guttural moan, low and deep, not the sound of a child.

Ellis is through the door before her, running across the hall to Booth's study. Flinging open the door he sees Booth knelt at the hearth, cradling one hand to his chest and, with the other, trying to smother the flaming edges of a piece of paper. He looks a madman, grey hair flying, eyes bulging and wild with panic, baying like a wounded animal.

Ellis crosses the room and stamps on the paper, the fire quenched by his damp woollen stockings. Dority runs to Booth and flings her arm around his shoulders. 'Master Booth! What have you done?'

Booth shrugs her off and rocks back and forth, clutching at his hand. Even by the dim light of the fire, Ellis can see a cruel red welt creeping across the palm.

Ellis bends to take up the paper. The corners crumble to ashes on the hearthstone.

'Do not touch it!' Booth says, but Ellis ignores him. The document is charred, only a few words remaining, and he cannot make out what it is that Booth has tried to save from the fire. In one corner, untouched by flame, there is a ruddy smudge, the colour of dried blood.

'Leave it be! Do not touch it!' Booth says again. 'Oh! Will they never let me rest?'

'Come now, Master Booth,' Dority coaxes. 'Let me see your hand. Did you burn it?'

He turns on her. 'Don't speak to me as if I'm a child! You think I don't know my own mind. But I do. I do. I'm not mad. They've come back, don't you see? After all this time. They've come back.'

Ellis steps forward. 'Let Mistress Garrick help you, sir.'

Booth looks at him and some flicker of confusion passes across his face. He grimaces, as the pain takes hold.

'Please, Master Booth, let me help you,' Dority says.

Booth tries to rise from the floor, legs weak as he leans heavily against her.

'What have they done?' he asks, as she helps him to the chair beside the fire and encourages him to sit. 'Why will they not let me be?'

'A light, please, Ellis,' she says.

Ellis goes to the desk where a candle burns, but is stopped short by what he sees there.

The desk is scattered with papers as usual, spilled across boxes and inkpots, an empty pewter cup dribbling liquid like a slug's trail. But the papers are all marked with dark red stains. On some there are smudges or spots but, here and there, he sees the distinct shape of a small red handprint, no bigger than a child's, as though someone has run their hands over everything, searching for something. He looks at the burned scrap he holds, at the same russet stain.

'The candle,' Dority says urgently.

He grabs it, and when he turns back, Booth is watching him. 'You see?' Booth says. 'Who else could it be? Who else could have done this?'

'Please, let me look at your hand,' Dority says, wincing as he unfurls his palm to reveal an angry scarlet burn. 'We must cool this with milk. Ellis, will you fetch some from the buttery?'

Just then Sam appears at the door, ashen and wide-eyed.

Booth falls silent.

'Don't be afraid, Sam,' Dority says. 'Master Booth has had an accident, but all is well.'

Booth stares at the child with a weird calculating look. 'Did you do this, boy?' he says.

Sam says nothing.

'Did you do this?' Booth pushes himself up from the chair, ignoring Dority's pleas, and gropes for his stick. 'Where have you been?'

Sam stares at the floor, jaw working as if he would speak, but no sound comes out.

'I said, where have you been?'

'Answer Master Booth, Sam,' Dority says.

'Come closer, boy.'

Sam takes a few uncertain steps.

Booth goes to the desk where he picks up a document riddled with ruddy handprints. 'Did you do this?'

'Sam wouldn't dare—'

'The boy can speak for himself, woman.' Booth draws himself

up, casting off the decrepit old man that Ellis recognises, seeming suddenly younger, broader and more fearsome. Then he bellows, 'Come here!'

Sam flinches and looks to his mother.

'Do as Master Booth says, Sam,' she says, cowed.

Sam does so, stopping just a few feet away from Booth.

'Show me your hands, boy.'

Sam hesitates, eyes darting to Ellis and back to Booth.

'Here, in the candlelight. Show me your hands.'

Slowly, Sam splays his fingers, palms up, a child's hands, small and uncalloused, the skin of his fingers stained a brownish red. Ellis knows that his own hands are the same – remnants of the ochre raddle that marks the backsides of all the tupped ewes on the fell. He knows that, no matter how hard you scrub, it takes weeks to fade.

There is a moment when he could speak up, when he could stop it, but he does not. He watches as Booth roars, raises his cane and swipes it hard against the boy's head.

Then Dority is screaming, tugging at Booth's coat as he rains blows across Sam's back and the boy crumples to the floor, covering his head with his hands.

For a few seconds Ellis is elsewhere, staring at his own reddened palms while the awful sounds of violence come to him from a distance, dredged up from memory – another place, another time, another small, helpless boy.

Dority's cries bring him back to himself and then he is pulling Booth away, pinning his arms by his sides, his own strength proving the better of his master.

Dority falls to her knees, protecting Sam with her body, wailing his name over and over. The child has not cried out once.

The strength of fury seems to go out of Booth. He buckles in Ellis's grip, drops his cane and stands panting and exhausted until Ellis releases him.

Sam uncurls and, pushing Dority away, climbs to his feet, unsteady, a thin line of blood trickling from his nose. Dority, trembling, reaches for him but he steps back and shakes his head, wiping the blood across his cheek in a grotesque smear.

He stares at Booth and his eyes are cold and sharp as shards of ice.

'Oh, see what they've made me do,' Booth whispers, looking at Ellis with horror. 'Lord, forgive me. See what they've made me do . . .'

He reaches out his burned right hand towards Sam. 'My dear child, forgive me . . .'

But Sam just stands there. He looks at each of them in turn. Ellis is shocked by the malice in his stare, as if all Hell's fury burns behind his eyes. Then he turns and walks out of the room.

'Fetch him back,' Booth says, pleading. 'Fetch him back at once.'

But by the time Dority has struggled to her feet and followed Sam out into the hall all she finds is the yard door unbolted and a splash of blood upon the step.

Chapter 33

'Two guineas is my final offer.' Owen leans back against the settle and takes a long drink from the tankard the tavern girl has just placed before him. Foam clings to his moustache. He wipes it away on his sleeve. 'Do we have an agreement?'

'They're worth four times that,' Ambrose says.

'They're only worth what a man is willing to pay, Garrick, and I am that man.'

'Master Owen,' I say, trying a smile. 'These lambs were bred on good hill country from strong stock. They're hardy and healthy – our very best. They'll do well on your land and, in a year or two, the ewes will make good breeders. We're offering you a reasonable price.'

He snorts. 'If they're your best, why would you part with them for any less than their worth? It makes a man suspicious. There must be some reason you wish to be rid of them.'

I don't answer. He knows my hand is forced.

'Only a fool would purge their stock of the best new breeders. I always said women have no head for this business.' He gives Ambrose a conspiratorial wink. 'Best stay where they're most useful, do you not think so, Garrick?' He has a purplish sore at the corner of his mouth. Every so often he worries at its yellow crust with his tongue. He does so now; my stomach turns.

'It's no use trying to win Ambrose to your view, Master Owen,' I say. 'I'm mistress of Scarcross Hall and your business is with me.'

He smirks into his mug, gaze sinking to my chest. 'I don't do business with maids,' he says. 'Especially those who would make themselves the image of a man.'

'Then perhaps I'm wasting my time,' I say, standing, but Ambrose catches my wrist and tugs me back down.

'We didn't come here to argue, Owen, but to strike a bargain with you,' he says. 'Let's all calm our tempers.' He shoots me a warning look. 'I'm sure we can come to an agreeable figure. Your offer is too low. What say you to five guineas?'

Owen laughs. 'I say you've not been listening to me. You'll accept my price and be thankful for it. I saw what happened at the auction. No one else will buy from you. You're trying to hide it but I know you're desperate, and a desperate man cannot make demands.'

Though my blood boils, I know he speaks truth. We would not be here, in this dank, back-street tavern, sharing ale with ragged farm lads and pox-ridden drunks like Owen, if the day had not been a disaster.

All morning I stood by our pen, with forty lambs jostling and bleating for the fells, waiting for the buyers to come. And some did, leaning over the fence, shooting curious glances my way, looking me up and down and sucking their cheeks at the sight of my breeches and boots. A few of the younger ones came just to stare. But none stepped into the pen to check for rotten teeth or fly-struck fleeces. No one asked my price. Even those I've known since I was a girl – those who used to pet and spoil me – did not wish me good day or ask the reason for my father's absence.

I've been coming here all my life and these people know me. Why would they act as if I'm a stranger, no longer one of them? As the day draws on, my suspicion grows – a hard, heavy millstone in my chest.

Perhaps I should have seen the signs when we were given a pen on the edge of the common, far from the flocks of wealthier stockmen, or when the first two inns we tried claimed they had no room for us.

Was I ignorant to suppose that word would not have spread so far? In the marketplace I see faces from villages and farmsteads near Scarcross Hall, neighbours I know from Pastor Flynn's congregation, people who will listen to Henry Ravens and his spiteful wife. Since the altercation outside the church, I'm sure Henry will have taken every opportunity to fuel the rumours in order to deflect suspicion and blame from himself. And gossip will spread down valleys and along roadways faster than the plague.

When time came for the auction and the teller called out the name of Scarcross Hall, there was a hush – silence except for the bristle of whispers and scuffling as men turned away. No one will buy from me today.

So, Ambrose and I are forced here, to this stinking den of scoundrels and thieves, to find someone willing to take the lambs off our hands. I cannot take them back. I cannot return without coin and the supplies we need. We will not come through the winter without them. I cannot face the crestfallen, despairing look on Father's face. Our survival falls to me and I must not fail.

Owen sits back, pursing his lips. He knows he has the better of me. A roll of white, lardy flesh, with coarse black hairs, like spiders' legs, protrudes above his breeches.

'Is this your doing?' I ask, though I can guess the truth. 'Have you poisoned others against us for your gain?'

'My dear girl, you credit me with more guile than I have.'

'Then tell me, what are people saying?'

He looks surprised. 'You don't know?'

I say nothing. I'll give him no leverage.

He scours the room, eyes alighting on a scrawny boy who lolls by the door, begging scraps from the tavern wench. 'Boy! Come here!'

The youth does as he's told and comes to stand next to the table.

'Do you know this woman?' Owen asks.

The boy shakes his head.

'Why don't you introduce yourself?' Owen says to me.

I don't understand his game but suppose I must play along. 'I'm Mercy Booth, mistress of Scarcross Hall.'

The boy's eyes go wide. He looks to Owen and back again. 'Truly? Is she the one?'

'You've heard of her?'

'I've heard of Scarcross Hall.'

'And what do you know of it?'

'Everyone knows of it. That's the house that's cursed. They say the mistress is a witch.' He stares at me, eyes popping with perverse fascination. 'I thought she'd be ugly, like the old one.'

Owen is clearly enjoying the exchange. 'That's enough boy. Away with you.' He flips a penny. The boy catches it and sidles away, never taking his eyes from me. He whispers to the tavern wench, who shoots daggers of pure disgust in my direction, and runs to speak to the landlord.

'So, you see, your lambs are bred under a curse, Mistress Booth. We all know the old stories. Word is you're the Devil's daughter. No one will buy a strand of wool or a stem of barley from you for fear of it. To think of the cunning – coming here on All Hallows Eve, hoping to witch us all. Do you think we're so easily tricked?' Again, he leers at me.

Ambrose has flushed fury-red. 'This is nothing but petty gossip and nonsense,' he says. 'And you know it.'

'Oh, I don't doubt that,' Owen says, lowering his voice. 'I'm not a superstitious man, Garrick, but I am a practical one. And if it suits my purpose for the rest of the world to believe in curses and witchcraft, then why should I put them right? So, you see, you'll find no other man willing to take your cursed lambs, for two guineas or for anything at all.'

Ambrose's fists are clenched on the tabletop as he takes deep breaths. He'll deny these tales. He'll defend me and will believe what he says. But he doesn't know the things I know. Scarcross Hall is not in his bones like it is in mine. He cannot begin to understand its secrets. He's never lain in bed and listened to footsteps in the dark and the breath of spirits, has not felt the malevolent, watchful eye upon the house. He cannot know that some part of what Owen says is true.

I see that Annie Ravens has had her revenge. My hope is shattered.

'Two guineas it is, Master Owen,' I say, quietly.

'No,' Ambrose starts, looking aghast. 'Mercy, don't do this.'

I put out a hand to shake Owen's. He reaches forward and puts his palm in mine. As he senses the resignation in me his gloating ceases. A flicker of doubt passes behind his eyes, fleeting but I catch it. He might think better and take his offer back. But then he releases my hand.

'A pleasure to do business with you, Mistress Booth.'

'They're good lambs, Master Owen. I trust you'll have no trouble with them.'

'Mercy, this is madness,' Ambrose says, but I cast him a glance that demands silence and he sits, brooding, while Owen counts out the coin. When he's done he slides the little pile across the table. I gather it, measure the pitiful weight of it. Two score of our best lambs and I can hold their worth in one palm.

A volley of shouting comes from the street. The boy, who's returned to his post by the door, darts outside. Drinkers crane their necks to peer through soot-smeared leads. A woman is shouting, high-pitched and excited, a mess of men's voices echoing I register the familiar sound of Bracken and Flint, barking and pulling at their binds.

I'm on my feet in seconds, stuffing the coin into a small leather pouch that hangs at my belt, Ambrose by my side.

Outside, I find Agnes cowering against the wall of the tavern, next to the stake where the dogs are tied. She's white-faced and shaking, her skirts spattered and filthy, as if she's fallen in the muck of the street drain. The dogs are straining at their ties, teeth bared and snarling.

The crowd surrounding them is not large – perhaps two dozen at most – but it's vicious. In the narrow street, they seem to press from all sides. There are faces I know among them – labourers who've worked our land, farmers I've done business with, wives I've supped with. At the fore is one I thought I'd never see again. I recognise her mean, half-starved face, the hanks of dirt-hued hair straggling from her cap, her shabby clothes and the vacant-eyed brood about her feet: Joan Goffe, the vagrant woman, the cause of such disruption on that hot harvest day when Sam's lamb was found dead.

She's screeching as if there's a demon inside her. 'How dare you bring your witch's curse among these good people? We don't want you here!'

A clod of horse muck sails through the air and strikes Agnes's shoulder. A cheer goes up. I push through the crowd to Agnes's side, Ambrose close behind, and when Joan sees me, she lights up with fervour. 'And here is the other one! As brazen as only the Devil could make her. Look at her in her fellow's garb – unnatural creature!'

I stand before Agnes, sheltering her. 'Oh, Mercy! What's happening? What have I done?' she says, fighting back tears.

'Nothing. That woman is mad.' My heart is beating hard. I long to strike Joan down. If anyone lacks Christian feeling, if anyone has evil in her soul, it's her.

Joan speaks to the crowd. 'I've seen their wickedness with my own eyes. I won't stand by and let them spread their witchery here. We must cast them out! Will you join with me?'

Again there's a chorus of agreement. More muck is thrown from the back of the crowd. It hits me on the chest. The stink of rotting meat and the privy is pungent. I do not think it animal waste this time.

Ambrose faces up to the crowd. 'Don't listen to this woman's lies. She's a firebrand, a troublemaker.'

But no one is listening. There's a scuffle to one side of the crowd and someone, though I do not see who, throws a rock. It arcs through the air and strikes Agnes on the temple. She puts a hand to her face, shocked, as blood trickles down her cheek.

A gasp goes up from the crowd but Joan laughs. 'Yes! Cast them out!' she cries. 'Stone the Devil's creatures!' The younger boys take up the call, scrabbling for handfuls of pebbles and grit. I see the lad from the tavern among them, grinning, wild-eyed and swept up, cattle stick in his hand.

I whip round to face the crowd. 'What kind of coward torments an old woman? Leave us be or I'll set my dogs on you!' I'm met with nothing but jeers.

A second stone is loosed. This time it hits the leads of the tavern and the sound of splintering glass is met with an outraged roar from inside.

Ambrose grabs my arm, pulling me behind him. 'Enough!' he bellows. 'Enough of this!' He raises his arms, addressing the crowd. 'You have your way. We're leaving and you'll let us go without trouble. We've no fight with any of you and you need fear nothing from us. I know what you've heard. Well, hear this now. I swear it on the life of my children. These women are innocent. There is no witch at Scarcross Hall!'

Someone spits at Ambrose's feet but he ignores it, turning to set the dogs loose. Ever loyal, Bracken strains on her leash, snapping at the ankles of those nearby.

'Hell's hound,' Joan says, glaring at me, eyes all spite and venom.

I long to fight back, to say my piece, but Ambrose grips my arm and pulls me roughly away. I know he's right. To vow vengeance now will only prove Joan Goffe right.

So we leave her there, free to spread her lies. Free to turn the whole world against us. I look back just once and see Owen, watching from the tavern door. He tips his hat to me with a mocking, self-satisfied smile.

And as we go, avoiding the throng around the swine stalls, heading for Gibbet Lane, rain starts to fall. The twilit sky is heavy with roiling cloud: a storm is coming.

Chapter 34

The candle lantern stuttered out a hundred paces back. Ellis struggles to relight it, crouching in the corner of a sheepfold, trying to shelter the tinderbox beneath his coat. His hands are wet, the flint slippery in his fingers, and sparks fall on dampened charcloth. He curses as the tinder glows for a moment, hissing and fading as raindrops splash in the pan. He gives up and leaves the lantern leaning against the wall, the wind rattling its catches.

He stumbles up the fell-side, ground sliding away beneath his feet, sinking in puddles and bog pits, trying to follow a ridge of heather that marks out solid ground. Every few minutes the sky burns with bright, crackling light and in those moments he casts about desperately, trying to find a bearing: there, the chasm of treetops that marks out the valley, and there, at his back, the stark chimneys of Scarcross Hall.

He had set off along the coffin path, but somewhere, somehow, has lost the track. A storm like this can remake the moor, opening chasms filled with slick, oily water and causing the bog to rise. He knows the moor by night, the safe paths, crests and gullies mapped in his mind, but this weather turns the land to something else – a shifting, living thing, savage and hostile. A wrong step can wipe out all traces of a man.

Another flash of lightning. The crossroads should be up ahead but he can see nothing in the dark, cannot gauge distances. He waits for the crash and rumble that follows, and when it fades he tries again, shouting into the wind: 'Sam! Sam!'

Dority had come to him, red-eyed and frantic, pawing at him like an animal, the baby mewling at her chest. 'I know there's something wrong,' she said. 'And Master Booth can't help. Please, there's no one else.'

It's true – the old man has retreated to his makeshift bed in the parlour and lies there, mad and moaning, muttering nonsense.

But what does it matter to Ellis if the boy has run away? Why should he risk his own life to find him? 'He'll have gone home,' he said. 'Or found shelter somewhere. Only a fool would go out on a night like this.'

But she is convinced. She'd checked the cottage earlier in the day, she said. No food was taken, Sam's things were untouched, the animals had not been fed. She's sure some terrible fate has befallen him. 'The White Ladies,' she said. 'He might have gone to the White Ladies.' Ellis knows why. She wrapped a shawl around her shoulders and threatened to search for him herself, trying to push the baby into his arms, but he refused to take it.

'If you go out there now, you'll likely not come back,' he said.

'But I must.'

'Then you leave me no choice.'

He labours on. The wind takes his hat and whirls it into the sky. He snatches for it but a gust takes it out of reach, the rain battering it back to earth and into the centre of a black patch of peat. He dare not step away from the ridge of heather so leaves it there, ignoring the icy rivers that begin to stream down his neck and inside his collar.

At last he finds a sheep track – or what's left of it – now ankle-deep in water as springs rise on the moor top, turning paths into streambeds. The way marker at the crossroads appears ahead – for a moment he mistakes the tall stone for a figure, waiting for him in the dark, and feels the familiar flare of unease.

From here, he should be able to find the path that leads to the stone circle. The darkness is almost absolute. He's made blind by the driving rain and has to wait for another flash of lightning before he can right himself once more. He sees a silvered streak of ground, winding away uphill through the heather, the path coursing with rainfall from springs further up the fell. If the ground has held, he can follow it to the moor top. He sets off, feeling the rush of water pulling at his ankles.

He thinks back to that morning when he had slipped inside Booth's study, as thin, grey light filtered through the panes. He had not been able to sleep but something made him wait until dawn, the night passing in long hours of listening: the scratch and patter of movement from empty chambers, the creak and sigh of the house.

By day, the mess of red-stained papers seemed less sinister. He gathered them, ordered them, began to read: letters from men he does not know, an unpaid bill of account from the butcher in the village, rough-drawn maps and sketches of Scarcross Hall in a spidery hand.

The burned scrap of paper that Booth rescued from the flames had disappeared. He suspects the old man has taken it. But what was it, he wondered, to cause Booth such distress? Nothing in these mundane fragments of life hints at anything suspicious. Perhaps it was the missing land deeds, proof of Booth's ownership of Scarcross Hall, the loss of which might thwart his plan to sell. But who else knows of Booth's addle-brained scheme? Who else would have reason to destroy them? There is Mercy, of course, but Mercy is not here.

Ellis studied the murky smudges of red that spread across the papers as if a small, bleeding creature had ricocheted across the desk in its death throes. Here and there, the shape of a hand was distinct. He measured it against his own: not a grown man, then, but a child.

If Sam is to blame, what reason could he have had? Standing there, Ellis thought of the boy, his quiet watchfulness, the fear and fury that seem to rise in tandem behind his eyes. He saw, once again, the blows of Booth's cane upon the child's head, the sticky scarlet trickle creeping from his nose.

A chill ran through him. He felt a presence and turned, expecting to see Booth in the doorway, but no one was there. He dropped the papers back onto the desk, suddenly convinced that he should not be there and that someone was watching.

He keeps his head down, feeling his way uphill. So long as his footing is sure, so long as he can feel the brush of heather against his calves, he will be safe, he will reach the moor top. He cannot think, yet, about how he will find his way back down.

The rain is relentless. As he reaches higher ground it is all around him, buffeted slantwise, from east and then west. He cannot see more than a few feet ahead and feels the land close around him as if it will swallow him whole. He feels the ground give a little beneath his left foot and trips, tumbling over a tussock. He falls to his knees and gropes for the heather but cannot find it. He feels the gentle give beneath him – a sure sign of bog. He was so sure he was on the path, on firm ground. How can he have lost his way? He was so careful. He pauses and breathes, telling himself not to panic.

Slowly he stretches, reaching for something solid, finding nothing but sodden bog grass. He feels the soft peat stir beneath him, the moment that the ground gives way and he begins to sink. He throws himself belly down and grasps for tufts of heather. He finds some, ignores the scratches as he buries his fingers into its roots and heaves himself forward, reaching a bed of the plant and draping himself over it, allowing the fear to rise and subside.

He stays there, blood rushing. This is an act of madness. Where is the sense in sacrificing himself? The boy is nothing to him. Booth is to blame for this. He should be the one to right it. He feels a swell of anger towards the old man. What kind of person beats a child bloody? But he already knows the answer to that. He remembers how it feels when wood meets bone. He closes his eyes, fury fuelling determination. The rain, running in rivulets down his cheek and neck, feels as if it could be his own blood.

Then the sky sparks and crackles and the world is lit once more. There, ahead of him, no more than fifty yards uphill, he sees the White Ladies.

He reaches the nearest stone and flattens himself against it, sheltering from the worst of the wind. In its lea he wipes the rain from his eyes and breathes deep, lungs burning, bile rising to taint his tongue. He shouts Sam's name, but there is no answer. The wind seems to snatch his words, shattering them against the stones. He waits for lightning, and when it comes, he moves to the next stone, then the next, intending to make his way around the circle. Up here there is less fear of the bog, but the rain has saturated the ground and he still does not trust it.

He pauses at the next stone, fighting for breath. He thinks of Dority, imagines her pacing before the kitchen hearth, afraid that there will be two missing souls to account for by morning. Her words come back to him: *Mercy cares for Sam a great deal. I thought that might mean something to you.*

It does. He's doing this for her.

He can still feel the way her hands pressed against his chest, see the look in her eyes: so bold and so certain. He wishes he could scour the image from his mind. Even with a quart of liquor inside him he cannot escape it. The Devil comes to him in dreams, shows him what would have happened had he not walked away. He wakes, hard and aching. It sickens him. Every time he thinks of that night he is tormented, and he can think of little else; that he should be the one to reject her, to cause her pain. But what choice has he?

He has prayed for relief, but God has not answered. There is a battle inside him that faith alone cannot fight. The Devil's grip is too fierce. He would rather face the raw, bodily pain of a pike wound, a musket shot, than this torturous anguish. There have been times, in these last days since she left, when he has taken the old flintlock pistol, and held it against his skull, imagining the sweet relief of pulling the trigger. But he will not be beaten. He will cast out these thoughts.

He grips the stone with both hands and dashes his forehead against it. The pain in his temple is bright and hot, flaring behind his eyes, and for a moment all else fades. He does it again, and feels the skin break, the sting of wound upon wound. Once more, and he feels the scrape of bone against stone.

There is nothing now except the pain and, when he opens his eyes, the black sky, rent with God's fire.

As the strike fades, something catches his eye: a pale shape atop the Slaying Stone. He makes out a figure – head, shoulders and thin white limbs – luminous before it fades, like the impression of a snuffed candle behind closed eyelids. He strains into the darkness, veins running cold. But when the light comes again there is nothing to see.

Once more the thought of Mercy, in her white nightgown, creeps to the fore. His mind is playing tricks on him: he has driven himself mad with the blows. He has seen marsh lights before and recognises the cool blue glow: the souls of those drowned in the bog, the lonely ones who crave the company of the living. He shivers, gripped by the conviction that someone else is here: someone or something. But then he sees a small bundle of rags, lying on the ground, at the foot of the Slaying Stone.

'Sam!' He stumbles forward, almost blind, praying for sure footing.

Sam is curled in a hollow beneath the stone. He could be asleep but when Ellis shakes him, his eyes roll and his teeth chatter. He is drenched, waxen and mud-streaked, cold as death.

'Sam!' Ellis shakes him hard. 'Sam! Wake up!'

There is no response – the boy is insensible – but Ellis feels the slightest beat at his chest, hears the rasp of feeble breath.

He gathers Sam in his arms and stands, head throbbing, struggling to see his way back to the path as blood blinds him. He waits for lightning, which seems to take an age to come. He edges away from the Slaying Stone, feeling dread build and a cold, malevolent eye on his back, until he is filled with a desperate urge to run. But to run would be to die, so he waits and waits until the sky is suddenly bright and he sees a furrow amid the heather that might be the path. He steps out towards it, across this Devil's land, into the black night.

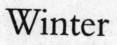

Winter

Chapter 35

I take a strip of damp linen and gently wipe the film of sweat from Sam's forehead. His cheeks are mottled with scarlet spots, his breathing shallow and thick. He does not seem to know me.

'What cure have you tried?' Agnes asks.

Dority gazes out of the bedchamber window, hugging herself. She looks deathly, face blanched, bruise-hued shadows blooming beneath her eyes.

'He was so cold at first that we just tried to warm him. When the fever began I gave him vervain and feverfew. I tried vinegar on the poultice, but nothing seems to make a difference.'

Agnes nods. 'You've done all you could. I'll find something more to ease him.'

Ambrose, kneeling on the floor beside the bed, clutches Sam's small, clammy hand. He's not moved since we arrived back at Scarcross Hall. 'Shall I go for help? There's a healer sometimes visits the village.'

'I need you here,' Dority says. 'Please don't leave me again.'

'Then Ferreby will go.'

'No. The man you speak of is a charlatan and I won't have him here. There's no one in twenty miles can give my boy better care than Agnes. Besides, we'd be wiser sending for Pastor Flynn.'

'Don't say that,' Ambrose says, squeezing Sam's hand as if he'll never let go. 'Don't even think of it.'

But, of course, we are all thinking of it.

'Why did you put him in this room?' Agnes asks, echoing my thoughts. 'We never use it. We keep it locked.'

'Ellis had a key. He thought it best to keep Sam away from the rest of the house, away from baby Grace, and the master, in case of contagion.'

'Ellis has keys?' Agnes glares at me, but I haven't the patience for questions.

'Who else should I trust? I couldn't leave them with Father.'

'I'm sorry if we did wrong, but we can't move him now. He's too weak,' Dority says. 'And don't blame Ellis. If it were not for him . . .'

'Where is Ellis now?' I ask.

'Checking the flock. He's been worried about them, after the storm. And he's done all he can here.' She inclines her head to indicate the changes about the room.

The trunks and boxes have been pushed up against one wall, the rusting farm equipment is gone and the floor swept clean. The fireplace smoulders, though the unused chimney sends the smoke back into the room. The broken shutter has been nailed up with a cross-hatch of boards. The split bolster has been replaced with clean linen I recognise from Father's bedchamber.

'He did all this?' I ask, remembering Ellis's words the last time we were alone in this room: *Whatever visits here, whatever its intent, you cannot keep it at bay with a locked door.* God knows I have relived that night enough times to understand his intention now – his attempt to face down whatever evil lurks here.

'He's been our guardian angel,' Dority says. 'I don't know what I would have done had he not been here.' She covers her face with her hands so we cannot see the tears well. Ambrose stands, goes to her and wraps her in his arms.

'I'm here now, girl,' he whispers into her hair. 'I'll not leave you again.'

She leans into his chest, seeming to shrink against him, and gives vent to the despair that must have been growing inside her these last two days.

I know it's wrong, but I feel a stab of jealousy. I cannot imagine how it must have been for Dority waiting for us to return, not knowing whether she would greet her husband with yet another tragedy, but what consolation it must be to have him back, to have someone to share her woes.

For many years I've assumed I'd never have such a thing. I've shared parts of myself with Agnes, and with Dority, and in my younger years I would have named Father my closest friend, but there's no one in this world knows the whole of me. I've shared my pains with God alone. I've whispered to the wind, let the rain take my tears, dried my eyes on the fleeces of my flock and never let anyone see how I've felt the lack of a true friend. I have not dwelled upon my loneliness. I never allowed it: I made my choice and must live by it. But the trials of these last months have stirred a craving I thought long dead.

'I'll prepare something for the boy,' Agnes says, 'and look in on the master.'

'Thank you,' Ambrose says, over Dority's shoulder.

But as Agnes reaches the threshold, Sam stirs. Dority is beside him in an instant. He turns his face towards her and blinks slowly.

She places a palm to his forehead. 'Sam? Sam, can you hear me?'

He blinks again, eyes vacant.

'What do you want, my love? Ambrose, fetch water. He must drink.'

Sam seems to focus briefly on his mother's face before his gaze wanders upwards and beyond her, to the wooden canopy of the bed.

Then he squeezes his eyes tight shut, a wail erupting from somewhere deep inside, a noise I've never heard from him before, more akin to the keening of foxes in the night. He tries to toss the covers aside and pushes his mother away, as though he cannot bear the sight of her.

'My darling, please be calm,' Dority says, trying to stroke his forehead, trying to soothe him, but he kicks and moans while I stand by, helpless, a cold hand squeezing my heart.

He struggles for some minutes, while we tend him with gentle words, compresses and water, but nothing gives him ease. Eventually he's spent and falls back into deepest sleep.

Dority is aghast. 'What's wrong with him? Why does he not know me? Why is he afraid of me?'

'His brain is fevered,' Agnes says. 'He does not even know himself.'

But I'm sure we are all thinking the same thing. It's not his mother Sam fears: he just does not want to die in the same bed as his brother.

I find Father seated on an old worn blanket on the floor by the fire in the parlour. He has one of Agnes's shawls draped around his shoulders. The air is stale with the stench of peat smoke, tallow, week-old sweat and an overflowing chamber pot. Bedcovers are caterpillared across the floor and the remains of a meal – a dry crust and flecks of crumbling cheese – are scattered where someone has upturned a plate. Two leather-bound books, treasures usually kept safe on the shelf in the study, lie open haphazardly. A pile of papers spills from the sideboard. A glance suggests most of these are covered with scrawled black ink and some have been screwed up and tossed aside.

Father is staring at the fire, whispering to himself. He seems not to notice as I slip inside and close the door.

'Father?'

He turns red-rimmed eyes towards me. 'Ah, there you are,' he says, as if he'd last seen me an hour since, and I'd not been gone near a week.

I cross the room and crouch beside him. 'Come, let me help you to a chair.'

'No . . . I'm comfortable here.' He shifts a little as if to prove it and gives me a weak smile. I'm taken aback by how frail he is. He looks so shrunken and old, skin grey and papery, eyes bloodshot and sore, as if he's not slept. The change in him, so marked in these few days, is painful to see.

He looks back at the flames. 'Come, rest with me awhile, child.'

I sit cross-legged next to him and, for a few minutes, let myself bathe in the warmth of the fire and the peace of the room. I notice there are no creaks or pattering steps from above, no chill air or sense of otherness; the house is quiet, as if, like all of us, it is waiting to know Sam's fate. When Father reaches over, takes my hand in his and closes his eyes, I do the same, imagining for a moment I'm that little girl again, suspended in silent prayer. How I wish that could be true. I'd like to lay my head on Father's shoulder and tell him about the horrors of the last few days, let him comfort me, let him make the world a safe place again. But I know it's impossible. That man is gone.

'Of course, Dority told you what happened,' he says, after a while. 'She told you what I did.' He sounds calm, no sign of the temper or fretting I've come to expect.

'Yes, she told me.'

'How is the boy now?'

'He's very ill, Father.'

'Will he live?'

'I don't know.'

He nods slowly. 'I've been praying that God sees fit to save him. "Take me," I say, "not the boy. It's nothing to do with him."'

'What do you mean?'

He looks at me with such sadness. 'Ah, Mercy. For all your years you're still an innocent. It's my own fault, I suppose, keeping you to myself all this time, away from the world. I just wanted you to be safe, you see. I wanted to make a life where nothing could harm you.'

'I'm no innocent, Father. You've taught me well. I know the ways of the flock, the land and the work. What more do I need?'

He shakes his head. 'I've been selfish. I've been thoughtless. Well, soon you will be free of me, free to do as you choose.'

'Please don't say such things.'

'No doubt you'll be glad to be rid of me, rid of a father who has failed you yet again.'

'You haven't failed me.'

'Oh, I'm afraid I have.' He lets my hand drop. 'I've something to tell you.'

My heart sinks. I'm not sure I can stomach more bad news.

'Yesterday Pastor Flynn came to see me. We prayed together for poor Sam. And afterwards we spoke of you, my dear.'

I've been waiting for this day to come. I gather myself, ready to argue against a marriage to Jasper Flynn.

'I'm afraid he did not agree to my proposal. He gave all the usual flatteries, of course, but he declined to ask for your hand. He said . . . he said that, given the current situation, it would not be in the best interests of either party. What did he mean, Mercy? Why would he refuse such an offer?'

I say nothing as this sinks in. Jasper Flynn, knowing the rumours, and some small part of the truth of them, has chosen to keep the goodwill of his parishioners over a future as master of Scarcross Hall. I'm sure, for him, the choice was clear. I am not a suitable wife. I cannot help but feel a great swell of relief and not a little gratitude.

'Is he afraid, do you think?' Father goes on. 'Afraid of the things we've told him? As a man of God, surely it's his duty to offer comfort and protection, not turn away in our hour of need. I cannot understand it.'

'I'm sure he has good reason,' I say.

'Well, I could not persuade him, and it seemed he could not wait to leave. And I thought that man was my friend. So, you see, I've failed you even in that.'

'I don't see it so. You must not blame him. It was too much to ask of any man.'

'But what are we to do now? Will you find another to marry, as I ask? You must act soon, my dear, before I'm gone. That time is drawing near. You must act soon or I'll have no choice . . .'

And with those words, the relief of my reprieve is quashed by the threat of losing Scarcross Hall. 'Father, please don't talk of that.'

'I must find a way to protect you, Mercy. It's all my fault, you see – what's happened to Sam and his family. What's happened to all of us. I'm to blame and therefore no one else can make it good.'

'You're not to blame. No one thinks so.'

'Oh, they do. I see it. I see it in Dority's eyes. If the boy dies, it will be my fault. The Garricks already know how it is to lose a son – there can be no greater pain – and they must have someone to blame.'

'I don't understand.'

'You will in time. We must all face up to our failings in the end, whether in this life or the next. And it's so clear – how I've made one error after another. I see it now, though I did not see it then. I just hope you can forgive me, child.'

'Why are you talking like this? Are you unwell?' But his eyes are clear, free of the confusion that has become so familiar.

'Can you forgive me?'

I think of the paltry collection of coin in my purse and of how I'm the one who has failed. 'There's nothing to forgive.'

'You are too good to me, Mercy. You put on a brave face to the world but you have a sweetness that reminds me of your mother. Any man would be blessed to have you by his side.' Then he shakes away his wistfulness. 'Enough maudlin talk. Tell me about the fair. Did you see my old friends? What news is there? Was the sale a great success?'

There is hope in his eyes. I cannot bring myself to crush it. 'Yes.'

'Then the Booths are not beaten yet.' He reaches over and squeezes my hand. I feel the slow crawl of guilt at the lie but, God forgive me, I do it to save him pain. The truth weighs heavy on me. If only my purse did the same.

Later that night, when Ambrose has gone to the cottage to tend the livestock and Agnes is dozing, exhausted, before the kitchen hearth, I sit up with Dority at Sam's bedside.

'You should sleep,' I tell her. 'I'll stay with Sam and wake you if there's any change.'

She shakes her head. 'I can't leave him alone, not for a moment. I can't risk it.'

I know what she's thinking. She was not there when Will breathed his last. I was the one who sat with him that night. The Devil has a way of tricking the living and she doesn't want to tempt him a second time.

I put my hand on top of hers. 'God won't let him go. He's too precious to us.'

'But if it were not for Ellis we would have lost him already.' She pauses, swallowing tears. 'Oh, Mercy, I've not seen a storm like it in years. He risked his life to save my boy.'

My throat tightens as I think of Ellis Ferreby. I've not forgotten my humiliation at his hands, the crushing of my hope that night in this very room. I'd been so sure of his intention, so certain of his response. I still burn with shame to think I was mistaken. Ever since that night I've avoided being alone with him and he's been surly and silent in return.

I had thought that my journey to the All Hallows fair would be a respite from the regret that torments me, but instead I found his absence a physical thing – an ache in my chest, as if I'd cracked a rib. I saw his features in other men, in one the fall of his dark hair, in another the long stride of his gait, in a third the broad stretch of his back, and I longed for one of them to be him. In years past I've joined the merrymaking and taken my solace with men now nameless and faceless to me, but this year, there was no one on my mind but him. And I hate myself for it.

Dority is watching me. 'He's a good man, Mercy. A little rough, granted, but there's a decent heart beneath.'

I say nothing but she puts a gentle hand on my shoulder. 'I see the burden you carry and you should not have to do it alone. You have Agnes, but Agnes is old. You have Ambrose and me, but we cannot be here always. And your father . . . Well, your father is not the man he used to be. A good husband by your side would be a comfort and a helpmate.'

Jasper Flynn's refusal crosses my mind. 'Men don't marry women like me.'

'You always say that but it's not true. It's only because you've kept yourself apart. You still have strength and youth for a family, should you wish it. Besides, he loves you, Mercy, I'm sure of it.'

I'm tempted to put her right but somehow I can't bear to disagree with her, not now. She always sees the best in people, always finds hope for them, even when her own is torn to shreds.

'What makes you think so?'

'Why else would he stay?' she says. 'And he almost admitted it to me, before all this.'

'Then why does he not speak up? Why does he not come to me?'

'That I can't tell you.' She pauses. 'But, Mercy, what's stopping you? I know you. It's not in your nature to hold back if there's something you truly want.'

Again I feel a surge of shame at the recollection of Ellis's rejection. I cannot tell her I've already tried with him and failed, as I seem to fail so much now. Though somehow her hope is infectious. I want to believe her. He turned away from me that night, but perhaps there was good reason. My head tells me one thing and my heart another.

'Don't waste this chance of happiness, Mercy,' she says, looking at Sam. 'You may not get another.'

She glances back at me and I see the memory stir behind her eyes. She looks away, back to her boy, chastened. She knows the reason I have *kept myself apart* all these years. She knows I had my chance of happiness and she stole it away.

Ambrose never made a promise to me, but I thought there was no need. It was understood. It was all there in his deeds: the shared dreams, the affinity with the land, the flock and each other, the passion we gave one another in snatched moments out on the fell. I was too young to understand that sometimes words matter.

On the day he told me he would be married to Dority, an iron cage clamped shut around my heart, barred and locked, and no one else has ever found the key.

When, after a time, I leave her, I take a candle to bed. I reach the small chamber next to my own and find fingers of candlelight creeping across the boards from beneath the door. I pause in their glow, holding my breath.

I raise my fist, meaning to tap gently but cannot do it. I stand there, halted by indecision, heart pulsing as if it might burst forth.

Before I can make my choice the door swings open and he is there, dressed in breeches and undershirt, unwashed, unkempt and looking half wild. There is a new angry, scabbed wound on his forehead.

He doesn't seem surprised to find me standing there. My hand drops to my side. Why do I lose all courage when we are face to face?

He stares at me a moment, with those dark, glowering eyes, then glances over my shoulder to make sure we are alone. 'Is it the boy?'

'No. I – I wanted to thank you.'

He continues to stare. I search for something to say, something that expresses what I feel, but fail yet again. 'Dority and Ambrose are grateful.'

'It's nothing,' he says.

I know that is not true. 'Is all well with the flock?'

'We lost some in the storm, as far as I can tell. I'll go out again tomorrow.'

I nod. 'Goodnight, then.'

'Goodnight.'

He stares at me a moment longer, as if waiting for more, then turns and closes the door. I hear the latch fall.

I go into my chamber where, despite my tiredness, I cannot sleep. Instead, I go to the wall that adjoins his. Like a foolish, pining girl, I press my fingertips against it, then flatten my palm and put my ear to the plaster, imagining that I can hear his night breath and the steady rhythm of his heart, imagining that he might be just inches away, on the other side of the wall, doing the same.

Chapter 36

He has good news at last: today is the first day in the week since the storm that he has not found more dead sheep. He has come across them drowned in becks, fallen where they tried to shelter against the folds, three of them yesterday, part buried beneath a collapsed peat hag. He has even found a couple of bedraggled carcasses down on the valley side, as if the rain had washed them there. But he has been out on the fells all day today and found no more. He feels an impulse to share this with her, something that might lift the black mood she has carried since she returned from Halifax.

He hears voices in the parlour – the room that Booth now rarely leaves – and goes there, thinking he will find her within. The door is ajar. Through the gap he sees the old woman and falters.

Agnes is standing, backlit by the dimming light from the window, while Booth sits on the chair before the fire. She strokes his shoulder with one hand – a gentle caress of care and reassurance. 'I can't believe it's true,' she says. 'You must be mistaken.'

Booth, agitated, reaches up and grips her wrist. 'Don't treat me like a simpleton. I know it's so.' He takes hold of her hand and brings it towards his lips, as if he might kiss it. 'Please, Agnes, you are the only one I can tell.'

She looks at him, pained. 'But why now? After all this time?'

'So that I might atone for my sins before the end.'

'What makes you so sure it's not the Devil's trickery?'

'I know it, Agnes, in my heart. I failed them, all those years ago. I know that and I've never forgiven myself. You remember what Pastor Flynn said? God allows souls to return only to carry out His will. He's giving me one last chance to make amends. But I don't know what I'm to do – I don't know how I can make it right.'

She sighs. 'Don't distress yourself. Be quiet now.'

'But I lost those coins. That was when it all began. I ask myself, did I will it somehow? Am I the cause?'

'You need to sleep.'

'But I cannot sleep. I am tormented.'

'Bartram, please . . .'

'That's why I beat the boy. God forgive me, I never meant to hurt him. I don't know what happened. I fear – I fear I'm losing my mind. They are with me day and night. They are driving me mad.'

'Then, please, take the draught. It will help you.'

He clutches at her sleeve. 'I dare not. I dare not succumb. They come to me in dreams and ask me to go with them. I don't want to go, but I fear I must . . . I fear I must.'

He hangs his head then and she draws him close, cradling his head against her hip and stroking his hair, hushing him as if he were a child. They stay like that for a while, Booth whispering into her skirts, things Ellis cannot hear from his watch post outside the door. He sees Agnes raise a hand and quietly wipe tears from her cheek.

He knows he should leave. He knows that to observe such a tender, private moment is not his place, but he senses the edges of something – an understanding – and cannot look away. His own heart is hammering, his mouth dry. He's not sure what he's witnessing but he knows it's important, secret.

Agnes crouches next to Booth and takes his face in her hands. Ellis watches her lips move as she whispers but again he cannot hear. Booth nods. She strokes his cheek with the gentleness of a lover. Then she straightens, slowly, awkwardly, and fetches a small cup from the sideboard. Booth drinks, pulling a face at the bitter taste of the contents, but he is already calmer.

Agnes drapes a blanket over him, stokes the fire, then waits until his eyelids begin to droop and his head nods.

As she leaves the room, Ellis presses back into the shadows of the stairwell, holding his breath as she makes her slow, shuffling way across the hall and into the kitchen.

Then he follows.

Mercy is sitting at the table, head in hands. The dog, Bracken, is with her, resting her scruffy brown head on Mercy's knee. As he crosses the threshold Mercy looks up. 'More today?'

He shakes his head. 'We have that to be thankful for at least.'

She does not respond and he is disappointed. Stupid, he thinks, to pretend that such a small blessing would cancel out the losses of the last week.

Agnes, grim-faced and frowning, goes to the table and begins slicing a small loaf of maslin, a greasy pat of butter beside her. She cries out suddenly, the knife clattering to the flags. Bracken barks at the sound.

'Can't you quiet that damned creature?' Agnes says, trying to stem the drip of blood from her cut finger.

Mercy guides her to the bench, where she sits, slumped forward, clutching her chest.

Ellis retrieves the blade, then takes hold of Bracken's rope collar and drags her to the door. What had Booth said to cause Agnes such distress, such distraction?

Bracken does not want to go. She whines and scratches as Ellis shuts her out in the cold. As he bolts the door, he catches a whiff of something burning and is reminded of smouldering match, the brimstone taint of gunpowder, the crackle of the barn alight. But there is nothing to see in the gathering darkness, save the fog coming down.

The cut is not deep and the bleeding soon stops, but the old woman has lost all colour and wheezes as she breathes, one hand pressed to her heart. 'Forgive me,' she says.

'You need to rest,' Mercy replies.

'How can I rest when there's so much to be done?'

'I'll help you.'

'You can't put barley in the mill and milk in the churns. You can't undo what the rain has done to the kitchen beds. How are we to manage through the winter, with no money for meat or grain?'

Ellis perches opposite. 'What of the money from the fair?' he asks. 'Will that not see us through?'

Mercy reaches into her waistcoat and brings out a small leather pouch. She unties the drawstring and spills the contents onto the table. A small handful of coins rolls towards him. 'It's not enough,' she says.

Though he's never been a trader he knows the value of lambs and those were good stock. She must read the disbelief in his frown because she tells him then, in short, angry words, what happened at the fair. As she speaks of the accusations that hounded them from the town, Agnes stands, waving away Mercy's protests, and pretends to busy herself by fetching a jug of beer and three cups. She's unsteady, he notices, pausing to catch her breath. Though she says nothing, he can see she's hiding pain and not just from a cut finger. The experience in Halifax has clearly wounded more than her pride.

'I had no choice,' Mercy says. 'I could not return with nothing, though this is little better. We had no chance to buy supplies, even if anyone would have taken our money.'

'And Garrick agreed to this?'

'I made the bargain, not he. Besides, he has other worries now.'

Her eyes flit above, towards the room where Sam still lies in his sickbed.

'What does the master say?'

'My father doesn't know.' She fixes him with a warning look. 'And you'll say nothing of it.'

Agnes returns, placing a cup of beer before each of them. He takes it gratefully and drinks.

'We shouldn't keep such news from him,' Agnes says. 'He'll know in time.'

Ellis thinks of the sympathy he observed between them and wonders if Agnes has already shared the news with Booth.

'I won't be the one to cause him more distress,' Mercy says, eyes fierce.

Ellis knows what she's really thinking – she will not give her father any more reason to leave Scarcross Hall.

'He's not well,' she goes on. 'We must wait till he's better.'

'But, my dear one, what if he doesn't get better? He's not himself. Not himself at all.' Agnes studies Ellis. He feels the weight of suspicion on him. 'Did you see it happen? Did you see him strike the boy?'

'Yes.'

'Was he in the wrong?'

'It's not my right to judge another man's conscience, but it was . . . needless.'

An unspoken question creases her brow. He feels her eyes rest on him as Mercy speaks.

'It would anger my father if he thought we'd been cheated. He has a temper.'

Ellis understands the fury that overcame the man's better instincts – he recognised the demon in Booth's eyes.

'If he knew what people were saying and the trouble we face, it might cause that rage to come again, and I fear he does not have the strength for it,' Mercy says, looking to Agnes. 'No, we must keep watch over him. Keep him calm and rested. Say nothing to disturb him. I'll find a way to keep us warm and fed.'

Agnes stands and goes to fetch the bread. 'More secrets . . .' she mutters, as she walks away, casting him a mistrustful glance.

'I'll find a way,' Mercy says again, under her breath: a promise to herself.

He slides a hand across the table and places it gently on top of hers. He had not intended to make such a gesture. He simply feels compelled to touch her, to reassure her. The urge to offer himself into her service, to protect her from the world, throbs in his chest.

Her fingers are cold to the touch. She looks up at him, surprised. Then, as Agnes turns towards them, she snatches her hand away, the thread between them torn once more.

Chapter 37

A strange hush descends upon the house.

Father confines himself to the parlour, surviving on guilt and prayer. Sometimes I press my ear to the door and hear him muttering to himself, bargaining with God. He does not mention Jasper Flynn to me again, though the pastor is true to his word and still visits weekly, when we all gather in the old bedchamber so that Sam might hear the prayers we say on his behalf. Flynn is distant and courteous to me, any old amity lacking, his presence clearly nothing more than duty. I wonder if he too is poisoned by Henry Ravens's lies. Or can he feel, as I do, the cold hand of death hovering above Scarcross Hall, like a red kite riding the wind, and the sense that we are all suspended, waiting for it to land, struggling to find comfort in the faith he preaches?

These prayer gatherings are the only time we come together. Father is not the only one to withdraw into solitude.

Dority stays at Sam's bedside for almost three weeks. She'll leave the room to feed baby Grace – fearing contagion forces her to bed her youngest in Agnes's room – but insists that Agnes or I take her place by Sam's side while she does so. She barely sleeps and eats little. I watch her already slight frame narrow, the shadows beneath her eyes deepen and her cheeks sink until she takes on the cast of a cadaver. She turns in on herself, all her usual life and energy drained, becoming watchful and silent, cooped up in that room, her world shrunk to a daily round of doses and chamber pots, her one concern the life of her boy. Even Ambrose cannot reach her and, after the first week, returns to the cottage by night, where his own livestock must be tended.

I begin to fear for her health. With Sam and Father to nurse, we cannot afford another invalid. So, in late November, I insist that she spends a night in my own bed, promising to sit with Sam till morning. I see the fear pass behind her eyes when I suggest it and know she's thinking of Will and the last time she trusted me to watch over her son, but I reassure her and, though she tries to fight it, I can see how her body craves the rest. After much persuasion, she gives in.

So, I find myself the nursemaid as night falls.

Sam is not much changed. The fever still has him in its grip. Though Agnes forces her best remedies and purges down his throat, he's insensible most of the time, stirring only to cry out or mutter the nonsense of disturbed dreams, his breathing thick and laboured. We feed him broth when we can, but he's not taken solid food for weeks and the flesh is dropping from him, bones beginning to show through translucent skin. If God does not save him soon, I fear he'll be joining his brother in the ground. Dority will not survive that.

After pacing the room awhile, banking up the fire and closing the shutters against the winter chill, I prepare myself for a night of wakefulness, sitting in the high-backed chair in which Dority catches her moments of rest. I listen to the sounds of the household as it settles for the night: Agnes's step upon the stair as she climbs to her bed, the familiar moan of wind in the chimney, the crackle and hiss of the fire. My body aches with exhaustion. There's a scratch at the door, a soft whine, and I recognise Bracken, slunk up the stairs from her warm spot by the kitchen hearth. I let her in. What harm can it do? She curls at my feet. I find comfort in her warmth, her gentle snores. Thankfully, Sam is silent and sleeping. And, despite my promises, tiredness overtakes me.

I wake with a start. Some hours must have passed. The candle has burned down, the wind got up. Bracken is on her feet by my side, teeth bared, making a low growl. She's tense, quivering, ready to spring, snarling as she does when a fox comes after our hens. I rub sleep from my eyes. 'What is it, girl?'

Then I see what has disturbed her – the child-shaped figure that plagued me in the summer is there beside the hearth: the fire screen. In the dim light and flickering shadow, its features take on form and movement, the boy's expressionless face weirdly menacing above the ruffed white collar and high-buttoned doublet of an earlier age. He seems to stare right at me.

I'm suddenly alert, gripped by fear and confusion. How can this be? I swear it was not there earlier. I thought the thing was gone – Agnes promised me she would destroy it.

Bracken growls, jaws beginning to foam. Sam stirs, mumbles something and I push myself up and go to him, forcing down the shock, trying to ignore the cold dread that slides up my spine: the child in my care is the most important thing now.

Sam's eyelids flutter and his lips work as he struggles to rid himself of the coverlet. I put a hand to his forehead and it comes back slick with sweat, so I reach for the fresh linen that Dority laid out, douse it in the bowl of cool water next to the bed, wring it out and press it to his forehead, trying to soothe him.

Bracken barks.

'Quiet, girl,' I tell her. 'You'll wake him.' But it does not help. She looks from me to the fire screen, barks again, louder this time.

Sam cries out – a high-pitched wail, laden with fear and sadness – the sound of nightmares. Again, I press the damp linen to his forehead. He begins to thrash about. I try to catch his hands, saying, 'Sam, it's me. It's Mercy. I'm here.'

Bracken is crouching now, ready to spring, hackles up, but Sam begins to moan and mutter words I cannot understand, jumbled sounds and cries of fear. He fights against me, pushes me away.

'Be still, Sam. Please,' I beg.

He opens his eyes but seems to look through me, a different boy, he does not know me. His face is vacant, a death mask. He starts to scream. There is such fear in his eyes, as if he's looked into the jaws of Hell and seen the Devil himself. But then he fixes on me and his expression alters: hateful accusation, burning blame, as if I'm the cause of his distress. It's just the fever, I tell myself, but, God forgive me, I'm frightened. I'm terrified of this poor child.

He starts to kick and shout, beating his hands against the bed, while Bracken barks and snarls. I shout at her to stop but it only makes it worse. She snaps at my boots, teeth sinking into leather. She tugs, growling low, as if she would pull me from the room. I kick her away. Then, from the corner of my eye, I see that the fire screen has moved.

It now stands about three strides from the fire, between the casement and the foot of the bed. And yet, it is still turned towards me, staring, eyes fierce with that same blameful look I've just witnessed in Sam.

Blood turns in my veins, icy as a winter brook.

Sam starts to cry, face flushed and sweating, while Bracken sets up a vicious barking, snarling at the screen as if it were a demon sent from Hell. And I swear, beneath the racket, I hear it, the noise that has tormented me for months: the dull *thunk* upon the floorboards, the horrid slow scrape.

Something inside me snaps, like a broken dam when the storms come. I press my hands over my ears. I cannot help myself. 'Stop! For God's sake, just stop!'

The door slams open and Dority appears, a look of utter dismay on her face. She runs to the bed and pins Sam's arms to his side. 'Sam. Look at me. It's all right. I'm here. Look at me.'

She brings me back to myself.

I stumble across the room and hoist the fire screen onto one shoulder. With my free hand I grab hold of Bracken's collar and drag her away. As I leave, Dority shoots me a look that says: *See? I knew I could not trust you.*

Outside, the night is clear, lit by a bright waxing moon. I toss the fire screen by the woodpile and pull Bracken, still frenzied, still barking loud enough to disturb any sleeping creature within a mile, towards the stables. As we reach the door she plants her feet, pulling against me, growling low, and this time directed at me. She rarely disobeys me and I curse at her, all my frustration and fear now embodied by this creature that will not bend to my will. She wriggles and twists, like a wild thing, turns her head to snap at my hand – something she's never done before – but I manage to drag her into a stall and tether her there with a length of rope.

'You'll stay there till morning,' I tell her, slamming and bolting the stable door as I leave, too enraged to care about the pitiful whining she begins, or the stamping and snorting of agitated horses.

I fetch the brazier and set it up on a patch of ground near the burned-out barn, out of sight of the stables, but still within earshot. I can hear Bracken, scrabbling against the door of the stall, complaining at her punishment. I fetch kindling and flame from the kitchen hearth and set a blaze. Then I take up an axe and chop the fire screen into pieces. Into each blow I pour all of my fury, railing against God as the blade splinters the wood. When the thing is split into a hundred shards, I feed them all into the flames.

I stay there some time, wanting to make sure the fire takes the thing whole, listening as Bracken eventually falls silent, until there are no more cries of anguish from Sam's chamber, until the flames have blackened and devoured every last fragment of that foul painted figure.

My mind is wild with questions, yet I find no answers. I run a list of all the unexplained things that have happened: the coins, still missing from the pouch beneath my bedchamber floor, the macabre death of the lambs, the noises by night, the footsteps when no one is there, the handprints in my father's room, the glimpses of that pale figure, just out of sight. I think back to the February day I first saw the figure in the fog and the threat that has haunted me ever since. I think of Father's speedy decline and the unfathomable guilt that has consumed him. Am I to suffer the same fate, driven mad by something I cannot understand? It's clear now: something wants us gone.

A wiser woman would flee. She would snatch hold of the plan to sell and wring any chance of a new life from it. But the thought is abhorrent to me. What others might see as escape would be the opposite. My very soul is entwined with this place – I feel I would perish elsewhere. The blood in my veins is the spring that silvers the fell, my breath the moor-top wind, my heartbeat the very pulse of the earth. I am bound to it and it to me.

Tears of anger and frustration begin to spill. I cannot go on like this and yet I cannot leave.

I do not hear Ellis coming but he's suddenly beside me, still dressed in his outdoor coat and hat, crook in hand, returning from his night-time vigil on the fell. He stands, face lit by flames, waiting for me to explain. But how can I?

I swallow tears – I do not want him to think he is the cause. I long to throw myself upon his mercy, to share my agony, to ask for help. But stubborn pride stops me.

He waits in silence then warms his hands over the blaze and says. 'Likely there'll be first frost tonight.'

I do not speak, for fear that a desperate plea will spill out of me. I leave him there and go back inside, trusting the flames to turn the remnants of the fire screen to ashes.

* * *

I cannot bear Dority's blameful looks, so I snatch what rest I can in the chair before the kitchen hearth, Bracken's blanket for my coverlet. Agnes wakes me at dawn. 'Come,' she says, beckoning me up the stairs and into the bedchamber where I find Dority, a new smile lighting her face, and Sam, milk-white and weak but sitting, the scarlet flush gone.

I think I must still be dreaming but Dority reaches out a hand and says, 'Our prayers have been answered, Mercy. The fever has broken. He's going to be well.'

The turmoil of the night before seems now a distant dream. A nightmare. A weird half-laugh, half-cry bursts forth, the feeling awkward and unfamiliar. I look around the room, at the thin winter dawn streaming through open shutters, the fire aglow, the small pale child propped against the pillows, and it feels unreal. Can this be the same room in which I witnessed such horror? How much did I conjure myself? I take Sam's small, chilly hand in my own. He looks up at me and whispers, 'Thank you.'

The sun rises bright and clear. I leave the house early and pause to watch the last of the curled brown leaves floating from the willows. The hens are scratching for worms in the leaf fall, squabbling and chuckling. The air is crisp, the sky pale blue as a starling's egg. Ellis was right – the hills are crowned with a dusting of frost, as if the world were made anew.

I pass by the brazier, burned out now, nothing left but ashes. Could it be so simple? Was it the fire screen that contained the curse? Sam's sudden recovery seems too strange a coincidence.

I make for the stables, my heart lighter than it's been for weeks. I will walk the fells with Ellis today. We'll go to the cottage and tell Ambrose the good news. We'll make a new plan for the winter. We'll discuss how to pasture the sheep and replant the kitchen beds with a winter crop. Perhaps I'll take Sailor, Father's old mount, down to the village and see if I can get a few coins for him.

or barter him for grain. Though his working years are done, someone in a kinder clime may find use for him yet.

I unbolt the stable door, expecting the usual enthusiastic greeting from Bracken. I've forgiven her, of course – after all, a dog will mirror her master and I cannot blame her for my own fears and tempers. But she's silent. There's no friendly yapping, no wriggling warm body, no wet nose pushed into my hand, no tail sweeping against my calf. It takes a moment for my eyes to adjust after the brightness of the day.

Her poor limp body is strung up from the post to which I tethered her, the rope looped about her neck. Her eyes are closed, tongue bulging, fleshy and sluglike, from her foam-flecked jaw. The post is covered with scratches and her claws are bloodied.

My legs give out and I sink to the floor, knees in a pile of Bracken's muck.

For every life, something else must die.

After a time, I pull myself up and gently, tenderly, bring Bracken's body down. The rope is twisted about her neck and twice around the post. There is no chance she could have done it to herself. This was no accident.

I remember that she fell silent as I burned the fire screen. The sounds of a struggle would have been drowned by the crackle of flame and by my own whirling thoughts. Everyone but Ellis was indoors. The image of him, appearing out of the darkness, comes back to me, but I cannot believe he would do this. There is no sense in it. Bracken trusted him and the bond between them was second only to my own. But, still, a seed of doubt is planted, takes root and begins to grow.

I tell no one what I've seen. I wrap Bracken's body in an old grain sack and carry her to the willow copse. There, I slowly dig a grave in the hard winter ground. It's customary to burn the bodies of livestock but I cannot bring myself to set her aflame. She'll not leave this life burned in the brazier in the ashes of that cursed figure. I want her to become part of the land that made her. So, I lay her out and cover her with earth, pausing only a moment to say my own silent prayers.

Then, I fetch a bucket of water and return to the stable to scrub away the traces of her end – the stinking muck on the floor, the traces of blood upon the post. I can do nothing about the scratches – they will have to stay, a reminder, till I can find a way to hide them.

I know that others would not do as I have done. Others might cry out their grief, hurl accusations and bring horror down upon the house, but this house already has its share of horrors. One more might tip the balance. I will shoulder this alone. I'll wait till I'm alone with Ellis and only then confront him. I will tell them all that Bracken died in peace.

It's not hard to tell the lie: instead of breaking, my heart turns to stone, as I lock it back inside its cage.

'Are you sure, Mercy? Are you sure he'll be safe?' Dority's gaze wanders once more to the casement of the bedchamber, where Sam still rests. We're standing by the gatepost. She's shivering in a thick winter cloak. Though Sam has made good progress, his mother has not. It seems that, as Sam gains strength, Dority grows weaker. She's giving her very lifeblood to him.

'Perhaps I should stay,' she says, searching my face for the permission she craves.

'We've been through this. Sam will be well looked after here, and you can come every day, but Ambrose and Grace need you now, more than he.'

She looks away, lips white and thin. 'Ambrose doesn't understand.'

'You mustn't let this come between the two of you,' I say. 'God has been merciful this time. Be thankful.'

'I know you're right,' she says, looking up to the window once more. 'It's just so hard to be parted from him.'

'He's still too weak to travel. He's better here.'

'But I want him close.'

I take her hands in mine. 'I'll look after him, I promise.'

She manages a rare smile. Since Sam began his slow recovery, she's forgiven me for much. Our old friendship is returning. 'There's no one else I'd trust. You know that, don't you?'

I nod.

Ambrose, standing a distance away with baby Grace, is growing impatient. He strides towards us, studying the sky. 'Snow's coming,' he says. 'We must go now.'

He's right – the clouds are low and flat, tinged with yellow. The air has the strange stillness that comes before snowfall.

Dority squeezes my hand. 'Look after my boy,' she whispers.

As she goes, she keeps turning back, eyes fixing on the bedchamber window. I cannot help but look up myself, and as I do, I catch a movement behind the glass, a pale figure, with a hand pressed to the panes: Sam, standing there, watching his mother walk away.

I go up to the room to make sure he's not upset but find him in bed, sleeping and peaceful. There is no one else in the room.

I go to the window and look out, press my own fingers to the glass. The air smells of burning, of tallow fat and bonfires. Ambrose and Dority make their way down the coffin path. I see Ambrose put his arm around his wife and draw her close.

As I watch, the first flakes fall, soft and white, drifting from Heaven like blossom on the wind. The snow does not stop for three days.

Chapter 38

They set out early. The snow is still falling in fat, lazy flakes but they cannot wait any longer. If sheep are buried in the drifts, they can last a day or two, huddled together beneath the snow, protected by the grease in their fleeces, but any longer and they will start to freeze or starve.

Mercy woke him at first light, already wrapped in thick worsted breeches and a long leather coat. By the time he reached the kitchen there was a pan of oats steaming on the hearthstone, next to a heavy iron shovel, and she had already cleared a path to the gate.

Outside, the air tastes like winter. The trees in the copse are snow-laden, low branches sweeping the ground. He pulls his hat down against the icy pinpricks on his cheeks and draws his woollen neckerchief up over his nose. The fell-side above the house is an ocean of white. Nothing moves except the wind, gusting snowflakes in flurries and whorls. All life is silent and still.

Ellis follows her as she struggles past the ruins of the barn. The snow comes up to his knees, much deeper where it has drifted against walls and banks. With the scorched ground hidden, the barn looks like an ancient ruin, something from a long-abandoned past, but he has not forgotten the urgent fear of that night, the stench of singed fleece and burning beams that finds its way into

his dreams. Neither has he forgotten Henry Ravens's triumphant
smile that day outside the church. He would like the chance to
confront him, to accuse him, though he knows that no one will
believe, now, that the fire was begun by mortal hand. He is not
even sure he believes that himself. Still, he is glad that Ravens is
gone, any ties between he and Mercy irrevocably severed; he has
won that battle at least.

As they make their way onto the fell he catches up with her.
'We need a dog,' he says. It could sniff out sheep beneath feet of
snow. 'Can we not fetch Garrick's?'

'It's too far. We'd spend most of the day getting there. Besides,
Flint will only work for him. She's not like Bracken.'

It is the first time she has said the dog's name since she told
him about its death, and he hears the catch in her throat. *Must've
died in her sleep*, she had said, in front of the others, fixing him with
a piercing stare. *I've already buried her.*

She has been withdrawn and sullen since. He's sure she's lying,
keeping something back, and he's been waiting for this chance
alone with her. 'What truly happened?' he asks.

She gives him a slantwise glance but says nothing. She knows
what he means.

'I know it was not as simple as you say.'

'Do you know something about it?'

'I know you've not told the truth.'

'And how do you know that?'

'It's clear to anyone who cares to see.'

'You were the only one abroad that night.' She says it quietly,
but he does not miss the accusation in her tone.

'You think I'm to blame?'

Again she looks at him, staring hard this time, searching for
evidence.

'How can you think that?' he says.

She does not reply. She's silent as they struggle over a ridge and across a frozen beck. It's impossible to keep to a path so they strike up towards the walls of a fold, where it's likely the sheep might have sought shelter.

He cannot let the subject drop. He may be to blame for other things, but not this. 'You admit what you told the others was a lie?'

She stops, breathing hard, and looks back the way they've come. Scarcross Hall is lost in the swirl of snowfall. They are totally alone. 'I spared the details.'

'You're wrong about me. But I'd hear the truth. I won't repeat it, if that's what you want.'

She pulls the neckerchief down, takes a fistful of snow and rubs it on her face, puts another handful in her mouth. Then she pauses, breath steaming. 'Someone strung her up by the neck and left her there to die,' she says, without emotion. 'I thought perhaps it was you.' She waits while he takes this in. 'Won't you defend yourself?'

'Nothing I say will make you change your mind. But tell me this: what reason would I have?'

She sighs, exasperated. 'If I knew that, you'd be long gone.'

'You should know me better than that by now,' he says.

She raises one sceptical eyebrow.

'You still don't trust me,' he says.

He knows what she's thinking – can see it writ clear – because he thinks the same: *I trust no one but myself.*

Lately, though, he's been doubting even that. Perhaps that's why he so craves her faith in him – to restore his own. It's pointless, he thinks, when he will betray her in the end, but he cannot help himself: he is powerless against this desire.

She's still staring at him as if trying to read his thoughts. If this is some sort of test, he's afraid he's failed it. Then she turns away and sets off up the slope. 'We've no dog. We do this alone.'

They find nothing at the first fold. Mercy sinks her crook almost to the bow, but there are no animals buried beneath the snow banked up against the walls. So they go on to the next, further up the fell.

The day continues like this. They find patches where sheep have nosed their way through to the heather, a gorse bush that has been stripped clean – signs of life amid the desolate whitewashed landscape. They find ragged little groups of sheep here and there, in threes and fours, sheltering in gullies, or on the leeward side of boulders and outcrops, some carrying a blanket of snow. They are docile, bleating for hay, made keen by the cold. There is nothing they can do for them except check them over and leave them to God's mercy.

They stick to the lower slopes, reasoning that the sheep will have migrated down to seek out shelter, and some time in the mid-afternoon they come to the abandoned cottage. As they draw close, Ellis is sure they'll find sheep buried here. This is exactly the kind of place they would wander, and its position catches the whip of the wind from the moor top, as it whistles down into the valley, so the drifts are deep.

They pause on the hillside, overlooking the crumbling walls of house and fold. He stands beside her, lungs burning, legs aching, feet and fingers turned blue and numb. She looks away, gaze sweeping the fell above, squinting into the wind, looking for something. Then she bends over, leans her weight on her crook and makes a rasping cough. He knows she will not admit that she's exhausted.

She wipes spittle on the back of her glove. 'We should turn back soon,' she says. 'Before night falls.'

'There's a good hour of light yet.'

'It'll take us that long to get home.'

An hour of struggling through snow so deep it's soaked his boots and breeches to the waist. 'Let me check here, then we'll go back,' he says, the conviction building that this place is important.

'No, it's useless. I can't see any tracks,' she says, impatient.

'Wait here, then.'

He leaves her, climbs and slides down the bank towards the cottage, landing in a drift. He loses his hat on the way and has to scrabble back up on his hands and knees to retrieve it. Mercy scans the fell, alert, agitated, keen to move on.

The snow is banked high on the windward side and he goes there first. It's too deep to stand, halfway up to what's left of the rafters, so he uses his crook to push down further into the drift. The wood goes straight through to stone. He tries again, working his way around the cottage to the gap where the front door once stood. He remembers this place on the night he found Bartram Booth with Silas and Joan Goffe and their ragged brood, and wishes that Booth had never encountered them. Still nothing.

Something tells him not to give up. He's had feelings like this before, perhaps when a ewe will lamb before her time, perhaps when the flies might strike or when a rogue dog is worrying the flock. It's a shepherd's knowledge, more instinct than sense. He had it the first time he saw her, that knowing, deep in his bones.

He makes his way to the far end of the building where a small barn once housed livestock. There is no roof at all here and most of the walls are crumbled away, but two still stand and it's in this corner that he plunges the crook once more into the drifts. And this time, it meets something soft and pliable that shifts when he presses gently against it.

He moves a few steps along and tries again, meeting resistance, about an arm's length beneath the snow: there are animals here. He unties the shovel strapped across his back and makes a tunnel. Sure enough, not two feet in, he finds fleece.

'Down here!' he calls, beckoning Mercy.

She comes, slithering down the slope, sees what he's found and, without a word, starts to dig.

★ ★ ★

They save thirteen sheep, most of them ewes in lamb and all suffering. As each one is released, it wanders away, dazed, to where the others gather against the wall of the cottage.

By the time they are done, dusk is falling. They have no lamp, no dog and no food. There is nothing more they can do. Ellis clears a way to the front door and, with whistles and crook, herds the wretched bunch inside.

Then they set off along the valley, hoping to meet the coffin path and the quickest way back to Scarcross Hall. As darkness falls, the snow starts to come down heavily and they tie themselves together with a length of rope. Mercy is silent for a long time, but he knows what she's thinking, because he can sense it, as he always can these days, and knows she must be able to feel it too: someone is watching them.

At last they reach home. At the gate in the wall that leads to the kitchen door, she stops. She unties the rope from around her waist and lets it drop. He collects it, unties it from around his own, a weird tug in his belly at their parting.

'I do believe you,' she says. 'I know you wouldn't hurt Bracken. It's just—' She stops short but all the things she won't admit fill the space: *It's just that I cannot explain the things that have happened, that I do not know who to trust, that I am afraid.*

'I know,' he says, wanting to reassure her.

She looks at him, questioning.

'But you do not have to face it all alone,' he says.

He manages a smile, and this time, he sees something shift in her eyes: desperate hope – gratitude – behind her cold, unfeeling gaze.

Chapter 39

I take Agnes's chair beside the kitchen hearth and Ellis pulls up a stool. We try to encourage some warmth back into our frozen limbs. Father is safe, nested in the parlour. Agnes has gone to bed. She's given Sam a draught that will keep him sleeping until dawn, and tells me he's been quiet ever since, so I leave him be. The house is stilled. There's no sound from empty chambers, no trip upon the stair, no patter across the boards by unseen feet. Scarcross Hall seems lulled by the blanket of snow and, for once, I'm glad to be indoors.

But the peace only serves to heighten my nerves. Today has been one of the hardest and most dangerous I can remember. Snowfall can hide deathtraps. I've known men fall into gullies and suffocate in the drifts or lie broken-backed and frozen, tricked by the ever-shifting landscape they thought they knew. My muscles ache and throb, my hands are chapped and raw, fingers pricking and burning as they thaw. But despite my weariness, my mind is wild as a tempest.

All day I've watched Ellis at work, been humbled by his skill, strength and sacrifice, witnessing what he's willing to risk for me. I was mistaken to think he could have had anything to do with Bracken's death. I doubted him because I could not face the truth – that her death might be a sign of more to come.

One coin marks the first to go . . .

I think of that first golden coin, found beneath Sam's pillow, and the boy who has, so far, escaped his brother's fate. But he's still weak, a shadow of himself.

A second bodes the fall.

The second coin, discovered by Ellis in the barn. Watching him today, I can hardly believe he's in any danger. But sturdy health did not help Bracken, or John Bestwicke.

The third will seal a sinner's fate.

Agnes. Poor Agnes – frightened, frail and distracted, but who refuses to leave my father's side. I understand why she'll not think of deserting us – even if the snow had not blocked her path, she's bound to this place just as I am, if for different reasons.

All day too I've been consumed by the question I must ask Ellis and how best to do so. Father's health is failing day by day. I'm running out of time. I'm certain now that my best chance of a future here rests with Ellis. There is no one else. But I fear he'll turn from me, as he turned from me before.

Agnes has left a pot of broth warming on the hearthstone, and after we've eaten in silence, Ellis leaves the room without a word. At first I think my moment has passed, but after a minute or two he returns, bottle of brandy in hand, fetched from Father's study. He shouldn't have taken it, but as he uncorks the bottle and pours two measures into pewter cups the smell is pungent and seductive. I take one gladly as he joins me by the fire.

'Drink,' he says, though I need no encouragement. 'It'll ease you.'

Can he sense the flurry of my heart?

I feel the heat of the brandy, like hot water flooding my veins, as it warms and loosens me. I do not know how to begin and do so clumsily. 'Thank you for what you did today.'

A shrug. 'I did my job.'

'Not many would work so hard without pay.'

'What kind of shepherd would I be if I abandoned my flock to the weather?' He stands briefly, fetches down a box of tobacco from the shelf. I take a pipe and fill the bowl.

'You're the best shepherd we've had.'

He looks at me with surprise, eyes flashing with something like pride.

'It's true,' I say. 'Even Ambrose cannot better you. How did you know where to dig?'

He's made awkward by my praise, turning away to kindle a rush light at the fire.

I push, wanting to prise him open, so that I might glimpse behind that inscrutable mask. 'You sensed it, didn't you? You knew where to find them.'

He avoids my eyes, lights his pipe, then hands the rush to me. 'It's not something I know by words.'

I put the flame to the tobacco and take a long draw, the taste charred, woody, reassuring. 'John Bestwicke used to speak of the shepherd's nose,' I say. 'He told me that a true flock man could sniff out problems at a hundred paces. Not many have the skill, but I think you do.'

'It's something like that, perhaps.'

'Well, I'm glad of it. I cannot do without you now.' I drain my brandy, reach for the bottle, fill both cups again. The stuff is doing its work, my fingers tingling with returning heat. It makes me bold – bold enough to ask the questions I must.

'Ellis, I must know – do you plan to leave come the spring?'

He shoots me a look of refusal but I will not let him disappear behind that silent wall again.

'You told me before that you choose to stay here because you've found somewhere that suits you, but till now, you've spent your life moving from place to place. It sounds to me as if you're running from something. And some might say Scarcross Hall is a good place to hide. But things have changed since you first arrived . . .'

He sucks on the thin white stem of his pipe, a fug of smoke blooming about his head.

'We live apart from the world here,' I go on, 'and I know you're not blind to the things that have happened. We're alone. Cast out. Shunned by those who should help us. And no man chooses to live alone, unless he has a reason.'

'You choose it.'

'I'm born to it. I know nothing else.'

'And why should I not be the same?' He looks at me at last and I see something stir in his eyes. 'Do you wish me to leave?'

'No. I'm trying to understand what makes you stay, when you know it's not safe.'

He rests his pipe on the hearthstone and takes a swig of brandy, stares into his cup for a long time, then places it carefully next to his pipe. Without looking at me, he reaches across and puts one hand on top of mine.

Seconds run by and neither of us speaks. My heart grows wild. He's staring into the fire, but I see the nervous twitch at the corner of his eye and know that this is his way of saying the things he does not have courage enough to voice. I will have to be brave for him.

'I've something to ask you.'

He withdraws his hand, still staring into the flames.

'Will you stay for good?'

He says nothing.

'Will you stay as my husband?'

He blinks, still refusing to look at me. No doubt he's shocked by my boldness but I no longer care. He knows me for what I am and will either love me or despise me for it, but I cannot go on any longer without knowing which it will be.

There is a long silence, disturbed only by the crackle and hiss of the fire. Then he stands slowly, careful not to touch me, and takes a few steps away, turns and plants his palms on the tabletop.

He is going to refuse me. My courage falters. I must make him understand.

'I must marry,' I say, the words strange and awkward in my mouth. 'And my husband will be master of Scarcross Hall. He'll be master here until our son can take his rightful place as my father's heir. What you told me about my father's plans – you were right.'

Ellis nods slowly, though he does not turn back.

'So, I must have a man who understands how things must be – a man who will be master in name but who will work alongside me, as an equal. I may not be a proper wife – I'm not made that way – so I need a man who knows me for what I am.'

Still he is silent.

'I'm offering you a great deal. I'm offering you all I have, in return for that understanding.'

At last he turns to me and his eyes are all turmoil. 'Why me?'

'Because I think you *are* that man.'

I push myself up from the chair and go to him. His gaze softens. I read in him the same longing that lives in me. Why does he not take me in his arms? I've laid bare my heart, yet he still will not open his. Surely he must see what it costs me to say these things. He must understand that I'm trusting him with so much more than the Hall and the land and the Booth name – I'm trusting him with my most treasured possession: my freedom.

He reaches out a single finger and strokes my cheek. Such a gentle touch for so calloused a hand. My hope takes flight. But then a cloud passes behind his eyes, his brow furrows once more and he hangs his head.

'I cannot,' he says, turning away and going back to the hearth where he leans against the mantel.

My heart is squeezed against my ribs and the words come out as little more than a whisper. 'Why not? What is it that you're hiding?'

'I cannot,' he repeats.

'Is there another? Are you not free?'

'It's not that.'

'Is it because of Henry Ravens? Because I'm not a maid?'

He shakes his head. 'No. You are the best woman I know.'

'Then why do you not wish it?'

'I wish it more than anything.' He spits the words as if they are a curse. There's no affection, just anger, as if he blames me for making him want this thing.

I can take no more. I go to him and force him to face me, one hand on each shoulder.

'What is it? What is it that you cannot tell me? I know there is something—'

I'm stopped short by the violence in his expression. I see the desire in him: a winter storm, raging and hungry.

Before I can speak again he grips my arms and pulls me roughly to him. There's no tenderness in his embrace, just desperate, ravenous need. His kiss is hard and urgent and steals my breath.

I had forgotten how it feels – lip on lip and mouth on mouth, the liquor-laced sourness of him, the scent of sweat and skin and peat smoke and sheep grease. It is like tasting the moor.

When I hear the crash of shattering glass I think at first it's the sound of everything falling away – all the walls I've built, all the lies I've told myself; that I want no one, that I've no need of love, that no man can touch my hard, unyielding heart. In that moment, when my soul speaks to his, and his to mine, I see the truth: the thing is already done. And it is beauty and pain all at once.

The sound comes a second time and he pulls away. I'm reeling, breathless, struggling to right myself. I'm speechless, beginning to shake – shocked by the torrent of feeling in me, but then the noise comes again and I'm tethered, pulled back down to earth. It's unmistakable this time: breaking glass, the musical cadence as it falls and shatters, a hundred discordant notes on stone flags.

He snatches up a candle and reaches the door of the kitchen before me.

The hall is made bright by moonlight on snow. Fragments of glass glint upon the flags. Three panes are smashed in the big leaded window. Amid the spill of glass lie three small pebbles.

The next startles me, like a gunshot. As shards of glass shatter I see the gleam of something metallic spin across the floor.

I start towards the front door, but Ellis catches my sleeve and pulls me back, shaking his head. 'Don't.'

Another smash, another shower of glass.

'I must stop it,' I say, trying to pull away, but he holds me fast and I know any action is futile. There cannot be anyone outside. The coffin path is blocked. There's no one about for miles. This is not youths from the village playing a cruel game, or our mortal enemies trying to scare us. A shiver of horror cascades down my spine and I strain to see through the window. Who – what – is out there?

There's nothing to see.

Another pane cracks and falls, splinters of glass exploding towards me.

A door opens above and Agnes appears on the gallery, in nightgown and shawl, washed ghostly pale, knuckles white as bone on the banister.

'Can you see anyone?' I call up to her, but she just stands there, aghast.

Another crash, a waterfall of glass. This time I watch a small round disc roll across the flags till it halts not three feet from where I stand.

The door to the parlour slams open and Father appears, barefoot, hair flying, eyes bright with shock. As he takes in the broken window and the mess of shards he looks horror-struck. So I run to him, glass crunching beneath my feet, dodging falling splinters as another two panes are shattered.

'Come back inside,' I say, trying to pull him away, but he's fixed on the window, eyes straining into the dark. He will not move.

'They've come for me,' he whispers.

'Please, Father, come away, it's not safe.'

'It's time. They've come to take me.' He turns to me and his eyes are those of another, conflicted with expectation and intense sadness: my father is not to be found there. I cannot bear it.

He pulls me towards him and holds me tight, as he has not done since I was a child. He whispers, so only I can hear, 'Forgive me, Mercy, but I must go to them. Forgive me . . .'

'Stop it!' Agnes cries into the dark space of the hall. 'For pity's sake, leave us be!'

As if in answer, there is a volley of three stones and three more panes cascade to the floor.

'God save us.' Agnes drops to her knees and starts to pray. '"O God the Father of Heaven: have mercy upon us miserable sinners . . ."'

Father releases me and takes up the prayer. '"O God the Holy Ghost: have mercy upon us miserable sinners . . ."'

There is another crash, icicles of falling glass, and a small golden coin spins across the flags, landing at Father's feet. I know what it is and what it means.

He drops to his knees, transfixed by the coin. He looks wild, terrified, on the verge of madness.

'"From all evil and mischief; from sin, from the crafts and assaults of the Devil; from thy wrath, and from everlasting damnation, good Lord, deliver us . . ."'

The sight of him pushes away any remaining sense. I kneel and join the prayer. There is nothing else to do.

'"Good Lord, deliver us. Good Lord, deliver us. Good Lord, deliver us . . ."'

I cannot close my eyes or bow my head – I'm too afraid, flushed cold with fear. As our voices swell above the moan of the wind, Ellis looks straight at me. I feel his stare as something physical, a brutal wound in my chest.

'"Lord, have mercy upon us. Christ, have mercy upon us. Lord, have mercy upon us . . ."'

Then, as suddenly as it had begun, there is silence. I feel the moment that it leaves, like the unclenching of a tight grip, an exhalation of long-held breath, and I know that it is over.

Some time near midnight, after hours of prayer, Agnes and Father are persuaded to their beds. Sam, lulled by the sleeping draught, has not stirred. When I look in on him, there's no sign of disturbance. The chamber is chill, still perfumed with the underlying taint of burning, but Sam is peaceful.

I go back to the hall. Ellis is there, leaning against the wainscot next to the hearth, as if he's been waiting for me. He's swept the broken glass into a pile by the window. All is quiet. A cutting night breeze whistles through the broken panes, and the bitter snow-bound air is sharp on my tongue. I go to the window, compelled to look out into the night, but afraid of what I might see. There is nothing, save the snow and the pale blue moon. Whatever was out there has toyed with us enough for tonight.

I turn to face Ellis, ignoring my frozen, prickled skin, and nudge the shards of glass with my toe. He knows what I seek and comes towards me, opening his palm. He has collected the stones, each a small round pebble, worn and stream-smoothed, the kind you find in the becks. Among them, three golden discs, patterned with strange horned figures. I pick out the coins. They are cold as midwinter on the moor top.

Ellis watches me in silence. I meet his gaze, waiting for him to speak, waiting for him to voice the fearful ungodly thoughts that poison my mind, waiting for an answer to the question I asked of him. He places the rest of the stones on the table, takes my hand in his and folds my fingers to cradle the coins. With the breath of the moor winding about us he looks at me as if he does not know what to say, eyes all confusion, then pulls me towards the staircase.

When we reach the door to his chamber, he pauses. I think: *this is it*. He will give me his answer now and I will take him into my bed, both of us finding the sanctuary we yearn for in each other.

But instead he brings my fingers to his lips and places a single kiss, gentle, chaste, all the wild passion of our moment before the fire gone.

He releases me. 'I cannot,' he says quietly.

Then he turns, goes into his chamber and shuts the door. I hear the latch fall.

I stand, dumbstruck, as my heart splinters, to lie among the glass on the stone flags of Scarcross Hall.

The next morning is dull, the sky heavy with cloud. Sleepless, I step outside at dawn, before the others rise, and taste the coppery tang of the snow-cloaked hills. The world is eerily quiet. There is no birdsong. Protected by the boundary wall, the snow is only ankle-deep at the front of the house. I stop outside the big window. On the glass I find small, child-sized handprints, etched in the frost. And there, in the snow, a set of child's footprints, leading from the window out through the gate and away towards the coffin path. There is a second set – larger, an adult's this time – following alongside.

Two hours later, I discover that Father is gone.

Chapter 40

As he follows her out onto the fell, the snow starts to fall again. At first the flakes are large and lazy, drifting as if a host of angels had shaken their wings, but soon they come thick and fast, settling on frozen ground and beginning to cover the tracks they are following.

A lone crow flaps in the willow copse, making a ragged, mournful cry as they pass. On far-off slopes he glimpses grey specks in the snow; sheep huddled under gorse bushes and beneath the crags. There is no scurry of small creatures through the heather, the moor birds are long since flown and the few that remain find shelter in the valley. Even the becks snaking down the hillside are silvered and solid.

She walks ahead of him, bundled in layers of wool, snow up to her shins, leather-gloved hand gripping her crook. She does not look at him. She has not looked him in the eye since last night. She has closed in on herself, seeming to have no other thought than for Bartram Booth.

He cannot blame her. He expects – even welcomes – the shunning because he deserves it. She gives nothing away but he knows she must be smarting the same as he. His own feelings are a blizzard.

He is angry with himself, for his recklessness, for doing the hing he swore he would not do but, at the same time, he clings to the memory, savouring it: the taste of brandy and tobacco on her lips, the hot, slick wetness of her tongue. She has not mentioned it again – the thing she said. She has been silent and grim since Booth was found to be missing. But the question she asked of him hangs in the air between them and twists in his stomach, like the gripe.

It would solve everything. She is offering him all the things he wants most. But at what cost? If he agrees he will never be able to tell anyone the truth.

Would it be so great a sin? Can he live the rest of his life under the shadow of such a secret? Would he pay for the lie when the final judgement is upon him? But, he reflects, his whole life has been a lie, so what difference would it make now?

She stops up ahead to catch her breath and checks he is still following. Her cheeks are flushed, snowflakes settling on strands of hair come loose from her hat. Her mouth is fixed, eyes cold and grey as the winter sky. He wants her. He wants to possess her – her and everything she stands for.

'The snow is covering the tracks,' she says, 'but no matter – I know where they will lead.'

There is only one place that Bartram Booth would seek. He looks ahead, up the fell-side, to the line where the moor begins. Everything is a sea of white, swirling flakes hiding the stones from view, but he knows they are there, pale statues, wreathed in a winding sheet of snow.

She turns away. 'Father . . .' she whispers, to no one but the moor, and sets off again.

Father. There is so much contained in that breath of a word – all the love, protection and guidance he never had. He had a father once but he does not like to think of him. Now, as he struggles in her wake, he's back there: a campfire, stuttering and hastily lit, the stench of men – sweat, shit, liquor and tobacco – the scratch of a lice-ridden blanket as he curls up in the shadows, keeping out of sight, a child known only as Boy.

'Go find your father,' Betsy had said, taking another man by the hand and leading him into the tent.

He followed his nose, because that's where his father could usually be found – on the other side of the camp near the cooking fires and the beer barrels, furthest from the officers' tents, where small trestles had been set up in a makeshift drinking den. He lingered by the cavalry horses, stopping to stroke the velvety muzzle of his favourite, a fine-limbed bay belonging to the captain, but was chased away by a groom. So he dawdled from fire to fire, watching men eating, arguing, smoking and sleeping, looking for Briggs. Some of the soldiers worked into the night, sharpening knives or cleaning muskets. Others gathered in groups, talking, eyeing the camp whores with hitched skirts outside their tents, listening to the animal grunts of fornication from within. Everywhere the familiar smell of unwashed bodies, the stench of carelessly dug latrines and the putrefying flesh wounds of the dying.

As usual his father was drinking, gaming with the men of his troop, and the one with the black beard who smelled of rotting gums and seemed always to win. Boy wandered over, hovering at his father's shoulder, reading his cards.

'What are you up to?' His father was already drunk – he knew that because the man turned and put his hat clumsily on Boy's head. The bedraggled plume of feathers in the hatband dangled like a shot pheasant.

He said nothing.

'Spying are you, Boy? Working for the enemy?' He aimed a punch at Boy's shoulder, a little too hard to be playful. Boy ducked and the other men laughed. His father didn't like to be laughed at: when he tried again, Boy took the hit and smiled along with the rest.

'Well, make yourself useful,' his father said, pushing a large pewter tankard towards him, slopping the last dregs of ale. 'Fill this.'

Boy took the mug and filled it at the tap. 'For Briggs,' he told the man who asked for payment, and was waved away.

A shout went up from the table as Boy returned. His father cursed. Boy could tell he was losing by the tone of his voice – that sharp edge cutting through the slur of drink.

'You sons of whores! We play again!'

'Come now, Briggs, you've nothing more to lose. Shall I take next month's pay too?' the black-bearded man said.

'No,' Briggs replied, as Boy put the drink on the table. Briggs slapped a hand on his shoulder. 'I'll play for the boy.'

A chorus of laughter.

'I mean it. I'll wager the boy.'

'What use is that scrap to me?'

'He'll fetch and carry for you. He'll do as he's told. He's a good boy, aren't you?' His father looked at him and Boy gave a cautious nod. It was always best to agree with Briggs when he was drunk, no matter what.

The black-bearded man sneered. 'That's not what you've said before.'

'He'll fetch your ale, clean your boots, bring you women. Show him the back of your hand and he'll do anything you ask. Anything at all.' Briggs raised a brow.

'You can't do that. It's not fair on the child,' another man said.

'I can do what I want with him. Who else is there to answer for it?'

'Betsy will have your balls.'

But the black-bearded man was interested. 'I'd have to feed him, clothe him.'

'Ah, he looks after himself. Eats scraps. Doesn't cost me a penny.'

'You can't wager your own son.'

'He's not my son.'

'But what about Betsy?'

'He's one of Betsy's castaways. God knows where he washed up, but he's not my blood, or hers either. But he'll do as he's told. You can do what you want with him. I care not. Be glad to be rid of him.'

Boy watched, wide-eyed, as the two men shook hands. Surely they could not be talking about him. But the black-bearded man studied him, a sly, greedy look in his eye. He watched as they began to turn cards, heard the raucous laughter and the back-slapping but he didn't understand what was happening because there was a buzzing in his head and a hollow feeling in his chest, as if the heart had fallen out of him . . .

When they near the White Ladies she tries to run, but the snow binds her. She stumbles and falls. He tries to catch up with her, to reach the stones first, to save her from what she might find there. Through the whirl of snowfall, he sees a pinpoint of black, stark against winter white.

'Please, God, no . . .' she says, as he draws closer. Then she puts her hands to her face, covering her eyes as if she cannot bear to look.

It is Bartram Booth, of course, leaning against the Slaying Stone, where Ellis had found Sam those few weeks before. The snow is already settling on his coat like a shroud.

'Fetch a horse.'

She has gathered herself but her voice is strangled. She squats next to the body of Bartram Booth, gently dusting snowfall from his shoulders. The old man clutches a small leather shoe in one hand. It is a child's, finely wrought and embroidered. Impractical. He remembers that shoe. He has seen it before. When Mercy sees it, the life seems to go out of her.

'I won't leave you here alone,' Ellis says.

'I'm not alone.' She lifts her fingers to Booth's face and tries to close his eyes. The lids are frozen in an unseeing stare and will not move. Her hand trembles before she snatches it away.

'It would take me hours, even if a horse could get through the snow,' he says, trying to reason with her.

'Do as I say. I'm still your mistress. Fetch a horse.'

'No. I won't leave you. It'll be dusk soon.'

She stares at him, nostrils flaring. 'You dare to disobey me?'

He crouches next to her. 'I don't want to find two bodies on my return.' The snow is still coming down. In less than an hour the light will start to fade. 'We need to go.'

'I won't leave him here.'

He puts a hand on her shoulder and feels her flinch. 'If we don't leave soon, we won't reach the Hall before dark. No one can survive a night on the moor in this weather.'

'I'll not leave him.'

He searches about, desperate to find something, anything, that might be of use, but the moor is swept clean by the snow. He curses himself for lack of foresight. He would give good money for a length of rope or a canvas. The turmoil of mind that consumes him has prevented any useful thought.

'Then we take him with us,' he says.

He pushes his crook into Mercy's hand and levers the old man forward to slide an arm behind him and gain purchase. Booth is too bulky in his thick coat, so he unfastens the buttons to peel it off. Perhaps he can use it to fashion a sled. Beneath, Booth is wearing nothing but a thin nightshirt. The man never had a chance.

He tugs and struggles to pull the coat off, Booth's limbs stiff and awkward. The leather shoe in Booth's hand tumbles to the ground. He sees Mercy look away, notices her lip tremble, but she does not break, and does not pick it up. She takes the coat and steps aside to make space for him to stand and hoist the body onto one shoulder. He slips and staggers under the weight – though Booth is shrunken with age, he is not a small man. Still she does not crack to see her father so mauled and degraded.

Through the nightshirt, he feels the press of bones, the shift of slack flesh. How strange, he thinks, that this is the closest he has ever been to him, and will ever be, in the indignity of death.

There are moments when he falls, when the body slips from his grasp and sprawls, limbs splayed like a carcass ready for butchering, or when they have to drag Booth by his arms or carry him between them. At one point when he falls, he finds himself suddenly face to face, the dead lips almost pressed against his own. But, through it all, she says nothing.

By the time they reach Scarcross Hall, the light is almost gone and every part of his body is screaming. His feet are frostbitten. Every step is a torment, every breath a dagger.

Agnes must be watching for them from Sam's bedside because the door flies open when they are still a hundred yards away and she comes running, stumbling and sliding in the snow.

'Go back inside!' Mercy shouts, but it's useless. Nothing can spare the old woman. Agnes sinks slowly to her knees, as if her legs have given out, skirts ballooning, making an anguished howl, like a fox caught in a trap.

Mercy reaches her, cradles her, rocking her to and fro as though she is the mother and Agnes the child, while Agnes lets out the despair that Mercy will not.

Midnight. The witching hour.

Despite his aching body, Ellis cannot sleep. He is too aware of the corpse on the other side of the wall: Bartram Booth laid out upon his old bed, in his old bedchamber, hands folded neatly across his chest, limbs thawed only to be locked in the grip of death.

He sits on the edge of the narrow bed, leaves the candle burning, listening to the night-time shift and sigh of the house. The snow is falling, the wind eerily still. There is no moan in the chimney, nor rattling at the casements, but Scarcross Hall is never entirely silent, and with each creak of floorboard, each scratch in the walls, he is listening, waiting.

He reaches beneath the bed and pulls out his pack, rummages through his few belongings until he finds the little scrap of cloth that holds the key. He unwraps it, dangling the leather cord so that the gold glints in the candlelight. Then he cradles it in his palm, runs a fingertip around the delicate metalwork, the curled letters, the arrow-straight backbones and the fat round bellies of the double *B*.

Bartram Booth has taken his secret to the grave. Who, now, is left to tell the truth? He supposes he should feel something – grief, perhaps, sadness at least – but there is a lack of these things. He cannot grieve for a man he does not know, a man towards whom he feels only bitterness and blame. But he does know how it feels to lose the one you love most. He knows how it hollows you out. There is a space where such sentiments should be and where, instead, she fits.

Though she thinks she does not show it, her suffering is writ in the crag of her brow, the desolation in her eyes, her bone-hard silence. He would save her that pain, if he could. He would take it as his own, if it were possible.

There is a gentle rap upon the door.

Quickly, he swaddles the key in its ragged cloth and places it back under the bed, heels the pack beneath too, stands and goes to answer.

She is standing there in the dark, in her white nightgown, hair loose about her shoulders. He is always stirred when she shows the woman in her, but now she looks like a girl, fragile and forsaken. Her eyes are red-rimmed, shot through with blood from crying, her cheeks blotched and tear-streaked. She is defeated after all.

There is a brief moment of confusion when he is unsure what she wants. He almost expects anger or accusation, but then she comes towards him and presses herself against his chest. She rests her head on his shoulder and his arms go round her and he feels tears soak through his undershirt to his skin. She does not sob or wail, just sinks against him until her arms creep around his waist and press into his back, pulling him closer.

She is perfectly still while he holds her. He feels her heartbeat racing alongside his own. She raises her head and meets his eye and in that single gesture he sees the open, broken heart that she is offering him and he knows he will take it.

Chapter 41

I rise early, slipping silently from Ellis's bed, making sure he does not stir, and go straight to Father's study. It's as cold as an ice house. Shivering, I lay the fire, bring a lit taper from the embers in the kitchen hearth and coax the kindling to flame.

The desktop is a mess of papers, pamphlets and documents, all smudged with russet stains, amid dried-up inkpots and snapped quills. I start here, taking each paper in turn, holding them up to the candle. There are letters, notes from Jasper Flynn, figures scratched in Ambrose's unpractised hand, maps, crude drawings of sheep that must be Sam's doing, but I cannot find the document that will determine my fate: my father's will.

When the snow melts and we carry my father's body down the coffin path to the churchyard, as we must, it will not take long for word to spread. Then they will come, the lawmen and the chancers, the meddlers and gossips, those with something to gain. But they cannot take Scarcross Hall away from me if they cannot prove Father's intent. When I find the document that confirms the entail, that names his heir, I shall burn it. This new plan, though precarious, is the best I have.

The idea came to me in the night, as I lay in Ellis's arms, bathed in the beams of a snow-bright moon.

'What will you do now?' he whispered, tenderly stroking my hair.

My torn heart ached. 'I don't know. Everything is lost.'

He was silent awhile. Then, 'It's not too late. Not if you marry. Not if you have a son.'

He kissed me deeply. My heart leaped, like a spring lamb. Has he changed his mind? Does he mean to agree to my proposal after all? Though he has not said so, his actions speak for him.

Breaking the kiss, I said, 'Even so, it's too late. I've missed my chance.'

'Then we'll find a way to buy time.'

'How?'

He propped himself on one elbow, running his fingers down my neck and across my throat. 'The name of your father's heir – have you ever seen it written?'

'No.'

'What if . . . what if no one can prove that Scarcross Hall does not belong to you?'

'There is an entail. A will.'

'What if they cannot be found?'

I paused, thinking.

'Your father kept that knowledge close. What if you say nothing? What would happen then?'

'But that would be a lie. A deception.'

'What does it matter, if it serves a greater purpose? Is it not God's will that you remain?'

A tiny spark of light seemed to flare in the darkness. 'You think I should stay silent? You think I should go on as before, as if I know nothing of the entail?'

'Who would question you? Only Agnes knows, and she will stay silent for you.'

'But there will be lawyers. As soon as word spreads—'

'Then we keep the news to ourselves, for as long as we can. And if anyone does come forward, they'll have to fight your claim. Without proof it would take many months, maybe years. And meanwhile . . .' He ran his fingers lower and gently cradled my belly, then bent to kiss me once more.

The memory of his flesh against mine is still vivid. The touch of his skin is on my fingertips, the taste of him on my tongue. He held me as if he would never let go.

In all my years and with all the men who have gone before, I did not know it could be like that – a gentle act, a thing of melancholy and sympathy that does not take away sadness but makes it beautiful, makes it sacred. I think of the care Ellis takes in tending an injured ewe, the deft cross-hatched stitches as he mends the flesh, and imagine he will do the same with my wounded heart. He is part of me now. We cannot go back. He is in my bones; in my blood.

I search for almost an hour, turning over piles of old pamphlets and newsbooks, burrowing through boxes filled with rocks, pebbles and brittle animal bones, becoming increasingly frustrated. I look in cupboards and trunks, even beneath the rush mats, driven by Ellis's words. I find nothing.

Even in my grief, I'm still defiant. I cannot forgive Father for the lies he told, for his weakness, for leaving me alone. I've given my life to this place, to this land and this flock. I cannot imagine a life elsewhere because nowhere else will have me: I simply would not fit. I'm a black sheep, an aberration, not suited to the world beyond. Leaving Scarcross Hall would be like opening me and scooping out my soul. I imagine I would shrivel and die, a thorn bush, deprived of all light. I would not be myself.

But what will it cost me to stay?

I ignore the chaos I've made, go to the window and look out across the white-draped garden, the low wall and the gateposts towards the coffin path. The snow is so deep I cannot make out the lip of the road, where carts and horses, sheep and men have carved their track in the land year upon year, generation upon generation I think of that poor doomed family, trapped here so many winter ago, and wonder if they suffered as we have suffered. I've heard th stories, I know the tales: the three golden coins found in th mouths of those wretched frozen bodies. It cannot be coincidence

My father is dead. The three coins, returned to us that terribl night, are hidden beneath my mattress. Their restoration can mea only one thing. But I understand why that family did not leav when they had the chance. This place is a battleground. The Devi stalks these hills. Whatever curse was placed upon this land bring death and despair and a path down to Hell. But there is also trutl and life. There are glimpses of God's work in the land, a chance c redemption in the rebirth of every spring, proof of His blessing Just like my father before me, I see both Heaven and Hell in th wild open spaces.

Father would tell me to hold on to my faith, to think of th eternal fight, even if, at the end, he surrendered to torment an madness. He would tell me that I must not let the Devil win.

I have to believe that Providence has brought us here. Ou Saviour must have His plan in bringing Ellis and me togethe Jasper Flynn would call me a heretic, a sinner, but I dare to thinl that a meeting of such affinity, of our twinned souls, must b God-given. Could it be a divine gift, strong and pure enough t withstand whatever evil stalks this place?

But if I tell the necessary lie, is the battle already lost? There i more at stake than the fate of Scarcross Hall: the true battle is fo the eternal fate of my soul.

The door opens and I think it's Ellis come to find me but it' Sam. He's still very weak and wasted, freckles bright like a rasl against pallid skin.

'Sam, what are you doing out of bed?'

He shivers. 'Agnes didn't bring my breakfast.'

Agnes has not left Father's side since we laid him out the nigh before. She keeps the vigil that I did not. I chose lust over prayer – yet another sin to add to my account.

'Come by the fire and get warm,' I say. As I lift the blanket from Father's chair the scent of him overwhelms me, my heart plummets, and I have to grip the chair-back a moment before I can move on.

Sam crosses the room, frowning at the littered floor, and takes the seat, wraps himself in the blanket and stretches his bare feet out towards the flames. I kneel and take his small foot in my hands, rubbing some warmth back into it. He watches me at work, his serious little face intent. 'Is Master Booth dead?'

The words are like knives in my gut. 'Yes, Sam.'

'Why did you not come to tell me?'

'You were sleeping. You need to rest.' The truth is, I did not have the strength.

Sam hangs his head and we sit in silence awhile. I expect him to weep but he does not. I take up his other foot to warm it.

'Is it my fault?' he says.

'Of course not. Why should you think so?'

His eyes dart about the room. He's afraid.

'What is it, Sam? Have you something to tell me?'

He leans forward, whispering, 'I thought it was Will.'

I drop his foot and take both his hands in mine. They are shaking. 'What do you mean?'

Again, he looks around the room, as if worried that someone will overhear. His gaze lingers at the window. 'There's someone here,' he says.

'There's no one here but Agnes and Ellis,' I say, though the familiar foreboding begins to worm in my belly.

'No – there's someone else. I thought it was Will, but it's not.'

I think of Sam's strange behaviour these last months, the way he's been distracted and withdrawn, the time I found him playing games with that cursed fire screen in the old bedchamber. I think

of the childlike footsteps in my room and the times I've wondered
the same thing about his brother.

'Sam, you must tell me what you've seen.' He looks uncertain.
'I promise I'll not be angry if you tell me the truth. Have you seen
Will?'

He shakes his head. 'No. But I could hear him. And I could tell
when he was near. I thought . . . I thought he'd come back.' He's
trying so hard not to cry that my heart tugs in sympathy. I know
how badly he must have wanted his brother back, how he must
have yearned for the impossible.

'You must tell me, Sam. When did this begin?'

'When it was cold. Just before this year's lambs came.'

February then – when I first sensed that sinister presence, and
when Ellis arrived.

'And what happened?'

'We'd play together on the moor, like we used to. It was good,
at first . . .'

'And then?'

He struggles to speak. 'He said . . . he said it was my fault.'

'What was your fault, Sam?'

'It's true,' he says, eyes flooding with horror. 'It *was* my fault.'

Shards of broken memory seem to reassemble. 'Are you talking
of Will's accident?'

He nods.

'What happened that day, Sam?'

Again he pauses. Then, quietly, 'I pushed him.'

I am silent, taking this in.

'I pushed him off the Slaying Stone, at the Ladies. It was a
game. I never meant to hurt him . . .'

I hold his hands tight, feeling him tremble.

'I thought he'd come back,' he says again. 'And then he told me
it was my fault he was dead. He was angry with me. He said I had
to make amends. He made me do things.'

'What things?'

He's silent. Button-lipped.

I think of the missing coins, the stolen inkwell, the dead lambs, the child-sized handprints – all the strange and inexplicable events of these past months. Could Sam have been the culprit all along?

'Sam, please. What did he make you do?'

Again, the fearful glance. 'He made me promise not to tell.'

'You can tell me, Sam. I'll not tell another soul.'

'I can't. He said if I tell anyone he'll hurt baby Grace. He'll take her away too.' A single tear escapes from the corner of his eye. 'I thought it was Will, but it can't be, can it? Will wouldn't hurt his sister, would he? Will wouldn't hurt anyone. Will wouldn't let Master Booth die . . .'

Then he breaks down and I hold him tight as he sobs and shakes and cries for his mother.

After a while he calms. He says he's sorry over and over but will not say what he's sorry for. I soothe him by making promises I don't know if I can keep. 'As soon as the snow clears, your ma will be here. Your pa and Grace too. And you can all live here with me. Would you like that? Would you like us all to be together?'

He nods.

'Good. Now, stay by the fire and keep warm – I've work to do.'

He watches, sniffing and wiping his eyes on the blanket, as I return to the desk and resume my search. An idea is forming, a way to banish whatever spirit stalks this place, a way to make a new future for us all. If I'm to have any hope of it, I must first destroy that will.

When a few minutes have passed and I've rechecked and discarded the papers on the desk, cursing with irritation, Sam asks, 'What are you looking for?'

'Something important.'

'Something lost?'

'Not exactly.'

'Something secret?'

'Yes, I suppose so.'

He slides from the chair and pads across the floor. He runs his fingers beneath the lip of the desk. I hear a click as he presses a small indentation. The front panel seems to shift. He takes up a blunt knife – the one Father used to break seals – and slides it into the new gap, levering the panel forward. The whole piece comes away, revealing a small compartment. In amazement, I peer inside. I find a roll of papers, tied with a black cord. I pull them out.

'How did you know?' I ask.

'The master showed me. You said it was secret. This is where secrets are kept.'

With trembling fingers I untie the bow and let the roll of papers unfurl. I clear a space on the desk and spread them out: three or four old documents, ink faded to brown but still clear, penned in a neat notary's hand.

My heart is racing, thoughts clamouring like a hundred church bells. And it's here, his last will and testament, a small piece of parchment, signed by my father and marked with his insignia, the double *B*.

My head swims. I struggle to read. I run my finger along the lines, past the long legal words I do not understand, past a list of property and belongings that I do not recognise, to Father's declaration. All he owns, everything that is his, he leaves to his rightful heir: his only son, Matthew Booth.

Chapter 42

Agnes is sitting by Father's bed, swathes of mismatched cloth spilling over her knees. She has cleaned him and laid him out beneath the coverlet, head resting on the pillow as if he's sleeping. He does not look like himself but like a badly done portrait or effigy. His face is without colour except purplish clefts beneath his eyes and lips black as ink.

As I enter, closing the door behind me, Agnes does not stir, or turn her attention from her needle. The air is icy, no fire in the grate. Frost on the windows gives the light a weird underwater taint. I'm trembling. My breath steams.

I walk to the bedside and look at Father. I want to shake him awake, demand the secrets that he kept from me, but it's too late. There's nothing left of the man I knew.

'How strange it is,' Agnes says sadly, still fixed upon her work, 'that your father made the wool that made the cloth that made other men rich, yet he must make do with a winding sheet of scraps.'

I turn to her. It seems that overnight she's become shrunken and small, half the woman she was, lungs wheezing, eyes rheumy. I've not noticed how, over these last months, she's become desiccated and frail, suddenly old. I've been so absorbed in my troubles I've not seen the changes in her. I see it now, as I'm beginning to see so much, but I don't care.

I hold the document out. 'What do you know about this?'

She rests her needlework in her lap and takes the parchment. 'What is it?'

'Father's will.'

She eyes it a moment, then shakes her head, handing it back to me. Sometimes I forget she does not have her letters. She picks up her sewing.

'Who is Matthew Booth?'

The needle stops mid-stitch.

'See here.' I point at the words on the page. 'It says that Father has a son, a son called Matthew Booth. I don't know anyone who goes by that name.'

Her hands drop to her lap.

'Is it true?' I ask.

She looks up at me, eyes deep wells of sorrow. 'Oh, Mercy . . .'

So, it is true.

The floor seems to tilt beneath me and I find myself on my knees at Agnes's feet. She puts out a hand to reach my shoulder but I move away. My whole body feels aflame. I cannot bear to be touched. 'Tell me.'

'Mercy, I—'

'You will tell me what you know.'

She exhales unsteadily, looking to the body on the bed. 'I told him many times you've a right to know the truth. But he'd never listen.'

I put my head into my hands – if I don't, my mind might split apart. I'm still clutching the will, afraid to let it go.

'I made a promise to your father and would not break it while he lived,' Agnes says. 'But now . . .'

I take a deep breath, trying to still my spinning thoughts. 'I have a brother?'

She's barely able to look at me. 'You did once. Long ago.'

'But . . . how? When?'

'He was a year your elder, a fine strong boy with dark eyes and dark hair. He was three years old when we lost him.'

'He died?'

She shakes her head, eyes downcast. 'No, we lost him.'

'What do you mean?'

She looks at Father again and her eyes spring tears. 'Forgive me, Bartram. She deserves to know.'

My heart is in my throat, my mouth dry as ashes.

'Mercy, your mother was a good woman. It was a terrible thing when she died. It was thirty years ago, last May just gone.'

'But that's nearly two years after I was born. I thought—'

'I know – you were told she died in childbed, but that was not what happened. Your mother bore you with no trouble. She cared for you and loved you.'

Again the room tilts, as if the floorboards are shifting.

'Mercy, my dear child, your mother was murdered.'

Pinpoints of white light seem to crowd at the corners of my vision and there's a sudden bright pain behind my eyes. I press a hand to my temple. 'I don't understand.'

Agnes puts aside the winding sheet. She's shaking. Her voice comes out strange and cracked. 'I haven't spoken of it in so long. I hate to think of it.'

'Tell me.'

'We were in the marketplace, when they came,' she says. 'God knows, I tried to save him. I tried to save them both.'

'Who? Who came?'

'The King's men. They gave no warning, no time to run or hide. We were in the marketplace. It was just an ordinary day.' She takes a deep, fractured breath. 'Oh, Mercy, I still dream about the horror of it. They slaughtered innocents, not just the townsmen who dared try to fight but women and children too.'

'Why?'

'Because Bolton had held out for Parliament, and we were punished cruelly for our rebellion.'

'She was killed by the King's men?'

Agnes reaches out, groping blindly for my hand, and this time I take hers. 'Your mother was found later, in an alleyway. The man who did those things to her must have been the Devil himself.' She stops and puts her free hand over her mouth. I see agony in her eyes as she remembers.

'And my brother?'

She pulls her hand away from mine and covers her face. 'God forgive me . . . God forgive me . . .'

'Please, Agnes, I must know.'

'To this day I don't know how it happened. One moment he was with me, holding my hand, and the next—' She stops, staring at her hand as if her own flesh has betrayed her. 'I searched for him. I searched and searched. God forgive me . . .'

'What happened to him?' My voice is small, like a child's.

She gathers herself and looks at me, eyes full of heartbreak. 'We never found him. We never saw him again.'

I search her face for any sign of a lie, but I know she could never invent such horror.

'Your father never forgave me. I never forgave myself . . .'

I see it laid bare then – the conflict between them, the unspoken guilt and blame, the shared secret, binding them together but keeping them apart for all these years.

I leave her weeping and climb to my feet. My body feels as if it's not my own. I feel apart, strangely detached from everything around me, as if I'm not really here, as if I'm drained of blood. I go to the window and look out through the tracery of frost. The sky is white and flat.

'How could you keep this from me? All these years I thought I was to blame for her death . . .'

'I made a promise to your father.'

'Why would *he* keep it from me?'

For a while she says nothing, but then, 'He wanted to protect you.'

'But he lied to me. All my life he lied to me. How could *that* protect me?'

'He believed it was for your own good. "She does not need to live a life so tainted," he said. "She will not remember them and so, in time, the loss will be nothing to her." He didn't want you to suffer the same grief as he.'

'And did he suffer?'

'Of course he did. He suffered terribly. For a time, he was under a sort of madness.'

'You mean, these last few months – that was not the first time his mind was adrift?'

'No, this was different – a fierce kind of madness brought on by grief.'

I turn back, eyes resting on Father's face.

'He refused to believe that Matthew was dead,' she says. 'He did nothing but search for him for a year, maybe more. It changed him, consumed him, sent him to the drink, caused him to have these black rages. Then, one day, he came home and told me we were leaving, that he couldn't go on any longer living with the memories of what had happened all around him. He told me he'd found a place where we could forget. And so we came here. He gave up everything – his business, his friends, his whole life – to come somewhere where there was nothing and no one to remind him. He made me promise I'd never tell you. I argued with him, but he was my master and I had no choice.'

'That's not true. You had a choice.'

She nods. 'You're right, of course, but I never saw it so. I've always done whatever he said.'

My whole life I've felt that something was missing. I've sought it in my work, in the arms of undeserving men, in my wavering, heretical faith. There has always been a sense of striving, of seeking to fill a space inside me that could never be filled, even by prayer: an empty chamber, echoing with the guilt of my mother's death. How could I ever find peace when everything I believed was based on deception?

'So, why tell me now? Why not continue the lie?'

Again, she studies Father's face as if she wishes he could answer for her. She looks beaten, worn out. 'Your father never stopped believing that Matthew was still alive.' She nods towards the will and I realise I'm still gripping it, so hard that my nails have punctured little holes in the parchment. 'I expect that's why he never changed his will, why he never pressed you to marry. He thought of Matthew as his heir, even after I'd long stopped hoping. But in this last year he changed his mind.'

'How so?'

Her voice drops and she looks unsure, frightened. 'He came to me, some time ago now, and said he believed that the spirits of your mother and your brother had returned, here, to Scarcross Hall. He said he recognised their footsteps. And the handprints he found, he believed to be a sign from your brother. He thought *they* were to blame for the things that have happened, that they were tormenting him, calling him to account.'

I remember the small footprints in the snow, the childlike handprints on the frosted glass, the patter of steps in my own chamber and that tall, pale figure in the fog. I recall the conversation with Pastor Flynn, many months ago, when Father had been so intent on matters of spirit and redemption, and his sudden plan to leave Scarcross Hall. Could he have been right? My mind is reeling with the remaking of my life and I no longer know what to think.

'Was that why he went to the White Ladies? To find them?'

'Perhaps. He said the time would come when he would have to go to them. And you know what they say about the Ladies.'

'But what do you think? Do you believe him?'

'He didn't want to leave you, Mercy, but he did want to go to her. He always did love her best.' She swallows deeply and looks at him once more. In her gaze I see everything she could never say – her loyalty, her steadfast devotion to a man who could never love her back. 'I hope he's right,' she says. 'He'll be at peace now.'

But I'm not satisfied. 'Do you really believe that?'

She turns back to me. 'There are more strange things at work in this world than we've the wits to understand. I don't know what your father saw or heard, but he believed it. Take some comfort in that, if you can.' She looks warily about the room. 'But me? It doesn't explain all that's happened here. This place has its own secrets. Its own soul. I've always felt it. I feel it still.'

As if Scarcross Hall is listening, there is a creak in the rafters above and a noise, as if something is skittering across the slates of the roof. But I'm beyond fear.

'And what of my brother? Do you think he's dead?'

Agnes interlaces her fingers and closes her eyes. When she opens them again, she looks at me with such pity, such tenderness, that I feel my heart shift.

'Please tell me the truth,' I say, suddenly breathless.

She gives a single nod. 'I tried to tell myself he was in a better place for a long time but, Mercy, when you've nursed a child, when you've held a baby to your breast, you don't forget them, even if they're not your blood. And if they go to God, you feel it when they go, as I did with my own poor bairn. I was wet-nurse to your brother and I've never felt that with him.'

'So you think he's alive.'

'I cannot be sure.'

She won't meet my eye. She's holding something back. 'Agnes, please, I must know the truth. All of it.'

'I've waited and waited, praying for a sign, hoping to be sure. Hoping with one half of my heart that I'm right, and with the other that I'm wrong.'

I stare at her. There is a strange rushing sensation in my head as thoughts battle one another, each too strange and too terrible to win. They crowd in on me, fragments of truth dancing and taunting like demons, then dropping into place. And before she utters another word, I understand.

'Do you feel it, as I do?' she whispers, fixing me with sad, anxious eyes. 'Do you know in your heart?'

I struggle to breathe. There is no air.

'I don't even know if he suspects. God works in such mystery, Mercy. Sometimes I think He's brought Matthew back to me. Others, I think he's the Devil himself, come to punish me for what I did.'

My whole world, my past and my future, seems to swim before me. I'm outside myself, high above, watching as I stumble forward and grab hold of the bedstead, unable to think, to speak, even take a breath. An image comes to me: a small golden key on a leather cord, glinting in the candlelight as I lifted it from beneath Ellis's shirt. The way he stopped me. Suddenly I know where that key belongs.

I leave the room without a word, abandoning Agnes with her head in her hands, muttering, 'God, forgive me . . . God, forgive me . . .'

I go to Ellis's chamber, pull his pack from beneath the truckle bed and tip the contents onto the floor. Amid grubby clothes, a box of tobacco, two broken pipes, and a metal flask there is a scrap of fabric, something hard inside. I unfold the cloth and find a leather cord, a golden key. The bow of the key is fashioned into two letters, the arrow-straight backbones and fat round bellies of a double *B*: Father's seal.

I take it to my chamber where I prise up the loose board and lift out the ebony box. It's still locked, as it has been these thirty years.

I go to the bed and sit, too afraid to try the key. I could undo all this. I could throw the key down the well or melt it in a blacksmith's furnace. I could pretend I never saw it. I could cut this moment out of my memory and lock it away, along with all Father's lies.

I put the key into the lock.

It turns.

A weird unbidden noise comes out of me: a cry of dismay, the revelation of long-held secrets.

I open the lid.

Inside I find a tiny portrait, a miniature of a young woman. She's well dressed in fine primrose-yellow silks but she's no beauty. Her hair is curled in ringlets, the drab hue of a thrush's wing. Her face is plain but she's smiling and her eyes are bright. She looks happy. She looks like me.

Beneath the portrait are two locks of hair, each tied with a faded strip of crimson ribbon. I lift them out, cupping them in my palm. One is fair and fine, baby-soft, the colour of new straw. I think it is mine. The other is dark and curled, black as peat. This must be my brother's hair.

And I am sure then: it belongs to Ellis Ferreby.

There is a dreadful screaming in my head and all Hell's fire in my belly. I double over and vomit onto the floor.

Chapter 43

'Come here, Boy.' Briggs sits at the table in Betsy's chamber, a half-empty bottle of spirits beside him. He's cleaning a pistol, the cloth, powder flask, shot and rammer laid out.

'Did you hear me, Boy? I said, come here.'

'Sir?'

Briggs puts the cloth down and takes a long drink from the bottle. He fingers the smooth wooden stock of the pistol. 'I've business tonight, but before I go, I've need of a woman.'

Briggs has been back in York three days – three days of liquor and gaming, spending whatever coin he's managed to steal and swindle in the year he's been away. Boy and Betsy have had some peace during that year. Betsy is starting to show the signs of her trade, so there is less money from tricks, but the old drab who runs the bawdyhouse is kind and lets them keep the room, provided Boy runs errands for all the girls. So he fetches in the coal, takes the soiled sheets to the laundress, collects the ointments and remedies from the apothecary, cleans the piss pots and makes himself invisible to the customers. In return he eats, drinks and once or twice in the last year, has spent a night beside Gretchen, in a tangle of sheets and sweat. But now Briggs has returned and, as always, Betsy is only too willing to let him into her bed.

'Shall I fetch Ma?'

'No, not her. Bring me that plump girl – the young one.'

Boy bristles. He means Gretchen. He hates the thought. It needles under his skin. But he's used to obeying orders so he goes to find her.

'Briggs wants you,' he tells her, avoiding the gaze of her clear blue eyes.

She sighs, pouts, considers. 'Very well, but he'd better pay up this time. He don't get any of us for free.'

She picks up her skirts and follows him back to the chamber. Once he's delivered her, he turns to leave.

'Stay there, Boy.' Briggs has finished cleaning the pistol and is loading it. He slides a small black round of shot down the barrel.

'Fetch you something?'

'No.' Briggs takes the rammer and pushes in the wadding. He slides the stick in and out of the pistol's mouth, eyeing Gretchen with a knowing, hungry look. 'Tell me, Boy, do you know what it means to be a man?'

'Leave him be, Briggs,' Gretchen says. 'Do you want me or not?'

'Quiet, girl. Sit down.' He points to the bed. 'I'm talking to my son.'

'Fine way to treat your own kin – you never even gave him a proper name.'

'I named him after Prince Rupert's dog. It's as good a name as any.'

Boy Briggs. It's the only name he has. He had another once but he cannot remember it. Besides, it must be his, he has the key around his neck to prove it – small, golden, and carved with a double B – so he can never forget who he is. He knows that now Gretchen has helped him with his letters.

Briggs puts down the rammer, takes up the powder flask and tips a small measure into the pan. 'Answer me, Boy. Do you know what it means to be a man?'

With Briggs you have to be careful. Say the wrong thing an
it'll hurt. You have to watch your words because he likes to twis
them and turn them into something they're not.

'I think so.'

Briggs laughs, puts the pistol down. '"I think so." Did you hea
that, girl?' He stands and takes a few paces towards the bed, wher
Gretchen waits. 'Well, perhaps you need a lesson.'

'No, sir.'

'I say you do. I'll show you. You stay there and I'll show yo
what it means.' He turns to Gretchen. 'Stand up. Turn around.'

She does as he asks.

'Now, lift up your skirts and bend over.'

She gives him a coquettish look over her shoulder and obey
slowly raising the faded and patched violet satin, revealing th
ivory skin of her calves, the dimpled flesh of her thighs and finall
her full, round buttocks.

Boy remembers the softness of her flesh in his hands, th
pillowy warmth of her, like sinking into a feather mattress. H
feels the rush and swell between his legs and moves towards th
door.

'Stay where you are, Boy.'

'But—'

'Do as I say or she'll pay for it.'

He doesn't know if Briggs means Gretchen or Betsy but h
knows that tone, so he waits by the door and tries not to watch a
Gretchen bends forward over the mattress and wiggles her cream
cheese arse, showing a glimpse of curled golden hair and pink we
slit. Briggs unties his breeches.

'Are you watching, Boy?' Briggs takes hold of Gretchen's hip
and pulls her roughly towards him. She lets out a false little squea
of excitement. 'I said, are you watching?'

'Yes.' But he isn't. He's trying to think of something else
anything else. He shuts his eyes and thinks about the stink o

the piss pot in the corner, but he cannot block his ears from the sounds.

Gretchen giggles as Briggs pulls away and flips her over, pushing her onto the bed. 'Get on your back.' He climbs on top of her.

Boy puts his hand on the latch. He does not want to see this. Cannot bear to hear Gretchen pretend like that – not with him. Does not want to catch the rank scent of the man. But as he lifts the latch he realises Briggs is watching. He's inside Gretchen but his eyes are fixed on him.

'You're not going anywhere.'

'Leave the boy alone,' Gretchen says, putting a hand to Briggs's cheek and turning his face to hers. 'Aren't I enough?'

'Shut up, wench.' Briggs puts a hand over Gretchen's mouth.

She struggles, half-heartedly at first, as though she's bored by this game, but then, more violently. 'Stop it,' she says, muffled by his thick, dirty fingers.

Briggs ignores her. He puts his other hand up to her neck and presses against her throat so she cannot breathe. She gasps, hitting his chest, trying to force him away, and still he is inside her, pushing into her.

'Stop it,' Boy says. 'Don't hurt her.'

'What are you afraid of, Boy?' Briggs says, bringing both hands to Gretchen's throat and starting to squeeze. She tries to call out, mouth opening and closing, but no sound comes, just a weird, strangled gurgling. Her eyes have gone wide and she kicks her legs, but Briggs is too big and too strong for her.

'Be still, girl,' Briggs says, teeth gritted, squeezing harder.

'For God's sake, you're hurting her!'

Brigg's face is contorted in a fierce, rictus grin, eyes burning like a demon. 'Get out of here, Boy. Get out now!'

Boy has seen him like this before and he knows it is dangerous. Gretchen rolls her eyes to his and she's pleading, afraid. Before he

can think better of it he dashes across the room and hurls himself
on Brigg's back. 'Stop it! Stop it! You'll kill her!'

In one swoop Briggs releases Gretchen, twists and swings a fist
connecting with Boy's jaw. It floors him, a hammer strike of pain
crashing through his cheek and temple, but he struggles to his feet.

Briggs climbs off Gretchen, cock dangling from his open
breeches, his attention now on Boy. Gretchen chokes and gasps for
breath.

'You little turd,' Briggs says. 'I'm trying to teach you a lesson
and this is how you repay me? Think you can hit me and get away
with it?' He swings again but Boy dodges this time.

'You were hurting her. She couldn't breathe. You might've
killed her.'

'And so what if I did? She's a whore. She's worth nothing.' He
comes at him again and this time lands a punch in Boy's gut. It
knocks the wind from him and he's left bent double, struggling for
breath.

'How dare you question me?' Briggs says. 'After everything I've
done for you and that whore you call mother.'

'We owe you nothing! You've brought nothing but trouble and
pain. I wish you'd leave and never come back. I wish you were
dead!'

Briggs swings for him again but misses. Boy backs up against
the wall. Behind Briggs, Gretchen stands, unsteady, clutching her
neck, and stumbles towards the door.

Briggs grabs Boy's arms and pins them against the wall. He
leans in close, so he can feel spittle on his face as Briggs speaks. 'All
I wanted was to teach you a lesson – to show you what it means to
be a man. Curses to God and damnation to the Devil, a real man
does what he will and to Hell with everyone else.'

Over Briggs's shoulder, he sees Gretchen reach the door, lift
the catch and slip outside.

'I don't know why I've wasted my time on you. You always

were a milksop. Well, if you can't stand up for yourself, you won't be needing this.' He raises a knee, full force into Boy's groin.

The pain shoots and spirals out from his centre. He crumples forward and Briggs lets him fall. He throws up a thin, stinking puddle onto the floor.

'She should've left you where she found you,' Briggs said. 'Or, better still, let me slit your throat like I wanted.' He takes a couple of paces away, tying his breeches, then turns back and aims a powerful kick at Boy's stomach. Boy curls into a ball, knowing what comes next. He knows there's no point in fighting because it only makes it worse. But today it's different. Something flares inside him, ignited by the pain – a burning, pulsing rage spreads through his limbs like wildfire.

'You know she stole you, don't you?' Briggs said.

No. No, he didn't know that.

'She could've taken you back, when it was all over. She could've given you back to whatever family you had left. But she didn't. "No one will ever know," she said. "They'll think he's dead." God knows why but that barren bitch had a hankering for a child.'

Boy rights himself, struggles to his knees.

'Bolton it was – the day we took the city for the King. Ah, now that was a day for sport.' Briggs smiles, remembering. 'So, you see, you don't belong here. You don't belong anywhere. You should be dead. You are nobody's son. You are nothing.'

Briggs laughs, turning away from him and Boy sees his chance. He launches himself at the man's back. Briggs staggers and falls, crashing down onto the table. The stool splinters under the weight of bodies, the bottle and the pistol spinning across the floor. But Briggs is bigger than him, and stronger, and he has no plan. Before he can do anything Briggs is on top of him, pinning him down. He's smashed his nose in the fall and blood streams from it and drips into Boy's eyes, blinding him. He can taste it – meat and iron. This is it, he thinks. Briggs will kill me now.

There is a sudden crash – the splintering of glass – and a shower of shards explodes from behind Briggs's head. He shuts his eyes, feeling fragments fall on his cheeks. Briggs roars and twists up and away from him. Through blood and tears he sees Betsy, broken bottle in hand, eyes wild and terrified. Behind her, Gretchen cowers.

'Don't you hurt him!' Betsy screams. 'I'll die before I let you hurt him again!'

Briggs is on her like a wolf. He sinks his teeth into her neck, almost lifts her off the floor with the force of it and she drops the bottle, arms dangling limp by her sides. Then, Briggs lets out a terrible howl, a battle cry. He tosses her against the wall. There is a bone-crunching crack as her head smacks against brick. She sinks to the floor and slumps forward, eyes rolled white, the front of her bodice already slick with blood.

Ellis has never been sure what happened next. He remembers it as if he'd dreamed it, or as if it had happened to someone else and he knows only the story, recounted second hand. But he remembers the furnace-hot fire of his rage because sometimes it still flares up in him. He recalls the gun in his hand, the force of the recoil as he pulled the trigger. Most of all he remembers the feeling – a whirlpool of elation, relief and incomparable pleasure – when, somehow, the bullet found its mark and gobbets of Briggs's brain splattered across the lime-washed ceiling.

And he remembers the words, Briggs's lesson, burned into his mind, the words that have led him here: *You are nobody's son. You are nothing.*

Chapter 44

Ellis comes in through the kitchen door, stamping snow from his boots. I'm waiting by the fire. I've banished Sam to his chamber and Agnes still keeps vigil by my father's body. I must be alone for this.

It all makes sense now – why Ellis came here, why he stayed, why he refused me for so long. In these last few hours, I've relived every conversation, every touch, every moment of connection between us, seeing it all with unveiled eyes. I think of the way he watched Father, silent and hawkish, the way I would feel his stare following me. He must have known. Has he been marking his time, planning, deceiving me all along . . . and to what purpose?

I feel betrayed, blind, angry and, most of all, lost. I cannot undo what has been done. The sin is too great. No amount of prayer and penitence will wash the stain from my soul or purge the evil I have let into my heart.

He peels off his thick coat, unwinds his neckerchief and takes off his hat, a dusting of snowflakes falling to the flags. He blows on his hands to warm them and comes towards the fire, reaching for me. He sees me flinch, must read my expression because he falters, confusion rising. The smile drops and the familiar deep creases appear at his brow.

'What's wrong?'

I say nothing. I look away, watching the flames as they take hold of a fresh clod of peat.

He unhooks the pistol from his belt and places it on the table. He stops.

I watch his face alter as he sees the ebony box, the key on the table beside it. I see the moment of shock, when all the lies fall away and he can no longer hide behind them.

He picks up the key.

'Open it,' I say.

'Where did you get this?'

'Open it.'

'This belongs to me.'

'Open the box.'

He stares at me for a few seconds. His hand shakes as he slides the key into the lock – the first time he's shown any weakness. He makes a strange moan as the key turns: disbelief, misery and elation, all at once. He lifts the lid, takes out the miniature and the locks of hair and places them one by one on the tabletop. Then he sits heavily, suddenly, with a sound as if the air has been punched out of him.

'How long have you known?' I say.

He looks at me blankly.

'Did you know when you first came here?'

'It's not so simple—'

'Don't lie to me!' I stand, unable to contain my anger. 'I'll listen to no more lies.'

He picks up the portrait. 'Who is this?'

'Answer me.'

'Is it your mother?'

The word is like a slap. 'You will *not* speak of her.'

'Your mother,' he says quietly, then, looking up at me, '*Our* mother.'

I am stopped dead as the last trace of hope fails, melting like the snowflakes on the cold stone floor. Some small part of me had hoped beyond reason that he was ignorant, that he'd acted in innocence, that some twist of fate could make us both blameless. But hope is a traitor.

'How long have you known?' I don't recognise my own voice.

He's staring at the picture. I feel the urge to snatch it from him, but I'm afraid to go too close.

'In some ways, I knew the first time I saw you. In others, I was not certain till now.'

He stands and goes to the sideboard, where a jug of beer awaits. He fetches a cup, pours, drinks. Then he waits, hands pressed flat on either side of the jug. I can see his mind racing, calculating. To my astonishment he laughs – a sound of bitter resignation, as if to say: *Of course, now everything will fall apart.*

My heart is pitching, my stomach alive with snakes.

'Did you find the will?' he says.

I don't reply.

'Did you find it?' His tone has a sharp edge. He turns towards me, flint in his eyes. 'Show it to me.'

I shake my head.

'It's my right. Show it to me.'

'You have no rights.'

He comes forward. 'Mercy, you must show me.'

'You've forfeited any rights here. Don't you see what you've done?'

'What *we* have done.'

'No. This is *your* doing. You have damned us both.'

'You think I don't know that? You think I've not spent these last months in torment? But *you* came to me, Mercy. *You* came to me.'

'I'm not to blame. I didn't know.'

He makes a sound of disbelief. 'Is that true?'

'How could I have known?'

'Ask yourself, is that true?'

He leaves a silence into which my mind spirals. I've questioned that very thing over and over today. Should I have seen it? Could I have known? Did I ignore the signs, choosing to believe he was one thing because, deep inside, I wanted that thing so badly?

'No – you are the liar here,' I say.

'Any lies I've told do not compare with those of your father.'

'Don't you dare speak ill of him.'

'He was a coward.'

'You didn't know him.'

'He abandoned his own son.'

'No. You're wrong.'

'You think you know better? You think you knew him? He deceived you. He lied to you your whole life.'

This, I cannot deny.

'Where is the will?' he says again.

'It's gone. I burned it, as I said I would.'

'You're lying.'

Yes, I am. But, I realise, that's exactly what I must do. I know what he's thinking: his true name is on that document, his true name as the rightful master of Scarcross Hall.

'You can't prove anything,' I say. 'I want you to leave here and never return.'

'Listen to me—'

'No. You'll leave tonight. Now.'

'I won't do that.'

'You'll do as I say. I'm still mistress here.'

'No, Mercy, you're not.'

'You cannot take Scarcross Hall away from me.'

'I don't have to take it. It's already mine.' He says it without triumph or emotion: a fact.

For a few seconds we stare at each other, defiant, dangerous, like wild dogs before the attack. I see the black fire spark in his eyes. And then I run.

I take the stairs two at a time and skirt the gallery.

As I burst into Father's bedchamber, Agnes is startled, a hand to her heart.

'Where is it?' I say.

She understands. 'Does he know?'

'I must burn it. Quickly!'

'Lord, save us!' She rises, putting aside her sewing.

I can hear Ellis following me up the stairs. 'Quickly!'

She slips a hand under Father's pillow. His head tilts towards me and for one horrid moment I expect him to open his eyes. She draws out the roll of parchment, tied once more with the cord, then turns back, recoiling as Ellis reaches the door. She's afraid of him. 'Mercy, please, there's more at stake than just your father's wishes.'

I snatch the will from her. 'I no longer care about his wishes.'

'Think about what's right in the eyes of God. He already knows the truth,' she says. But I'm consumed by one thought alone: I must destroy the will. No one will take Scarcross Hall away from me.

Ellis steps into the room. 'Give it to me.'

'This,' I say, brandishing the scroll, 'this is a lie. My father has no son. I'm his only heir.'

'Give it to me,' he says again, and in his persistence I hear a tremor of desperation.

I make a dash towards the candlestick – the only flame in the room – but Ellis gets there first, pushing Agnes aside.

'Let me see it.'

He tries to grab the parchment but I duck away from him, heading for the door – the only lit fires in the house burn in the kitchen hearth, and in the old bedchamber where Sam now rests.

But Ellis is quick. He catches me, gripping my arm, dragging me backwards with such force that I cry out. I drop the scroll and it bounces across the floorboards to Agnes's feet. She stares at it as if it might burst into flames.

I struggle to free myself but Ellis holds me fast. I kick at his shins and he twists one arm behind my back until it burns. He hauls me across the room, my shoulder screaming.

'Please, stop!' Agnes begs.

'Burn it, Agnes! For God's sake, put an end to this!'

She hesitates, eyes darting to the candle behind us – there's no way she can reach it.

'Do it for me – please!'

She bends, picks up the will and takes a step towards the door. Ellis sees everything slipping away from him. He shoves me so hard that I fall, breath knocked out of me, reeling with pain.

Agnes makes it as far as the gallery. Ellis lunges for her, grabs her skirts and pulls her back. She holds the will out of reach, leaning out over the empty hall below.

As I stagger to my feet, the door to the old bedchamber opens and Sam appears, shock-haired, clutching a candle.

'Go back inside, Sam!' I shout, my voice coming out strangled. 'Go back in your room and lock the door.'

The boy freezes as he sees the struggle, eyes wide and frightened.

'Sam! Do as I say!'

Hearing my panic, he obeys.

Ellis grabs the laces in Agnes's bodice and tugs her towards him. He draws back a fist, eyes all thunder and lightning. He looks like Father when the black temper descends. Why did I never see it before? But Ellis falters. He cannot do it. I snatch up the candlestick, the tallow bouncing across the boards, flame snuffed, plunging us into milk-blue moonlight. I bring the stick down on the back of Ellis's head, feeling hard bone beneath flesh.

He roars, shoving Agnes away. She falls awkwardly against the banister. I hear the sickening crack of brittle bone and she cries out, clinging there, unable to stand.

Ellis is panting hard, towering over her, menacing. 'Just give it to me.' He stretches a hand out for the parchment, fingers smeared scarlet with his own blood.

Agnes whimpers, swooning with pain, leaning out over the dark hall below. I should go to her. I should protect her.

There is a sudden rush of icy air. I sense someone just behind me. A flood of dread steals my breath. I feel a cold hand on my shoulder, holding me back. I cannot move.

Then, the sound of breaking wood, a great splintering, like a branch brought down in a storm. Agnes looks right at me and I see her terror, and the moment she knows.

Then she's gone, skirts flying over her head as the banister splits and she falls, taking my father's will with her.

Chapter 45

He sees Agnes fall, feels the brush of her skirts, her boot as it grazes his thigh, the swift air, like a gust of wind on the moor top, followed by the awful sound. Then silence.

He knows what he will see, because he's seen it before: the awkward splay of limbs, the tangle of petticoats, the unnatural tilt of the head, the blood, already seeping, inky in the moonlight.

But he looks anyway, gripping the splintered banister, because what else can he do? It is just as he imagined. Then Mercy is by his side. She turns to him, face twisted and ugly with blame.

This is not his fault. He had not meant for any of this. He stretches out a hand towards her, anger and savagery dissolved into something else – this double-edged sword for which he has damned himself. But she's away from him, running down the staircase into the hall. When she reaches Agnes's body she sinks to her knees and covers her face. She stays there until he joins her.

Up close, there's no doubt: Agnes has broken her neck. She's belly down, one cheek angled against the flags, one eye open and staring, a horrid grin of cracked brown teeth.

Mercy drops her hands to her lap. Her eyes are dry, expression hard as a millstone. Slowly, she reaches out and picks up the scroll of parchment, now lying in the old woman's blood. She climbs to

her feet and without acknowledging him, walks towards the
kitchen.

He stares at the old woman and feels nothing, hollow, an
absence where there should be something else. She's probably the
only one who could have told him everything. If the truth has died
with her, what does it matter now? He does not feel shock or guilt
or any of the things he might expect but only a sense of dreadful
inevitability. He must follow this path to the end.

By the time he reaches the kitchen, Mercy is already at the
hearth, feeding the scroll into the fire. It flares as she drops it into
the heart of the flames. She looks at him, defiant.

'No!' He runs to the fireside and falls to his knees, tries to
rescue the burning fragments, but all he does is scorch his fingers.
The stench of singed hair rises and he gives up, watching as the last
pieces of old, dry parchment ignite and curl to ashes.

'Why did you do that?' he says, but she just stares at him, eyes
like icicles. Suddenly he cannot bear it – cannot stand for her to
look at him like that, for the bond to be broken, not after everything
that has passed between them.

He climbs to his feet and takes hold of her arms. She does not
react, does not pull away or move closer. He gathers her to him,
expecting her to collapse, to weep, as she had last night, but she's
limp, lifeless, a dead thing in his arms.

Something snaps inside, some thread that has been holding
him back, some last shred of conscience: he will do anything now
to get what he wants.

He pulls back, clasps her hands, the idea gripping him. 'I can
set this right.'

She does not respond.

'Don't you see? There's nothing to stop us now.'

She snatches her hands away.

'I'll make no claim to Scarcross Hall,' he says. 'We'll go on as
we planned. No one need ever know the truth.'

She is incredulous. 'You must leave at once.'

He must make her understand. 'Don't you see? There's no one left to hinder us.' Again he snatches up her hands, brings them to his lips and kisses them fervently. 'We can live as man and wife. That's what we shall be to the world. No one need ever know the truth.'

Her fingers begin to tremble in his. 'You are mad . . .' she whispers. 'Do you not see what we've done? God is punishing us.'

'No. God has brought us together. He's cleared the way for us.' Again she pulls her fingers from his, throwing him a look of disgust, turning her back. He's losing her. 'I know you feel as I do. You cannot deny it.'

'You're a liar. No – worse than that. I knew it from the start. I was a fool to trust you.'

'Mercy, please . . .' He spreads his arms in supplication. 'Please listen to me . . .'

She turns back and he sees a tiny sliver of feeling. 'Why?' she says. 'Just tell me why you came here. Did you mean to ruin us? To destroy us?'

He shakes his head. 'Never.'

'Then why?'

He can hardly remember now what his intention had been. How can he explain it – the years of grief, guilt and torment, dogged by the question that gnawed at his soul, extinguishing the goodness that Betsy had tried so hard to teach him? The slow painful death of hope. Then, a chance encounter, the tale, told over a pint pot, of a man named Bartram Booth who had lost a wife and son at Bolton and taken his daughter to live like a wild creature on the moors. The wife was dead, but the boy? No one knew what had happened to the boy. What was the boy's name? he had asked, but no one could remember.

Bartram Booth. Boy Briggs.

You are nobody's son. You are nothing.

Briggs's words, branded into him like a tar mark: not true. And he would prove it. He would find this man and the daughter who had taken the place that should have been his. He would have his revenge upon them for abandoning him to a life of poverty and violence. He would claim his birthright and with it redemption, for Briggs, for Gretchen, for Betsy.

But that was before he met her, before she cast her heathen spell upon him, before the Devil cursed his body and mind with temptation and sin, and by the time he was sure he had found them, it was too late: his desire, his love, had grown stronger than his hate.

'I came to find you,' he says simply. 'God sent me here, to my rightful place.'

'How can you say that?' she says. 'When God has abandoned us?'

'If that's so, then what does any of it matter?'

He sees the moment she begins to doubt herself, when her eyes spring tears and she no longer has the strength to fight. He seizes that chance, slips a hand to her face, cradles her jaw and lowers his mouth to hers. He feels the hard crags of her heart open to him and thinks: *She will understand, as I have come to, that this is the only way now*. He fought it for so long but now he sees it differently. When they lay together he felt no guilt or misgiving, just something strange and wonderful. There can be no wickedness or shame in something so sacred. She will come to see that in time.

But then she pushes him away. 'No . . . I cannot.'

His own words echoed back to him – how they wound him now.

'Don't you see?' he appeals to her, losing patience. 'You can be free, just like you wanted.'

'Where's the freedom in living a lie? Where's the freedom when death will bring certain damnation? No. No, you must

leave.' Her face is flushed. He sees her struggle, knows she
fighting the same battle he has already lost.

'I won't go.'

'You must.'

'Think, Mercy. You can have everything you want in this life.

'But what of the next?' She puts her hands to her face, mout
yawning in an anguished, silent cry.

He recognises the conflict in her: the fear of Hell's flames, c
eternal suffering, competing with the human need, the desperat
yearning and the wilful spirit in her that will forsake all con
sequences, if only she will let it win.

'No!' she cries out. 'No – you must go!'

Why can she not see how simple it is? He feels the dark twist c
anger in his belly, the blackness pressing in on him. He will nc
give up now, not when he has come so far, not when he is so close

'You must trust me,' he says, struggling to keep the frustratio
from his voice.

'Trust you?' she exclaims. 'How could I ever trust you again?'

'You will come to. You'll see – we are the same, you and I.'

'I'm nothing like you.'

The anger burns in him now, raw, dark and untamed. 'You ar
mine,' he says, determined. 'And I *will* have what's mine.'

As she searches his face, her expression alters. 'What ha
happened to you?'

'You *will* do as I say.'

She understands him then, understands that if he is forced tc
he will leave her no choice. He sees fear flash behind her eyes.

'My God . . . you are the Devil himself,' she breathes.

'No, only the devil in you.'

He pushes her up against the wall next to the hearth and presse
his mouth to hers. She struggles, bites and kicks, but he's stronge
than her, and the rage makes him more so. It burns within, all
consuming, black fire scorching any other thought to ashes.

His hands go up to her neck. She tries to push him away, gasping, trying to call out, so he squeezes to quiet her. He forces his mouth to hers, presses harder so her tongue begins to bulge forward. He takes it into his mouth and she is kissing him back, her arms around him, pulling him closer. Her heartbeat becomes his. Her breath is his breath. This is what he wants, he thinks, sinking into darkness, and he *will* take it.

The sound is what pulls him back: a shot, ringing so loud that he feels the shock of it all through his body. He releases her, spins round.

Sam stands by the table, holding the pistol out before him, half hidden in a plume of gun smoke. He had forgotten about the boy.

He looks back at Mercy, sees the red weals on her throat. My God, did he do that to her? She's staring at him, eyes bright with horror and shock.

There is no pain at first, just a seeping wetness beneath his waistcoat and a creeping awareness that something is wrong. He puts a palm to his right side, just beneath his ribs.

It comes back bloody.

Chapter 46

I watch the knowledge register on Ellis's face as he stares at the blood on his fingers. He holds his hand out towards me like a question: *What is this? What does it mean?*

There is a clatter as Sam drops the pistol, face stark white, a smudge of gunpowder grey across one cheek.

I stumble away from Ellis, gasping for the air that he forced out of me, bright points of light glittering before me like snowflakes. I grab a knife from the sideboard.

'Keep back.' My voice is choked, tongue dry and heavy. I expect Ellis to fall but he just stands there, reaching out his gore-smeared hand.

The wind rises, whistling down chimneys and howling through broken panes in the hall. One of the boards that we nailed to cover the gaps comes clattering down, echoing like a second gunshot.

'Mercy . . .' Ellis takes a few steps, winces and doubles over, clutching his side. Blood begins to drip onto the flags.

I brandish the knife. 'Stay back.'

But the fire has gone from his eyes. Again, I'm reminded of Father – the impassioned, violent rages, followed by confusion and dismay, then desperate contrition. The kinship is clear now Ellis has shown his true colours: hellfire-red and brimstone-black.

I skirt the edge of the room, making for the door into the hall, and pull Sam into the passageway with me. His eyes are wild with fright, his whole body quaking. I must get him away from here. He stares across the hall to Agnes's body. Even in darkness, she seems to stare back.

'Look at me,' I tell him, turning away. 'Don't be afraid.'

I know the words are absurd, worthless, but I don't know what else to say. I grab a pair of my old boots, cast aside by the door.

'Put these on.'

He looks at me as if I'm mad.

'Please, Sam. Hurry.'

'Don't make me go out there,' he says, teeth chattering.

'You must. Put them on, quickly.' Over his shoulder I glance at the door to the kitchen, but there's no sign of Ellis.

Sam steps into the boots, eyes welling. 'I didn't mean to hurt him, only to stop him hurting you.'

I crouch so we are face to face. 'Listen to me. You must fetch help. You must run to your pa. Do you understand? Fetch your father. Tell him to come at once.'

'But the snow's too deep.'

'You can do it, Sam. I know you can.'

He looks at me with such sorrow it takes my breath. 'I won't leave you here. Come with me.'

'I can't.'

'Why not?'

How can I explain? I know if I leave now I'll never return. I've no idea what Ellis might do, what might be in his power. To leave would be to forsake Scarcross Hall for ever, to abandon Father and Agnes to an unholy fate, to give up the one thing I have fought for my whole life. I cannot do that. 'You must do this for me, Sam. Please.'

I fetch down a coat, far too big for him but there's no time to find better, and bind one of Agnes's old shawls around his shoulders. Then we go to the door and I slide back the bolt.

Outside, the snow has stopped, but the wind sends drifts spiralling and shifting in the moonlight.

Sam looks up at me with those sad eyes – eyes that have seen far more horror than a boy of his years ought – and a wave of guilt sweeps over me. I wrap him in my arms, hold him close for a few seconds, feeling his sickroom breath on my cheek.

'You must hurry. Keep running – whatever you do, don't stop. Do you understand?'

His face takes on a determined cast. I see all the grit of his father in him. Then he steps out into the snow. I watch as he struggles through the drifts to the gate, towards the coffin path. He could make the journey blindfold – the moor is in his blood, as it is in mine – but as he disappears into the night, I remember the coin found beneath his pillow, and what it foretells.

I shut the door and reach for the small leather pouch at my belt, feel the cold metal discs inside, fetched from beneath my mattress. While I have the coins close, I reason, surely Sam will be safe.

I pick up the knife, stand and listen. The house creaks and groans, wind moaning in the rafters. I go back to the kitchen, expecting to find Ellis lying, bleeding, before the hearth, but the room is empty.

I check the kitchen door and find it bolted. He must still be in the house. Besides, I know it. I know he's waiting for me.

I take a single candle from the mantel and, knife gripped tight, creep out into the hall. Everything is darkness and moon shadow, the golden glow of the candle stuttering as my hand shakes. My heart pounds so loud I feel sure he'll hear it.

I cross the flags towards Agnes. Snow is gusting in through the broken pane from the tree outside the window, dusting her body. There's still warmth in her, the flakes melting on her arms. The grief that racks me when I look upon her is stifled only by fear. I think of Ellis, his hands about my neck, that dreadful look in his eye. It has taken hold of him – this thing, this evil – as it has possessed and poisoned all of us.

If it has the power to make him a killer, what else might it have done? All this time I've sought answers for the terrible events of these past months in the commonplace. But it seems clear now that such malevolence, such corruption, is the work of something unholy. And it is not done with me yet.

A vision rises in my mind's eye like a deep-buried memory, an echo of the past – a pale figure at the Slaying Stone, a pact with the dead, as bodies burn and curses are sworn. Searing flames. Roasting flesh. The screams of those slaughtered in the name of old forgotten gods. My blood runs chill. I hold up the candle, casting light into shadowed corners, but find nothing. For a moment I think I see a face at the window but it's only my own reflection, distorted in the leads. Still, I know it's here. I know it's close.

A noise makes me start: a low *thunk*, something heavy, hitting the floor in an upstairs chamber. I wait, barely breathing. I know what comes next. Long seconds run by. And it comes – the sound that has taunted me all these months – the slow scrape of something dragged across the boards.

I make my way up the staircase, my whole body thrumming.

Thunk . . . ssshrrrrrrssssst . . .

I feel insubstantial, apart, as if I'm watching myself from afar.

Thunk . . . . ssshrrrrrrssssst . . .

I reach the threshold of the old bedchamber. The noise stops.

I step inside.

Silence.

The air is strangely still and midwinter-cold, despite the embers of Sam's fire glowing in the hearth. There's a strong smell of burning, tinged with the sickly scent of animal flesh. I cross the room to the casement, place the candle on the sill, press my forehead against the panes and peer out – nothing but the snow and wind against the glass.

I know when he finds me. It's not the sound of his laboured breath, or the unsteady step along the gallery, but the familiar sensation – the shiver down my spine, the watchful eye upon me.

He stops by the door. He has no weapon that I can see, just the small golden key from the ebony box, clutched in one hand.

I hold out the knife. 'Come no closer.'

But he does, one step and another.

The candlelight throws shadows across his face. He is pale, deathly. He has removed his waistcoat and I see now the large red stain flowering his shirt, the slick of it down one leg. He falters, bending, hands on knees, taking deep, ragged breaths. 'Where is the boy?'

'Somewhere you cannot hurt him.'

'I won't hurt him. I promise.'

'Your promises mean nothing.'

'If you sent him out there, you must go after him. Bring him back.'

'So you can take your revenge?'

'He'll never survive.'

'Yes, he will. And he'll fetch help. People will come.'

He shakes his head. 'You've sent him to his end.'

'How dare you lay blame on me? I'm the only one who has not lied.'

He gives a grunting, humourless laugh. 'There are different kinds of lie, Mercy. Those meant to deceive, those made out of good intentions and those we tell ourselves. Before you condemn me, ask yourself, which have you told? Which are you telling now?'

'How can you speak to me of truth?'

'We've all been lying,' he says. 'We're all damned by our secrets. But I'm done with it now.' He grimaces and sucks in a breath. 'Put the knife down. I won't hurt you. I never meant to hurt you. Besides, I've not the strength.'

I can see he's truthful about that at least. The violence in his eyes is gone, faded, along with his anger. He seems a different man from the monster with his hands about my throat. The man who took me to his bed, who held me and comforted me, in whom I placed all my hopes, is returned. How can one body contain both?

Slowly, I place the blade on the sill next to the candle. Despite my caution, part of me aches to see the life leaking from him – the part that desperately wants him. My heart, which I thought dead as a winter tree, finds feeling in its depths. Is he right? Have I been lying? Was I already damned by my secrets, my past sins, before our sin secured it?

Despite everything, the devastation and betrayal, I cannot deny that I have loved him. I felt a bond between us from the very first, but have been too afraid to own it. Instead, I buried it deep, where it took root and grew, until it became this terrible, beautiful, poisonous thing – a winter hellebore blooming in the snow.

He reaches a hand towards me. 'Come . . . please . . .'

I'm spent, nothing left to give.

'Please, Mercy . . . We are blood.'

He keels and collapses, legs giving out, head hitting the floor with a hard *thunk*. The key tumbles from his palm.

And all my anger, all my bitterness, leaves me in the face of one simple truth: he is my brother, my love, and I am losing him.

I drag him to the bed, his boots making a long, low scrape across the boards.

He comes round as I struggle to heft him onto the mattress, leaving a fresh streak of scarlet on the coverlet.

His breath is shallow, all colour drained, cheek sticky from the wound on his skull – the wound I made – a deep red gash, a slice of bone. I prop him gently against the bolster and sit beside him. He reaches for my hand. His fingers are slick with blood but he brings mine to his lips.

'Be kind to the boy, if you see him again,' he whispers.

I hush him. For a few moments, he lies there, thin breath wheezing, lost to all sense. If God were kind He would let him go now, I think. But God does not hold sway here.

He stirs again, looks at me, and there's no temper in his eyes, no blame or fear.

'Mercy, what is my name?' he asks softly.

'Ellis. Ellis Ferreby.'

'No, my birth name . . .'

'What does it matter now?'

'I am nobody's son. I am nothing . . .'

So that is why he was so desperate to see the words written in faded brown ink on that cursed piece of parchment. I search for kindness in my scoured-out heart.

I lean in close and whisper, stomach knotting as I say it: 'You are the son of Bartram Booth. You are my brother . . . and your name is Matthew.'

The furrows melt from his brow. 'Matthew,' he breathes. 'Matthew Booth . . .'

Then he closes his eyes.

He does not wake again.

It is near dawn when I rise.

I held him until the warmth began to leave his body, his skin started to turn grey and his blood hardened on my breeches. Then I laid him out – Ellis, Matthew, I'm no longer sure what to call him – and rested my head upon his chest. Only one day has passed since I lay just so, his arms about me, soothed by his heat, his scent and the steady beat of his heart, seeking false hope in the dream of a new future.

Now I pick up the golden key and slip the cord about my neck, where it hangs, cold against my chest. I do not want to leave him for a moment but there is something I must do.

I go to my father's bedchamber. Standing by the bed, I take the leather pouch from my belt, choose a single golden coin and slip it onto his tongue.

I say goodbye.

Then I return to the hall, where poor Agnes lies in a frozen pool of blood. I cannot bring myself to disturb her, but I crouch and slip a second coin into her mouth.

As I do this, I sense that I am watched. It is here. It is waiting for me.

But I do not pray. There is no need. I am not afraid any more.

Back in the old bedchamber, I slip the third and final coin onto my brother's tongue.

The Devil take them all . . .

I go to the casement. The sky has that dull, heavy look of more snow to come. I open the window, feel the midwinter chill, the ever-present wind, and breathe it in. Drink deep. The air is knife-sharp, slicing my throat. I push the casement wide. The breeze whips hair across my face. I lean out, craving more, filling my lungs until they hurt – the wind that carries the soul of the moor.

The moor.

When my father chose this place, he sought proximity to God. He longed for redemption. He hoped for forgiveness. He came to forget his sins, but the moor would not let him. He tried to teach me to find Paradise among the moss-cushioned rocks and rust-hued becks, in scar and fell and cloud-scattered sky. But as we are closer to Heaven so we are closer to Hell.

The moor is a wild and lonely place, a refuge for the broken and the tainted, a Bethel for the damned. The Devil hides in peat bogs and speaks in the tongue of curlew and nightjar. I see witch-brew in the storm clouds and hellfire in the sunsets. It is a place for those who have fallen from grace. And now I am one of them, I am become part of it.

I am the moor-top wind; the setting sun and the rising moon;

the red kite, soaring with talons primed; the rushing becks and the hard, unforgiving crags. I am the ancient stones of Scarcross Hall, the black peat bog, the pulse, the lifeblood.

I can see the tracks that Sam left in the snow, not yet covered, leading through the gates, towards the coffin path, where they disappear, lost in the drifts. Perhaps he will reach home. Perhaps not.

What will they find, when the snows thaw? Will they carry me down the coffin path in a makeshift box? Will they lay me down by night, in that corner of the churchyard, beneath the horse-chestnut, where the ungodly are left to be forgotten? Or will they vilify me? Will they brand me a heretic, a witch, a sorceress, and bury me at the crossroads with a stake run through my heart so I cannot come back and haunt the moor? Will drunks in the tavern scare strangers with tales of the mistress of Scarcross Hall?

I place a hand on the windowpane and look out across the snow-bound hills.

I become aware of a presence at my shoulder.

But I do not turn. There is no need.

I no longer have anything to fear. Nothing can hurt me now. I've found the freedom I sought. I understand my fate and it is what I've always craved.

It comes closer, grave-cold breath wreathing about my neck, creeping down my spine to my centre. I welcome it: there is pleasure in it.

A hand, pale and gossamer as moorland mist, covers mine. Fingers interlace.

My heart is shattered glass, a key turned in a lock, a skylark.

I will stay where I belong. I will never leave.

Scarcross Hall is mine.

Author's Note

The Coffin Path is a work of fiction and all characters are of my own invention. However, the story of the Booth family is rooted in a real event that took place during the English Civil War: the storming of Bolton.

In May 1644, Bolton was a staunchly Puritan town of parliament supporters, known as 'the Geneva of the North'. Charles I's commander, Prince Rupert, hoped to take Bolton for the king as he led his troops through Lancashire on the way to relieve the siege of York, then a royalist stronghold.

Rupert's army arrived at Bolton on 28th May and attacked immediately. This initial onslaught was repelled, albeit with about 300 royalist casualties. Rupert's forces then became enraged when the townspeople hanged a captured royalist soldier who was believed to be an Irish Catholic. Bolton would pay the price – in blood.

Fuelled by sectarian anger, a second attack led by the Earl of Derby successfully breached the walls and carried the fighting into the streets. Exactly what happened next is unclear. Parliamentarian propaganda and 'eyewitness accounts' framed the incident as a massacre, with wild, bloodthirsty troops committing the indiscriminate slaughter of hundreds of innocent men, women and children. Here is a taste:

> At their entrance, before, behinde, to the right, and left, nothing heard, but kill dead, kill dead was the word, in the Town killing all before them without any respect, without the Town by their horsemen, pursuing the poore amazed people, killing, stripping, and spoiling all they could meet with, nothing regarding the dolefull cries of women or children, but some they slashed as they were calling for quarter, others when they had given quarter, many hailed out of their houses to have their brains dasht out in the streets, those that were not dead in the streets already, pistoled slashed, brained, or troden under their horses feet . . . The massacring, dismembring, cutting of dying or dead bodies, and boasting, with all new coined oathes, swearing how many Roundheads this sword, or they had killed that day, some eight, some six, some more or lesse; armes, legs, yea the braines themselves lying distant from their heads, bodies, and other parts.

> *An Exact Relation of the Bloody and Barbarous Massacre at Bolton in the Moors in Lancashire*, R.W., 1644

Royalist apologists argue that local burial records do not back up this story and that the majority killed or captured must have been soldiers. The numbers dead, reported by both armies, range from 200 to 2000; we can be reasonably sure that at least 1000 lost their lives, making the incident one of the worst atrocities of the war. Already famed as a man of small mercy, Bolton served to cement Rupert's reputation as a brutal, ruthless leader.

In a rather satisfying postscript, the Earl of Derby was captured in 1651, tried for treason and eventually executed in Bolton, the very town that surely most enjoyed his fate.

A precursor to the famous battle of Marston Moor, the Bolton massacre is a mere footnote in a larger conflict, but one that exposes the full horror and long-term consequences of the English Civil War for ordinary people. This novel is, in part, written in remembrance of 'All those of Botonn slayne on the 28 of May, 1644' (Bolton Parish Register).

Acknowledgements

I would like to thank John and Mary Pearson for an unforgettable weekend in the lambing shed at Lovesome Hill Farm; Diana Rowsell and her husband Ken for welcoming me into their home and showing me the old coffin path that runs through their idyllic Sussex village; and Simon Davies for early research advice on seventeenth-century hauntings.

Huge thanks to the whole team at Headline: to my extraordinary editors Mari Evans, Claire Baldwin and Frankie Edwards; to Caitlin Raynor, Jo Liddiard and Hazel Orme; and to my agent Annette Green.

I raise a glass to all my writing colleagues, especially members of the Historical Writers' Association and the Prime Writers, whose encouragement and camaraderie is unparalleled; and to the Royal Literary Fund, whose Fellowship scheme enabled the writing of this book.

My gratitude, as always, to friends and family who continue to give tireless support. Special thanks must go to Ian Madej, Caroline Clements, Jeremy Prosser and Claire Holloway; to John Clements for influential discussions on the Book of Common Prayer; to Jan Clements for her indefatigable red pen; and to Paddy Wells, to whom this book is dedicated, for holding my hand through it all.